PROCLAMATION

IN the name of Her Majesty Dona Juana,

Princess of the Kingdom of Portugal.

WHEREAS I have it in my command from His Majesty King Joao II that Her Majesty the Princess has this day given birth to a son and heir to the throne who will henceforth be named Prince Sebastian of Aviz. Due to the tragic and untimely death of his father Joao III be it known that Prince Sebastian stands next in line as King of Portugal and her dominions.

With licenses of the Holy Inquisition, Ordinary, and the Palace.

IN LISBON

By Pedro de Magalhães, the King's Printer, anno 1554

Also by Greg Barron

HarperCollins *Publishers* Australia

Rotten Gods

Savage Tide

Lethal Sky

Voodoo Dawn (short fiction)

Stories of Oz Publishing

The Hammer of Ramenskoye (short fiction)

Camp Leichhardt

Galloping Jones and Other True Stories from Australia's History

Whistler's Bones

Red Jack and the Ragged Thirteen

Outlaw: The Story of Joe Flick

The Time of Thunder

The LAST DAYS *of* DOM SEBASTIAN

GREG BARRON

STORIES OF OZ

First edition published 2021

by Stories of Oz Publishing

PO Box K57

Haymarket NSW 1240

ABN: 0920230558

facebook.com/storiesofoz

ozbookstore.com

© 2021 Greg Barron

ISBN: 9780648733881

Proof reading/editing: Catriona Martin

Cover design: Nada Backovic nadabackovic.com

Printed and bound in Australia by IngramSpark

Cover background: iStock

Cover photography: Catriona Martin

18102021r1

Dedicated to the memory of my mother,
Faye Marlene Barron
1938 – 2016
In our hearts you live forever.

Myth is the nothing,
That is everything.

Fernando Pessoa

PRÓLOGO

The young woman's pain resonated in the air and walls, the act of bringing life into the world drawing power from all the elements. This was a moment more beautiful than dawn, more powerful than death.

Sixteen years old, already a widow, Doña Juana clenched her jewelled fingers. Her dark hair spread over the silk pillows that padded her shoulders. Candles burned down to stubs, and her bare knees trembled under the comforting hands of the midwives.

Doña Juana stared at the vaulted ceilings of her chambers — the painted scenes of deer hunts, contests of valour and nobles dressed in coloured cloaks. Forcing down the bile she pushed again. At the limit of her endurance something tore inside her, followed by a slippery rush as vibrant, kicking life eased through the barriers. At first she tried to see, but hooped skirts frustrated her efforts until, exhausted, she fell back against the pillows.

'He's dead. My baby's dead. I know he is,' she wailed, certain that no living thing could have survived such an ordeal.

A drawn-out cry filled the room. A midwife appeared at the

Princess's side, holding the infant in her arms. The child was blue, streaked with bruises and larger than the doll-like baby of her dreams. His eyes were dark-lashed and half-closed.

'Let me hold him,' she demanded, and nothing could have prepared her for the feeling of that child in her arms, sucking her fingers and seeking the breast.

Word passed from the midwives into the rooms beyond. There waited a crowd of nobles and courtiers, falling to their knees to thank God that an heir had come to the House of Aviz, keeping Portugal safe from the grasping hands of Spain.

The news filtered from the Royal Palace, into the square, where tens of thousands gathered. A procession of clergy began at the Sé, moving at a slow walk, singing hymns of thanksgiving all the way to the Monastery of Saint Domingo. Families filled the cobbled streets, laughing and giving thanks. The baby, born on Sebastian's day, in the year of our Lord Fifteen Hundred and Fifty Four, would be named in honour of that Saint.

When Doña Juana had bathed and dressed she received visitors in her chambers. The sleeping infant wore a suit of linen, embroidered in blue with the pale discs and blue shields of the quinas.

So began the life of Dom Sebastian. In the early afternoon I looked on him for the first time. I was a young man then, untouched by tragedy and loss, a humble Blackfriar. With me came the Castilian astrologer, Rui Chanoca, who had lately arrived at court. We must have seemed like an unusual couple – thin, bleakly dressed Chanoca, and myself, in my coarse woollen cassock.

Doña Juana welcomed me with her eyes, for we were friends,

yet she stared curiously at the stranger. Rumours abounded about him – that he held heretical views and had been hounded from Spain. As with all rumours, truth lurked among the embellishments.

The young mother was, understandably, tired and drawn, her brown hair pasted to the skin below her ear. Bending at the waist I kissed her cheek. 'Congratulations, Doña Juana.'

'Thank you, Padre. We are blessed.' Her eyes were red with fatigue, yet proud nonetheless.

'Doña Juana,' I went on, 'Senhor Chanoca has cast Prince Sebastian's horoscope. Perhaps you would like to hear it?' The Papal bull, *Terrae et Coeli Creator*, had recently denounced astrology, and I personally disapproved of it, yet the royal families of Europe were besotted with the practice, and King João himself had ordered the preparation of this chart.

The young woman smiled with bloodless lips. 'We have not met, Senhor Chanoca. You are Spanish?'

'A native of Castile, Doña Juana.'

The Princess was also a Spaniard, sister of King Philip, come willingly to Portugal to marry the prince she loved, now dead of diabetes just two weeks past. 'Tell me,' she asked. 'How did you learn the secrets of the stars?'

The astrologer waved one hand in a circular motion, as a potter might throw a jar. His eyes glowed white. 'The silken threads that bind us to God's heavens – to the stars, moon and tides have long intrigued me. I learned my trade at the elbow of true masters – seers without peer. Over time, our Lord God has blessed me also with a small measure of ability.'

'I would like to know how you interpret the stars for my son, Senhor.'

Rui Chanoca bowed low and shuffled a sheaf of papers. 'It

is my honour, Doña Juana, to share my findings with you. I have used the relative positions of the stars and planets, and the concepts advanced in Ptolemy's Tetrabiblos, to sketch the path Sebastian's life must take. The eminent astrologer Doctor Fernão Maldonado has checked my findings for accuracy and agrees with my conclusions. Shall I begin?'

The young woman said nothing, fingering the medallion of Saint Isobel that hung on a filigree chain beneath the curvature of her neck. Nostrils flared, she appeared to focus with every sense on the mysterious Spaniard, who drew breath audibly, as if about to leap into dark and murky water.

'Mars and Mercury,' he began, 'are in the twelfth house, with the Sun opposite Leo. Sebastian's childhood will be fraught with illness and insomnia. The night hours will prove difficult for him.'

The young woman's eyes creased with sadness as she stared down at her infant. 'Go on.'

'Mercury is in the twelfth house and the Moon in the sixth. Sebastian will be a man of good judgement—'

Doña Juana struggled to sit up in bed. 'Dispense with your reasoning – allow me just your conclusions.'

'As you wish. Sebastian will enjoy a good memory, a patient disposition and a love of letters. He will be popular with the opposite sex and display an aptitude for music. His temper will be uneven and passionate.'

'So like his father,' Doña Juana whispered, eyes downcast. She and the young Prince João had shared a heated and obsessive love before his untimely passing.

'In adulthood Sebastian will enjoy good health, and as his sun sign is Capricorn – the goat – he will be sure footed and direct. He will overcome obstacles in his path.' Senhor Chanoca exhaled and let his hands hang limp, as if to indicate that his dissertation was complete.

'That is all?' Doña Juana asked.

'There are other, minor, divinations. The full chart will be drawn up and delivered to your chambers.'

The young woman frowned. 'You have not told me everything. I command you to do so. Will my beautiful Sebastian live to hold his grandchildren in his arms?'

A flush spread across the astrologer's face. 'Doña Juana, your son is ruled by Saturn. It is a difficult planet, one of boundaries and sometimes an indicator of premature mortality.'

'I command you to answer. Will Sebastian die a natural death?' Her brown eyes, still fixed on him, moistened.

Taking the trembling man's arm, I attempted to lead Chanoca away. He, however, fell to his knees beside the Princess, face contorted with grief. His eyes became as white as moons. Spittle flew from his lips and his voice choked with emotion. 'Sebastian will be a famous king. He will change the world. Poets will sing of his greatness. Our ancestors will yearn for him across the ages.'

Doña Juana raised her chin, as if she expected no less of her offspring. 'Yes, but will he die young?'

'Millions will weep for him – future generations will look to him for leadership.'

The young mother, nerves stretched beyond endurance, covered her face with her hands, tears flooding from between her fingers, shuddering deep in her chest. 'Tell me, please.'

The astrologer cowered before her, 'Forgive me, Doña Juana, but the stars tell me that your son will know the nightmares of madness. That he will die a violent death, and lie cold in the earth before his time.'

The wind freshened with the promise of dawn, swinging the *Josephine* on her anchor line, and carving the waters of the channel into sharp wavelets. The dark shapes of nearby islands lay silhouetted against the East Kimberley sky.

Francis da Costa gripped the flybridge rail with brown, work-hardened hands and stared out across the sea, gooseflesh rising on his bare arms. Expectation mingled with the melancholy longing of the saudade, the curse of his Portuguese blood. Dark figures moved across the cockpit – shadows under the glare of the LED floodlights. Men and women carried SCUBA tanks and plastic crates, passing them over the transom into the rigid-hulled-inflatable-boat that would carry them out to the site.

The sound of feet on the ladder vibrated through the deck, and Lauren Hart came up beside Francis, her wild sun-blonde hair and shoulders silhouetted darkly against the sky. There were three volunteers on the expedition – all students, but Lauren was a consulting archaeologist, and was paid accordingly when in the field.

Francis moved against the forward rail and pointed out at the sea, where tendrils of mist rose from the surface before being whipped away by the breeze. 'There are ghosts over the sea this morning,' he said.

The tension was palpable. Just before sunset on the previous day, minutes before darkness forced them to haul in the sensors, Lauren had picked out a signal on the magnetometer that might well be that thing that they had scarcely dared name, and had searched for, over so many months and years.

Before she could answer a third figure appeared on the bridge, the boat skipper, Jeff Dunn. 'Not ghosts,' he said. 'The ocean is a few degrees warmer than the air. That's all. We're almost ready.'

Francis hugged his chest with his arms. 'My God Jeff, I can almost feel them. We're treading in their footsteps.'

'I hope you're right.' Jeff's singlet gaped open, revealing a silver rijksdaalder coin on a chain of the same metal, nestled against the tanned skin and curling hair of his chest.

Francis moved his gaze to the cockpit where the dive crew waited. 'Okay then, let's get out there, and see if those ghosts are real.' He turned away from the rail, as frightened of failure as he had ever been in his life.

They left the *Josephine* behind, piling into the RHIB with Francis at the wheel and Jeff standing watchfully beside him. The run through the channel between the islands was comfortable enough, the RHIB's sharp bow knifing through the chop, maintaining twenty knots without fuss. They motored on past pebbled beaches, tidal flats, and rocky sentinels where nesting boobies and terns formed crying hordes on the least exposed faces.

Approaching the open sea, Francis eased back on the throttle. Droplets of spray appeared on the screen, and the hull rolled, a movement he absorbed with flexed knees. White surf broke to seaward on reefs and shoals that lurked just below the surface, and the sea was lumpy through the only practicable route to the survey area.

'Damn,' Francis said, tightening his hands on the wheel. 'The sea's come up – visibility underwater will be shot to hell.'

Jeff's lips were white as he spoke, 'That's the tropical low I was talking about, and it's moving in. I was just watching it on the radar. Your call, but it doesn't look good.'

'It's too late in the year for a bad cyclone,' Francis said. It was May, and so far they had been blessed with three weeks of hot but otherwise perfect weather.

'Maybe, but it's still a powerful cell.'

Francis ignored him, easing the throttle forward and bringing the RHIB onto the plane, the hard chop slapping into the hull as he found a good compromise speed of around fifteen knots. He navigated by feel, and with an eye to the chart screen; a track laid over weeks of travel.

Fifteen minutes of hard running followed before the way-point they had marked late the previous evening loomed up, and Lauren came forward to watch, as if with jealous pride over the spot.

'We should deploy now and try to pick up the signal again,' said Francis, and he throttled back, a hundred metres off a reef that reared from the sea like the back of a whale. It was a dramatic sight, with water running off the face to reveal kelp, sea urchins and living coral.

'Let's get it happening, guys.' Then, to Jeff, 'Can you take the helm please?'

Practiced hands went to work on the cable reels, while Jeff provided enough way for the towed magnetometer and sonar probe to drift out behind the boat. Further adjustments became necessary as they moved in and out of the strong current generated by the tide.

'Moving to running speed now,' Francis shouted, cursing the wind that blew out of the northeast with steady force. As the instruments went out, Jeff brought the speed up to five knots, the maximum at which data from the instruments could be relied upon.

A pressure wave tilted the boat and the occupants of the craft lurched with it. Voices fell silent now, and Francis saw something new in the eyes of his crew – wariness, confidence in his decisions fading. He found himself hating their timidity, wishing he was alone with the sea and its secrets.

The boat inched on. All eyes remained fixed on the instrument console.

'Two degrees starboard. Steady. One hundred metres off the rocks. Ease up.'

With the outboard barely ticking over it became more difficult to keep the vessel straight, as the surging water tried to drag them broadside. Jeff gunned the motor in an effort to bring the nose around.

'That's good. Fifty metres. Steady. Now, dead slow. Passing overhead now.' He paused, and then breathlessly: 'That's it – regular on two sides – almost damn perfect with a strong signal on the magnetometer to boot. This must be it.' The group broke into a round of laughing and congratulations. Even so, Francis recognised a nervous ring in those voices. He turned to look at Lauren, sharing a grin of excitement.

Don't forget, her eyes said, *I was the one who spotted it.*

'Let's bring the gear in and head down for a look,' Francis said, glancing at the sonar unit. It showed a depth of seventeen metres – under sixty feet. Decompression stops, he calculated, would not be required for short dives, only after long cumulative times underwater.

Looking across at the others he chose the two strongest divers. 'Lauren and Nick can come with me. Marinda, you stay with Jeff.' The volunteers in the crew were interns from Charles Darwin University, happy to come along for the experience and fun. All were handy in the water and good company.

The SCUBA equipment consisted of Faber 12.2 litre steel tanks, Oceanic regulators, and an octopus integrated into each BCD. Pressure and depth gauges completed the instrumentation. None of the gear was new, but had been maintained in perfect condition.

Working the harness around his chest, buckling up tight, Francis added a couple of weights to the pockets then rinsed out his mask. Finally, he slipped on his fins and inflated his BCD. With the regulator between his lips, air hissing in and out, he ran his eyes over the crew before turning to Jeff. 'It's as rough as hell, and the current's probably three knots across the face, but hold us here until we're in the water, then get out of it like a bat out of hell. Stand off at a safe distance. Give us half an hour. No more. No less. Watch out for us on the surface.'

'Aye aye Captain.' Jeff mock saluted.

Francis turned to the other divers. 'You ready?'

'Sure.'

'Lauren?'

'Yep.'

'Let's go then.' He turned to look at the chart plotter and saw that they had already drifted fifty metres off the mark. 'Get us back on the spot if you can.'

Eighteen inches of stainless-steel propeller bit deeply into the water and the bow sliced into the waves. Francis admired the skill with which Jeff used throttle and wheel to work with the sea. They went in so close that spray saturated hair and clothes alike. Surf pounded like cannon fire.

'That's it,' Jeff shouted. 'Thirty minutes.'

Francis lifted one hand to his mask, nodded once at the others, and back-flipped over the side. He had always loved this moment of immersion, morphing from one world into another, senses reeling. It always took a few seconds for that underwater being to kick in, his breathing steadying, hearing the reassuring hiss of each inward breath and the rumbling of bubbles as he exhaled. Even in the wild conditions, the water was much clearer than he had expected – enough to see every detail of the sea floor.

Using the deflator button to bleed air from the BCD, he descended through effervescent surface layers, the clarity improving as he equalised pressure with a squeeze of his nostrils. A school of tiny silver fish appeared, bright as diamonds. One hand extended, Francis watched the school panic, dancing sideways before resuming their pattern at a safe distance.

Reaching the bottom, Francis took the lead, his fins beating with practised regularity towards a bright coral bombora, patrolled by larger fish – coral trout and emperor, queenfish and spotted tuskfish, tinged with electric blue. Some of the larger individuals sped off, others zigzagged, as if torn between curiosity and fear. Some seemed not to react, but continued their slow cruising, mouths closed with a faint expression of disinterest.

The divers rounded a curve of coral-encrusted rock. The sea floor fell away by several metres, creating a deep pool surrounded on all sides by walls that rose at least halfway to the surface.

Crayfish antennae waved in the current from cracks in the pool edge and when the divers swam too close a moray eel thrust its head from a hole and opened its mouth in a silent hiss of disapproval at these interlopers from above. Was it Francis's imagination or could he see a series of regular but rounded protrusions, lying against the floor of the pool?

He did not hurry, but swam slowly, while seagrass strained at its roots with the surging and receding waves, and small shells and detritus skittered along the bottom.

Now he hesitated, as if a headlong rush might make the thing disappear completely. The other two divers, however, had no such inhibitions. Nick turned and lifted both thumbs, grinning behind his mask, while Lauren darted around the area like a butterfly.

Only then did Francis swim in, touching the coral surface with one gloved hand, moving cautiously, judging distances and measurements. These shapes were too perfect, too regular to be natural.

Francis knew straight off that this was no Portuguese não: no great galleon, but a small vessel of six or seven metres in length, fully calcified and coral-encrusted with age. The boat had a high sweep to her bows. The shape was unmistakeable.

In that moment the past reached out to touch the present. Francis embraced it with both arms. Humans had died here; he knew with certainty. He saw the burst of spray over the bows, men and women packed like sardines on the decks, sick and desperate. He sensed fear, and felt the crash as sharp stone and coral burst through timbers, followed by white water. Screams of fear and helplessness filled his ears. For a fleeting moment he knew what it was like for them. He saw the same wild sea that now pounded these reefs begin to tear the boat apart.

The divers burst through the surface together, climbing aboard and laughing while the RHIB whisked them out of danger, beyond the reefs, there to indulge in a frenzy of back slapping, everyone talking at once, hugging and shouting.

Lauren said it first, 'One of a much larger ship's boats. It has to be.'

Francis felt his skin prickle with the deep excitement of that moment. 'Yes, a ship's boat – barca. Sixteenth century Portuguese.'

'Is it from the *Santo António*?'

'Maybe, or part of Cristovão de Mendonça's lost fleet.' Francis stood tall and bowed with a flourish, 'Ladies and gentlemen, we may well have just discovered the vessel that brought the first Europeans to Australian shores.'

The applause was long and loud until Jeff, who had, until then, joined in the celebrations as eagerly as the others, tapped his watch. 'I hate to say this, but if we don't get through that channel in the next twenty minutes we'll be stuck out here until the tide rises again tonight – and I need to get the *Josephine* back to Darwin by the day after tomorrow.'

Francis grinned, 'One more little dive – just a quick one.'

'You are the most single-minded, reckless bastard I've ever had the misfortune to work with.'

Francis grinned back. 'You love it.'

This time Francis carried the SeaLife DC2000 underwater camera, taking digital frames of the boat from all possible angles. These shots would be instrumental in planning the recovery of the vessel.

With almost a hundred frames in memory, Francis descended to the level of the wreck and circled it slowly, looking for damage, trying to visualise how the vessel must have struck the reef. At the same time Nick used a coring tool to drive through the coral and take samples of the wood underneath.

Finally, glancing at his watch, Francis decided reluctantly that it was time to leave – they were cutting things fine as it was. Then, just as he signalled to the other divers his eyes fell on a short, roughly cylindrical object in the coral, embedded in the lower wall beside the small boat. The growth and substrate around it was stained by the tell-tale iodine colour that often surrounds a long-submerged iron object.

He almost finned away, leaving the object for later recovery, but then he hesitated. Months might pass before they could return, depending on funding and logistics. He reached out a gloved hand and touched the area, before waving to Nick, who carried a small iron jemmy bar.

Together they chipped away at the object before it broke free in Francis's hand. He smiled, and pointed to the surface. It was time to get back up to the RHIB, and through the channel before conditions made that impossible.

DOTS

When Jeff's F150 pulled up outside Francis's house in the Darwin suburb of Parap it took them a few minutes to haul the crates, tanks and bags from the tray, piling it all up beside the two strips of concrete driveway. They didn't shake hands, but bumped their fists together in Jeff's post-Covid version of a high five. The big ute roared away, and Francis turned his attention to getting everything stowed and organised.

The main part of the house, like so many older Darwin dwellings, was elevated, with the bottom half divided between a lock-up garage and a flat. By the time Francis had his first load in hand, the screen door had banged on the latter, and Camille was standing in the doorway, watching him with a smile on her face.

'Hi there,' Francis said. He put down his load and kissed her cheek.

'You were gone a long time,' she said, a note of reproach in her voice, yet her brown eyes were aglow with happiness.

'Four weeks, like I told you. Anyway, here I am.'

She beamed. 'I'll open the garage door and get the trolley.'

With a duck and deft action of her arm Camille rolled up the door and used the trolley to help Francis carry the rest of the gear inside, stacking it neatly on the shelves. He owned most of the equipment used in the course of the expedition – tanks, regulators, electronics – and she knew their places as well as he did.

'Did you find anything?' she asked.

'We sure did, a small boat. It looks Portuguese, and might end up being really important.' He held a finger to his lips. 'Don't tell anyone.'

Camille smiled, 'Mum would have been proud of you.'

Francis squeezed her arm. 'I think she would. I really do.'

Making a face and squashing the end of her nose with the tip of her forefinger, Camille said, 'You need a shower, Francis, you do stink a little bit.'

'Sorry, I know I do. Come upstairs and put the kettle on while I scrub up, and I'll tell you all about it.'

With a carpet bag in one hand, and a cardboard box under the other arm, he walked up the steps with the iron frame clanging underfoot and Camille prattling along behind him.

'What's in the box?' she asked.

'Wait until I've had my shower and I'll show you.'

The upstairs interior was musty from weeks without ventilation, and Francis opened the double sliding door to the verandah before he headed to the bedroom, where he undressed and laid out clean clothes before enjoying his first truly hot shower for a month. He followed up with a quick beard-trim and general tidy before dressing and heading for the kitchen.

Camille was waiting at the dining room table with two steaming cups of tea, the yellow Lipton tags hanging over the rims. She was staring at the box, unable to hide her curiosity at the contents.

'You smell better,' she said. Then, 'Can we look at the thing in the box now?'

Still standing, Francis took a deep sip of his tea, smiled and opened the box. The contents were thickly wrapped in bubble wrap and newspaper. Like a child at a party playing pass-the-parcel he removed one layer, then placed it in front of Camille to do the next. With a wide grin of anticipation she did so.

'It's very heavy,' she said, and it made his heart swell to see her so excited.

Francis raised his eyebrows, and removed the last layer of paper. The object sat revealed on the table, heavily crusted in coral and not recognisable as anything in particular.

Camille's face fell. 'What is it, Francis?'

'I don't know yet,' he said, 'maybe not much, but we know there's metal in there because we used a detector on it. You'll be the first to know. I promise you.'

'Good.' She screwed up her face. 'Is *she* coming around to-night?'

'You mean Lauren?'

'Yes, that's who I mean.'

'Well she might, I'm not sure.' Francis scratched at his face.

Camille flashed her eyes. 'Now tell me everything about what you found, and I'll tell Mum when I pray to God tonight.'

Francis smiled, and inhaled the fragrance of his tea as he drank deeply.

Later, when Camille had gone back downstairs to her flat, Francis carried the object into his office and sighed with pleasure. He loved every part of this modest little room – the shelves of books, the Fernando Barata prints on the walls, and the quality furniture.

Everything here was manifestly his, and he loved those possessions with the intensity of a miser.

He sank into the chair with pleasure, looking around the room as if checking to see if anything had changed during his absence. Then, he set about making an official notification of the finding of the barca, under the terms of Western Australia's Historic Shipwrecks Act. This oft-despised legislation required registration of finds and provided a complicated system in which the discoverers are entitled to a small financial reward for the wreck along with other claimants. The lion's share, however, belonged by default to the Australian government.

On completing the list of 'removed artefacts' he looked across to the coral-encrusted lump sitting on its bed of soft linen. Then, in a scrawl he wrote NIL, for it had not yet proven to be any kind of artefact at all.

His legal responsibilities discharged, Francis carried the item over to the work bench, where most of the interesting work got done.

Twin fluorescent tubes glowed white, and in that light he used a loupe pressed to his eye to study all the visible surfaces. Having been submerged for hundreds of years, in a tropical location, the object was not only coated with coral growth, but was saturated with sulfates and chlorides.

Satisfied that the best course of action was to physically chip away as much coral as possible, Francis settled the object into a bed of clean rags, then selected a twelve-millimetre chisel and rubber mallet. Using these tools judiciously, he removed mere fragments of material at each pass.

Two or three hours went by before he heard the sound of an engine in the drive, feet on the steps and then the front door swinging open.

'I'm in here,' he called out.

Lauren blustered in, accompanied by the sound of plastic bags and the smell of Thai food. It was only then that Francis realised that he was hungry.

The food thumped down on the kitchen table and she breezed into the office as if she owned it. 'I brought food because I knew you'd be busy. Any luck?'

Francis looked up. She too had taken the opportunity to groom herself. Her sun-bleached hair had been cut and styled, and she wore jeans and a loose blouse. Unusually for her, she wore lipstick and light foundation. 'Not yet, just more coral,' he said.

'Any guesses?'

'As I said, not yet.'

She came up beside him, her shoulder touching his.

'A cluster of small iron cannonballs?' she suggested. 'Like for a verso gun?'

'Possibly, but according to the electronics there's a non-ferrous component. Hard to explain that.'

'Okay, keep at it, I'll get some plates out.'

'There's a bottle of shiraz in the cupboard.'

'Right, I'll get it.'

They ate at the table, with the wine dark and reflective in crystal glasses, and the Thai food spooned onto brown china plates, an old Wedgwood set with battle scars on the rims, and the maker's name almost worn away from the back.

'Sorry if I'm not great company,' said Francis. 'I'm a little weary.'

'You must be exhausted,' Lauren said. 'I've been asleep all day but I bet you haven't.'

The journey back to Darwin in the *Josephine* had been dogged with stormy seas, and long periods of sleep had been impossible.

'I was thinking,' she said. 'Have you considered maybe giving me a bigger role in all this?'

'For example?' he said between mouthfuls.

'Like making me a partner in the company?'

Francis stopped chewing and stared as she went on.

'It'd save you having to pay me between trips.' She paused. 'And it was actually me who spotted the barca on the screen first.'

Francis took umbrage at this. 'Just because you happened to be first to see the signal on the screen, on a boat paid for by me, and an expedition planned by me, doesn't make you the discoverer.'

'No, but it means something, doesn't it?'

'You're a great archaeologist and you bring a lot to the team.'

Lauren shook her head and snorted softly through her nose, shaking her head sadly to herself as she finished the meal. When it was over and they washed up together, she looped her tea towel around his waist and pulled him close to her. 'Partners or not, why don't we go to bed,' she said.

He shook his head. 'We complicated things once before. I don't think we should do it again.'

She released him, 'Whatever. Let's get back to work.'

Francis rubbed at his temple with the middle fingers of his left hand, 'I'm sorry to be pouring cold water on everything, but I think you probably should leave that to me as well if that's okay. To be honest I'm pretty much done for the evening.'

'Fair enough,' she said, 'it's been a big few weeks. Any idea when we'll get out there again?'

The tension evaporated, just like that, and Francis felt himself breathe easier. 'Late June provided I can raise the finance. I'm also thinking of a quick trip to Portugal if the bank balance allows.'

'Can I come?'

'Sorry again, but no, and I'm sure you can pick up some work at CDU.' Charles Darwin University had a small but robust marine archaeology department. 'It might even be fun.'

'If you can call marking Archaeology 101 essays fun, yes. ThoughI might have two weeks at a new Ubirr dig in September.'

'That's something, anyway,' he said.

When Lauren had gone Francis worked for another hour on the object, then went through the mail that had accumulated during his absence. One item was a book he had ordered before his departure, a brand-new Portuguese-language work written by a lecturer in history at Lisbon University. The title was *Os Marinheiros de Portugal do Século XVI*, loosely translated as *The Mariners of Sixteenth Century Portugal*.

By the end of the fifth chapter Francis knew that the author had a rare gift of imparting facts, but also at looking beyond dates and names. He found himself flicking from the text to the author's biography towards the end. Her name was Dr Nicolá Massane. She was surprisingly young, with huge dark eyes that seemed to look right at him, all the way across the world.

It was past midnight when he reluctantly laid the book on his bedside table and switched off the light. He turned onto his side to sleep and knew nothing more until the morning light stole in through the curtains and Camille started tapping on the front door.

'Francis, time to get ready for Mass,' she called, and although swinging his legs out of bed and heading for the shower was an effort, it was worthwhile when he reached the pew and sat down on the polished hardwood surface. Strangely, it was something he needed – the comforting and gentle resonance of the priest delivering his sermon – and the youth group strumming their guitars to the latest evangelical hits. The methodology of it all: rising to sing, kneeling to pray, appealed to his sense of ritual, and he enjoyed the atmosphere of the relics that lined the walls and filled each niche – crosses, virgins and babes.

Camille's face was shining, for this was one of the times that she came alive, when she was as clever and capable as any young woman in the room, knowing every response and standing with dignity. Now, Francis could almost see their mother in her eyes.

At the end they went to the hall for scones and pancakes smeared with jam, making small talk with good people and Francis grounding himself, letting his mind leave the past for a while.

Two more days of gentle chipping away at the object followed, before Francis felt justified in moving onto the next stage, soaking the object in dilute hydrochloric acid for a week until it became possible to wipe away the remaining coating with a cloth.

The final stage was the use of a dilute sodium carbonate solution as an electrolyte, an action that would discourage further corrosion as well as cleaning the object, removing all salts from the metal surfaces.

Francis did all the work himself, lights burning late into the night, watching the thing take shape before his eyes, while the shuttle bus arrived for Camille each morning and brought her home each afternoon. He finished reading his copy of *Os Marinheiros de Portugal do Século XVI* then turned back to the start and began reading again. Already the book was helping him narrow down the list of ships that may have launched the barca they had found here, fifteen thousand kilometres away from the River Tagus.

With almost all the contaminants removed, a final scrubbing with a paste made from gel and grit revealed a cylinder of silver, and a gold-plated guard. The suspicion that he had found the hilt of a sword, the iron blade mostly rusted away, was borne out at last.

True to his word, Francis ensured that Camille was the first to see it. She was entranced, gently shaking her head to see the beauty of precious metals so perfectly wrought and aged by time into a new splendour.

'It's beautiful,' she purred, her eyes like green moons. 'Will you go back to the boat and see what else you can find?' she asked.

'Soon, but I have to arrange the money. Just to get a full crew out there again will cost twenty or thirty thousand dollars.'

The final polishing process then revealed the greatest treasure of all. Francis's heart lurched with excitement as he slowly revealed a series of letters, engraved along the guard by some ancient metalsmith. Many were indecipherable, but he made a note of those that he could discern by eye.

--t---a-m---ão s – ra--o e s----e me nã   em h---ra

Francis transcribed the pattern onto a locus sheet that he prepared to record the details of the find. When this was done he allowed himself the indulgence of lifting the object by the hilt.

Fingers curling over that cold metal, Francis closed his eyes, remembering a childhood promise, knowing that he would not rest until he knew the name of the man who had once wielded that sword.

'You have to go public,' said Lauren, perched on the edge of a chair like a cat ready to spring. Her initial frostiness had thawed with the sight of the hilt, and she had regained some of her usual enthusiasm. 'Maybe start with the ABC for the cred and the others will follow suit. I'm pretty sure I met one of the Darwin journos at a party last year. After that you'll have no trouble getting finance.'

'I don't want publicity yet,' said Francis. 'I need more information first. Besides, every treasure hunter for a thousand kilometres will swarm in as soon as the news breaks.'

Lauren shook her head. 'It's such a remote area, Francis. There might be one or two intrepids, but they don't know the exact location. Besides, if we don't break the story ourselves it will leak out of its own volition – those kids we had out there will talk – of course they will – and even Jeff knows as much as we do.'

'I agree, and I'll break the story when I'm ready. I'd just like to be sure of the details – what ship that barca came from, for a start. At the moment we know very little. We don't even have the C14 results for the samples we took from the boat timbers yet.' He paused. 'I'd like to do the research, and as I said the other night, I'll probably need to go to Portugal.'

As well as booking flights he also began the application process for his own company to begin an initial, non-invasive exploration of the wreck. This involved the West Australian Museum, the Kimberley Land Council and two other agencies. By the end of it all he had a splitting headache, and still had to send emails to the three benefactory organisations who kept the operation afloat. Even to them he could not bring himself to disclose the existence of that wonderful, amazing artefact. *Not yet*, he told himself.

Camille frowned when he told her about the trip. 'Do you have to go away again so soon?'

'I think so. I want to know how that barca might have come to be there before we explore the area again. Are we looking for more small boats, or a towering carrack? I think I'll find some answers in Lisbon.'

'Okay,' said Camille. 'But please hurry back.'

Before getting into the final round of packing, Francis fired off an email to Dr Nicolá Massane, the author of *Os Marinheiros de Portugal do Século XVI*, asking for an interview the following week. He gave her a carefully selected overview of what he had found, and included a photograph of the patchy text from the relic, knowing that he needed to provide something to pique her interest.

He did not, however, give any reference to the discovery's location, not even by country, though he could not avoid stating his sphere of work.

Within a minute an autoreply found his inbox. It was a short, formal message, with a signature line in Portuguese identifying Dr Massane as Senior Lecturer in Maritime Archaeology at the University of Lisbon. It did not say where she was, or the date of her return, only that she was currently out of the office and not reachable by telephone.

Francis felt a combined disappointment and thrill at that robotic contact. He was looking forward to meeting the author of the little book very much, if it was possible to do so.

TRES

With the sword hilt stored securely in a bank safe-deposit box, Francis flew overseas in this world barely recovered from the worst pandemic in a century. Masks had become a matter of choice. Some passengers wore them and others did not. He endured the take-off rather than enjoyed it, then half-watched the track of the aircraft towards Singapore, the first leg of the flight.

Even as Francis rocked gently against the restraint of the seatbelt, his mind wandered back to the beginning, to when the sails of his imagination had first billowed full in a Fremantle classroom, a teacher's words transforming chalk dust and a faded world map into ships, exotic ports and the spice-laden Portuguese carracks of the Age of Discovery. His heroes were adventurers voyaging into an uncharted and dangerous world – determined, bearded mariners, eyes haunted by tragedy and misfortune. Cannons fired; alliances were struck. Holds were packed with pepper, cinnamon and nutmeg. Overloaded ships went down with all hands, and pirates waited off the horn of Africa to board and plunder.

Most afternoons, when he cycled home and parked his bike near the back door, he would hear the stuttering notes of a student at the piano. Some days, however, the instrument remained silent, and Portuguese fado music drifted back from the stereo system in the front room – the plaintive cry of the guitarra, and the languid sadness of the fadista. Perhaps once a month his mother turned inwards. This was a time to tread softly.

The front room would smell of red wine and Alpine cigarettes, a vinyl disc spinning on the turntable. Avelina da Costa's brown eyes would run with tears as they always did when the saudade, the yearning sadness, was upon her. Camille was three years older than he, spending her days at 'special' schools, inhabiting a world of rag dolls and silence.

Francis remembered how he would stand near the piano, waiting until his mother looked up. 'Are there no lessons today?'

'Not today. Did you learn anything new at school?'

'Today we studied history. Portugal discovered the world. I did not know.'

Avelina's eyes were both wise and sad, for she had fled the bitter memories of revolution to raise her children in this new country. Standing, she took his hands in hers, thumb resting on his wrist. 'The blood of the mariner runs in your veins,' she whispered urgently, as if it were the most important information in the world. 'Five hundred years ago the people of Portugal built ships greater than any in history. Can you picture masts so tall they might pierce the sky? Can you imagine a young man's fear as he sailed away into darkness? Can you feel the beat of his heart?'

Francis closed his eyes and longed for that age of courage and sacrifice, when Portugal's youth sailed beyond safety and reason. 'One day I will learn of these brave adventurers,' he said.

Avelina da Costa touched Francis's cheek with the palm of

her hand. 'The saudade touches you already. Some of us feel the yearning more deeply than others. Sometimes it is too poignant to bear.'

In high school, Francis remained a loner, warming a seat in the Perth library on Hay Street, reading of the Age of Discovery, interspersed with displaying a rare talent on the soccer field. As centre forward, he scored goals with ease, roaming the field with a flawless grace that invited comparisons with greats of that position like Jan Koller.

Francis's lack of true passion for the game prevented the state coach from drafting him into the team, but did not stop him from dominating the scoring at school and district level. At fifteen he joined the adult competition, pulling on a jersey for the Stirling Lions Soccer Club, where he set a club goal-scoring record. He attended university with a full scholarship, yet still, football was just a diversion. He had already decided on the course his life would take, and he worked single-mindedly towards it.

Francis neither sought nor avoided the company of his peers, but his mind was always elsewhere, moving on, as if there was something more interesting just out of sight, beyond that which most people could see and notice.

At the age of thirteen, he bought himself a mask, snorkel and fins. After a practice session at the city pool he plunged into the blue waters off Cottesloe Beach. There amongst the waving kelp beds and black reefs he found adventure and mystery. By his mid-teens he had his own SCUBA apparatus.

Always there was his mother, Avelina, in the car, holding a burning cigarette between index and forefinger, trailing smoke out the window, waiting while he snorkelled behind the breakers, or devouring Mills and Boon bodice-rippers at the library as he delved into thicker and more complex sources.

Avelina was the constant. No effort was too great. In return she expected obedience, help with the household chores, and shared ownership of his dreams. In addition, she required he and Camille's weekly attendance at Mass. It was easy for Francis to see his mother and God as a partnership. The painting of Jesus' crucifixion that hung in the lounge room showed a bearded man ill from pain and disappointment – always on the verge of passing into death – in that middle ground, so that the grieving could never end.

On weekends, they went together to a favourite Swan River sandbar, collecting crabs and shellfish for bait and casting them out with fishing line wrapped around glass bottles. If passers-by stared at the squat middle-aged woman, cigarette in her mouth, line held in her fingers, it did not worry Francis, for he loved her without reservation.

Avelina was contemptuous of government size and bag limits, along with the nervous little men who enforced them. She was not above wrapping undersize whiting in her shawl and secreting them in the cavernous leather handbag she carried everywhere. These she filleted on the sink at home and cooked with bread-crumbs, crisp and salty.

Sometimes, when all the students had gone for the day she would play the piano just for herself. Francis would sit at his bed-room desk working on his algebra, music resonating through the walls – pathos-laden melodies that would haunt his dreams unto death.

The memory made Francis, staring from the window of the plane, feel warm inside. The boy who had loved his mother was inside him. Loving her still.

After school, Francis began a Bachelor of Archaeology degree at the University of Western Australia, and gave up sport for study, travel and volunteer work on wrecks scattered along the Western Australian Coast. University opened Francis's eyes – lectures with scribbling students and lunches on sunny days on wooden picnic tables around the student union building. He paid his fees by instructing tourists and adventurous locals on dive charters working off Rottnest Island.

Twenty-three years old, his freshly printed PhD thesis still being considered by a panel of three professors, Francis flew to Portugal for a week. At the city museum on the Campo Grande, Francis found a pre-revolution photo of officers from the Fifth Infantry Regiment. The young captain in the middle rank, left side, was his father. Strong features made him seem noble and honest. The tingling began in Francis's feet and rose to his neck. His father had been a member of the *Movimento das Forças Armadas,* which, weeks after the photo was taken, brought the fascist regime to its knees in the Carnation Revolution.

'Your father was a hero,' Avelina had told him earnestly. 'He was wounded in those terrible weeks, seeking to free his people from the chains of fascist tyranny, and was never the same again.'

Francis visited his father's grave, weeping for a man who had lived on for just fifteen years after the revolution, forgotten and crippled. The following day, with renewed pride in his past, he returned to Australia, the dream as strong as ever.

Seven years at the Maritime Museum in Fremantle followed, during which he rose to the position of Assistant Curator. Still he was restless, unable to pursue his dream to the exclusion of all else. Then, just past his thirtieth birthday he quit and staked his future on an unlikely theory of Australia's European history, based on the proximity of Portugal's colony on Timor to parts of Northern Australia.

Using his savings, he launched a private company called Procurar Pty Ltd. The first six months he spent raising funds from the corporate sector, and with promises of full support from his old employer, he commissioned an aerial survey, using the most sophisticated equipment, over tens of thousands of square kilometres of the Western Australian and Northern Territory coastlines.

On the cusp of an expedition into one of four likely sites, Avelina was diagnosed with Stage Two, non-small cell lung cancer, and for five months he stayed home, bathing her, making peppermint tea and tempting meals on plastic trays.

In the final days she coughed incessantly from what was left of her lungs. He remembered the room, death smell thick in his nostrils – how she lay on the sterile cot – a tube clipped to one nostril. Her skin had turned sulphur yellow, wrinkled and loose over a skeletal body.

'Francisco,' she whispered through lips cracked and lifeless.

'Mãe, please, do not exert yourself—'

Avelina, however, went on, as if aware that she had only moments left to speak. 'Seek out the truth with everything you have. It is important for its own sake. Make the world understand what it was like for them.'

And in the last hours Francis watched Avelina go from vibrant expressive life, to something beyond, somewhere he could never reach her. The spark left her eyes. He felt like he carried a gut full of stone – a dam wall holding back a tide of terror.

Now he understood the essential frailty. Avelina's head sagged back against the pillow and her lower lip fell away from her teeth to leave them exposed.

Francis allowed a doctor to move him aside, leaning against

the rear wall, scarcely breathing, aching as if he had been beaten with a stick.

'I'm sorry, but your mother is gone,' the doctor said.

Francis grieved as if he had been torn in two. While trying to maintain a semblance of normality for Camille's sake, he wandered the empty rooms, where the piano sat silent, never to be played again. The dreams he had cherished for so long seemed meaningless.

The saudade became a black tide, sometimes receding, sometimes so high and painful that to walk to the kitchen and make tea became too great an effort. Dark fingers of liquid despair inched across the windows of his mind, and the pain was too much to bear.

It comes from the mist, his mother had once said, *and like the mist it has no form.* At its strongest, Francis felt as if the sun was as cold as the sea, and the air as bitter as poison. All his being, even the muscles of his arms were filled with a strange, undirected rage, like a bull seeking out a shadow to charge.

Months passed before he turned his thoughts back to the survey – the dream of finding a Portuguese shipwreck, this time with a renewed sense of purpose. With Camille's blessing he called a real estate agent and asked him for an estimate on the house.

The money from the sale allowed for a move to Darwin, the closest large city to his main area of interest – a neglected five-hundred-kilometre stretch of the far North Eastern Kimberley coastline, close to the Northern Territory border – the nearest parts of the Australian coastline to the medieval Portuguese colony on Timor.

Camille needed stability, and Francis found a house they could buy, with funds left over.

He planned a search of the areas pinpointed by the aerial surveys — calling for volunteers and screening them carefully. After considerable research he also hired Jeff Dunn and his boat, the *Josephine*. A man in his mid-forties, Jeff's wild blonde hair was streaked with grey, and his skin as weatherworn as that of a lifelong fisherman.

Over two exciting years the loose and ever-changing group of volunteers and professionals had become a team, sharing the hardships, facing the future with confidence. Now, finally, they had found something, and a dream was within reach.

QUATRO

Baggage handles sharp on his palms, Francis walked through the sliding terminal doors of Lisbon International Airport and towards the bustle of cars and crowds outside. As with previous visits, he had the sensation of treading on the bones of his own past. Men and women chattered away in his mother's tongue, unafraid to raise their voices. Tourists moved in ovine flocks, shepherded by lively young men and women.

Humid, perfumed air filled Francis's senses as he approached a row of taxis. Engines roared, horns sounded, and drivers cursed. Vehicles came and went at a rapid rate. Many were Fiats and Renaults, a large proportion of them electric. Before Francis had time to order an Uber or cab, a man hurried to meet him. He was tall for a Portuguese, his features elongated to match. 'You want taxi, senhor?'

'Sim – yes.'

'Your bags please.'

Francis gave up his overnight bag, but made no effort to part with the briefcase he clutched in one hand.

'Your destination?'

'I have a booking at the Hotel Vitoria.'

'Easy. Good choice. Very central.'

Once inside the cab, the driver smelled of garlic and onions. Freeways gave way to busy and hilly streets. Houses five or six centuries old stood close, leaning together for strength like tired old men. High-rise apartments heightened the impression that space was precious, though jacaranda and cypress trees grew between stone and pavement, and in every square.

The taxi driver, holding the wheel between his thumb and first two fingers of one hand, scarcely glanced at the road as he drove, reserving all his attention for Francis. He was, like most men of his profession, a ready conversationalist, beginning with a prompt on the weather, then European football.

'Your English is very good,' said Francis.

'Ah, I watch Sesame Street on the television almost every day. That's why.'

Francis stared at the other man, who seemed so serious he could not laugh, listening instead as the driver recounted the names of his six children, the various ailments of his elderly mother followed by his deceased father's cause of death and general failings. Finally, the taxi slowed outside a neat, white-painted hotel. Sunflowers burst from stone pots on the pavement.

Francis waited while the driver lifted his bags from the boot. 'Muito obrigado – thank you,' he said. The driver smiled and pulled away with a polite wave, leaving his passenger to carry his bags towards reception.

That evening Francis took a stroll, watching couples walk past on the grey-paved streets, arm in arm. Music poured out of café doors. The tiled walls of many of the older buildings gave the streets colour.

The yellow Tagus River in the distance reminded him of those long-ago mariners who had crossed the globe in conditions that seem inconceivable in this modern world. The Portuguese had opened up the East to Europe, landing on the shores of India, Sumatra, and Java, more than a century before the first timid excursions by the English and Dutch. By the time the Dutchman Willem Jansz in his Duyfken touched Cape York, five generations of Portuguese colonists had already lived, loved and died on nearby Timor.

Someone, perhaps fifty or even a hundred years before Jansz, had occupied the small boat Francis and his volunteers had found on the sea floor, and wielded a sword that had once been a fearsome weapon. To Francis this was not merely a matter of finding names and dates. He wanted to know everything. He wanted to close his eyes and *be* that long ago mariner.

When Francis returned to his hotel room he opened his laptop, sorting through the emails that had accumulated over the previous days. An answer from Dr Nicolá Massane caught his eye.

> Of course I would like to meet you. The item you have found is extraordinary, and I have some information to share. I know that this is an unusual request, but would you meet me at dawn tomorrow on the terrace below the Castle of São Jorge?

Francis fired back a response, replying that of course he would, and the next morning, he did as she had asked, shivering in the predawn cold as he walked the Rua do Limoeiro, reaching a bougainvillea-lined miradouro with views over the narrow alleys and ancient dwellings of the Alfama to the River Tagus, white with fog.

Advancing across the terrace Francis saw a ragtag group of men and women leaning on the rails, staring out into the gathering light. The group numbered at least three hundred. Some were elderly, some young. Many were dressed in suits as if ready to head off for a day's work in offices and businesses.

'You see them, Senhor da Costa?'

Francis turned to find a young woman at his side. The way she looked appealed to him. Her hair, brown overall, was streaked with lighter and darker shades. A mauve band held the strands away from her ears. The analytical part of his brain told him that she was not classically beautiful – that her chin was too short, and her brown eyes too dominant, yet she drew his attention and made him feel something that had not stirred in his heart for some time.

'You must be Francisco da Costa,' she said. 'I am Nicolá Massane.'

'Good morning.' The hand he shook was capable, yet neatly tended, her nails painted a pale shade of pink. 'What are those people doing?'

Nicolá's eyes widened, 'They are waiting for the King, Dom Sebastian, to return, after half a millennium, from across the sea.'

Francis hissed in wonder, 'Sebastianists?'

'Yes, the last living members of a strange and ancient sect who believe that the king, Dom Sebastian, who supposedly fell on the battlefield in 1578, will return to save Portugal.'

The four-hundred-and-fifty-year-old legend of Dom Sebastian was one Francis had digested with his mother's milk. 'Surely this is myth.'

'Myth? Oh no. Look. Does it not seem real to them?'

Francis focussed on an old man – one of many individuals of both genders staring out through the fog at the river, just starting to shimmer with the first glow of daylight. It was not difficult to imagine the returning king on the deck of his warship, crossing the river bar to safe anchorage, cannons spewing black smoke and sails ballooning with the light morning breeze.

Nicolá went on, 'As you probably know, Dom Sebastian was prophesised to return on a foggy morning, to save Portugal in her hour of need, and usher in a new age of prosperity and greatness.' She used her hands in a circular gesture to communicate the passage of time. 'Just two or three centuries ago, the Sebastianists numbered in the tens of thousands, and constituted a major political force, long after the King's natural life must have ended. Their numbers dwindled after World War Two, but the hard core remained – still yearning, still believing. Twenty years ago, just ten or twenty Sebastianists gathered here in the mornings. After the pandemic, however, with a sense of hopelessness awash in the city, the idea of a saviour resurfaced, and the movement gained traction. This is just an average crowd here this morning.'

Francis creased his eyes, 'Why are you showing me this? What is the connection?'

There was no trace of humour or irony in her eyes. 'There is an open café in the quarter of Santa Cruz. If you like we can buy coffee and breakfast while we talk.'

Francis shivered with both cold and a kind of religious awe at the faith that made these people rise at dawn and stare out at the river, waiting for the arrival of a long-dead king.

The quarter of Santa Cruz was a place of tight cobbled streets, and housing so condensed it might have been squeezed from a tube. The café nestled beside a compact police station. The dark interior was busy with those who work when others sleep – delivery men, truck drivers and members of the policia who obviously found the café more congenial than their offices next door. Nicolá led the way to a solid timber booth near an open fire. They talked little until the coffee arrived – and even then the young woman seemed content to hold her mug with both hands, palms open to absorb the warmth.

'Dom Sebastian,' she said, at last, 'was the last king in the line of Aviz. His father died of diabetes just two weeks before his birth, making him the only chance for a bona fide heir to the throne. He became king at the age of just three years, on the death of his grandfather João III. Until his majority his grandmother Catarina and Uncle Henrique acted as regents. Sebastian was raised by Jesuit priests, and came to see himself as the avenging sword of Christ against Islam.'

Francis sat, spellbound, eating the spicy pastries and drinking coffee.

'As King, he let the Jesuits run the country, and devoted himself to manly pursuits – hunting, the military – and set about fulfilling his dream of a crusade, three hundred years after the rest of Christendom had given up. Barely twenty years old, he led a first, exploratory expedition to Morocco. This encouraged him. A few years later he raised an army of eighteen thousand mercenaries and went back to – how would I say? Finish the job.'

'But of course he was killed,' Francis added.

'Not necessarily. He disappeared. Dom Sebastian was not a normal man, but a mystic – deeply religious, schooled in theology and the mysteries of his faith, and a skilled warrior. This is our greatest legend – our King Arthur if you like. More than just a story, it's a matter of the heart.' The colour rose in her cheeks and to Francis she was beautiful.

Francis felt the hair rise on the back of his neck and he shivered with superstitious excitement. 'Why are you telling me this?' he asked.

'Because the sword hilt you found … is a very special one indeed.'

He said nothing. Just stared at her.

'Francis, the sword hilt carries the remains of an inscription famous to we who have studied such things. Extraia-me não sem razão e sheathe me não sem honra: Draw me not without reason and sheathe me not without honour. In Portugal I know of only one such sword ever made. It was originally the property of King João III, and was passed down to his grandson, Dom Sebastian. Beside that inscription is the crest of the Royal House of Aviz.' She paused to draw breath. 'From the time King João died, Dom Sebastian owned that particular weapon – it may have fallen out of his hands at some stage, in Morocco for example, but it was his sword.'

Francis's breath caught in his throat. 'Are you telling me that the sword hilt I found was once carried by a King of Portugal?'

'Not just any king, but the most famous of them all. If there were any doubt I have, in addition, determined that the weapon was manufactured by one Diogo Lopes de Sousa, ironsmith to the house of Aviz.' She paused, 'Where on earth did you find it?'

Cold fingers walked Francis's spine. 'Can we just say the Australian coastline – the Indian Ocean side. The exact location must remain confidential at this stage.'

'That's, well … incredible.' She rose, gazing at Francis as if she wanted to devour him. She slipped her bag over one shoulder. 'I have to go to work now, but can we catch up soon? Perhaps at the library, the Biblioteca Nacional? Today is crazy, but my last lecture tomorrow is at one, so I could meet you at three, does that suit you?'

'Of course. I'd like that very much.'

When she had gone, Francis left the café and walked back to the miradouro. The Sebastianists had gone. A woman sat alone on a bench, reading a paperback novel with a pursed, almost critical expression. Her glasses were huge on her face, her greying hair restrained by oversized pins.

Moving past her, Francis took his place at the rail, standing so the cold iron pushed against his midriff. Staring out at the river he almost hoped to see the king, but instead a roaring filled his ears.

While rolling fog swallowed the eerie river mouth he heard voices, and conjured faces from the deep sense of history that pervaded the harbour. The saudade, ever close, enveloped him in fingers of mist, choking thick and white.

The vision, when it came, was that of a madman, but yet the truth. Ancient fingers entwined with his own. Five hundred years fell away.

Francis had learned to feel the past, and would never know peace again.

CINCO

The smell of burning flesh filled the square. The screams reached a tragic crescendo, and the gorge rose in my throat. I counted eighteen pyres, each with its own burning, living human being, tied to a stake in the centre.

Amongst the carnage walked the Grand Inquisitor – Henrique the Chaste, Cardinal of the Church and great uncle of Dom Sebastian, the King. Henrique wore the scarlet robe and biretta of office. That he would display the accoutrements of his position while he presided over savage death chilled my heart.

Even over the screams Cardinal Henrique's voice was raised, the Latin words unintelligible at that distance. In his fat hands he carried a golden incense pot, and it jingled as he walked and sang.

The Royal Square was packed with onlookers all the way to the river, patrolled by the gold-visored knights of Henrique's private army – the guarda-costras. Tears fell from my eyes at what happens when unscrupulous men are backed by both church and state.

The burning men and women were dying now – no longer

cringing from the flames, but sagging, the fat from their bodies making the fires burn still hotter – creating a vaporous blaze that seared to the bone. My eyes returned to Henrique, hating his bearing, his self-righteousness, and his smug superiority. I knew that my Portugal was changing – that power to this man was a fuel, and that even then he was reaching out for the greatest prize of all.

Remaining at the rail until the flames died low, I saw slaves, under the direction of the heartless guarda-costras, remove the blackened remains of the dead and shovel them into horse-drawn wagons. Still the spectators lingered, watching this process like ghouls.

Henrique's litter appeared, borne on the shoulders of eight massive Angolan slaves. His high-pitched voice needled this vehicle into position and then, with the aid of portable steps, he ascended into the curtained interior and was whisked away.

Only then did I turn, heavy of heart and limb, whispering to God under my breath, knowing with all my soul that He had not willed the death of those poor souls in the square below. I prayed for my country, and for my king. Terrible things lay ahead for us – the Sea of Straw was filled with the traffic of war – boats from lean caravels to hulking great carracks of five hundred tons or more.

How can I rest until this story is told? Can I let such a tale slip unnoticed into history, or allow men to take liberties, inventing lies about that which is precious to me? I, Luis Pereira, Dom Sebastian's friend and confessor, can alone let the truth stand for posterity.

I am but a Dominican priest, and a priest's life should be one of order, solitude, and reflection. Instead I have seen blood and death, fighting and loving. To my shame I have spent half a lifetime on my knees begging for forgiveness. Now it is time to record the things that I have seen.

The years muddle me with distance. Moments both great and humble clamour for my attention. Images rise and fall before my eyes like paintings in a gallery. I begin this account as one close to the king. An observation post, if you will, to the calamitous events of our time.

The Palace, as I approached it across the square, was the envy of Europe. Tall spires and arched vaults told the world that Portugal owned the Eastern trade, that Portugal was fat with profit. The library held seventy thousand volumes collected over three hundred years of unbroken dynastic rule. One thousand clerks, assistants, slaves and entertainers toiled between her walls. The Palace was itself a small city, with theatres, barracks, living quarters, eating places and meeting halls. It had its own rules, and enough intrigue to keep our playwrights busy indeed. The palace crowded against the river Tagus – yellow, wide and the key to an empire.

Nearing the entrance to the Doña Maria wing of the palace, the smell of burning flesh receded. Couples strolled, and officials hurried by with papers under their arms. I walked on to the marble steps of the main entrance. At the summit a pair of Palace Guards waved me through, and I marched with an outraged stride down the corridor, a thoroughfare floored with marble apart from a central strip of blue carpet. On both walls hung tapestries and displays of arms and armour. Arched doorways led in all directions.

Still I walked on, ascending more steps, until a guard admitted me into a courtyard, floored with stone. A water fountain, complete with lily-filled pool, dominated the centre. Plants both exotic and native grew in bursts of colour from earthenware pots.

Reaching the doorway I heard the shrill sound of steel on steel. This noise was common here – one of Dom Sebastian's favoured haunts. Our young king preferred the sun on his shoulders to the dark throne room, and martial arts to pushing a quill along a page.

On a stone bench sat a group of exhausted warriors. Foreheads ran with sweat, and more than a drop or two of fresh blood trickled down arms and legs, stoically ignored by the sufferers. All eyes followed the movements of two men sparring in the open space.

One I recognised as the captain of the Palace Guards, Tonio Fonseca, a good friend of the king. The other was Dom Sebastian himself – a tall and rangy young man, arms thick with muscle and twined by veins, revealed by shorter than usual sleeves. His neck was tight with sinew and his hands larger than those of normal men. His face was compelling, through fierce, pale eyes, and the strong jaw of a born athlete. The close-cut auburn hair spoke of his royal bloodlines, for reddish locks had long manifested themselves in the House of Aviz.

Like most men, Dom Sebastian did not spar in armour, but wore tight-fitting breeches, a loose shirt and a leather chest-guard fixed by straps. A bracer shielded his sword arm. His opponent wore a short length of chain mail to protect his neck, and a wrist band of beaten iron to deflect any stroke that might pass through the blurring defences of his blade. Damp patches at the under-arms of both men betrayed their exertion.

If Dom Sebastian was the most skilled swordsman in the country, Tonio Fonseca was not far behind. His father had died when he was young, and though raised by his mother, he became a protégé of King João. He was less tall than the king, yet stocky, and swarthy of skin, with thick eyebrows and vigorous facial growth that needed shaving twice a day. At birth he had been afflicted with a minor cleft palate, yet the palace surgeons had done their best, and the only remaining sign was a scar below his nose that few men would dare draw attention to. It was most visible when he became anxious or upset.

When those blades struck, they did so violently, yet with speed and grace – the warriors advancing and withdrawing over twenty square paces of the courtyard – conscious of and responsive to each other, moving in concert like the most graceful dancers.

Yet, those who have been at the receiving end will understand just how fearsome a hand-held sword can be. The largest are as heavy as axes, and a strong man can demolish a wooden house with one. King Richard the Lionheart once cleaved through an iron bar with one stroke. The men who wield them for a living are inordinately strong, and sparring can be a life-threatening past time.

Not daring to disturb the pair, lest I distract one and precipitate an injury, I waited until, with a clever feint, Dom Sebastian over-extended his opponent, mesmerised him with the bright blade, then dexterously kicked his shins out from underneath him. Tonio landed hard, elbows and knees bearing the brunt of the impact. Breath oomphed from his lungs.

Dom Sebastian lowered his weapon, smiling as he helped the fallen man to his feet, then threw one sweaty arm around his friend's neck and pulled him close, playing to his audience. 'This man is like a brother to me,' he laughed. 'But still I can lay him on his arse any time I like.'

I must have been one of the few who noticed the momentary dark scowl that crossed Tonio's face before he recovered, smiled and returned Dom Sebastian's embrace. The crowd clapped and laughed, while the young king disentangled himself, passed his sword to one page and accepted a towel from another. Using this to mop sweat from his forehead, neck and cheeks he walked towards me, smiling.

'Ah, Padre, did you see?'

'I saw.' Dom Sebastian's need to draw attention to his actions had irked me in the past, but now I understood that need, and accepted it as part of him. I loved the sum of those parts like a father or brother might. Dom Sebastian was an unfinished masterpiece, and it was a delight to watch him grow in stature and wisdom as the months and years passed. Like most men in their middle twenties, he was somewhat self-absorbed, and besotted with chivalry and honour, yet still there was much to admire about him.

'Where were you earlier?' he asked. 'I felt the need for absolution.'

'I'm sorry, but I was busy.'

A slave hurried across with a mug of whatever tonic Dom Sebastian's quack doctors had lately prescribed for him. He downed it in one draught, belched so loudly that his sycophants across the courtyard laughed, then clapped a hand on my shoulder. 'Isn't it a wonderful day?'

At that I gripped his arm and led him away until we were out of earshot. 'Not such a lovely day for those men and women just this hour burned to death in the square, while your Uncle Henrique preened amongst them, singing and scattering incense smoke as if it might perfume over the stink of his guilt.'

Dom Sebastian reached out to the blue flower of one of the

Brazilian calatheas plants that adorned the courtyard, plucked a petal and rubbed it between thumb and forefinger. The aromatic remnants he sniffed delicately. 'My uncle is the Cardinal of Lisbon, and the Grand Inquisitor. What he does is outside my control, and besides, the burning men are New Christians. They have only themselves to blame.'

The term 'New Christians' referred to Jews who had pretended to convert to Christianity to escape the Inquisition, yet wore their tallit and yarmulke in private, their hidden rabbis continuing to promote their faith. It was indeed these unfortunates that Henrique had burned in the square, for he considered himself an expert in rooting them out. I frowned, 'Yes, but when will Henrique stop? The day after tomorrow, you, me, and every soldier loyal to you sails for war in Morocco. You cannot leave Henrique here unfettered.'

'My uncle is a pious man—'

'He is a butcher.' I wanted to tell Dom Sebastian how I had watched Henrique seek power for thirty years – seen him thirst for it like a drunkard for his next goblet of wine. 'Your place is here. Send the ships away, and the troops home to their families,' I implored. 'Morocco is not our fight.'

The good-natured smile slipped from Dom Sebastian's lips. 'Tell, me then, Padre, when do we fight? When the Ottomans land on our shores? Their advance must be stopped – Morocco is merely an excuse for the Muslims to once again push the boundaries of their empire outwards. Besides, we were victorious last time.'

Grimacing, I recalled how two years earlier Dom Sebastian had set off with an expeditionary force, landed at one of our forts on the coast near Tangiers and satisfied himself with pillaging a few unfortified Muslim towns and outposts, embarking for home before any real opposition formed. Now, however, he would fight for real – on the pretext that the Moroccan ruler, Abu Abdullah Mohammed Il Saadi's throne had been stolen by his uncle, Abd-Al Malik, backed by soldiers supplied by the expansionist Ottomans.

Eighteen thousand men waited in tent barracks on the outskirts of our city – many of them knights of our three great military orders, along with Papal troops from Italy, mercenaries from France and England, and our own regular troops. The first units were already embarking on the ships that filled the Sea of Straw.

'I will not argue with your motives,' I said, 'but implore you, on all we have shared, to reconsider. Deal with Henrique first – send him to Rome, out of the way, while you are gone, and the da Câmara brothers with him. Or better still, stay here – let Philip of Spain fight the Ottomans.'

Dom Sebastian, however, smiled with that frustrating, patronising expression that said – *I am not listening to you.* 'Padre, don't you remember your own lessons? You taught me yourself that Islam has ruled Portugal before, that her kings have stood where we stand now. Would you have them here again? Do you want to see the Umayyad Dynasty rule in Lisbon? For eight hundred years we have fought them, and now we have the chance to deliver the commanding blow.'

Knowing myself misguided in thinking I had a chance of persuading him, I lowered my head in submission. 'To go to war or stay is your decision, but please, do not trust Henrique and Martin da Câmara to administer Portugal while you are away – instead appoint a committee of your most trusted noblemen.'

'I have full faith in my Jesuit brothers.'

I seethed – the Jesuits – that most recent and conservative order of Holy men had wormed their way into every facet of

Portuguese government. Frei Martin da Cãmara was Chancellor, and thus head of the civil service. Dom Sebastian increasingly placed major decisions in his hands, and those of his brother Luis.

At that moment, one of the poets who, like stray dogs, followed Dom Sebastian's every move, climbed a stone bench and shouted for quiet. He had composed a verse honouring the King's success in the sparring circle. I was forced to wait, listening to this rhyming nonsense until the applause died away.

'One last request,' I said finally, 'and please do not refuse me this time. Leaving the contents of the Royal Treasury here with Henrique in control would be a grave mistake. Allow me to spirit the most special items away temporarily, to a monastery I trust. You have enough gold to fund your war. Some things are too valuable to allow your uncle unfettered access.'

Dom Sebastian's broad forehead creased into a frown. 'Would this transfer be a difficult thing?'

'No. I have already made arrangements and could begin within an hour.'

'Very well. Do it. But I hold you responsible for its safety.'

I wasted no time in setting my plan in motion. As Dom Sebastian's tutor and confessor no part of the palace was barred to me. I first called at the barracks room, to gather my hand-picked team, and I led them to the treasury, where Dom Sebastian had sent a messenger with the news that they should expect my visit.

The clerks, as always, spluttered and carried on, full of self-importance and bluster. Yet none dared argue with the word of the king, and within an hour the most important part of Portugal's riches were on their way to safety.

It would be many nervous hours before news of the operation's success came back to me. I intended to pass those hours in my quarters, comforted by my books.

As I made my way to my room, the stone corridor was dark, but for candles fluttering with a breeze that must have wafted through cracks in the blocks themselves. I hurried on, passing slaves and courtiers, reaching the wider, marbled thoroughfares of the royal wing of the palace, where Dom Sebastian's rooms occupied an entire floor.

Below this level, yet above the lowly slaves' quarters, were a number of rooms that housed men who Dom Sebastian might require at a moment's notice. Foremost among these were several physicians, a nurse, an astrologer, poets, and an artist, who might be called upon to pick up his charcoal whenever the king performed some action deemed worthy of posterity. My own room was located here, and when I opened the door I felt the gentle warmth of sanctuary as I invariably did upon entering my abode.

The room was of stone block construction – twenty paces square. One double hinged door, now open, led to a balcony overlooking the river. Another hid a discrete closet that was serviced by running water, raised by hand pumps to a reservoir high in the Palace. True to my vows, however, there was nothing luxurious about my furniture. A sleeping pallet lay in one corner; a hard oak table and three chairs in the centre. Beside the table lay my prayer mat, woven from river reeds. Numerous shelves held books and manuscripts – one of the few luxuries I allowed myself. The candles sat in cheap brass holders and were of market quality only.

Having filled a mug with water from an earthenware jug, I moved to the balcony. From there I watched my ten handpicked men board the punt that would take them across the river. With them were three nondescript cases that looked like luggage. On the other side they would be met by a carriage and more men, ready for the journey to the hiding place. All were Dom Sebastian's most loyal guards. Men he trusted like brothers.

Pleased with my work I moved back into the room, taking up my seat and opening one of my Bibles. This version was in Ancient Greek, a language that I made sure to keep touch with regularly. All written scripts require practice, and this one more than most.

Less than an hour passed before footsteps sounded outside, a slow dragging gait that I knew well, followed by a knock on the door. Upon opening it I looked into the single good eye of Luis da Câmara.

I greeted him formally, yet made no effort to invite him inside. He was an unusual man: legends abounded of his days in the African hellhole of Tétuan, providing spiritual aid to Christian prisoners there – and his time as amanuensis to Ignatius de Loyola, the founder of the Jesuit order. Now, however, he was a ruined wreck. The remnants of his hair he had greased and combed over the bald sections of scalp. He made no effort to cover his one empty eye socket, and his skin had the pallor and texture of a dead cod drying out on a beach.

The nature of da Câmara's illness was subject to public speculation, for his symptoms were consistent with the venereal disease, gonorrhoea. According to rumour he had, on occasion, performed the act necessary to contract it.

'I hear that you wasted no time venting your precious conscience to the king,' he said. His voice was unsteady from illness, and he reeked like death.

Of all the Jesuits, da Câmara was the one who hated me most, for it had been I, on the orders of the king's grandmother, who had replaced him as the then teenage Sebastian's tutor and confessor. When Dom Sebastian acceded to the throne he was but three years of age. His mother, Doña Juana, had been forced back to her native Spain at her brother's insistence.

Henrique, and the young Sebastian's grandmother Catarina ruled together as regents, despite a bitter rivalry. When the time came to appoint a tutor Henrique chose da Câmara and Catarina chose me. At first the Inquisitor had his way, however, when the young king was thirteen, with a suddenness that had surprised me, an outraged Catarina informed me that I was to replace da Câmara.

Though Catarina had since passed away, whether from natural causes or otherwise I know not, Dom Sebastian and I were close, and da Câmara, for all his scheming, had not yet found a way to resume his former relationship with the young man. Instead, he hovered in the background, manipulating and influencing.

I tried to keep my voice even. 'There must be a better way of dealing with New Christians than taking them from their homes and burning them to death.'

Da Câmara sneered, 'You so believe, do you? Well who cares? You bask in the King's favour, for now. That will not always be the case. One day you will find yourself unprotected by the young fool.'

'Dom Sebastian is young, yes, but no fool, and despite your own and Henrique's efforts to fill him with hatred and misogyny, he is smart and bright. You have failed at moulding him to your own image. Every day I help bring him back from the far boundaries of reason where you took him.'

'You have had your day, Dominican, ours is dawning.'

'And on that day, I imagine, the streets of Lisbon will be thick with smoke from the fires you build. How many of her citizens will burn if Henrique and his Jesuits take control, I wonder?'

'They burn themselves,' da Câmara sneered. 'We but apply the spark.'

I have long observed that a man's eyes display much of what he carries inside his heart. The advantage of dealing with those who have a single optic is that this tendency is somewhat magnified. When I stared into that dark orb of Luis da Câmara, I shuddered at what I saw there, for this was a man in love with power, and with a grudge against youth and beauty. 'There is no goodness left in you,' I said. 'You hope for death and suffering.'

His voice now hissed from his throat like that of a snake. 'You know nothing, Dominican.'

'Indeed? Then why waste your time here? Tell me, does this visit have purpose?'

'I came here to bring you a message,' da Câmara growled. 'A warning that you ignore at your peril.'

'Then hurry – say what you have to say, and go. Unlike you, I am a busy man and have much to do other than scheming and creeping around corridors—'

'Beware, Padre, of the sins of yesteryear. That which you believe is not known, has come to the ears of men who are tired of your troublemaking ways. Cease your agitating, go quietly on the fleet with the King, or harm will come to the one whom you love most.'

With those words he turned away, his idiosyncratic gait still echoing in that narrow space. I did not move until he had gone, until the stink of him had cleared from the corridor and no vestige of it could enter my chambers.

SEIS

y favourite prayer was Lauds, for it ended with the sun rising over the far bank of the river. On this morning, from my balcony, that summer fireball seemed brighter and more intense than usual – climbing with the glowing heat of a forge-fire from the horizon, dancing over the unruffled waters.

As soon as it rose clear I hurried back to my chambers and dressed. All night I had considered Luis da Câmara's words, and was cognisant that I must act before it was too late. The secret he had alluded to was far too precious to risk, and I could not sail away without taking steps to protect her. Only one full day remained before I would join my king on the flagship as she took her place at the head of the war fleet.

Donning a clean robe, I hurried down through the Doña Maria entrance, and into the square, where the only signs of the executions from two days previously were blackened patches on the stone. There were now, in the midst of Henrique's latest pogrom against the New Christians, some hundreds of these marks, a record of the church-sanctioned savagery that held sway in this land – and Spain too, for the Inquisition was a cancer of the whole Iberian peninsula, and as far as I knew, the Christian world.

My mind was so fraught that I ignored my surroundings, though summer in Lisbon is a wonderful time of year. After all, she was one of the world's great cities, straddling the river Tagus, drawing life from the safe harbour she provided for our navigators and fleets. Beyond the river the seven hills of our city rose, each topped by a castle, church, or miradouro.

I hurried on past buildings and temples older than the days of the Caesars, and others that reflected the architecture of the Moorish occupation. The best and most recent constructions, hewn of stone and oak, represented our new and prosperous age, buildings such as the massive Jerónimos Monastery taking shape on the riverbank at Belém.

Deep in the Alfama, the poorest quarter of Lisbon, I climbed the steep Alley of the Cross, jammed with rickety stone buildings and multi-storey apartments where the inhabitants live virtually atop one another. The stench of sewage mingled with that of rubbish and here my natural desire to move on was defeated by the increasing physical effort of climbing that hill. At this point, on my regular visits, I would smile, for there were few aspects of my life I enjoyed more than that of Patron of the Orphanage of Saint John.

Today, however, my thoughts were of just one among the orphans. Sixteen years ago it had been I who touched holy water to her head and named her Aletia, a popular girl's name that means, 'the honest one.'

My hands shake as I try to find words to describe Aletia as she was then. So many aspects of her crowd for attention in my mind. I know well how she entranced those of us lucky enough to know her. The way she walked, hands lifting the sides of her skirts so they did not hamper her, darting forward as if loath to waste a moment of her time on this earth.

Picture a slim young woman with long dark hair that fell in waves of velvet. Picture eyes of glossy green, a poem in every glance. Youth in all its curious devilment – bewitching and blissfully naïve all at once.

At the crest, level with Leitão de Gamboa's butchery store with its blood stench, I paused to catch my breath. Just ahead I saw that Senhor Valadares the fruitseller had set up his cart, and beside him stood Aletia herself.

Valadares's wooden trays carried an abundance of citrus from the Algarve, apples from the Trás-os-Montes. Lettuce, carrots and beets from the market gardens just out of the city. The fruit seller, a toothless man who smelled of donkeys and rotten fruit, was busy picking out the delicacies that would not keep until the following day and filling Aletia's basket.

When I walked into view she picked up the overfull basket as if it were nothing, skipping across to meet me. 'Padre,' she cried, 'Frei Aguiar is not expecting you. He will be ashamed that he has not made preparations.'

I knew my Dominican brother well. 'Aguiar will recover. Let's go in, for I am leaving the country tomorrow, and have much to do.' Her frown of concern made my heart weak, and I yearned to take her in my arms and comfort her. Of course, that was not possible, so I made my face kind. 'Don't fret on my behalf. I'll keep away from danger and be back soon.'

'I'm pleased to hear it. Now just wait until you see Belchior, I swear he has grown another span in the last week, and young Maria has painted a watercolour of the Church of Santa Lucia that you will not believe—'

Children! How I loved them, scampering through those corridors until my throat grew hoarse from telling them to slow down. Small boys with sleeves too long for their arms, and faces and knees that, no matter how many times they were wiped, soon became grubby once more. Girls that huddled with their wooden dolls, dressing them with rags cut from cast off attire of their own.

Children were my passion. Children of all sizes. The youngest were mere babes, crying through the night until an older child or priest arrived with a mug of warm goat's milk and a rag to suck it from. Most, however, were between four and eight years – mere urchins – but with questioning minds and growing bodies, already seeking to understand their place in the world.

On this morning, as I entered the dining hall, the greetings were noisy and enthusiastic. Aletia de Calvez shared her donated fruit with scrupulous fairness, and, eating without decorum, the smaller children clung to my legs and competed to hold my hands. Frei Aguiar watched, wispy hair clinging to his pink scalp, the knuckles of his left hand white on his cane, ready with a word of praise or stiff rebuke depending on what action a particular child's behaviour warranted.

Throughout that hectic morning, I first sought to spend time with Frei Aguiar, then Aletia, a difficulty considering how busy she was with mothering the younger orphans. When I managed to corner her, she was in the kitchen adding flour and eggs to a porcelain mixing bowl.

During Aletia's formative years I had made time each day to arrive at the orphanage and teach. She had been a bright and inquisitive student, particularly fond of the most tricky word games I was able to invent.

These games had become a tradition with us, and almost every conversation was preceded by one.

'I heard an interesting tongue-twister yesterday,' I said.

Aletia paused in her mixing, already smiling. 'What is it, Padre?'

'Try this,' I said, 'and say it quickly – A aranha arranha a rã, a rã arranha a aranha – the spider scratches the frog, the frog scratches the spider.'

She was so earnest, filling her lungs with air, eyes dancing with delight as she stumbled over the repeated vowels. 'A aranha, aranha a rã, a rã arranha … oh just let me try that again … A aranha, aranha … oh please don't laugh at me Padre. I'll get it, you know I will.'

'Indeed you will, but please practise it later. For now, while we're alone, I wanted to have a word about something else.'

'Yes?'

'I have a gift for you.' During the night I had thought out how I would approach the subject with her, without divulging the sudden necessity to place her out of harm's way.

Aletia did not pause in her labours. 'Gifts are not necessary, Padre.'

Never once, over the years, had I neglected her birthday. This gift, however, was something else. I cleared my throat. 'You and I have sometimes talked about the countries in the East, and the opportunities there.'

Aletia ceased her work for long enough to look into my eyes suspiciously. 'That is true, Padre.'

'And you know that I have promised to use all my influence to ensure that you have the best possible chance at a good life.'

'Yes, you have made that promise, though I am happy here.'

'This is an orphanage, and you are almost a woman.' It was

true, for in the last twelve months her breasts had grown from grapes to pears, and her hips broadened. 'You cannot stay here. As you know, the India Fleet will not sail until next Easter, but there is a smaller, provisioning fleet being assembled for September, as soon as the winds serve for them to sail. By then I will have finalised arrangements for you to sail as an orfâs d'El-Reia – a crown orphan, with a dowry sponsored by the King. A dozen rich merchants in Goa or Malacca will vie for your hand.' The men I spoke of were indeed amongst the richest in the world – with profit margins measured in the thousands of percentage points. They cared little for the social norms of home and would compete lustily for the hand of a young, pretty virgin such as Aletia. Her life, as the lady of a spice tycoon, would be richer than anything she could expect here.

Aletia stared, 'I am to leave Portugal?'

'Is your head made of rotten garlic, or haven't you been listening? Yes, you will leave – in order to live a better life.'

Tears sprang forth at the corners of her eyes, and this physical sign of her distress made me soften. 'I realise that this is a shock to you. Rather see it as an opportunity. You will live in luxury, and perhaps one day return to Lisbon with your wealthy husband. Staying here you could never fly so high. That is good news, isn't it?'

'Yes Padre. Yet it will be hard to say goodbye.'

'The children are your family, I know, but you have outgrown them.'

'Will you be going to the East with me?'

'No child. My place is here.'

'I might never see you again.'

'Yes, and that will be as hard for me as it is for you. Still, it is the least winding path to a greener pasture.'

Aletia returned to her mixing bowl, stirring furiously. At this point I should have left her to her thoughts. I lingered instead, studying those alert brown eyes of hers. They were so tragic that it broke my heart to know that I was the cause of her pain.

Ceasing work now, she regarded me seriously. 'Thank you Padre, but I am frightened.'

'The Lord will give you strength,' I said.

When I left the orphanage, it was with a heavy heart. Indeed, once on the street, the tears that I had long denied myself flooded down my cheeks, and the burning sensation in the back of my throat turned to fire. Thus afflicted, I dawdled across town, oblivious to the street chatter and bustle of trade that made Lisbon such a lively, prosperous city.

Approaching the Alley of Saint Helena, however, I heard shouts and jostling. This sound emanated from a group of guards pushing and shoving citizens from the roadway, thus allowing the passage of men on horseback, one being Martin da Câmara. Next came the open litter that carried his brother Luis, my visitor from the previous night, that hideous one eye not looking my way.

The da Câmara brothers, I well knew, seldom left the safety of their usual haunts and this alone was enough to arouse my suspicions. Rather than heading back towards the Palace, I followed at a discreet distance as they moved on past the Sé, to the sumptuous apartments of Cardinal Henrique.

Halfway down the next block, in the shade of a grove of street-side persimmon trees I saw a figure hurrying towards me. As we closed on each other I recognized Dom Sebastian's best friend Tonio Fonseca. Up close we clasped hands.

'You are just the man I would have wished to see,' I said. He and I had never been close – he was a strange and very guarded man, but his pedigree was beyond reproach. His father had been a loyal friend of the long dead King João, a friendship cut short by Cortes Fonseca's tragic death in a boating accident on the Sea of Straw. Of course, prior to the death there had been rumours of a most unfortunate nature, though Tonio had either never heard tell of this long-ago scuttlebutt, or if so, had never given any sign.

Both late father and son enjoyed the nickname, royally bestowed, of Leal, the loyal one. I trusted Tonio absolutely.

'Have you seen the strange and suspicious procession just ahead of us?' I asked.

'I could hardly miss them,' he said. 'They are like circus clowns. What do you make of it?'

'I am not yet sure, but I intend to find out. Will you join me?'

The scar on Tonio's upper lip was white and glaring against the brown, bristled skin of the rest of his face. 'Unfortunately, I am on urgent business of my own. Leave it Padre, they can do no harm with their scheming. You are too suspicious of them.'

'Perhaps so, but I think I will continue on, just in case.'

'Go with God then Padre.'

'And you also.'

Without a backward glance I left Tonio to his errand and continued in pursuit of the unorthodox group as they reached Henrique's apartments. Upon reaching the gates I was further intrigued to see the liveried coach of the Bishop of Coimbra, Manoel de Menezes, arriving also, that personage himself being escorted inside by the guarda-costras. I made myself invisible behind a pillar as the da Câmara brothers were also admitted.

Waiting, loitering, wondering what to do, I watched the group enter Henrique's lair. Here were at least three powerful political figures, all with suspect motives, converging on the source of the threat to the one whom I loved most. Not only that but this gathering was occurring just one sunrise before Dom Sebastian would sail to war. Could I afford to walk away?

Once the da Câmara brothers had disappeared into the building, I walked the path through the gates, bright with flowers on either side. Tall, thick hedges had been trimmed into perfect geometric shapes. Green lawn surrounded the garden beds, interspersed with Romanesque statues.

As I approached the main door, three guarda-costras stood in my path. These were the highest paid and best treated men at arms in the nation, answerable only to Henrique. The regiment had been created under licence from Pope Paul IV some twenty years earlier, and from the start had been endowed with freedoms not available to other men. It is my belief that the consequent excesses, along with copious idle time, like children with no restrictions or limits, had placed them outside the normal moral sphere.

'Move aside,' I demanded. 'I wish to enter.'

The centre man responded by placing one hand on the hilt of his sword. 'We have orders that none may pass this point.'

'How dare you!' I blustered, 'I have urgent business with the Cardinal, and it cannot wait. Do you know who I am?'

The man looked at his fellows, then back at me. 'Wait here, I'll check with the Steward.'

The man who had spoken disappeared inside, and while I waited, to avoid the baleful stare of the others, I turned and looked out at the garden and the cathedral, with its towering twin bell towers in the background. The normality of that vista calmed me, and helped time pass until the guard returned, accompanied by Henrique's steward, a Greek by the name of Milos. This man studied me with jerky eyes, his mouth a bloodless slit above a plaited beard.

'Blessings of the day, Padre, but the Cardinal has requested that he not be interrupted while his meeting is in progress.'

While looking at Milos, I inclined my head at the guards. 'Can we talk in private?'

'Yes, come with me.' He turned to the guards. 'This is a man of God. I will vouch for him.'

Milos led me inside and out of earshot, behind the oblong, deep green leaves of an Indian rubber tree, a popular indoor plant. I turned on him with all the sanctimonious rage I could manage. 'Are you stupid? Henrique will have you whipped, for I am late.'

The Greek frowned so his brow reddened and furrowed like ploughed earth. 'I did not realise that you are one of them.'

'Did you not think that they need me to succeed?'

'I did not think, Padre. Many apologies.'

'I assume they are in the Reunião Room?'

'Yes, I will take you—'

'No, I know the way. Stay here and keep a better eye on the door than those buffoons out there.'

Before the Greek steward could respond I was already stepping away across the marble and down the corridor, praying that Milos would not rush after me, or worse, call the guards. Only once I had turned the corner did I relax enough for my chest to rise and fall in its regular pattern.

Over the years I had visited the Cardinal's apartments enough to know each framed image that adorned the walls – famous images by the greatest artists of our age, and the blue tiled brilliance of the corridors. My intimate knowledge of the place took me past the main door to the room I was seeking. There I found a side corridor and a double door. This led to a caterer's kitchen. Moving on inside, using my hands to feel my way forward in the dark, I reached a cubby-hole through which foodstuffs and drinks could be passed to staff on the inside. Here I stopped, able to look through that empty space while remaining in darkness myself.

The Reunião Room was panelled with teak, inlaid with ivory, sandalwood and rosewood. An oak table large enough to seat twenty noble couples dominated. Just six robed figures, however, now occupied the carved chairs. These were, as I had supposed, the da Câmara brothers and de Menezes. The latter was an important man, Rector of the University and Bishop of Coimbra, with sharp features, and soft white hair spilling from his mitre.

The Grand Inquisitor himself, Cardinal Henrique, occupied the head of the table, bovine and heavy, his washed out brown eyes assessing each man in turn. The Cardinal was not a young man – having seen perhaps sixty-five winters – and his hair, never thick, was all but gone, though the red galero on his head hid that bald pate. Liver spots and moles marked his skin, and his lips were pink and bulbous beneath a thin moustache.

A stranger, olive of skin, with a nose shaped like the fin of a shark, was speaking. He looked Moorish in both appearance and dress, and spoke what I recognised as Darija Arabic through an interpreter who stood at his shoulder. This was a presence I had not counted on, for the man must be from far away, his skin marked with the sun of desert summers.

This stranger launched into a long and involved explanation that included gestures as complicated as those of a music conductor. The interpreter then translated that harsh tongue into broken Portuguese. I quickly learned the dark stranger's name, for the interpreter preceded every statement with 'Abdul Samad says ...' before detailing what he had said.

Words are innocent in isolation, yet together these added up to such obscenity I could scarce draw breath, especially when

Cardinal Henrique spoke also, at the same time passing over an unbound sheaf of papers which the man who called himself Abdul Samad then examined in consultation with his interpreter.

Treason! And it was happening before my eyes. I knew I had to get away intact, and warn Dom Sebastian, for Henrique had just sold our battle plans to the enemy.

With this realisation, however, came a knock on the main door. The Greek steward, Milos, appeared. His eyes searched the group assembled at the table and I knew that he was surprised to see that I had not yet made it to the table. He was no fool.

I was already backing away from my hiding place. Too late, I turned to the sound of footsteps. Grim-faced men crowded into my hiding place. Raising my arm in a vain attempt to fend off a blow, I was conscious of a sharp impact on my skull, and then the loss of power from my limbs and mind.

I remember strong arms cushioning my fall, then nothing.

SETE

Back in childhood I had a nurse, for my parents were moderately wealthy. Her name was Augusta – an Italian woman, broad of hips and face. Sweet by nature, she was inclined to spoil me. As I grew into a rowdy toddler she would sweep me up in her arms and walk the gardens around the Castle of Saint George, describing each rose and thrush in soothing tones. The gentle motion of her arms would lull me to sleep, and when I woke it was to see her smiling face and feel comfort such as I have not known before or since.

My waking shattered a dream that had been so pleasant I might have let it continue forever – safe and warm in Augusta's embrace, secure and happy. The waking was a strange one, however, for the lulling, gentle motion continued, and I became confused as to where on God's earth I might be.

Sitting up, I found that the motion that had so appealed to my senses was the rocking of a horse-drawn cart, and that it was dark outside. I realised also, from the smell of unwashed male bodies, and the murmur of conversation, that I was not alone.

Hardly had I woken before the man beside me responded. I felt the razor-sharp prick of steel against my neck, then a gruff voice, 'Do not breathe a word, nor try to escape. Henrique does not wish to kill you, yet we have his permission to do so if it becomes necessary. Do you understand?'

'Sim.' I was surprised to find my throat so dry I could scarcely form the word. 'Where are you taking me?'

A hand struck my other cheek, leaving my skin stinging. 'No questions. Just shut your mouth.'

My eyes became accustomed to the darkness and I thus saw more of our surroundings – deep forest for the most part, with moon-blanched mountains in the distance. Knowing that we could have travelled only a few leagues from Lisbon, and calculating from the position of the North Star that we were moving away from the city, I judged us to be west of Sintra somewhere, deep in the forests and mountains there – an uninhabited and empty place frequented only by timber cutters, beasts and hermits.

Another hour or more passed, the track growing narrower. Wheels now clattered over stony ruts, so that the journey was no longer the gentle lullaby of a nurse, but the fierce shaking of an angry father. Ahead was a light in the darkness, and my two minders stirred. One produced a rope and fastened my wrists together, so tight that I gritted my teeth with pain. I dared not complain, lest this precipitate still worse treatment.

The trees drew back somewhat. The man who had earlier threatened me with a knife gripped my forearm while the other left the carriage. I heard voices from outside, and then my other guard returned and barked an order through the open door.

'Get him out.'

This was achieved by dragging me bodily until I thumped

to the earth. Since my hands were fixed together by the wrists I was unable to use them to soften my fall. Instead my thigh and shoulder took the brunt and breath left my lungs. Dew-wet earth smeared my body.

'Get up,' one of my captors roared, and when I failed to respond a boot lashed out and caught me in the ribs. Fear ruled my movements then, and anxious to avoid more pain, I rolled to my feet and stood, coughing. My tied hands hung abjectly below me.

One of the two guarda-costras reached out and propelled me forward. 'Walk, priest.'

We had indeed reached a clearing, for the sky was now brilliant with stars. Ahead stood a low stone building with a single lantern hanging adjacent to an entrance. A hand pushed me again and I staggered. Only fear caused me to keep my balance.

Nearing that isolated building, a terrible sound emanated from it – a moaning, pitiful complaint of humanity, that swelled and receded in some complex rhythm. From somewhere inside a man shouted and a whip cracked.

As we came into the light and a guard opened the door I recalled where I had heard such a racket before – in the dungeons of the Fortaleza at Peniche, when inspecting conditions with the king. This was the low and mournful dirge of men who long for freedom. Here in the mountains, a short distance from Lisbon, was surely Henrique's secret prison. At that realisation, I tried to struggle, but the nearest guarda-costras tightened his grip.

Inside, I found an antechamber lit with stinking tallow lamps. Rough hands pushed me against a wall, then scuttled like crabs along my person. While I suffered this indignity I regarded my three captors – one must have been the gaoler himself, a rough and cruel looking man, short of stature and dressed badly. The guarda-costras were healthier specimens, clad like arquebusiers in cloaks and breeches.

'This way,' ordered the taller man, and I found myself propelled down a stone alleyway, a bare and dank place relieved only by barred enclosures from which emanated a dreadful stench, accompanied by the noise I had heard from outside.

Driven down the passage, I stared in all directions like a cornered rat seeking an escape route. Finally we paused before yet another barred door and with a spark of desperation I turned, summoning all the bluster I could manage. 'You have no right,' I began, 'I am a man of God.'

'And you have no right to trick your way into business that does not concern you. A man of God should not enter a house by deception, nor spy on his betters.' The guarda-costras nodded to the gaoler, 'Put the priest in with the others while we wait for *him.*'

A heavy iron door swung open and strong hands dragged me through, my senses overwhelmed with the reek of prison, as cloying and repugnant as sewage.

The cell was so crowded with men that some time passed before I found room enough to stand without touching another prisoner. Positions against the walls had been taken by the strongest, for men feel safe with stone against their backs. The centre, conversely, was a place for the weakest, many of whom lay groaning in pain from their injuries or illnesses.

The cell was windowless and airless – the smell of death, sweat and decay so strong I gagged with each breath. Those dozens of figures in that room, must surely, I decided, be rapists and murderers. My chances of surviving even a short stay seemed slim indeed.

Images of Dom Sebastian sailing away without me, and of Portugal seized by a circle of traitors filled me with despair. Sinking to my knees I wept again – for my country, my king and my own pitiful self. Curiously, however, having sobbed for some minutes, I felt a gentle hand on my shoulder. I stiffened, and my sobs choked off in the night.

'Do not weep, brother. You are not alone.'

The sound of an educated voice cheered me. 'Thank God for that – a man of learning in this cesspool.' I turned to clasp his hand.

'Oh, more than one,' he said, 'beside you is Frei Amador, a teacher from Lisbon, and behind him Compte Rebelo.'

My breath hissed in my throat. 'A priest and a nobleman locked up in this place?'

My new friend went on, 'Many of the men in here are clergy, nobles and intellectuals.' He paused, 'Do you know what men call this hellhole?'

I shook my head.

'The Anus na Florista.'

'The what?'

'The Arsehole of the Forest. It is Henrique's private hell – the graveyard of truth and goodness.'

I did not wish to endorse the crude humour, yet appreciated the aptness of the parallel. 'Tell me, friend, who are you and why are you here?'

'My name is Jorge Cardoso, my crime was to hide a family of New Christians in my basement. A groundsman betrayed me to Henrique for thirty centi.' The man sighed in the darkness. 'The guarda-costras came in the dawn – twenty or more, pounding down the doors, screaming out their threats, forcing me to take them into the room where the New Christians, a wonderful family, were sleeping. Henrique's men took me also, and forced me to watch my friends burn that very morning. When it was over they brought me here, and I have been here ever since.'

'What of your wife and children?'

'As far as I know they are at home still, yet without me they have no money – no food – I wonder how they manage, and when, if ever I will be released. In my early days here I shouted at the door for answers. I was beaten, and had to stop. They tell me nothing, have charged me with no crime. What can I do but wait, and pray for our Lord's intervention?'

I listened, amazed at how the man betrayed no emotion whatsoever in the telling of that harrowing tale. 'How do they feed you all?'

'They throw bread through the doorway, hoping we will fight for it. Instead we share it equally between us.'

'Water?'

'There is plenty – a trough that they keep full from the outside.'

'Is there no way out?'

'Not even a window, nor a loose stone anywhere. We have tried.'

'How many gaolers are there?'

'Just three, and a half-witted turnkey.'

'So few to guard so many?'

'The bulk of the men in here are priests, as I told you. No one wants to fight or has the gall to try a violent escape. Instead we help each other, hoping that somehow, someday, Henrique will fall.'

A carriage arrived far out in the darkness, with the stamp of horses. Men shouted, others talked, their voices deadened by the thick stone walls. I was certain that this arrival was important to me, for had not the guarda-costras said – put the priest in with the others while we wait for *him*?

I did not have to wait long – a few minutes later the gaoler opened the door and walked inside. One hand held a burning torch, paraffin smoke adding to the stench of that cell.

'Frei Pereira?' he called in an abrupt yet disinterested voice. 'Frei Luis Pereira of Lisbon?'

I looked at my new friends. 'Should I answer?'

'There is no way out but through that door. Go, and take whatever opportunities God offers to you.'

After shaking the hands of those around me I blundered towards the gaoler. 'I'm coming,' I called, 'please give me a moment.'

Near the end of a long, dark corridor, the gaoler opened a door and pushed me through. The space was no larger than a clerk's office, and contained a single table surrounded by chairs.

'Sit down,' this abhorrent human being commanded, pushing his loathsome face close to mine so I could see the gaps where teeth had once been. His nostrils flared like those of an old stallion, long gone to pasture, forced to exert himself against his will.

When I sat, trembling and quiescent, the gaoler stepped aside to admit another man. Though I had suspected it must be him, I was surprised to see Henrique himself, pushing into the room in that bulky, momentous manner of his. The air that swept along from the entrance carried the scent of his perfumes with it, filling my senses until the prison stench and these new heady odours mingled to become something repugnant yet powerful.

When Henrique's eyes fixed on mine he worked his throat once, as if swallowing something distasteful, then breathed heavily through his nose as he too, sank into a chair and stared. As was his way he made no attempt to make small talk, instead saying exactly what was on his mind. 'You meddle in things you do not understand. Things that do not concern you.'

'Treachery is the concern of every patriot.'

Henrique raised his eyebrows. 'You have caused me much inconvenience. As you have probably surmised, however, even I must be careful with one so close to Dom Sebastian as you, yet how can I let you return with what you know?'

'I will not traffic with traitors. As you have said, Dom Sebastian will be looking for me – he expects me to sail with him in the morning. If you kill me he will bring you to account.'

'Oh do not be so sure. Make no mistake, Padre. Dom Sebastian can live without you, and a credible accident can be arranged. Or, conversely, you can rot here – imagine that you have seen the last shining sun you will ever see. There is another way, however.'

'What might that be?"

'Swear an oath. Swear a holy oath that you will say nothing of what you saw and heard and my men will take you back to Lisbon, ready to sail with Dom Sebastian in the morning.'

'Never,' I spat. 'I will tell everything – I will shout your guilt from the rooftops.'

'You will not.'

My heart lurched, 'Why wouldn't I tell of treachery and evil?'

'Because I am a suspicious man and have made inquiries – ones that date back many years. I know everything of your past. There is a girl, is there not? One you love very much.'

My heart seemed to stop beating. My efforts to remove Aletia from the city had come too late. 'I have not the slightest idea of what you are talking about.'

Henrique reached down to smooth his cape with one hand, running his forefinger over the fine cloth like the tongue of a grooming cat. When he spoke again it was without looking, as if thinking aloud to himself. 'Beware the sins of the past, my good

Padre, beware that when you least expect it they will rise again.'

My face burned as if with fever, and my mouth dried to the consistency of chalk, for Luis da Câmara had used much the same words. My pulse hammered at my forehead as if with an iron mallet. 'You are mistaken, there is nothing—'

The next words Henrique spoke chilled me like ice. His tone was monotonous. 'Sergeant?'

The tall guarda-costras stepped forward 'Yes, your Grace.'

'Ride now to the Orphanage of St John on the Alley of the Cross and ask for a girl called Aletia de Calvez. I am told she is an exceptionally pretty child. Bring her here.'

I stared, aghast. 'No!'

Henrique rocked pleasurably on his buttocks as he realised his power over me. 'My men will take her back to their barracks. Can you imagine what she will be like after a hundred muscled warriors of the guarda-costras have made her theirs?'

'You and your associates are deviants and animals.'

'Your insults mean nothing. Understand though, that I will carry out my threat without hesitation. You will say nothing, of what you have seen or heard, Padre, or the image I painted for you will become reality. Understand?'

The world swirled around me like a black snowstorm. My anger built as if I faced the very devil himself across that room. Looking Henrique in the eye, I made my voice as cold and hard as iron. 'What kind of man do you think I am?'

His eyes flickered with uncertainty. 'I do not know, Frei Pereira.'

'Then I will tell you that my answer is no. Not under any circumstances. I will not play your game.'

If I could live for a hundred years and see that expression on his face every day I would never tire of it – the smugness wiped from those flaccid features, replaced by surprise, for men of low morals expect others to suffer the same weaknesses. That pink tongue appeared, wiping along his lips nervously. 'You are making a mistake, priest. The girl will die, and you will be responsible.'

My rage was a rising tide over which I now had no control. I saw only the evil of the man before me, and wanted to crush him – not physically, for back then I still believed myself to be a man of peace, but with all the force of truth and righteousness. Slowly, I rose to my feet, my body stiff and rigid. 'You touch that girl in any way and you will be cursed for all time, and those of your minions who do your work will be struck blind and will burn eternally. You are evil, and I expose you in the name of Jesus Christ. Satan inhabits your mind.' Oh, how well I knew this man – knew his fears and weaknesses intimately, for I have studied him as a scholar pores over the scriptures. Under the force of my words he cowered now, drooping towards the ground under the fire of my rage. 'How dare you beckon me towards treason with your threats. I curse you with the certainty of eternal fire. Never will I bow to tyranny. You are evil, yet there is no power in it, and you will die alone and friendless, afraid as you journey into Hell.'

The Grand Inquisitor's eyes widened like planets.

Few men know what I know. Henrique, almost certainly through some form of possession, was prone to the Falling Evil, the sacred disease of the Greeks that Aristotle once likened to sleep, and Hippocrates blamed on depletion. This was indeed the thunder of Paracelsus that he recommended be treated with such specifics as Oil of Vitriol, fragments of human skulls and the blood of a decapitated man.

Slowly, as I continued to harangue him, Henrique slipped to the floor and began to froth at the mouth and moan, thrashing from side to side, eyes rolling back in his head. Still I did not let up.

'Die, and let demons kiss both your cheeks and hold you close – let Satan embrace you and welcome one of his own.'

Fearing my words, the two guards who had stood behind Henrique ran from the room, leaving me alone with him. I had a strange and terrible feeling of power, for the evidence of his possession was now plain to me as he danced a dance choreographed by his interior devils.

I knelt beside him and placed one hand on each side of his face, turning it so his eyes returned to mine. 'I speak to you and the demon within. You will never win.'

Satisfied, rising to my feet and dusting off my cloak, I walked through the open doorway, and down the corridor, there finding the gaolers huddling together, terror filling their eyes as I approached.

'We have done no harm, Padre, please, bless us,' they wailed, 'do not harm us.'

'Open the prison,' I demanded, and watched as they did so, throwing open the doors. At first nothing happened, but then slowly the man I had earlier befriended, Jorge Cardoso, appeared, followed by others, wide eyed and filthy, blinking in the strong torchlight.

'You are free to go,' I said, 'all of you. We will find what horses we can. The power of the Grand Inquisitor is fading.'

Even as this rabble shouted thanks and sought to hold my hands and bow at my feet I had a terrible premonition that I was mistaken. That, in fact, Henrique's time of power was only just beginning, and my precautions to protect Aletia would not be sufficient to ensure her safety.

OITO

At the Biblioteca Nacional on the Campo Grande, Francis dug out every reference to Dom Sebastian and the Sebastianists he could find.

For two days he remained immersed in Antero de Figueiredo's *Dom Sebastião, Rei de Portugal*, and Sales Loureiro's 1972 work, named simply *Sebastião*.

Skimming through João Lúcio de Azevedo's study – *A evolucão do Sebastianismo* – *The Evolution of Sebastianism*, he stopped more than once to savour the power of the words, the full significance of this aspect of history now dawning on him: *Born of suffering, nourished on hope, Sebastianism is for history what yearning is for poetry; an inseparable part of the Portuguese soul.*

At noon he spent an hour on a bench staring at the riverside beauty of the Praça de Comércio. This had been, before the earthquake and devastating tsunami of 1755, the site of the Royal Palace. Gazing out at the stone jetty Francis pictured the India fleets leaving for the East – pennants flying, crowds cheering – praying for the fleet's safe return.

His mother's words filled his mind: *Five hundred years ago the people of Portugal built ships greater than any the world had seen.*

The square was white, dominated by a statue of King José I on horseback, and surrounded by the Marquês de Pombal-designed government office buildings, with their distinctive arcaded first floors and royal yellow and white paint work. At the river end the Tagus lapped stone barriers, where a procession of ferries disgorged passengers onto the jetty, and at the other a patchwork of ancient buildings stepped their way up the hills behind the river.

After lunch Francis visited the Museu Nacional de Arte Antiga, a seventeenth-century palace turned art gallery in the Bairro Alto. There he found a portrait of Dom Sebastian, suited in close-fitting armour to the waist, one hand on the pommel of his sword and the other resting close to the pointed muzzle of a hunting dog. Francis stared at that ethereal face, with its close-cropped reddish hair for another hour before catching a crowded bus back to the library.

There, returning to his reading, a little after three he felt a presence behind him and turned, looking up into the eyes of Dr Nicolá Massane. She carried her laptop and a slim manila folder.

'Hello again,' she said.

'Pull up a chair.' Francis was surprised to find his pulse racing, for she had taken pains with her appearance – a green chiffon blouse matched with a skirt that suited her slender legs.

'You confided in me, and now I will return the favour,' she said. 'Here is something that might interest you.'

The page Francis took from her hands was a photocopy of a microfilm.

'I found this by accident some years ago in the journals of Pedro Barreto de Magalhães, a viceroy of Timor. It has always intrigued me.'

Francis looked at it. He read Portuguese fluently, yet difficulties arose in any medieval text in that language. For example the early Latin alphabet did not contain the letter u, and therefore v was used in words requiring the u sound. The letters i and y were also used interchangeably up until the nineteenth century, as were i and j. Doubling up letters was also common.

> *March the twentieth, in the year of our Lord Fifteen Eighty One, by the hand of Pedro Barreto de Magalhães, Viceroy of Tymor and Larantuka. At noon we calculated our position as six degrees twenty minutes south, one hundred and twenty-four degrees east. Sailed with the tender Andorinha to make landfall on the mainland. To our surprise, there we were greeted by a bedraggled Portuguese man. The pitiable fellow, apparently a eunuch, communicated that he had lived on a continent to the south for many months before building a seaworthy raft and crossing the ocean. He appeared to be quite mad, and spoke of a river he called the Rio Grande. He also told us of a valley rimmed with walls of stone. We would have taken the man with us but he ran away into the trees.*

When Francis had finished reading his voice was no longer steady. 'That was written in 1581. Dom Sebastian disappeared in 1578. The time period is perfect. So what missing ship might this castaway have been a survivor of?'

Nicolá gestured at the library shelves. 'In here we can find out.'

Together they consulted the log of India-bound ships leaving Lisbon in the years 1578 and 1580, twenty-eight vessels altogether. Rather than skimming through, Francis read each entry carefully, for the stated destinations might not, necessarily, have reflected the final landing place.

The first ship to catch his attention was the *São João*, which set sail from Lisbon's Sea of Straw under the Captaincy of one Miguel de Arruda. The story sounded promising until a footnote revealed that the vessel had been lost at the Baixos of Pero dos Banhos. The *São Pedro*, likewise, sailed in 1578, but it too had been lost far from Australian shores.

Only the *Nossa Senhora dos Anjos*, part of the same fleet, had gone missing at an unknown location, the others had all returned safely.

'Look,' he said, 'this one fits.'

Nicolá came close and read the text above his finger. '*Nossa Senhora dos Anjos*,' she repeated, '*Our Lady of Angels*.'

Francis mulled the name over in his head. The Portuguese had named many ships and churches after the Virgin Mary… *Our Lady of the Ascension, Our Lady of the Rosary, Our Lady of Light, Our Lady of the Conception…*

'Okay, let's try to find out more about her,' she went on. 'As you know, the 1755 earthquake destroyed most of the old maritime records. The kind of information we need is gone, though the records probably wouldn't have told us much – just how many pipes full of olive oil and wine each vessel carried in the hold.'

'There must be something somewhere,' Francis prompted.

'Perhaps, but the one really annoying thing about shipwrecks is that people don't always come back to tell the tale. On the other hand, if Dom Sebastian went East on a ship there must be a record of it somewhere.'

A curt female voice came over the public address system, announcing that the library would soon close.

'That time went fast,' said Francis, glancing at his phone screen.

Nicolá planted one elbow on the chair's arm rest, and reached up with her hand to cup her chin. 'Since we are both interested in mysteries, and because you are a visitor – perhaps we can dine together tonight? Purely, of course, as a professional courtesy.'

Francis felt his cheeks burn, then, realising that his mouth was wide open, closed it. The young woman, however, was waiting for an answer, and he fumbled for words.

'I would like to have dinner with you – very much.'

'I'm pleased,' she said. 'I like a place called the Latina on the Rua da Conde. It has a wonderful menu. I could meet you there at eight o'clock?'

Francis beamed at her. 'That's fantastic. I'll see you then.'

The Latina was a University hangout, the clientele young and talkative, sitting in couples and small groups. The food was plentiful and cheap, but wholesome and traditional, with a strong selection of local wines on the list. The blue tiles on the floor and walls, Francis decided, were genuinely medieval, and the room had been furnished to suit.

Nicolá met Francis at the door in a loose summer dress, the white fabric looking cool against her glowing skin. Braided hair sat neatly behind the nape of her neck. He was enchanted by the way she rose on tiptoe to kiss his cheek as though they were old friends. Francis was unsure what to say, instead just looking at her, pleased to feel the intense physical reaction again. She wore a plain silver necklace and earrings with a sparkling stone at the centre of each.

Seated beside a curtained window, Francis cast his eye over a menu that listed dishes derived from the simpler fare of his childhood – marinated pork with clams and peppers, and a tripe dish seasoned with meats and vegetables. He settled on a grilled steak, flavoured with port wine, while Nicolá chose a mushroom and pasta dish without consulting the menu.

'I am almost a vegetarian,' she explained.

'What does an "almost" vegetarian eat?'

'Red meat and pork tastes rank to me so I avoid it. I therefore indulge in occasional fish and free range chicken.'

'That's a pragmatic way to go about it.'

'Oh but let's not talk about food.' Her face was constantly moving – endlessly expressive. Dimples appeared and disappeared. Her eyes, of the deepest brown, enlarged and glowed and her lips were glossy with lipstick. 'I'll tell you about my work, and you tell me about yours.'

As he ate, Francis listened to Nicolá's stories of Late Pliocene cave sites and a summer in Egypt's Valley of Kings. 'I explored many paths,' she explained, 'but I became interested in the Age of Discovery and settled on the technology of the period as a speciality.' Rather than seeing her resume as that of a seasoned professional, however, she apparently regarded herself as having much to learn, despite experiences that most of his Australian colleagues would have traded their honours degrees for.

'Now, Francisco, you have said very little about yourself. Your mother was Portuguese?'

'Both parents, from Lisbon.'

Something in his expression must have warned her. 'Sorry, I don't mean to pry.'

'No, it's okay. My father was wounded in the Carnation Revolution and apparently never recovered fully. After he died my mother emigrated with my sister and I to Australia.'

'You sound bitter.'

'Maybe I am. As a child I always wished that I came from a normal family, instead I was a dark kid with a mother who cried all the time. I lost her, not long ago.'

'How?'

'Lung cancer.'

Her hand crept out and covered his. 'That's terrible.'

'That's what two packs of Alpine menthol a day does to you. I can't tell you how important she was in my life. When we first got the news I decided that when she went I would have no re-grets. I cared for her myself. She was alone so much in her life, and devoted to me. It was the least I could do.' Francis looked into Nicolá's eyes, then away, unsure why he was sharing so much of himself. 'After her death I thought I might lose my courage.'

'Did you?'

'For a while. Then it came back.'

For dessert they ate wafer-thin chocolate and ice cream, ac-companied by strong coffee. Nicolá took control, asking the wait-er for a bill, which she examined like a departmental budget and split with scrupulous fairness.

'That was a pleasant evening,' she said, 'thank you. Now, do you really want to go home? It is only ten o'clock.'

'Do you?'

'Not yet, perhaps. You have been to Lisbon before, haven't you?'

'Yes, once.'

'Have you been to a fado club?'

'Not yet.'

Nicolá rolled her eyes. 'Oh dear! You have Portuguese heri-tage but you have never been to a fado club?'

'Sorry.'

Standing, she reached for his hand. 'I know a good place. You are so lucky you met me … I can be your tour guide.'

The sound of fado music provoked a chill that began deep down in the base of Francis's spine and drilled its way to his neck and brain, bringing the hairs erect on his arms. Each note was an emotion in itself, each musical phrase a journey, each line a beginning and an end.

The club was on the Alley of the Holy Spirit, accessed by a nondescript door manned by a tall and muscled Greek, who greeted them in accented but polite Portuguese. Inside, the lights were dimmed low, with a murmur of voices from perhaps two dozen tables arranged in close proximity to each other. The music swelled as Nicolá led the way closer to the stage, where a trio were performing.

The fadista was a big woman, with the size to let her notes resonate. As with other fadistas Francis had heard on recordings, her lips whistled as she formed soft consonants. Beside her sat the musicians – one stroking the mandolin-like guitarra, and the other playing a flamenco-style acoustic guitar.

Reaching an empty table, Francis allowed Nicolá to usher him into a seat, yet still not taking his eyes off the performers.

'This is a very famous song,' Nicolá said. 'It's called, Trago Fado Nos Sentidos – Bring Fado in the Senses. The great Amália Rodrigues sang it first.'

A waiter arrived with a tray of wine glasses. Francis took one and sipped appreciatively – the bold but subtle blend of flavours was, he decided, a perfect accompaniment to the music. For more than a minute he stared, feeling the emotion coming to the surface. When tears formed at the corners of his eyes he wiped them away, annoyed that Nicolá had noticed him do so. To his surprise she touched his hand.

'Do not be ashamed to shed a tear. The strength of fado comes from saudade. If you can feel it you are blessed.'

Smiling now, Francis sipped a little more wine. The song ended, and another began, this one more upbeat, lacking the intensity of the previous number. Nicolá moved her hand and he felt somewhat disappointed.

'See how the fadista wears a black shawl?' she asked.

'Yes?'

'All fadistas do so, in memory of Maria Severa, one of the first great cantoras. Her story is very sad, do you want to hear it?'

'Why not?'

'Well, Maria fell in love with a nobleman called Conde de Vimios. It was a terrible scandal, for he was a married man. He was forced to break it off with her, leaving her shattered. At just twenty-six she committed suicide.'

'That *is* a sad story.'

'Yes.'

The musicians took a break, and conversation swelled, laughter breaking out here and there. Waiters hurried to supply wine to the tables. 'I'm quite tired,' Francis said. 'Do you mind if we get going?'

Nicolá slipped the strap of her handbag over one shoulder. 'Not at all. I have to work tomorrow anyway.'

Outside, Francis ordered a car from Uber. While they waited he was content to watch Nicolá surreptitiously – her long legs and wide shoulders. 'I'm pleased that you suggested dinner,' he said,

'It's been a long time since I went out like that.'

When the car arrived, speeding through the quiet streets, Francis became lulled into a warm emotive state, remembering something that his mother used to say.

> *One day you will find someone, and there you will see a beauty that is unique to your eyes; the wonderfulness of them will be your secret alone, and that is love, when you see someone in a way that the rest of the world can't see. You will know things about them that no one else can know. So it was with your father and I. Not even his death could make me stop loving him.*

Nicolá took his arm and leaned against Francis for a brief, wonderful moment. 'We are on the trail of something special, you and I.'

It was all too soon when they parted outside a modern apartment block sandwiched between older buildings. Francis left the car and walked her to the door.

Their lips met for a brief goodnight kiss – enough to stir his heart. Before he could attempt to prolong the moment, however, she turned and went through the door, the smell of her perfume lingering like an echo. A curious sense of elation filled Francis's heart, and on the short ride back to the hotel he replayed the evening over and over again in his mind – the way she spoke, the fierce intelligence, the utter changeability of her.

Something had altered – like the way sound carries more clearly after rain.

DOVE

According to Francis's notes, Sebastianist beliefs stemmed from three primary sources, and he recommenced his research the next day with the most recent of these, the *Mensagem* of Fernando Pessoa. The poem was a cryptic one, dense with imagery, divided into forty-four sections.

Francis worked through the first chapters, the Coat of Arms, and then, the second, the Portuguese Maritime, detailing Portugal's age of seafaring power. It was the third part, however, O Encuberto, The Hidden One, that had the hairs at the back of his neck rising and prickling.

> *Carrying aboard the King, Dom Sebastian,*
> *And raising atop, like a motto, the pennant*
> *Of Empire,*
> *The last galleon sailed away, under a sun of*
> *ill-omen*
> *Forsaken, 'mid weeping of anxiety and ominous mystery.*

Noon passed, then half the afternoon. Francis raised his head and wiped his eyes. The poem was interesting enough, but a dead end in many ways, bringing him no closer to understanding how such an important relic had arrived off the Kimberley coast.

Nicolá, meeting him for coffee at a café in the Bairro Alto, listened to his frustration. 'Francisco, you have neglected the most important source of all.'

'Who might that be?'

'Bandarra, of course.'

'Who?'

'Gonçaleannes Bandarra. The shoemaker. You need to read his most famous work, the *Trovas*. It was he who first prophesied the rise and fall of Dom Sebastian.'

'Is there a copy in the library?'

'I imagine so, but it would be more fun to hunt such a volume down.'

'What do you mean?'

'There are two old bookshops in Lisbon that specialise in this kind of thing. Both are said to have Sebastianist links. Perhaps we should go and look together.' She paused. 'That is, if you don't mind me coming with you?'

'No, of course not. After reading on my own all day I could do with the company.'

The bookshop Paradisiaco occupied a tiny frontage on a shabby block in the Chiado, its existence acknowledged by an ageing, hand-painted sign. A bell rattled as Francis pushed the door open.

The store resembled a labyrinth formed entirely of books — dark timber shelves rising from floor to ceiling. Francis had always been conscious of the way old books could smell. Never, however, had his senses been so filled by the reek – the stink of old paper. This was an elephants' graveyard of books, where the titles might be anywhere from one hundred to six hundred years old – from an age when manuscripts were hand copied and illustrated by monks who might spend a week on a single page.

Francis walked those old floorboards, polished by the feet of ten or twenty generations, the weight of a thousand years of words heavy on his shoulder, as if such ancient knowledge as abounded in that shop was too much to bear.

Two genres made up the bulk of these titles; theology, and Portuguese history. As Francis, with Nicolá silent and watchful behind him, approached a plain desk piled with books, he felt a quickening of his pulse – this was a place of secrets, hidden under an overwhelming blanket of uncountable words.

In one corner an old man sat in a chair, rocking gently, a rug on his lap, and a book on his knee. One hand held a pair of reading glasses. Spiders might have spun their webs over the immobile skin of his face. Even as Francis passed, the man said nothing.

Reaching the book-laden counter, Francis gave Nicolá a nervous glance. A woman sat nearby, working at a ledger. She barely looked up. An open door led to a darkened space behind, and a man appeared at the threshold. He too was old, with weathered skin. Strangely familiar, his eyes appeared out of focus so that one stared in a different direction to the other.

'Can I help you?' he asked.

'I am looking for a book,' Francis said, casting a tentative glance at Nicolá. 'It is called the *Trovas*.'

The old man lurched through the doorway, returning some minutes later with a package wrapped in brown paper. The price was less than Francis had expected, and he counted the notes from his wallet, then waited patiently for the handwritten receipt.

They had barely left the shop when he turned to Nicolá. 'That old man – I recognise him from the miradouro the other morning – he is a Sebastianist.'

'I told you – this shop is one of their enclaves.'

'Would you like to come back to my hotel and look at the book together?'

'Of course. If that is what you would like to do.'

Francis's hotel room was equipped with a circular glass table, and two upright cane chairs. Francis took a seat and opened the package.

Inside two cardboard protectors sat a thin bound manuscript, the leather cover cracked and brittle with age. The title was calligraphed in Portuguese. The inner pages had been printed in lead alloy moveable type. The rag paper was perhaps a century old, though no date marred the cover or frontispieces. A dark stain on the binding and first few pages might have been blood.

'So who was this fellow?'

Nicolá leaned so close that he could smell her perfume. 'Bandarra was the first Sebastianist prophet – a shoemaker. He lived in the village of Trancoso, in the Beira Alta, fifty years or so before Dom Sebastian. His works were banned by the Portuguese Inquisition.'

Turning the first few pages, after a short dedication, Francis found that the book consisted of double quatrains, or trovas; rhyming verse, each eight lines long, organised into verses, or 'dreams.' At first, when he started to translate, the words did not appear to make sense. 'This is crazy,' he said, reading softly,

'Generations innocent of purpose will crawl ... an angel longs for him ...'

Nicolá took the book from his hands and studied it. 'Bandarra's meaning is not easy to absorb. Just keep in mind that the subject of the poem is a hidden king, or *rei encuberto*.'

Armed with this information, Francis read on, soon coming to understand that the subject of the poem was also referred to as Leão, or the Lion.

> *A great lion will arise,*
> *And will bellow grandly,*

Some of the passages were so cryptic as to defy interpretation:

> *The dreaded flag of Portugal,*
> *As five Coats of Arms in the midst ...*

Though real meaning eluded him, Francis felt a deep and unusual empathy with those words, as if he were listening to the voice of an old and dear friend who was speaking behind a barrier through which no meaning could pass.

'Start again,' Nicolá said, 'We'll go through it line by line until we have it.'

This process required concentration, and together they studied the text, yet remained far from discovering the real truth behind the words. Hours passed in a kind of isolation, where normal things did not seem to matter.

'He is predicting,' Francis breathed, 'the birth of a great king who will be defeated, then rise again, returning from exile to save Portugal. He will preside over a fifth and final empire – one that will bring peace and prosperity to the world for all eternity.'

Nicolá smiled. 'That, in a nutshell, is it. Oh, it's unbelievable,' she cried. 'I feel so close to him – that I could touch him,' she said, 'I can almost see his face.' Her eyes flew to the bedside clock. 'It's ten o'clock. I'd better get home.'

'I'll walk you to the station. We could talk a little more.'

'Of course.'

For much of the way, Nicolá directing Francis through various short cuts and the occasional scenic detour. The night was, Francis agreed, balmy and comfortable, and he felt that he could have walked with her forever.

'I'm going home the day after tomorrow,' he said. 'Will I see you again before that?'

'I don't know. Maybe not.'

'I wish you would come out to Australia and join our team to fully investigate the barca. By law we're not allowed to raise any part, the museum will have to do that, but we can sift through the sands all around it.'

'I'm not sure if the timing is possible for me, but I would love to. Are you inviting me?'

'Yes.'

'For how long?'

'The next trip will be four weeks.'

'I may have trouble getting the time away from work, but I'll let you know. Let's make sure that we have each other's details.'

They kissed goodnight again, just a brief contact as it had been the previous night, and when she had gone Francis scarcely dared to move or breathe.

$$\mathcal{O}\mathcal{E}\mathcal{S}$$

The African landscape was the pale shade of mackerel flesh, adorned with stones and thorny argan bushes so tough even our mules found them unpalatable. Beyond the crest of each dune-like hillock, the vista included only rocky plains and yet another line of hills, dimmed with distance and the ever-shifting dust and sand. Above all reared a sky anaemic with this same dust.

Dom Sebastian called me in the early afternoon from the highest of our fortified peaks, a place he had chosen as a command post. He bade me study the western horizon, where an hour earlier it had been possible to make out the distant foothills of the Rif Mountains. Now, unnatural darkness filled the western half of the landscape – men on horses, swarming beneath a ball of dust as if they were insects.

Behind the enemy cavalry came a creeping mass of infantry that filled the horizon from one side to the other. We felt it in the ground and in our ears as a deep, powerful growl. Clattering armour. Spear against shield. Men talking in a score of discordant tongues.

It seemed that the advance would never stop, that the colourful tide of horses and men would overrun our ridge like a wave. Horns sounded, however, and the massive army halted. As the dust dispersed, the host of Abd-Al Malik made their camp. A sea of tents appeared on the plain.

Dom Sebastian had five trained men plotting the numbers and locations of the enemy units. For this task he also employed the services of the deposed Moroccan king, Abu Abdullah Mohamed Il Saadi, who became useful for the first time in the campaign, standing with robes billowing, scenting the air with his perfumes.

'There, on the left flank,' Abdullah informed us, 'those are Sipahi cavalry. They carry a bow, thirty-six arrows, a scimitar and a round shield. They ride like the wind, but just as happily in either direction. Put fear in their hearts and they will turn tail and run. Behind them, the pennant is that of the Jusham warriors of Arabia. Behind the Jusham, a mass of Turks advance – see their red trousers and coloured cloaks? They are the yeniçeri.'

I had heard of these most famous of Ottoman warriors. The yeniçeri were boys plundered and plucked from Christian homes, or surrendered up from the Balkans. These unfortunates were trained as war machines and schooled in the fanatical teachings of the Dervish Saint Hajji Bektash Wali, a most poisonous strain of Islam.

'The yeniçeri seek a martyr's death as a normal man might seek his next meal,' our ally told us.

'What of the artillery?' Dom Sebastian asked.

'Abd-Al Malik has forty cannon with mouths like devils from hell, and to serve them he has recruited Christians who have come to bask in Allah's love.'

An uncomfortable silence followed. Stories had circulated for some time of Christian artillerymen who had turned to Islam and now fought against their own. Such a thing was terrible to contemplate.

'When will they attack?' I asked.

Tonio Fonseca's dark eyes narrowed, eyebrows black and fierce, standing beside Dom Sebastian with his arms crossed. 'They will not have the opportunity,' he said, 'for in the morning we go down to fight on the plain.'

I turned to Dom Sebastian for confirmation. 'Really? You will leave these impregnable cliffs to face a much larger force on equal terms?'

'We have a plan, good Padre.'

'Yes,' I said. 'Plans that are in the hands of the enemy. A good general alters his plan according to circumstances and conditions. Julius Caesar would have fortified these cliffs and let those vast hosts come to him.'

Nervousness flickered across Dom Sebastian's eyes, but his voice was deep and steady when he answered. 'We will fight on our feet, on the plain, with God giving strength to our arms and hearts.'

Ah, chivalry, that code so beloved of poets and knights. Dom Sebastian had been besotted with honour and chivalry since his teens, and never once had I seen him take unfair advantage of another man. An enemy, once he had lost his feet or his weapon, was no longer an enemy. Tonio, too, was no less in love with this admirable, yet pointless conceit.

Pointing out at the massive forces encamped on the plain I hissed, 'Look at them! As many cooking fires as there are stars in the sky. Please do not sacrifice so many lives for pride.'

This was too much for Tonio, who clutched at my shoulder

with one mailed fist. His eyes were fierce, and his voice intense. 'It is not productive for you to question the judgement of the king.'

Dom Sebastian looked at me, his eyes liquid with worry, 'I will not be a coward, hiding on a hilltop.'

To whom will you prove your courage? I wanted to ask, though even then I knew the answer.

Later, when I retired to my sleeping mat, there were so many things on my mind that sleep seemed impossible. I had sent a message to Frei Aguiar at the orphanage before leaving Lisbon, warning him that Aletia might be a target and asking him to spirit her out of harm's way, but I could not be sure that he had received this letter. I was also of course, desperately worried at what the next day might hold, in a battle that was both ill-advised in the first place, and to be held on ground advantageous to the enemy.

In the end, however, exhaustion had weakened my reserves sufficiently that I fell into a dark and featureless slumber. Scarcely, however, had I explored that unconscious world but I wakened to find one of Dom Sebastian's pages poking my side, silhouetted by candlelight flickering on the tent walls.

'What is it, boy?'

My tone shocked him to the extent that he rebounded away from me like a leather ball struck by a foot. I felt contrite and so lowered my voice. 'I'm sorry. What is the problem?'

'My master, is suffering,' he said, 'I was told to fetch you.'

At times, a bad dream would provoke Dom Sebastian's need for confession. Occasionally, the reason was more serious. I sighed, 'I am awake now, go back while I prepare.' This was a ploy I sometimes used to snatch more sleep.

'No, I was told to wait and not return without you.'

Sitting up, I saw genuine worry in his youthful eyes. 'You are a dutiful boy, and must love your master. Please tell me, what is the nature of this emergency?'

'I do not know for sure, but when the médico, Dom Barreto, asked me to fetch you, he was pale in the face at what he had seen.'

Drawing my cloak over my head, I located the satchel that I kept ready at all hours of the day and night, then burrowed through the tent flap and out into the camp. Watch fires burned all over the hillside, but the majority of our army was asleep, resting ahead of the coming battle. The smell of cooking horse flesh pervaded the air, for Dom Sebastian had ordered that the mounts that had faltered on the long desert journey should be slaughtered so the men could fight with full bellies of meat.

The king's tent was made of sail canvas on the outside and lined with calf skin on the interior. The structure took thirty men one hour to erect, and contained seven rooms, each floored with woollen rugs imported from England. Their simple, bold designs and rich colours befitted this mobile palace. Each dawn, the massive tent was broken down into multiple sections, each of which could be carried by two or three porters.

First we entered an antechamber, passing through a ring of guards who granted the right of entry to me, used to years of my comings and goings. Once there, I swept through a series of narrow passages and into the sumptuous sleeping chamber. The walls were lined with the fur of lion and antelope. The floor was soft with the pelt of a black bear. Dom Sebastian had, on the day of his twenty-third birthday, stabbed this giant beast through the heart. The necessity of it travelling to Morocco with us was past my understanding.

A chandelier of burning candles lit the centre of the room, where a bed sat on four wooden pillars. On the edge of the mattress sat Dom Sebastian, weeping volubly, surrounded by a pair of physicians.

My own confusion lasted only moments. This was a scene I had encountered many times over the years. As I entered, Dom Sebastian lifted his head, wringing his hands and looking plaintively into my eyes. I felt the physical jolt in my chest that pain or grief in loved ones often provoked in me. Moving closer I took one hand. It was cold and trembling.

The young man returned my grip with the power of iron, eyes as deep and sorrowful as mountain lakes. 'The emptiness has come.'

At the remove of some years it is hard for me to describe just how deep my feelings ran for Dom Sebastian. That young man was exceptional in all respects, yet weighed down by our Lord in his wisdom by an internal sadness so deep it is somewhat difficult to understand. Like the faulty heel of Achilles this was the impediment that kept him from the greatness he strived for. The timing of these episodes had at first seemed almost random, but over the years it transpired that they came almost always before, during or after times of unusual stress.

'Pray with me, Padre, I beg you.'

Falling to my knees, I examined him carefully, seeing with relief that I had arrived in time – that he was unlikely to slip deep enough for this visitation to take on the perilous and frightening form I had seen several times in the past, each of which had almost ended his life. I knew, however, from past experience that he needed time and patience for this milder distress to recede. Clearing my throat, I lifted my Bible, watching Dom Sebastian's face run with tears and the great chest heave as I read from the book of Psalms.

> *God is our refuge and strength, a very present*
> *help in trouble ...*

I had not intended to, yet since the words appeared to help, I continued on to the end of the chapter. When it was done I said, 'So you can see that God is all-powerful – that we should not fear. You wish for His forgiveness and He will freely give it.' I looked down at the face I loved so well and saw the pain there. 'It is only that God has gifted you so mightily that He must test you so sorely. Never question your worth, Dom Sebastian.'

For a time he was silent, but then he began to weep – breathing as if he had run the twenty-five miles of Pheidippides. 'This visitation cannot be a good omen,' he said. It is a sign that God is not with us.' Before I could interject he had turned to the page who remained at his post near the door. 'Boy! Fetch Senhor Chanoca, the astrologer.'

This development appalled me, and as the lad scurried away I rounded on the young king, 'Do you think that is wise?'

'Yes. I must know. I need to know.'

'The stars do not always tell the truth.'

'Perhaps not, but Senhor Chanoca can see the future in other ways.'

When the page returned, Rui Chanoca followed, shoeless, with his shirt hanging over his breeches. He was a tall man still, rather bent as he advanced through middle age, with eyes that darted in all directions.

Dom Sebastian turned on him. 'Senhor Chanoca, will you cast the points for me?'

'Yes my Lord.'

This was an interesting skill, the science of geomancy or the divination by earth. First Chanoca prayed in silence, before removing paper and a charcoal stub from a canvas bag he carried. On the white surface he drew sixteen lines of points in groups of four, and then in pairs. In this way he produced the geomantric figures – the mothers, daughters, nieces, the witnesses and judge.

'Ask me a question, Your Highness,' Chanoca said.

'There is but one thing I need to know,' Dom Sebastian replied. 'What will be the outcome of tomorrow's battle?'

For some minutes Chanoca bent to his task, on his knees like a child with his drawings. As the process continued, however, his lean face reddened, and he muttered the Latin word *rubeo*, over and over. This word was familiar to me, for it means 'red,' and in geomancy indicates violent death and destruction.

Dom Sebastian grew impatient with the man. 'What is it?' he cried. 'I command you to answer me.'

Chanoca's eyes rose like red orbs to fix on the King's face. 'I see death,' he cried, 'God has abandoned us. I see our destruction on the plain of Alcácer Quibir.'

'No,' Dom Sebastian stammered. 'It is not true.'

Rui Chanoca said nothing else, yet looked stricken, flinching as if expecting a blow from the King, who was now as angry as I have ever seen him.

Chanoca lowered his head, 'I am sorry, forgive me, please.'

Dom Sebastian drew a thin azcumas dagger from the bedside and whipped it around the astrologer's neck. 'How dare you!' he cried. 'Are you in the service of the enemy?'

My surprise at this development was such that I could do nothing. I knew also, that any movement on my part might precipitate the killing blow.

'No Dom Sebastian, I serve only you.'

'Liar,' Dom Sebastian cried. 'Creature of the Devil!'

Rui Chanoca's life hung in the balance, though he did not seem afraid. The King's anger, however, faded swiftly. Dom Sebastian sheathed the knife and looked down on the man he had almost killed. 'Leave tonight,' he hissed, 'and do not come back. The rumours from Spain that I have long ignored must be true – you are a heretic and an affront to God. Did King Philip send you here to ruin me?'

'No, sire. I serve no one but the Lord God and Portugal.'

'If the Moors kill you no one will weep.'

Chanoca gathered up his implements and withdrew, bowing low. In moments he was out the door and scampering away. When he had gone I looked at Dom Sebastian. To my relief he had come back from the brink of that most extreme of physical manifestations of God's special love. Yet fear filled his eyes at what he had almost done; at what he was about to do with twenty thousand worthy lives.

ONE

In one passage of the sun across the sky, from dawn to dusk, my world changed irrevocably. I woke in the headquarters of a mighty army, and by sunset I was a broken creature in a foreign land, prostrated with grief and guilt.

The smell of death saturated my throat and nostrils, and wounded men shrieked into the night. Even now, I remember the sound of sand, driven by a dry desert wind. I remember the bodies of the fallen. Night creatures fed on the dead and living wounded alike. I could hardly comprehend the enormity of our defeat, yet when I looked towards the ridge, I saw no twinkling of watch fires. There was no haven or reserve force to save us.

Down on the plain, that huge Moorish army had encircled and crushed us. Despite the courage of our men, individual heroics that will remain stamped on my mind like bright lights in the darkness, the enemy were too numerous, and our much smaller force had been destroyed or captured in eight hours of cataclysmic fighting.

Dom Sebastian lay beside me against a mound of earth, his

eyes closed to the darkness. His body was limp, yet he appeared to be but lightly wounded. I examined his eyes by peeling one eyelid wide between thumb and forefinger. The process was well advanced and it would take urgent action to stop it from proceeding further.

'We must go,' Tonio hissed at me. 'Parties of the enemy keep finding us in the dark. Soon there may be too many for us to handle.'

'Give me another moment, please.'

By the light of a candle and with the help of two men I removed the young king's armour and chain mail. I noticed more cuts. Most were not serious, but one on his upper arm was deep, as was another in his left shoulder. I dressed these quickly.

'Hurry,' Tonio urged again.

Ignoring him, I took Dom Sebastian's hand and prayed as I have never prayed before, beseeching our Lord to bring him back to our world, and out of the darkness where he must surely be hurtling. *Not now, please*, I repeated under my breath.

Tonio gripped my sleeve. 'For the love of God, Padre. Would you rather he died a slow death from this madness or from the razor slice of steel? That is what will find him soon if we do not get away.'

I rubbed my aching head. 'Yes, yes, you are right, and perhaps he can walk, even if he cannot speak. Here, help me to get him up.'

Between us we dragged Dom Sebastian to his feet, and as I had hoped, he walked along like a dog on a rope. When I held his hand I felt a trace of blood trickling down from his wrist and hoped the others would not notice. That blood came not from a physical wound.

I stayed close beside him, trusting the guardsmen who led the way, for it was they who knew the shortest route to the river, and they who sensed when roving bands of the enemy neared, and adroitly led us out of danger. The broken ground, however, was treacherous, and more than once I blundered over shallow clay banks, despite the warnings from those who went ahead.

The terrain made my task of leading the helpless man difficult, particularly when we crossed a shallow sweep of that foetid river Mahkzan, mud sucking at our legs, coating us to our thighs. Two strong men dragged Dom Sebastian across, and on the far bank, hidden by a thicket, we rested. Here I bathed his face with water and whispered prayers.

For the first time, reflected moonlight in his eyes showed that he was following my movements. He murmured in a language unintelligible to me. When I placed an arm around his shoulders he cowered away, and said the first clear words I had heard him utter since the battle.

'I am not afraid.'

'No, I know you are not,' I replied, 'and fifteen thousand men have died to prove it.'

Dom Sebastian resumed his babbling. This I suffered with a sense of dread, squatting on my haunches until Tonio touched my shoulder.

'We must move on,' he hissed. 'Now.'

Manoeuvring Dom Sebastian back to his feet, we set off into the night.

Hours later we stopped again, between two desert dunes with the night wind hissing sand off the crest. At this point Dom Sebastian had regained a good portion of his wits. 'I cannot go on,' he said.

'I would rather sit and die.'

'That is not your choice to make. You have a responsibility to your people. The Sea of Straw will run red with the blood of Henrique's enemies, and who knows what Martin and Luis da Câmara will do with unfettered power. Hurry now.'

Dom Sebastian stood, devoid of the energy that so character-ised him. 'Henrique will save me.'

'I have told you a dozen times. Henrique is your enemy. Even now he will be manoeuvring to steal your crown.'

'No.'

'Yes! Now walk, before the Moors catch us and leave us dead on the sand.'

'I will run from no man.'

That empty, pointless, arrogance brought anger to my cheeks and to my lips. 'Damn your pride,' I shouted. 'You will do what you have to do.' Our eyes met, and what I saw there made me soften. 'So often you have spoken to me of courage and honour – those are not qualities you can prove with a weapon, but with your actions when things seem bleakest.'

The words helped. Facing the western sky, within a few strides he outpaced me, and I sighed with relief.

Swift ships carried news of the Battle of Alcácer Quibir, that great calamity, along with the first few battered survivors, back to Portugal. I am told that in Lisbon a procession formed, two leagues long, of mourners, men and women alike, their bodies draped with black. Pope Gregorius declared a week of mourning throughout the Christian world, and Saint Theresa of Avila is said to have wept when told the terrible news.

Hundreds of desperate bands like ours fled across the desert, bringing news of defeat to the fleet, whose captains waited for survivors to carry back to a country so deep in shock it might never recover. On the Barbary Coast we were lucky enough to find a bleak and uninhabited beach between low sandstone cliffs. On the white sands we lit a fire of driftwood and thereby attracted a two-masted caravel, a vessel of around a hundred tons, with her stern towering higher than her bow, rigged in the lateen style favoured on our coasts.

This one boasted eight guns and a draft shallow enough to anchor just beyond the beach and send a barca ashore to collect us. The caravel was commanded by a young man of just twenty, with a crew still in their teens. The master could not hide his joy upon seeing that Dom Sebastian was still alive.

Taut sails propelled us northwards towards our homeland. Sea air, fresh water, wrinkled apples, olives and cheese had a miraculous effect on the men. Most talked of home, and wives and babes. Dom Sebastian, however, remained inconsolable – praying constantly, staring out at the ocean as if it were a balm to soothe his torn heart.

For my own part I worried about dear Aletia, and not only the fear that Henrique might have harmed her. I also fretted about how she must feel upon news of the battle. I knew that she might well think that I was dead. Yet how in the name of heaven could I let her know that I still walked the earth?

God's answer was the thump of each swell against the bow, and the whistle of wind in the stays.

The winds, while light, served us well, bringing us within sight of a pale brown Spanish coast on the second day. The next morning we lined the rail to view the Portuguese village of Tavira.

The young captain professed a desire to stop there, desperate for water and supplies but I prevailed on him to continue to the port of Faro, less of a backwater and thus more likely to yield current news of the political situation. Four hours later we tacked past the islands of de Faro and de Culatra.

I found Dom Sebastian in his cabin, lying on his bed, staring into space.

'I am going ashore,' I said.

'Of course we are,' he responded. 'I will commandeer the fastest ship in the harbour and—'

'Pray, Dom Sebastian, do not reveal yourself hastily. We need to know what Henrique has done now that news of the battle must have reached Lisbon. I think it is better that you stay aboard.'

The young man looked at me as if I were ill. Such subtleties did not occur to him. 'Why?'

'Because you may be in peril. I beg you, please allow me to go ashore first. If all is well, then we will talk again.'

'I trust you,' he said simply, sagging back onto a chair. 'If you think that is the right thing to do then let it be so.'

While the ship's barca, rowed by six crewmen, carried me shoreward, I looked around with interest, never having set foot in the city of Faro. The Bishop's castle sat in a commanding position on the hills, and handsome stone warehouses verged the azure water of the Gulf of Cádiz. Crowds lined the wharves, and fishing boats swung on their moorings. Weeping was audible from a distance, and lines of wounded men lay on the paved earth.

The barca bumped against a jetty. 'Tie us off,' shouted the coxswain. Strong hands made us fast to a bollard, and as I stepped over the gunwale a crowd gathered.

Please, they asked, *are you survivors of the battle? Have you news for us?*

The wharf precinct had been set up as a makeshift hospital and emergency accommodation. Carmelite nuns tended lines of wounded, white headgear shading them from the sun as they kneeled to the task. The few uninjured survivors attracted dozens of listeners anxious to hear their stories.

Many priests were already at work with the nuns, so I did not linger, looking for someone who might be in a position to answer my questions. Continuing across the precinct I made for a man in the garb of a minor local official – an Italian doublet and white ruff collar. I walked towards him. Up close I saw that he had a goatee and hooded dark eyes. An unhealed scar on his left cheek added to the air of danger that accompanied him. He looked at me and sniffed, revealing tiny rabbit teeth and cavernous nostrils.

'You have returned from Morocco?' he asked.

'Yes.'

'Was it as great a tragedy as others have said?'

'Worse,' I told him. 'A calamity beyond description. What news here, though? What has happened to Portugal in our absence?'

'Have you not heard? Cardinal Henrique has quite rightly taken the throne. He is now king, lord of Portugal and her dominions.'

'The old fox did not waste any time.'

'Why would he? Dom Sebastian is dead, and King Philip of Spain waits for an opportunity to annex Portugal. If we had remained leaderless he would have pounced. Henrique did what he had to do.'

'How does Henrique know that Dom Sebastian is dead?'

'Word of his death is everywhere. Philip of Spain claims to have the boy-king's body. Henrique grieves for his beloved nephew.'

Someone, I decided, had been hasty in identifying a body as that of our king – as those with vested interests might well be. Yet I did not see any value in telling this man the truth. I bowed. 'Thank you, sir, for your time.' I started to walk away, but the official called me back.

'Wait. Identify yourself,' he said.

The question wrong-footed me and I had no time to prepare a subterfuge. 'Frei Luis Pereira, of the Lisbon Dominicans.'

'Indeed,' he said.

Walking back towards the jetty I turned and saw him watching. When we rowed back out to the caravel he was visible on the dock, staring after us. With some trepidation I saw him turn and walk across the courtyard towards what must have been the civil offices.

Before we could set sail from Faro, a weather front rolled up from the ocean, forcing us below into the open hold, squatting on the stone ballast and upturned pipes while the rigging squealed and planks groaned with strain. For three days we remained at anchor, and my unease grew in line with Dom Sebastian's impatience.

My tiny berth was squeezed between the main cabin and the bulkhead. Sleep came hard to me on that narrow shelf of oak, so on that third night I scarcely had my eyes closed when I heard shouts, then the creak and stamp of running feet on the deck above. I sat up, drawing in a lungful of disturbed air, annoyed at the interruption.

'Unidentified vessels,' a lookout cried. 'Approaching fast … captain to the deck … captain to the deck.'

Taking a gulp of air I swung my legs off the bunk and wrapped my cloak around my shoulders, reaching down to slip my feet into leather shoes. In the dark I felt my way along a narrow crawl-hole that took me into the main cabin and from there onto the deck.

In the dull, clouded light, I saw the surrounding waters covered with small boats – all filled with fighting men – edged weapons pointing skyward like the quills of some deadly urchin. Men from the closest of these vessels were hurling grappling hooks and swarming over our gunnels.

One of our deck falconets discharged in a flash of lightning and a bellow of sound so fierce my ears rang and I staggered for lack of balance. Soon after firing, however, this worthy gun crew were overcome by our attackers, and the weapon fell silent.

Already Dom Sebastian's guardsmen were rising and engaging the enemy. They were joined by the crew, also armed, many of them veterans of conflict at sea.

Grappling hooks continued to strike the deck, some bouncing off into the water, others finding purchase on rails and chainplates, ropes drawing taut as they did so. I watched, frozen with fear, as an attacker gained the deck, a big man, swinging a broadsword almost as mighty as that of Dom Sebastian. In the light of our lanterns I saw the muscles of his arms and neck bulge as he swung; his unshaven face, and the dark woollen headband around his brow.

I regained sufficient composure to duck back towards the main cabin, while two of our guards moved to engage the dark figure that had seemed to spring from the sea itself. My concern, now, however, was for the still bigger man barrelling towards me from the dark of the companion ladder – Dom Sebastian.

'No,' I said, grasping his arm, 'you are in no condition to fight.'

He shrugged away from me, running and ducking to avoid the boom, unsheathing his sword as he ran, making for the nearest of the wraith-like shapes at the edge of the caravel's deck. More of the crew, those who had been sleeping below, had risen and armed themselves, joining the fray enthusiastically, the young captain swearing under his breath as he plied a heavy naval cutlass.

A rallying cry was raised above the din of battle, and perhaps a dozen of the enemy joined ranks in an attempt to carry the decks. A sword struck the main shrouds. Ropes parted, whipping and cracking as they did so. The mainmast groaned and leaned with the sudden lack of support, and somewhere, up high, more rigging snapped.

The enemy piled onto our deck in numbers, gaining a foothold at the stern. I saw Dom Sebastian holding his weapon high and charging into our attackers, flinging them away through sheer force.

All through the battle there were shouts of bravado, expressions in currency at the time. Tonio fell back from the fray, gripping his upper arm and grimacing in pain.

'It is sliced deep,' he said to me grimly. 'Kindly bind it for me so I may fight on.'

I did as he asked, ripping a length of cloth from his own shirt and wrapping it around his upper arm. Blood still seeped through, but to a fighting man of his calibre it was a mere inconvenience.

'What manner of men are these?' I asked him as I worked.

'I was going to ask you the same question. These are no sailors or hack marines – they fight like seasoned professionals – almost a match for we Guards, man for man. Bless me, Padre, for I go back to kill some more.'

By then the stern portion of the ship was in enemy hands, and our fighters fell back steadily, against the weight of numbers, for this was a force many times the size of our own. New fighters appeared on deck constantly, and our own number dwindled until only Dom Sebastian, and Tonio at his back stopped us from being overrun.

Finally, a new boat loomed close in the night. An armed caravel, bow coiled like a sleeping cobra, with three dark gunports on the starboard side, and another twenty or more fighting men in position to protect a figure on deck I recognised – a mature man, heavy in the body, cloaked and dangerous.

The vessel must have been piloted well, for it came alongside perfectly, nudging against us at the waist. The reinforcements jumped aboard and made a corridor through which walked Henrique himself, heavy and smug, nonchalant of the power he wielded so carelessly. Men ceased fighting and stood, chests heaving.

'There is your enemy,' I cried out to Dom Sebastian. 'Can you see it now? Henrique wants you dead – he has caused the lost battle of Alcâcer-Quibir. It is he who has stolen your crown and enslaved your people.'

Dom Sebastian looked back at me, and I saw understanding come. His grip tightened on the hilt of his weapon. He lifted it high and screamed with killing rage. The usurper, however, was well protected. A crossbowman at his flank fired his weapon and the quarrel buried itself deep in Dom Sebastian's upper leg.

Triumph filled the Grand Inquisitor's slitted eyes as he focussed all his attention on the wounded man. 'I am pleased to find you still alive, dear nephew, contrary to those unpleasant rumours.'

Dom Sebastian fell to his knees, his drawn sword on the deck before him, chest rising and falling. As I watched he clasped the quarrel buried deep in his leg and struggled to snap the shaft from his flesh. His face contorted with effort and pain. When it was done he threw it away and stared at his tormentor.

'Get up,' I cried, 'get up, and stop him.' I looked for Tonio, but saw that he too was down, lying unmoving, near the mainmast. This sight multiplied my despair. 'You must kill this traitor now,' I screamed. 'That is the only way to free Portugal from the rule of a tyrant.'

Cardinal Henrique saw me then, and his eyes narrowed. 'Gag the priest – do not let him speak. He has the tongue of a serpent.' While callused hands, then a filthy kerchief covered my lips Henrique advanced on Dom Sebastian, raised one heavy leg and kicked the wounded man to the deck.

'Get down before me, weakling,' he said, 'you should feel shame for what you have done. You are not a man but a child.'

Dom Sebastian, who I had thought was afraid of no one, shook like a palm frond in the wind as his uncle went on.

'You have driven your country to the brink of ruin and must pay for what you have done. You are no leader of men, but a fool who guides them to death and ignominy.' He turned to the guards that flanked him, pointing towards Dom Sebastian. 'Finish this pitiful man, send him to hell.'

Despite my efforts to struggle forward and prevent the blow, the nearest guarda-costras drove his sword into my king's chest, seemingly pinning him to the timbers. Blood seeped from the wound and around the blade. The swordsman then leaned forward to check his handiwork.

'The heart is pierced, your Grace.'

I choked with helpless rage, crying from the pit of my soul.

'Burn the ship,' Henrique shouted. 'Let Dom Sebastian and

his confessor be together in death. Let this be their funeral pyre.'

I was scarcely conscious of what was happening as they set their fires and the ship became an inferno. I heard the seamen's shouts as they loaded their fighters aboard and took them back from whence they came, leaving me there on the deck to be consumed. In truth, at that moment, I welcomed the arms of death. With my king lying broken and dead on the deck my life had lost meaning.

Prising the gag away from my lips I kneeled beside Dom Sebastian's body and beseeched the Lord to take me also.

A shadow appeared beside me. He must have been close to the flames, for smoke rose from his breeches and shirt.

'Tonio,' I cried. 'You are alive – but I saw you dead on the deck.'

'Stunned only,' he said, 'but what's this evil I have woken to? Is this Dom Sebastian lying here? Can he really have fallen?'

Singed with flame, weeping now, I reached out and placed one hand on the centre of Dom Sebastian's chest, to where that sword stroke had rent through clothing and skin. My fingers touched the wound itself. The bloody gash was not cold, as it should have been, but warm, and the flesh beneath pliant and vital.

Uncomprehending, I leaned forward and placed my ear to Dom Sebastian's lips. At first I was unsure if I was mistaken, but then I could not deny the soft easing of breath between the cracked, pale lips.

My face turned to stare upwards, like a child desperate to thank his father for an unexpected gift. 'My Lord God,' I croaked. 'He is alive. Not one miracle but two – your kindness is beyond comprehension.'

Already I was probing, assessing, checking for wounds. Apart from the near mortal rent in his chest, there was the wound from the quarrel above the knee, skin swelling like puckered lips around it.

'Beat, heart,' I implored, 'and lungs, breathe. Lord, grant me time to heal you. Grant me time to take you back to your people.' At that moment I remembered the barca we had earlier used for our journey ashore, tied up by a painter to the stern, where the ship's carpenters had been tending a cracked timber.

'Help me to carry him,' I pleaded.

Dom Sebastian was heavy, but together, coughing in the thickening smoke, Tonio and I dragged him along the deck, while the flames climbed the sails and my face burned as if from a brazier.

The ordeal must have lasted only minutes, or the flames would have claimed us. As it was, while we shifted the true king down and into the boat, the caravel began to settle more deeply. Water, I imagined, was rushing through her planks, distorted from heat and fire.

Untying the painter and drifting away, I was faced with a dilemma – try to seek sanctuary ashore in the bay, or face the tempest outside the harbour where at least we might be free of further discovery. Either choice was a risk, but I had no friends in this town, and our enemy might still be watching.

'Row,' I hissed at Tonio, and once we were out of sight of other vessels I stepped the mast, and let the sail billow full. She was a handy little vessel and set off like a hunting terrier on the scent of game.

The bay was not large, and we soon thumped into a steep and inconstant swell. That, however, was nothing compared to the open sea we encountered once we had cleared the islands. The gales had not yet moderated, and the tops of waves whipped into my face, drenching me through my cassock so the cold made me chatter like a madman.

Not being a sailor, and overcome with fear of the dark sea, I feared the worst. The tiller under my arm was my only comfort, and succour for the desperately ill man lying athwart the boat my only aim.

DOSE

It was one of those times when the universe seemed to conspire against Francis. First, Nicolá Massane, who he was very much looking forward to seeing again, sent through an email regretting her inability to attend an Australian expedition at that time. Then came the news that Jeff and his *Josephine* had been booked for late June and early July by an ornithological party heading to Croker Island. The long semester break at Charles Darwin University also meant that many of the usual volunteers had already made plans or headed off 'down south' for the duration.

With these setbacks delaying any departure, it was mid-July before Francis was able to head back to the East Kimberley with a full crew, confined by a 'window' of just fifteen days. Camille assisted with the food-shopping, and packing the dive gear. On the morning of his departure she ticked off a list of things that he should and should not do when he was away, and he left her with a tight embrace that made her complain gently.

'Hey Francis, I can't breathe, you know, when you hold me

like that.'

Despite the tight time-frame, Francis was cautiously hopeful as the *Josephine*'s bow sliced through the Arafura then Timor Seas. The company's corporate benefactors were pleased with his progress, had happily transferred funds, and the holds and eutectic fridges were loaded with supplies.

When Jeff took a breather from the helm and left Francis on the bridge, Lauren stood beside him and helped keep watch. With the autopilot set it was merely a matter of looking out for uncharted shoals or the unlikely passage of another vessel.

'You haven't been very forthcoming about your Portugal trip,' she said. 'What did you actually find out?'

Francis felt a pinprick of guilt. He had said nothing about the possible history of the hilt. 'Well as I told you. My theory is that the barca was originally carried by a ship called the *Nossa Senhora dos Anjos*, that left the Tagus River in 1578. She was bound for Timor and Larantuka.'

'What about the sword hilt?' she asked.

'What sword hilt?' he smiled back.

Lauren couldn't resist a smile. They both knew that he had still not declared the item, and that he was already liable for a significant fine for not doing so. 'You're a nutcase,' she said, 'and you'll get us all in trouble.'

'I just can't bring myself to hand it over – not yet – not until I know everything.'

'I understand,' she said. 'But I wish you'd share things with me like you used to.'

The following day, after running through much of the night and another day, they dropped anchor in the lee of a small island, eased the RHIB down from the davits and began preparing for work. In the evening, with the sun glowing red over the western coast, Francis called the volunteers together for a briefing.

'Without going into details I believe that we have established beyond reasonable doubt that the barca is Portuguese. We have the chance to prove that the Portuguese were the first Europeans to set foot on this country, and the Carbon 14 results on our samples date the hull to somewhere around 1550 to 1600. No one, however, is going to take that as evidence. We need to collect a range of artefacts that point to the time-period and hopefully the identity of the ship itself.'

'We'll be famous,' someone suggested.

'In a way, yes, but more importantly we will have corrected an error in the history books. There are several possibilities as to how this barca got here. Mendonca's fleet was a little too early. Mendana's expedition in 1595 is a distinct possibility, and there are other ships, from the 1570s onward, but my money is on a não called the *Nossa Senhora dos Anjos*. Would you like to hear a little more about her?'

The next morning, out on the shining blue-green surface of the sea, Francis took the RHIB in close to the reef, dropping the pick when Jeff, reading data off the GPS, said the word. 'Okay Nick, Marinda, get ready,' Francis said, turning until his eyes rested on Lauren. 'You too.'

Francis strapped rubber fins over his neoprene bootees, watching Nick flip his lengthy torso over the side. Rather than follow his lead, Lauren sat on the transom and eased in. As her head disappeared below the surface a reassuring trail of bubbles appeared.

When she had gone Francis also climbed over the transom onto the step, then slipped into the water, lowering his head, taking the first artificial breaths, and beginning the descent. The other two divers were already at the site. Once again, the wreck looked unprepossessing until, like a 'magic eye' pattern, it drew into focus. That first dive passed in reorientation, poking around at the wreck, re-establishing the lay of the land and registering the effect that currents and surf might have on their investigations.

That was the only unencumbered dive Francis would allow himself. After returning to the RHIB, they went to work in earnest, surveying the site. Nick held the stadia, and Francis hovered behind the theodolite – a version of the instrument developed for underwater use. Marinda took detailed notes on a slate – information which, back at the *Josephine*, would be added to the map that had been developed with the help of a photomosaic back in Darwin.

The basics done, it was possible to begin the creation of a grid network using prefabricated, weighted, plastic bars. This grid, numbered from one to sixty-two, would allow a record of the provenience – the exact three-dimensional location – of each and every object found.

Almost as soon as the first grids were lowered via ropes and snapped into position, Francis, using his hands like pointers, supervised the positioning of an airlift line that appeared from over the gunwale of the boat far above. Powered by the air compressor on board, it would lift a continuous stream of sand and bottom detritus to the surface, passing through a sieve before falling back to the sea floor.

The team dived in relays, returning day after day, trying to make the most of the limited time available. Black tubes ran down from the surface like snakes. Compressed air, flowing at eighty pounds-per-square-inch powered the dredge, forcing sand from the substrate around the barca wreck, grid-square by grid-square up to the boat.

Francis, working on the sea floor, held the vacuum tube in his right hand, directing the flow of sand and shell grit upwards, looking for likely places – traps where heavy objects might have accumulated. He constantly moved the tube to the hard corners and plied the tube underneath, feeling the heavy rattle as coral fragments, sand and hopefully relics moved up to where the resting diver was poring over the sieve.

In the evenings they drank beer, risked quick swims, spotted crocodiles on the sand bars and fished. For the younger members of the party, this kind of working holiday was a dream come true and there was always time to discuss theories on the wreck and its location. All the crew became used to gritty coral sand between their toes, deep in their scalps and in every crease of their bedsheets.

Yet, for all the intensity of their labours, day after day they faced disappointment. Amongst the debris in the sieve they found some buttons, a few glass beads – all consistent with a sixteenth century Portuguese vessel, but not uniquely so.

'If this was launched as a lifeboat,' said Francis, in an attempt to explain the lack, 'there would have been precious little aboard.'

'Maybe,' countered Lauren. 'But if the great não she came from was sinking wouldn't the people crowding into lifeboats have grabbed their most precious possessions? Jewels? Coins?

Trinkets?'

'True,' Francis breathed. 'Unless it was an exploring party.'

Lauren shrugged, 'That's possible of course.'

Towards the end of the trip – under a perfect sun, but after three sleepless nights, Francis reached breaking point.

Having worked his way around a coral-encrusted stone, he tucked the tube under his arm, braced himself and lifted a small boulder with both hands, exposing the underside, sending it tumbling over. He had been underwater for some forty minutes, and this was his third dive of the day. Exhaustion and a desperation for results combined to change his perception.

In the swirling storm of sand and dust that erupted – not exposed to light for five hundred years, he imagined that he saw the corpse of a man long dead. The vision wore scraps of what must have once been cloth. It sat up, gripped in the power of disturbed water, a seaman's amulet around its neck, still wearing the woollen jerkin that would have been worn week in, week out, for years.

For a moment Francis stared at death itself, grinning hideously back at him, laughing at the joke of it all. He shivered, as if that claw of a hand might reach out to pluck his soul. As he tried to back away an arm stretched out to touch him. It became impossible to move fast enough to avoid the claw hand that opened to strike.

Now came the unmistakeable concussion of a gunshot, along with the image of a head snapping back from the impact of a heavy lead projectile. He became aware of the fragility of his existence, of how each shallow breath carried oxygen to his blood and onto the brain – at how any break in this complicated and vulnerable process would bring his life to an end. It seemed so pointless, at that moment, to live at all, if not to connect with those who had gone before – their struggles and lives.

The *Trovas* of Bandarra echoed inside his skull, as if the significance was just beginning to dawn on him. Dom Sebastian was important to Portugal. Not just then, but now. There was a deep significance to what he was doing here.

In seconds that seemed like years the vision disintegrated, falling like rubble, dissolving into a swirl of fine calcium dust. Francis wanted to shout his disappointment, wanting to know the man – his name and where he grew up – whether he liked music, or animals. He wanted to ask how that medieval sword hilt had come to be there.

Gripped in a vice of fear and confusion Francis signalled to the others that he was going up. Yet as he ascended towards the RHIB, colour leached from the underwater world, for a capillary in his nose had burst, filtering his vision through a red layer of his own blood.

He slowed his ascent, not wanting any sudden pressure changes that might make the situation worse. Lauren detached herself from the others, and rose with him, bubbles flowing from the valve in her BCD as she dumped the expanding air.

They surfaced next to the boat together, and he reached up with his right hand and tore the mask from his face, revealing his blood-streaked nose and cheeks.

Nick leaned over the side, eyes wide. 'Jesus. What happened?' he asked.

'Just a bleeding nose.'

Lauren dropped a hand on his shoulder and squeezed. 'Let's get you out of the water before every damned shark in the Kimberley comes for a look.'

Back in the RHIB, diving gear removed, the bleeding soon stopped, but still Lauren insisted that he sit up, head forward, while she crouched beside him with her arm around his shoulders and wet body pressed close, holding a tissue to his nose, catching the last of the flow.

'We'd better get back to the *Josephine* for an ice pack.'

Francis struggled out of her grip. 'No. Give me five minutes. I'll be fine.' The other two volunteers surfaced beside the boat. Francis turned on them. 'It's nothing, right? Just a little nosebleed and we've got work to do.'

TWELVE

The waters of the Rio Sada were as dark and oil-calm as the dregs of an olive press. Over the bows I saw the lights of Setúbal – a thousand candles, lamps and cooking fires. Tonio, who must have been at the limit of his strength and endurance, rowed like a machine.

For five days we had sailed north, bailing constantly, surviving on rancid, stale water from the emergency pipe from the bows, and biscuits so infested with weevils they tickled the throat as they went down.

Looking aft my eyes creased with worry. Dom Sebastian lay athwartships, dying on a bed of soft rags, head lolling to one side, his fever-riddled mind causing him to emit the occasional moan of pain. I feared for him then – feared for the trust we were about to place in other men. His wounds were terrible, and it was only through the mercy of Our Lord God that he had survived.

Turning back to Tonio I smiled, but there was no warmth in that gesture. I did not feel connected to him emotionally, after all he had done. Despite our days at sea together I had no idea went on behind those beetling dark brows. I was grateful to him, but he remained a mystery to me.

My thoughts were cut off as the barca's keel kissed against mud, and swinging out over the gunwale I felt the soft riverbed beneath my feet. Advancing to dry ground I surveyed the area. Behind the Cais de Embarque a long thoroughfare ran. Even now, after dark, it was populated with fishermen and their fires, along with occasional strolling lovers.

'They will not come,' Tonio said.

'Have faith, my friend. My message was despatched. They will come.'

As if in response to my optimism, the youth I had waylaid earlier that day, on a visit to shore, appeared from the darkness. 'I passed the message,' he said. 'They are on their way.'

'Well done,' I said, pressing the promised coin into his hand. He disappeared back into the darkness without a word.

My eyes moved to a cart waddling down the road, a tired looking mule in the traces. Two monks walked alongside. As I approached the cart, I saw that it was driven by a lad of fourteen or so. Behind him sat the Prior of the Monastery of Arrábida, whose lean frame sat tense on the bench, I recognised his wide shoulders, and the taut sinews of his neck.

'I am pleased to see you in good health, brother.' I greeted him with clasped hands.

'Likewise, I am honoured by this visit from such an important personage.' His words carried a hidden meaning. Of course he was not referring to me, but to the rightful king who lay close to death in the barca. 'We must be quick,' he hissed. 'We have a visiting Jesuit with us. His name is Frei Sereno, and I'm certain that he is an agent of Henrique. He insisted on accompanying us tonight.'

This news caused my near relief to evaporate. 'Where is this spy?'

'I managed to send him on an errand, but he will expect us to collect him in a moment. As soon as we have the True King on board – and a load of fresh fish.'

'Then let us hurry,' I said.

With Tonio silent at my shoulder, I followed the monks down to the boat. Together we lifted Dom Sebastian over the gunwales and up to the cart. There, in the shadows, we laid him on the platform of boards before dropping a calico cover, kept raised by a pair of buckets around his head so he could breathe.

Only then did the monks carry up crates of mackerel from the fleet on the shore. Some specimens were still kicking, they were so fresh. The monks poured them carefully into the cart, arranging them around and over the wounded king so as to cause the least pressure on his body.

As I climbed up onto the seat beside Brother Martinho, the mule dragged his feet forward, driven by the Prior's novice. The cart dawdled through the streets, scarcely worthy of a glance by housewives throwing slops out into the street.

One block distant from the docks, a darkly dressed figure waved us down.

'That's him,' the Prior hissed. 'The one I warned you about.' Then, to his novice. 'Stop, please, Duarte.'

The boy did as he was told, bringing the cart to a halt. The monks loaded the bundles of olives that sat on the pavement on top of the fish, then the Jesuit climbed up between the Prior and I. The priest's face was pinched, his body somewhat rigid so that his arms swung with a hunchback-like lack of grace. His eyes bored into mine.

'Ah, Frei Sereno,' the Prior said. 'You did well with the olives.'

'I always do. And who might this be?' he asked, still looking at me.

'An old comrade in the service of Jesus Christ,' the Prior explained.

'You look and smell like a corpse,' the Jesuit exclaimed. 'From whence do you come?'

Before I could invent a reply, the Prior stepped in. 'His name is not to be spoken, and he has been on a special assignment for his order.'

This was a master-stroke, for it invoked the confidentiality of one Holy order against another. Even this strange creature knew better than to enquire further. Besides, the Prior followed this up by turning on his novice, who held the reins in his hand.

'What are you waiting for, Duarte? You foolish and lazy boy. Get us back or we will be late for Compline.'

The boy looked back with a start, then flicked the reins urgently. I felt somewhat sorry for him. The Prior was a good man, but was well known for his sharp tongue.

Leaving the city of Setúbal, we passed farmland, with bleating goats and sheep in their pens, and market gardens, the produce of which was shipped north across the Tagus to feed the ever-growing populace of Lisbon. Before long the sea appeared again on my left, and ahead, the Monastery of Arrábida, white and stately, high above the ocean. The Franciscan order there were staunch supporters of the House of Aviz. One or two of the monks were superb physicians.

As we approached I recalled the legend of the monastery's origins. Apparently, some three hundred years ago, an English trading galley had struck stormy weather off the coast. A substantial stone image of the Virgin Mary was lost over the side, though the ship and her company survived. They took shelter, lying at anchor below where the monastery now stands, and were surprised to see an unearthly light shining on the hillside.

The ship's captain climbed the foreshore in search of the light. To his surprise he found the lost stone Virgin, glowing with heavenly fire, moved by a miracle from deep water to ridge. Overcome with Grace, he sold everything he owned to fund the construction of a monastery on the site.

Approaching it now, I saw that the brush fence that surrounded the main enclosure was not guarded. The driver dismounted and opened the gate while the mule munched on coarse grasses. We saw no living soul until the cloister, where curious monks huddled in groups.

These men wore plain cloaks of spun wool and like the Prior, had the gaunt features of men who feasted little and laboured much. They carried candles that flickered against the chapel walls and illuminated a stone representation of Saint John in the centre of the courtyard.

We were forced to wait until after Compline in the monastery chapel, when Frei Sereno was safely at rest, before we could carry Dom Sebastian to a cell adjoining that of the Prior. I watched with the worried gaze of a parent as two monks laid him on a mattress of linen stuffed with fresh straw. One of the eldest monks kneeled at his side and removed the coverings to view the wounds by the light of two candles.

At some length he looked up at me. 'Who dressed the wounds?'

'I did.'

'I congratulate you. Dom Sebastian would not have survived without your good work. Even so, the wound in his thigh is deep and poisoned. His chest wound is clean, however, and if the blade had pierced a lung or his heart he would already be dead. I can only imagine that the man who Henrique ordered to kill Dom Sebastian made his stroke intentionally shallow and non-mortal. Dom Sebastian owns the loyalty of many men, even perhaps, some of those in the guarda-costras.

'There is hope?' I asked.

'By the Grace of Our Heavenly Father there is hope.'

The Prior touched my shoulder. 'Leave the rightful king now. He is in safe hands.' His voice became stern. 'You and I need to talk.'

Back in his office we settled into hard chairs. Duarte the novice brought mugs of broth. I accepted the sustenance gratefully, though the Prior took one sip and turned on the boy.

'You careless child. This broth is cold. How dare you show such discourtesy to a guest? Take it back and heat it up.'

I saw how the lad's face fell at the reprimand, and his brown eyes moistened. Duarte had an open, honest face, with the promise of a dimple on his chin. Of average height, he had a raw-boned musculature – all swinging arms and bulky shoulders – like a grown man in miniature. Supporting this impression, his hair, cut close to his skull, appeared to recede on either side of his temple. When he had collected the mugs and retired to do his master's bidding I commented, 'You are hard on the boy.'

'You know that is my way. Slovenly work will make his life hard. Strict standards are the best thing for youth.'

I wanted to comment further but I knew it was not seemly. Besides, the boy was soon back, with soup of a temperature that pleased his master, and we were free to talk.

'Frei Sereno is a problem,' the Prior said. 'I believe that he and other Jesuits have been sent out to monasteries sympathetic to Dom Sebastian to search for that which you had the foresight to hide here before the King sailed for Morocco. Somehow we have to neutralise Sereno.'

'That may not be so easy,' I warned.

'I agree. But our country's future, and all our lives, depend on us doing so.'

'We'll think of something,' I said. 'But first, what are we going to do with Dom Sebastian? He can't stay here forever.'

'Of course he can't, but you and I alone lack authority to make weighty decisions about his future. We need help.'

Our deliberations lasted almost an hour, and by then we had decided on a course of action on the matter of Dom Sebastian. My fatigue was obvious – my eyes almost closed several times.

Finally, the Prior touched my shoulder. 'Come now. You need to rest. I've had a cell cleaned out for you, and your belongings carried there.'

The cell was spotless but small, hewn from stone centuries earlier, and the walls were etched with the names of previous occupants and snippets of Holy Scriptures. It was furnished with a small desk and a sleeping pallet. The Prior called Duarte to bring a cloth and bowl of warm water mixed with white wine.

The novice also brought me a fresh cassock, hanging it ready on a wooden peg impregnated into the wall.

'Leave us now, Duarte, and be ready for Matins,' the Prior said. When the boy was gone he undressed me himself, and I felt no shame in my old man's body – my paunch, the white hairs of my sunken chest, my flaccid little member and hairy testicles.

The Prior began to wash me. It was an act of respect. A necessary rite, that we both knew I had been too long without. He rinsed the cloth and started with the top of my head, a gentle dabbing of my eyes and face, long slow strokes down along my neck, my chest.

Neither of us spoke, but at times I closed my eyes. His scrubbed the sweat from my armpits, and that wine and water mixture dripped down the sides of my body like cold fingers. Down my back he went, and when the cloth smoothed my spine I could not control a shiver that ran through my body. He cleaned all the way down the backs of my legs to the balls of my feet. The silence in that cell was so thick that I could hear the snores of sleeping monks, and the scratching of a rat somewhere in the corridor.

The Prior dropped the cloth into the bowl and stepped back. 'Now,' he said, 'you must sleep. We will talk further after Matins.'

'Thank you,' was all I could blurt as the Prior left the cell. When he had gone I sank down onto the pallet. Within a few moments I was fast asleep.

CATORZE

The house at thirty-seven, Rua Carneiro, in the Lisbon suburb of Estrela, held special memories for Nicolá Massane – the domed basilica on the hill, and elm trees lining the narrow-paved street. Always she remembered the sound of a window sliding open and her mother's voice.

'Nici, come inside at once.'

Behind the glass-panelled front door, Mãe brushed at her dress with work-hardened hands. 'What kind of boy will be interested in a dirty girl with her head full of stories of Romans and Greeks and the Lord God knows what else?'

'I don't know, Mãe.' The smell of boiling mackerel from the kitchen permeated the hallway.

'The wrong kind of boy, that's who. Have you prayed since school?'

'No Mãe, not yet.'

'Then wash your hands and do so now.'

'Yes Mãe.'

'Doña Valadares mistook you for a boy last Wednesday. That

would never have happened with your sisters. I concede that God did not give you their beauty, but you could at least try. Even your brother managed to keep himself out of the dirt.'

Nicolá was the youngest of four siblings, all high achievers, two already married. To the others she was constantly and unfavourably compared. 'I'm sorry, Mãe.'

'No you are not. Now hurry before your Pai gets home.'

Pedro Massane was an engineer with the Lisbon City Council. Each evening he caught the Metro, then the number twenty-eight tram, walking the final four blocks to arrive home at six-thirty. In one hand he carried an oversized brown leather briefcase and often a tube of rolled blueprints in the other.

Nicolá, scrubbed and ready, waited on the front step, bony knees knocking together with anticipation. The first sign that he was close came from the widow Ribeiro's barking dog. The gate would creak and slam closed and his shoes slap on stone as he ascended the path. Pai would smile and ruffle her hair, his round face beaming with pleasure.

'May I take your case, Pai?'

'Of course Nici, did you find anything interesting today?'

Some days there were stories to tell, and fragments of glass or terra cotta nestled in cotton wool. Other days there were not. 'Mãe made me come in early.'

'Well, she wants you to be a young lady, and so you should.'

'But I want to look for things in the earth.'

'Then you must be a young lady who looks for things in the earth.'

That night, lying in bed, Nicolá heard her father remonstrate with her mother. 'You must remember, Elena, that Nici's IQ has been tested in the top one percent of the population. A brain is there to be used.'

'I have no problem with the girl using her intelligence, but I object to her grubbing in the garden. I swear that her knees will never come clean. Why does she have to be so different to the others?'

'Because that is how God made her. She needs to follow her interests.'

At school Nicolá was first to volunteer to clean the blackboard or sharpen pencils. She spent hours colouring pictures in exceptional detail. By her teenage years she was consistently placed in the top three of her class and in the tenth grade she was chosen to attend a selective government school.

In her mid-teens Nicolá dealt with the trappings of womanhood – periods and awkward health checks with an organised irritability, as with anything that slowed her down. She made sure that she had the required hygiene product on hand, and carried on with the business of life.

Nicolá's mother was not the only one who suggested that she lacked femininity. In her senior years at school other girls, dressed in the latest fashions, giggled behind their hands as she passed. At first she feigned indifference, but then, guided by a new friend, Vidonia, she developed a unique style in dressing.

'You don't have the classic face,' Vidonia told her. 'But you have beautiful hair, perfect skin, and a nice body. Draw attention to them.'

Wearing a dress at her friend's insistence, at an end-of-high-school party, she met Miguel, who played his guitar and sang like a pop star, with sensuous lips and loving eyes that focussed on her face as he sang. When the others danced to compact discs of American R&B music on the stereo, Nicolá talked with Miguel on the veranda. He was studying medicine at university, was two years her senior and would one day save lives, perhaps in some foreign country. Refusing his invitation to walk back to his shared unit, she left her telephone number. To her surprise and delight he called before nine the next morning, inviting her to a club that night.

Sensing her inexperience, Miguel did not rush her, showering her with kisses and gifts, always leaving her wanting more, giving her time to consider their relationship before it deepened further.

Three months into the affair, Miguel appeared at her door one morning, happy and smiling, taking both her hands in his.

'Nicolá, you will never guess what has happened. I have been accepted as a volunteer, a humanitarian worker.'

'Where?'

'Angola.'

'But your studies?'

'I have deferred them for six months. Say you will come with me, please.'

Laughing, Nicolá waved her hands in an attempt to explain. 'I am going to University. I have a scholarship.'

'Put it off for six months. What do you say?'

'I say maybe.'

This was the first time Nicolá had gone against her father, and strangely, it was Mãe who argued for her. The older woman had welcomed Miguel from the first, spending hours producing enchanting food – feioada and rojoes for him to eat, fussing over him while Nicolá sat back, excluded from the conversation.

'Let her go out and see the world, Rafael, before she faces those dreary halls at university. Africa! How exciting it will be for her.'

The young couple made love for the first time the night before they left. Nicolá had consumed just the right amount of red wine to numb her Catholic guilt.

Nicolá wanted to take it seriously, but the image of naked, serious Miguel straining against her, every muscle proud on his long torso, made her want to giggle. The act ended with his frantic shudders. Both hands on his back, now she felt, if not pleasure, some proprietary pride that it was her body that had induced such a reaction in him.

As the tremors subsided he rolled off, breathing deeply, the sides of his hairless cheeks dusted with perspiration. 'Was it good?' he asked.

'Yes.'

'That's nice. I'm glad your first time pleased you.'

They lay in silence for a few minutes before Miguel spoke again. 'Do you think we should go back to the party?'

'I'm happy here.' Nicolá snuggled up to his chest. Something serious and adult had passed between them. Their touching bodies, dusted in sweat, gave rise to a delicious sensation.

'I think we should go back, people will be looking for us. Come on.'

Nicolá sighed, 'If you think we have to.'

They dressed in silence.

In Angola, Nicolá promised silently, *I will make it better for us.*

In Africa, however, Nicolá was trained as an emergency nurse and posted to Calumbo, just south of Luanda in the Bengo Province. There, in that dry coastal strip she found herself under the control of a domineering doctor who gave orders with a harsh Dutch accent.

A week passed before she was able to climb a small hill and call Miguel with a cell signal that hovered between non-existent and scarcely usable.

'I thought we would be together,' she said.

His voice sounded strange. 'So did I. I'm sorry. I'll see what I can do.'

On a rare day off, Nicolá was able to visit the ruined walls of a fort that mariners from her country had built three hundred and fifty years earlier, on a wild and remote headland south of Cabo Ledo.

Here, with the breeze off the Indian Ocean lifting the hem of her skirt she felt the importance of the Age of Discovery and just how far away from home her mariners had sailed. Wrinkling her nose at the freshness of the sea air, she wished that she too, could have sailed far away, into the unknown.

Soon after arriving back at the camp, in a borrowed four-wheel-drive with an Angolan assistant at the wheel, she was summoned for a telephone call. This time Miguel's voice sounded even more distant.

'I have to tell you something.'

'Yes? Have you found a way for us to be posted together?'

'No, sorry querido. That's not it.' He told her that he had fallen for a young Italian nurse he had been working with. 'I'm so sorry.'

Her throat ached. 'I'm sorry too.'

Nicolá spent another month near Luanda, but her heart was no longer in it, and she arranged to cut short her stay. The regional director was sympathetic.

'It happens all the time,' he said. 'Young people arrive as couples but their relationships cannot survive the rigors of life here.

What can we do?'

Back in Lisbon, her father made no attempt to hide his pleasure at her return, while Mãe folded her arms, 'You meet one decent boy and let him slip through your fingers.'

Nicolá said nothing, yet her lips assumed a determined expression. 'I am early enough to start university in the first semester. That is better for me.'

In the second year of her degree, Nicolá let herself fall in love again, with a professor from Coimbra nine years her senior who was assigned to Lisbon for a term. Tears ran from his eyes when he first told her of his feelings for her, and this time the lovemaking was more pleasurable. After three weeks of strangely-timed sexual adventures, however, he broke down and told her that he was married – making no pretence that this was a temporary situation. Yes, he and his wife were happy, yes, they had children, and no, he could not understand what had possessed him to lie to her. Was it not possible to love two women at the same time?

Nicolá considered the question thoroughly. When she replied it was with a light shake of the head. 'No. I am sorry. That is not possible. Not in the way a woman needs to be loved.'

Increasingly wary, Nicolá graduated with honours and launched into a PhD thesis on fifteenth and sixteenth century Portuguese metallurgy. The research took her to remote villages and regional centres where sometimes men, of all ages and stations, expressed an interest in her. Before long the game bored her, and in the presence of interested males she became aware of the signs and found a reason to move away.

At twenty-six years of age she was on the University teaching staff, living in her own unit. Acquaintances stopped trying to line up blind dates. An aura of inapproachability built up around her, something that she both welcomed and regretted. Seldom moving outside her circle, Nicolá accepted the occasional dinner invitation, but the men she went out with were not interesting to her, and she discouraged any attempt to take the relationship further.

Instead she sought out platonic friendships with men she respected, spending three weeks with such a man one summer. Together they travelled through Southern Portugal and Spain. The vehicle was a Ford van with a mattress in the rear and her companion a French linguist who wore his hair in a ponytail, and used his deep voice in carefully constructed sentences.

One night she woke to find his hand down the waistband of her pyjamas, and when she told him to remove it he pleaded that her refusal would leave him in physical agony and that while they were mere friends, surely she felt sorry for his predicament. 'Why cannot friends be affectionate in a physical way?' he asked.

'Because they can't,' she said.

Feeling contempt for him, she rearranged the crowded van so that his guitar case lay between them and went back to sleep. Nicolá was proud that she would not bow to pressure – that she could live without the complications of sex and romance.

There was one problem – her heart was not cold, but warm and loving. Only the barriers around it were cold.

QUINZE

Before we could put any plan for Dom Sebastian into action there was still the vexing problem of Frei Sereno. He knew that something was going on, but was not yet sure what. Three times I caught him following me, and on each occasion I had to invent an innocent errand to throw him off-track.

Funnily enough it was Duarte, the Prior's novice, who provided the answer. I was deep in thought, pacing the cobbled path outside the chapter house, when I heard the Prior's raised voice, admonishing the lad as he so often did. When I came upon them, the youth was holding a partially-full jute sack in one hand.

'Where have you been, boy?' the Prior was shouting. 'I have a dozen errands for you.'

The boy stuttered and stammered, displaying the contents of his bag. It was filled with field mushrooms. I could smell the stale fungi smell of them. 'Parvo from the kitchen sent me to collect them.'

'And is Parvo the idiot your superior?' the Prior thundered.

'No sir. But … he says that Frei Sereno is partial to mushrooms, and insists on a serve of them every night before Compline.'

The Prior harrumphed, but it was hard to argue with catering for the whims of a powerful visitor. He took the bag and sent the lad off on some mission or other. I stepped forward as soon as Duarte had gone and held out my hand.

'Here,' I said, 'I'm heading for the kitchens. I'll take the bag of mushrooms with me and deliver it to Parvo.'

The Prior was a busy man, and did not mind as I carried the bag away. As soon as I was out of sight, however, I headed not for the kitchen, but detoured past the fishpond with its hungry mouths kissing at the water surface. My route took me through the back gate, and down the hillside into the forest.

There, as I had expected, I found a different kind of mushroom. Its name was the Pale Rider – not deadly – but known to produce a serious stomach disorder that lasted for days. I picked more than a dozen of them.

Pale Riders look different to field mushrooms, so I crumbled them up in my hands and spread them throughout the bag so they would mingle with the others.

I carried the bag to the kitchen and handed them to Parvo. 'These are for Frei Sereno's supper. No one else, do you understand?'

Satisfied that I had made at least some forward progress I retired to my cell and wrote a long letter to Frei Aguiar, beseeching him for intelligence on Aletia's safety and the general situation in Lisbon. By chance a contingent of Royal Mail horsemen had just come through with a delivery, and I entrusted my missive to them, with an extra coin to expedite its delivery.

It was midnight when I heard a shout of pain and anger. I soon discovered, hurrying down the corridor, that our honoured guest was bent over in his cell, sobbing with pain.

'I've been poisoned,' Frei Sereno shouted.

I looked in with some sympathy, because even by the candle-light I could see the calibre of his agony. I started forward to wish him some comfort, but was forestalled by an even greater excla-mation of pain from down the stone corridor. I wended my way in that direction to investigate this new problem, and came to the Prior's room, where he was similarly doubled over, his face pink with pain.

I was confused, and since both sufferers already had several helpers on hand, all as good or better at first aid than I, instead of giving comfort to the afflicted I instead went straight to the kitchen, where I located Parvo, likewise prostrate with pain, sob-bing.

'You idiot. I told you only Frei Sereno was to eat the mush-rooms. Who else ate them?'

'I … planned to give them only to Frei Sereno as you said,' he gasped between spasms, 'but then the Prior smelled them cook-ing and asked for some. There was a small portion left so I—'The sentence was cut off by a powerful contraction of his gut.

As I walked back towards the monk's cells I could hear the Prior, voice cut off by waves of pain at intervals, remonstrating with Duarte.

Certain that there was nothing to be gained by intervening, I crept back to my cell and laid my head down. I consoled myself with the knowledge that at least the primary objective, keeping

Frei Sereno from prying, had been achieved.

The following morning, while the Prior, Frei Sereno, and the monastery cook remained prostrated with vomiting and diarrhoea in their cells, seven messengers rode out on what poor mounts the monastery could spare. I watched them go, then hurried inside to make my preparations.

Over the next twelve hours the respondents came in a trickle, then a stream – thirty priests and noblemen with their entourages, riding in from as far away as Cascais and Grândola. They came with serious faces and grim determination, greeting me with promises of help and friendship.

Not trusting Frei Sereno to stay in his cell, I posted Duarte at the Jesuit's door. 'If he emerges, run and tell me immediately.'

'Yes Padre.'

I studied the lad for a moment. I knew he would take this duty seriously. My mind at ease, I led groups of new arrivals into the presence of Dom Sebastian. The last rays of the sun touched him through the window, just as it set fire to the mountain behind us. That glow gave his fever-ridden body an unearthly quality, as our visitors kneeled to kiss his sleeping lips.

This procession filled my heart with hope – Dom Sebastian's supporters were so fervent, so serious, that together we must surely make the correct decisions.

We gathered in the Chapter House, and after a meal of goat meat, fish and wine, I stood before the assembly, peering out between the oak posts and tables in the candlelight. I was pleased to see Frei Amador Paiva beside the Duke of Braganza, for he was one of many that I had been unsure of reaching.

Continuing to study the group I noted the presence of Luis Vaz de Camões, the most acclaimed Portuguese poet of all the ages, who had dedicated his immortal seafaring epic *Os Lusiadas* to Dom Sebastian. He, like Luis da Câmara, had lost an eye, though in his case from cannon shrapnel. A patch covered the empty hole in his skull. Beside him sat our supporter Balthazar de Barbuda, radiating patient strength as always.

Those gathered allies were not only men, either. I recognised my friend, the influential merchant Ana Horta, sitting beside Rosa de Almada, daughter of one of Lisbon's most powerful banking families.

Man or woman, each member of that group was a patriot. All knew what the usurper King Henrique and the da Câmara brothers were doing to our country. They had seen guarda-costras in the guise of tax collectors. Men slaughtered for a pittance before the eyes of their children. Public executions were, apparently, common. No one was immune from the visit of armed men in the middle of the night – not knowing if a friend or neighbour might have reported some implied criticism of the new king.

'My friends,' I said, after a short prayer. 'Thank you for coming here. You have travelled at great personal risk.' The Chapter House was so quiet that I heard the lamp wicks hiss in their fat. 'I am a learned man, yet remain at a loss as to what to do. Dom Sebastian cannot stay here. One of the many pilgrims who travel here to see the Stone Virgin might at any time betray his presence.'

A staunch nobleman I knew as Dom de Tovar cleared his throat. 'To nurse Dom Sebastian back to health is not enough. Henrique will soon learn that he is alive and seek him out.'

The door opened, and all eyes turned. It was Duarte, eyes filled with worry. He hurried across to me and I leaned down so my ear was close to his lips.

'Padre. Frei Sereno has left his cell. He can scarcely walk, but—'

I looked out the window and saw that the Jesuit was indeed out in the yard. He was clutching his gut with one hand as he moved. At that point he stopped and sat down, looking around balefully. He knew something was going on, but his body would not obey his need.

'Carry on,' I said to my gathered friends. 'But keep your voices low.'

A fellow priest was the next to speak. 'My brother is prior of a remote monastery in the Trâs-os-Montes. Dom Sebastian would never be found there.'

Ana Horta rose from her seat. 'That may be true, but what then? Dom Sebastian does not need monk's robes, but an army. He does not require prayer beads, but iron and men. Do you think Henrique will give up the throne without force? We know he has been building up his resources for some time, while men loyal to Dom Sebastian lie dead at Alcácer Quibir or remain captive until their ransom is paid.'

My friend Balthazar took up the argument. 'Doña Horta is right,' he said, 'I know that even now Henrique is recruiting, building up his forces, buying loyalty with gold. The only way Dom Sebastian will return as king is at the head of ten thousand men.'

'Where will he raise such an army?'

'The East.' I looked at the speaker – de Andrade, the bookseller, a man both learned and respected, slump shouldered as if bowed from the weight of stacks of manuscripts. He went on, 'There, in the shipbuilding centres of India, Dom Sebastian can gather an army and the ships to bear them. I know of three or four

Eastern potentates who will support Dom Sebastian with money and men in return for future alliances.' De Andrade lowered his voice with the skill of an accomplished performer. 'A fleet waits at anchor in the Sea of Straw. Even as we speak she takes on supplies and men. Dom Sebastian must sail with her.'

De Tovar took up the idea. 'In Goa and Malacca Dom Sebastian has many friends, and there he will find money and allies. Dom de Oliveira, the captain of *Our Lady of Angels*, the great não at anchor in our harbour, is a fervent supporter of Dom Sebastian, from whom he gained his commission.'

The conspirators nodded and muttered, 'Sim,' at this idea, for it was an inspired one. At the other side of the world we would find support, for our people had been colonising the Indies for five generations. Goa was populated by more than twelve thousand of our families, many of whom boasted great wealth and would value the opportunity to support Dom Sebastian in return for trading concessions. Their sons would enlist as soldiers and sail to Portugal in glory.

The poet Luis de Camóes rose, twisting the waxed tip of his moustache between thumb and forefinger as he did so. 'As you know, I was, many years ago, banished to Goa, and spent eight years there. I know the city intimately – and can assure you that it is the natural refuge for the True King. I have a proposal. Let us consider ourselves a band of brothers and sisters united in common purpose. Each of us will have a task to perform.'

The poet's voice was high, and somewhat effeminate, yet it carried throughout the room, brimming with good sense and recognition of the gravity of the situation. 'Each of us will swear an oath in the sight of God. Let us call ourselves the Sebastianists – men who devote their lives to protecting Dom Sebastian and restoring him to the throne.'

The assembly cheered in a muted but powerful fashion. My own contribution was tinged with a personal and selfish excitement. If Dom Sebastian went with the fleet I was bound to go with him, and also with Aletia, whose fate I still did not know – only that she was already committed to the journey.

I glanced through the window. Frei Sereno must have heard our raised voices, and he was staggering towards the main Chapter House door with a steely-eyed determination.

'All of you,' I hissed. 'Leave now – out the back door – and hurry yourselves.'

They were all smart people, and trusted that I would not give such an order without cause. They rose and began to file out the rear entrance, out to waiting servants and willing horses.

The Duke of Braganza waited until the last, then took me aside and said, pitched so that even Duarte would not hear. 'Henrique is furious that the *Parcela* is missing from the treasury. Somehow we must get it onto the ship. Few of our comrades have calculated how many ships will be needed to carry an army such as the one Dom Sebastian would need to bring back to Portugal. Thirty at the very least. India now boasts some of the biggest shipbuilding enterprises in the world, but a war fleet will cost a fortune. Dom Sebastian possesses the fortune required, but we need to make sure it goes with him.'

'You're right, of course,' I said. 'There must be a way.'

'There will be, if we are bold but cautious.'

He too then moved for the exit, leaving just myself and the novice.

A moment later the doors flew open, and Frei Sereno stood in the entrance, hardly able to stand, with a look of pained outrage on his face. Then, scanning the area, seeing the empty seats, his expression changed.

'Why hello,' I said, in unconcerned tones. 'I have been helping young Duarte with his public speaking. One day, I'm convinced, he will deliver marvellous sermons.'

Henrique's man looked from me to the boy, and back again, then let loose his bowels with a thunderous sound. A foul liquid escaped his robes and flooded around his feet.

'Oh dear,' I said. 'It seems that it was not a good idea for you to leave your cell.'

Later, I sat at Dom Sebastian's bedside. The fever conjured mad ravings from the deepest recesses of his mind.

I valued those hours – alone with the young king and his random vocalisations. At times he called for his mother, at others for Tonio who, bored like any fighting man would be at a monastery, had left on some errand for a few days.

I comforted my king with damp cloths and thin soup prepared to my own recipe. This I dribbled between his lips, stroking his neck until he swallowed. Occasionally his outbursts summoned the dead – Alvaro de Castro, his best and truest friend, who had died of a fever – or his grandmother Catarina, whom he had feared. Other vocalisations were meaningless, though his eyes would narrow and limbs thrash as though he fought Satan himself. At those times I would pray, or recite snatches of scripture over and over again. I am sure my words penetrated into that unnatural slumber.

Yet my mind was on Lisbon. Not just the fleet, but the girl who was precious to me. Now was the time to get my own plans in motion, before Sereno recovered from the mushrooms; before he could send word back to Henrique that the stirrings of rebellion were afoot here.

The arrangements I made were ready not a moment too soon. By Matins the next morning Frei Sereno was gone without trace, his cell left befouled and untidy. It offended my good nature that he left without a word to his hosts of many weeks. Even so, this turn of events made my plan much simpler.

I spent much of the day and night preparing the ruse, necessitating some time in the monastery crypt, then the careful and very private packing of a plain pine coffin. If the long-dead monk I selected had guessed that his body might one day be the resting place of a vast fortune he might have given up his chance of eternal life for a few days on earth to enjoy it.

After virtually no sleep, the next morning we set off after breakfast. There were five of us in the party, walking beside a wagon loaded only with that coffin.

The Prior had loaned us Duarte to drive the cart, and his horse to bear it – much swifter, at a pinch, than the usual mule. We took the road towards Lisbon, damp of eye and downcast, occasionally breaking into hymns. I had taken pains to disguise my appearance. Since Morocco I had, partly by circumstance, partly by design, allowed my sparse grey beard to grow in its strange wispy and wilful manner. Today I had shaped what I could into a sharp goatee beard and moustache, and one of the monks had plucked my normally wild eyebrows into neat little arches.

To complete the transformation my head had been shaved to the smoothness of an egg. When examining my new self in a looking glass I must admit to a moment of sinful pride, for I looked younger. Many of my cares and the tide of advancing years seemed to lie on the stone monastery floor along with my silver locks.

In any case, we attracted little attention as we trudged our way along the track that followed the south bank of the Tagus. It was a maudlin little procession, cloaked in black and singing. Many of the monks had some physical disability or other. One was club-footed, another had lost a hand in a farm accident as a boy. The monasteries were filled with men who would have found other employment difficult, shunted off by their families into houses of God.

Occasionally someone would stop to ask us the name of the occupant of the coffin. My speech had been well rehearsed. 'Herein lies the elderly father of a wealthy merchant in Goa, India, may God rest his soul. The son has requested, at great expense, the sending of his father's body, heavily embalmed, so he might view his beloved parent one last time and bury him with ceremony.'

The idea had occurred to me because just such a thing had happened the previous year. When trying to sell an untruth, all born liars know, the more the teller can drape it with truthful baubles, the better it will carry.

Reaching the jetty just before noon, we left the cart and horse with a trusted local priest and carried our burden to one of the many ferry boats that ply the Sea of Straw to and from Lisbon.

In our case I paid the ferryman extra to take us not directly across, but past the Palace to where the India fleet was waiting at anchor.

The pale-yellow water passed under our bow with a hiss and occasional puff of effervescence. I studied every detail of Lisbon's shore – each strolling figure, each slow cart trundling away with goods unloaded from the ships at the jetties. Seabirds hovered and squabbled around fishing boats. Rotting hulks lay aground in the shallows, and weather-scarred old men rowed their boats, fishing or arguing in loud voices.

The tall spires of the Sé dominated the skyline, along with the solid, imposing ramparts of the Castelo São Jorge. The narrow streets and crowded buildings of the Alfama drew my eyes, along with the beauty of the seven hills. Street merchants plied their wares and gutter children enjoyed the sunshine on the shore. Lisbon was my city. Her music was in my heart. I had missed her.

As we neared the fleet I saw that it was attended by hundreds of small boats, provisioning and loading goods. The great não, *Our Lady of Angels*, stood out amongst them like an eagle amongst sparrows.

With a displacement of more than a thousand tons, she had been built of Indian teak in Baçaim, and had only recently arrived on her maiden voyage. Dom Sebastian had approved the plans himself. Her masts soared fifty varas high, with such a vast and complex array of rigging that the boat seemed more like a work of God than of man. Her hull supported three internal decks – the cable deck and two gun decks. Fore and aftercastles towered high above the waist, with lights winking from the galleries and gun ports. The beakhead carvings were of Roman warriors, dolphins and fearsome titans along with biblical scenes and images of angels. She carried a brace of small barca on davits, to be used as tenders and lifeboats.

At that moment, rowing towards that great ship with a coffin on board, my plan seemed ridiculous, particularly as the ferryman shipped his oars beside her and we looked up at a man-at-arms and a civilian in clerical garb standing at the top of the nets.

'Who are you and what are you doing?' the guard demanded.

'We are priests, accompanying an embalmed cadaver bound for Goa, by account of the family of Dom Barrate.'

'Nothing goes aboard without customs clearance.' The man-at-arms removed his helmet, cradling it in his arms as he spoke. With his free hand he pointed across to the shore. 'Take your burden for checking to the landing yonder, and return with it sealed and ticketed.'

'Thank you, kind sir. We will return directly.'

I gave the ferryman this new direction and he grunted at me. 'Ten centi extra for the diversion.'

'Fine, fine,' I said loudly. 'Dom Barrate will reimburse me.'

Still with a strong and steady stroke, the ferryman took us towards the shore to where a crowd of boats and clerics stood in disorganised bunches. Civilians in lines carried items to be sent on their personal account, most likely to brothers, fathers, and cousins far away in Goa, Tymor, or Larantuka.

We touched the jetty and the ferryman skipped over the gunnel in time to prevent a scratch on his vessel. He then produced a leather baffle that he wedged between hull and stone, then made us fast to a bollard.

I felt a shiver of fear as I saw that two gold-visored guarda-costras were supervising the customs officers as they went about their work. Whether because of our priestly garb or the obvious and sudden interest on the part of the crowd in our burden, a customs man moved across to appraise us.

'Who died, Priests, and why carry the body hither?'

I repeated my story about the Eastern merchant desiring his father's body.

He wrinkled his nose. 'Does it stink? Let's face it, a ship is a stench-filled place enough without carting bodies aboard.'

'Oh no sir. I assure you that this old man has been embalmed by experts, there is nothing to rot.'

'Do you have paperwork to prove your story?'

'Yes, of course.' I was prepared for this. The letter I produced had been wrinkled, folded and unfolded many times. It also carried a few artful water stains. 'This was sent to me via the captain of a Spanish caravel, then from Castile via personal courier.'

The customs officer turned to spit on the ground, near my sandalled feet. He read the document with a look of distaste on his face. The words were convincing, I had composed them carefully, gilding the lie with irrelevancies that soon bored the reader.

'Alright then,' he said, and it was only when my chest heaved that I realised I had been holding my breath.

'Thank you,' I said.

He narrowed his eyes suspiciously. 'We'd better have a look at him then.'

'Who?'

'The dead man, of course, Padre.'

My heart hammered against my ribs. 'But the lid is nailed down – he is ready for transport—'

But the official was already calling for one of the carpenters who had been busy hammering crates together, and one such man hurried across, gripping a hammer and pinch bar.

The word passed around the crowd of the coffin's opening and people craned their necks to watch as the carpenter stepped into the boat. I cursed the fixation that the living hold for the dead. Like our fascination with cliffs and high places – that we climb solely to stare at the drop – we love to see the beyond, to taste it from a safe distance.

The ferryman looked less than impressed at all this attention, scampering back to the stern, where he sat on the transom.

'Is this necessary?' I asked.

The customs man ignored me, but smiled wickedly as he moved closer to the boat, while the carpenter used his pinch bar to lever up the lid. He worked with care, with no splintering of the vulnerable pine.

Finally he lifted the lid aside, with a gasp from the crowd, but there was a layer of linen shroud yet. The customs officer stepped down into the boat itself, and used a small knife from his belt to cut the shroud aside. The wizened face of a very old man appeared. He had indeed been embalmed: his skin had that strange, dried out consistency. The job had been done well – I had selected him carefully from the monastery crypts for that reason, praying that God would forgive me disturbing an old monk's rest.

The crowd oohed and aahed at the sight, particularly as the customs man again used his knife to peel down the simple white robe that the corpse wore.

'Can we cease this maudlin act?' I snapped. 'I'm sure that Dom Barrete would be horrified at the treatment his father's body is receiving at your hands.'

I heard the jangle of metal as one of the guarda-costras elbowed his way through the crowd. 'Let the man do his job, priest. King Henrique has ordered that they be thorough in our duties.'

'Yes, yes, of course.' I said, yet I was berating myself as a fool. In my pride I had thought this a foolproof plan, but now I had half of Lisbon interested, including at least one member of Henrique's personal guard and a customs man with a knife. I could not have attracted more attention if I had shouted my intentions from the rooftops.

The customs officer exposed the hollow chest and belly of the cadaver, and pointed at the rent in his abdomen. 'Why has he been opened?'

'Ah,' I said, as calmly as possible. 'That's part of the embalming process. I thought you would have known that. We slice a corpse open.' I placed an undue emphasis on the word slice, in order to get their attention. 'We use our bare hands to bring out the intestines, kidney, liver. We pickle them in strong spirits as well as the interior of the body—'

The customs man wrinkled his nose, catching the lingering scent of those spirits, but also in distaste, for my graphic description of the process had turned many of the watchers away, depriving him of his audience.

He turned to the carpenter. 'Seal this thing up.' Then to me. 'Let's hope that this rich man's fancy of sending a corpse across the world does not become popular.'

The remainder of the audience tittered at the observation then wandered off. Five minutes later our burden was sealed, tied with an official ribbon and we had a certificate of carriage. Even so, it wasn't until the coffin had been carried up into the ship, and stowed down in the holds, where it would soon be jammed in by many tons of crates and casks, and we were on our way, that I believed that our plan would work.

DEZASSEIS

As the ferry boat again nudged land, but further down the river, I handed over the coins that I had promised, enough for the tireless oarsman to take the monks to the south bank. They would return to the monastery. Only the Prior's novice, Duarte, would wait with the horse and wagon for my own return later in the day.

Alighting from the boat, I adjusted my robes and climbed the steps towards the square. There I saw how the new ruler of Portugal had begun his reign of terror. On the stone pavement a row of gibbets had been erected. Two dozen dead men hung from ropes, while crows delved with bloodied beaks into their necks and faces. The courtyard, once so beloved of lovers and strollers, was peopled by a staring crowd, mesmerised by the bodies.

'Who are they?' I asked one man. 'They must be murderers and rapists, surely?'

He narrowed his eyes. 'No, Padre, these were intellectuals who printed a letter criticizing the new king.' After sharing this information with me he hurried away, looking over his shoulder as if someone might be watching.

Haunted by those drooping dead faces I walked on across the square and east into the Alfama. Streets that had once been vibrant and filled with laughter were hushed and frightened, and men of the guarda-costras loitered at all the main intersections. I pulled my hood closer around my face and persevered.

Turning into the Alley of the Cross, heart pounding, sweating with exertion despite the cool day, I feared the worst. My pace did not slacken as I tackled the last hill, and then at the orphanage itself I found the door locked.

Frei Aguiar answered my knock, smiling with pleasure at seeing me, clasping my arm. 'You are alive, thanks be to God.'

With the streets quiet and the populace ruled by fear, the orphanage larders were but lightly stocked. The portions of bread at the noon meal were small, and there was scarcely enough olive oil to flavour it.

'Times are hard,' Frei Aguiar explained, 'but we manage.'

'I'm sure you do, for you are a resourceful man. Please now, tell me. Did they come for her?'

The good man's face creased as if with the memory of a nightmare. 'A short time after your message reached us, a dozen men of the guarda-costras forced the door, as angry as any men I have ever seen, demanding that I give Aletia de Calvez into their care. I told them that she wasn't here, but they terrorised the children and searched every closet and under every bed. When they could not find her, they…' He lifted his sleeve to show a series of burns on his forearm, deep festering things that he had smeared with some kind of grease. 'They used a hot poker on my skin.' His chin lifted. 'I told them nothing.'

'I give thanks to God for the day I met you,' I said, 'you are my brother until death. So she is safe?'

'Just three days ago I had word that she is well. So far as I know that situation has not changed – you can be with her in an hour from here, and please, give her my best wishes for she is missed.'

My relief was stronger than wine, and I carefully noted the address he gave me. 'Now, to politics. What has happened since Henrique took the throne?'

'The whole country weeps. They know not where to turn. Since Dom Sebastian was lost—'

Now I took his arm and whispered. 'He is not dead, but wounded. In a year or two he will return with an army to restore his rightful throne.'

'Praise God. It is true?'

'Of course.'

'Oh, you have brought such joy today – your own survival, and that of the king.'

We clasped hands and I lowered my voice. 'Now, there is no time to waste. I have to go away again, and I must take Aletia with me. She is still in danger.'

'Of course, but please say farewell to her, from me. I miss her presence, so very much, and I will miss you too.'

The distance out to the fields and green hills of the Alcântara Valley was not so very far, yet I was delayed by the business of finding and engaging a cart and driver. It was mid-afternoon when I bade the driver wait, and walked ahead into the gardens, fields and trees of the smallholding where she had been billeted.

I was halfway across when I heard singing, and my spine tingled. Ahead, sitting on the clover and grass I saw her, fixing a flower in her hair, the sunshine so bright through the trees that it pained my eyes.

The song was a popular one at the time, with a melody that stuck in the mind like glue, hummed by everyone from boatmen to ladies. 'Sweet Maid of Nazaré.' It was the kind of song that appealed to all – one that sounded bawdy when sung by a sailor, hopeful by a lover, and despairing by a lonely traveller.

Even though by now I was close, she still had not seen me, and I was able to watch as, the flower now in place above her ear, she shook her head so that her hair shimmered in the sunlight. Finally I could bear the silence no longer.

'Aletia,' I called.

Despite my altered appearance, Aletia recognised me in an instant. Leaping to her feet, smiling even more widely than before, she cried, 'Padre! You are safe after that terrible battle.'

'Of course I am.'

At a distance of perhaps five paces she stopped what had begun as a headlong rush for me. There had never been physical closeness between us, and the gulf was too great to bridge now.

'Your hair is very short,' she said at last, as if to fill the moment.

'So it is. But we have very little time. You must come with me back into the city. Soon our ship will sail.'

'Our ship?'

'Yes. Plans have changed. I will accompany you on your journey.'

Aletia's voice became grave and joyful at the same time. 'That is good news. Very, very good news.'

After a visit to the farm cottage for Aletia's belongings, and to bestow my thanks on the family who had cared for her, we moved with haste back to Lisbon, both of us hooded lest we be recognised. Dusk was upon us as we hurried along the Rua da Assunção to the store where de Andrade the bookseller plied his wares. Once there, I pretended to browse while a customer haggled over an old edition of Procopius's Secret History.

The potential buyer maintained that the book had been affected by water, a charge that my fellow Sebastianist denied. De Andrade, however, caught my eye, and ended the business, giving the customer a better deal than he was entitled to. As soon as the buyer left I hurried to the counter.

'Frei Pereira,' de Andrade cried, wringing his hands. 'It is risky for you here. Why did you come?'

'I had no choice, believe me.'

'How goes Dom Sebastian's health?'

'Improving, slowly.'

'Now that you're here, I have news. Your Dominican colleague Frei de Sousa has asked that he might bring a fugitive from King Henrique aboard to travel in your company. A man in fear of his life.'

'What is his crime?' I asked.

'A heretic.'

I hesitated. My order held orthodox views, and many of my brethren supported the inquisitions both in my own country and Spain. Yet, an enemy of Henrique was already halfway to becoming my friend. 'What is this man's name?'

'Rui Chanoca. It is said that he fled Morocco before the battle, and Henrique is attempting to blame him for the disaster.'

My eyes widened, remembering how Rui had foretold Dom Sebastian's defeat, and his subsequent dismissal from Morocco. 'I know the man. Tell de Sousa that his refugee will be welcome among us. What of Henrique?'

'Rumours that Dom Sebastian is still alive have reached him, and from all reports, his rage is apoplectic. The guarda-costras are on the move – hundreds of them. I never dreamed that Henrique had so many. They are looking for you … and we both know what he really wants!'

'I know. I will be careful.'

'Please, do so.'

'Now, I too have a favour to ask.' With these words I brought Aletia forward, her eyes downcast with shyness yet also betraying a profound interest in these new things and people she was seeing. 'This is Aletia de Calvez, I have arranged for her to sail with the fleet as a crown orphan, yet she is also in danger from Henrique. Can you hide her and make sure she boards the ship in time?'

'Of course.'

'Please,' I cautioned him, 'look after her like you would your own daughter.'

'I will protect her with my life.'

I looked into his eyes, knowing that he would.

Kneeling in front of her, seeing crystal clear droplets nestled on the perfect skin of her cheeks, I wished I could dab them away. 'Please, do everything Senhor de Andrade tells you. I will see you again before you know it.'

After shaking my friend's hand I prepared to leave the shop. 'Keep out of sight,' he cautioned, 'Do not let yourself be seen.'

While I sat in the bows, deep in reflection, the ferryman stroked his oars through the smooth surface of the Tagus. The air was as still and waxy as candle smoke. Far ahead loomed the dark southern bank, and in my impatience the journey passed as slowly as a sleepless night.

Finally the opposite bank neared, with a lantern burning on the jetty. The riverbank was so silent that I heard the impatient stamp of a horse in the shadows.

Duarte was waiting on the jetty, with the Prior's horse in the traces, hobbled by the forelegs. As I stepped up to the bow he moved forward and extended a hand to help me out. I brushed him away.

'Leave me, boy. I'm not decrepit yet.' I was tired, and let my fatigue get the better of my natural courtesy. 'I'm sorry for my lack of manners, young Duarte,' I said. 'The day has been long and difficult.'

The youngster's smile lit his face. 'The moon is full, Padre, and the wind stirs not at all. Not even a grey cat rests easy on such a night.'

Having paid the ferryman, I moved to the cart, where I sat up next to Duarte. He urged the horse into motion without any perceptible instruction or movement, his hand never straying to the whip. Being a native of the Ribatejo, he was skilled in the handling of animals. Indeed, children of that district are born astride a horse, and can bunch and herd cattle before they learn to walk. With little fuss, we were thus on our way south on the Setúbal road.

Even on land the eerie atmosphere lingered. We entered the forest, where cork oak trees rose to the heavens, throwing shadows across the path. Noises, such as the moan of a barn owl, that might have been comforting, served to heighten my unease. A mist crept in from the river, and Duarte and I no longer spoke, concentrating instead on the journey.

The sound of hoofs came from behind soon after we left the village of Moita. Duarte and I exchanged glances, for this was a strange hour for any traveller to be on the road – most would be curled up at a convenient inn.

'Draw to one side and let them pass,' I advised. 'They must be either in unnatural haste or on official business.'

Duarte did as I advised, using his clicking tongue and light pressure on the reins to coax the horse off the path and onto the spongy grass of the verge. As he stopped we heard grinding teeth as the animal took the opportunity to feed.

The sound of hooves continued. I waited, holding my breath, for those unknown horsemen to pass us by. When this did not happen I looked back over the body of the cart. There, in the dim misty light I noted two armoured men. First one, then the other, spurred his horse forward, drawing broadswords as they rode.

'Go!' I shouted to Duarte. 'They mean to do us harm.'

Duarte is a bright young man, and both he and the Prior's horse, which also showed signs of intelligence, missed nothing from my tone. The beast went from feeding to a lightning bolt of energy in the time it takes to blink. I felt a sudden lurch, then a tearing acceleration as we jolted into flight. At that same moment one of the armed men came alongside, his weapon outstretched to slash at Duarte. Our sudden movement, however, caught the man off balance. He fell back, though I heard thudding hooves as both he and his companion spurred their mounts. Being lone men on horseback, though heavy with armour, I suspected that we would not shake them off with mere pace.

'Who are they?' Duarte turned to ask.

Leaning close to his ear I shouted, 'Only one breed of men wear helmets with golden visors. You have just met the guarda-costras.'

Duarte crossed himself. 'Thanks be to God, there are just two of them.'

'Foolish boy! Those two are more than a match for ten normal men. How do you think one old priest and a boy might fare against them?'

As soon as those words had left my lips another of the horsemen thundered up, this time on our left. The narrowness of the track saved us, for the low branches of the cork oak forest forced him to drop back. I risked a look behind.

'They will wait until the path widens,' I shouted into Duarte's ear.

'Have you a weapon?' he asked.

'Of course not, and even if I did I could never raise it against another man.'

Later, on the other side of the world, another man's heart blood splashed on my arms, I would remember those words. At that time, however, prayer was my weapon, my lips moving and the words emerging so fast they flowed into each other. Still we raced on, with the pursuing men holding back, waiting for a widening of the path so they could manoeuvre. From what I remembered of that road they would not have long to wait.

'Hold the reins for me, please Padre?' Duarte asked, and before I knew what was happening he placed the leather in my hands. The Prior's horse slowed, sensing that the boy was no longer in control.

'What are you doing?' I asked the novice.

Ignoring me, he attacked the wooden body of the old cart with his hands, levering up a single rotten plank before throwing it back towards the two horsemen riding close behind. The missile flew from his hands and struck the leading guarda-costras's mount hard on the forequarter. The animal stumbled and almost fell as Duarte cried out, taunting the men.

The next plank fell to one side, but the third struck one of the men low down in his body armour, landing with a strong metallic clunk. I noted that Duarte's target practice had opened a gap, and when the path did widen the two men took some seconds to catch us, one riding on each side, swerving to avoid the missiles that fell upon them.

My young friend's efforts soon denuded the old cart of moveable timber. Only the main planks remained. These oaken members were bolted into place.

I turned to look where we were going. The track ahead was filled with men and their mounts. One of them was Tonio, armed and warlike on a horse, returned from his excursion. Hoping to avoid a collision I pulled hard on the reins to the left. That brave horse did not hesitate, leaving the road and speeding off the track. Faced with a stand of trees and no way of stopping in time, the horse, with little direction from myself, aimed between two trunks.

There was room for the horse, but not the cart, I covered my head as it struck unyielding oak on each side, and splintered apart, throwing me up into the air like a boulder from a trebuchet.

Coming to my senses, I blinked with surprise. A bed of leaves pressed against my left cheek. The Prior leaned over me. I realised that I must have been knocked unconscious for a short time.

'What happened?' I asked.

'You drove off the road. You and Duarte were thrown from the cart.'

'The horse?'

'He is grazing nearby. No damage.'

'Duarte?'

'A cut on his hand. Grazed knees. Nothing a lad won't swiftly recover from.'

'The cart?'

'Wrecked.'

I sat up, and rubbed my neck. 'What of the guarda-costras?'

'As soon as they saw us they melted away. I had a feeling Henrique might have you followed, since Frei Sereno left the monastery with the results of his spying. I suspect that we have only met the advance party — there will be more to come.'

Back at the monastery we held a council of war, and sent a fast messenger back to Lisbon. Balthazar and his sailing boat — a manchua — a fast, single-masted pleasure boat common on the Tagus, were soon heading out through the river bar and around the coast to collect us. In just hours we would make our escape.

When I marched off to pack my things I found that the novice Duarte had been waiting for me. 'There is something I need to speak to you about,' he said.

I responded impatiently, anxious to finalise preparations for our departure that evening. 'Hurry then,' I barked, 'I am busy, and important things are happening.'

'I want to go with you on the India fleet,' he blurted.

'How do you know that I am going with the fleet?'

'I listened at the door when you spoke with the Prior. Please, Padre, I believe that God has ordained this course for me.' The hands that twined and intertwined with each other as he spoke were brown and strong.

'I doubt the Prior will be happy for you to sneak away when there is so much to be done here.'

'He will understand that this is God's will.'

'Do not presume, boy, to know our Lord's intentions. It is not often clear, even to your elders and betters.' Hurt filled his eyes, and I softened my voice. 'I will ask the Prior to release you. But please understand that this is his decision alone.' Duarte started to walk away from me. 'Where are you going?'

'To pray that the Prior will agree.'

'Have you thought this through? Your parents – your family? If you journey with us you may never see them again.'

'I know that, and it pains me. Yet I feel compelled.'

Often, in later years, I wished that I had made him stay. A life of tedium would have been far preferable to the fate that awaited him in the nether regions of this world.

DESOTO

On the last morning of the expedition, while sunset lent red fire to the stony hinterland, Francis stood at the bow of the *Josephine* and studied the deep-riven headlands, encircled beaches and patches of mangrove. He recalled the written account that Nicolá had shown him at the library in Lisbon – the story of the 'bedraggled' man – the eunuch – who had arrived in Timor, speaking of a 'valley rimmed with walls of stone.'

Was it somewhere nearby? Was the expensive, drawn-out but exciting nature of underwater archaeology leading him to ignore the possibility of stronger clues ashore?

Walking aft, he found Jeff with a mug of coffee and a plate of toast at the stern rail. 'What time do you want to get away?' he asked.

Jeff finished his mouthful. 'Mid morning if we can. You can sneak out for one last dive if you want to.'

'No. That's it for this trip,' Francis said. 'I think we've done everything we can and another hour won't make any difference.'

'It's a shame we can't try to bring at least some of the frame up – maybe the sternpost?'

'The Museum would hang me out to dry if I did. I'd say that they or UWA will have a team up here next dry season to do just that.'

'Alright then, we'll start packing up when everyone's awake.' Some of the younger members of the team were notorious for staying in bed as long as possible.

Francis felt unusually keen to get back to Darwin – just to have a cup of tea with Camille, and sit in his office and think. 'I'll start organising the gear in the RHIB.'

'Sure, let me know when you're ready and we'll lift her up.'

And while Francis packed regulators and masks into tubs, Lauren came across to join him, yet she was unusually silent, and a little absent-minded in the packing. Clumsy, even.

'Is something on your mind?' he asked.

It was a strange place to talk, kneeling on a boat deck pitching with the sea. Lauren did not look at him, 'I might be out of whatever comes next,' she said. 'I applied for a job as a junior lecturer in Maritime Archaeology at James Cook University in Townsville. An email came through late yesterday – I'm on the short list and they're interviewing next week – though that's not yet common knowledge.'

Francis wasn't sure how he felt. 'Congratulations. Is it what you want?'

'I've given you a lot of time,' she said. 'Some of it paid, some not, and I kind of felt that we were building towards something.'

He sensed the double meaning behind those words.

'It hasn't really happened,' she went on. 'And I need to think about myself.'

'I hope you put me down as a referee?'

'Of course I did.'

'I'll miss you,' he said, 'and one day, when the site truly opens up – when they find the main wreck, I hope you'll come back and be part of it.'

'I hope so too,' she said, and there was a tear in her eye that flowed to her cheek and remained there until she wiped it away.

Back in Darwin Francis found comfort in the accoutrements of home, especially Camille's gentle friendship, the rituals of life and church and the solace of his books. He read again some of the works of Australia's greatest wreck-diver, Hugh Edwards, and his stories of two Dutch wrecks in particular, the Batavia with its infamous mutiny that involved both massacres and pitched battles, and the Zuytdorp of 1712, where the survivors lived ashore for weeks, leaving cliff-ledges near Kalbarri, Western Australia, scattered with glass and pottery fragments, clay pipes and belt buckles.

Had something similar occurred with the *Nossa Senhora do Anjos*, if that was indeed the ship they were dealing with? It was possible, and the thought of some on-land survey work appealed after years of focussing on the sea.

More towed-array surveys of the coast looking for a mother ship were inevitable, whether undertaken by Francis or one of the museums, but the prospect of years spent doing so, along with the onset of the wet season likely to come before any such survey could be launched, made this option fade as the next course-of-action.

Francis began to plan a survey of likely shore-based locations in the area: beaches, cliffs and the hinterland. All were part of the Balanggara Indigenous Protected Area and he had to apply for permission to enter through the Kimberley Land Council in Broome. This process took several days, and involved a number of emails.

The search for any land-based reminders of long-ago visitors would be exacting, slow work, and might extend into the heat of the build-up season. It was too much for one person, but when Lauren came around to inform him that she had been offered and accepted the Townsville job, he found himself wondering who he might take with him. Nick, Marinda and the rest of the usual volunteers would soon be back into university life.

'I wish you could come with me,' he told Camille.

It was a joke, but of course she took the invitation seriously, shaking her head. 'I have to go to work,' she said. The facility where she spent her days had a way of making her feel valued, even indispensable. 'How would I go to work if I was out in that wild country with you?'

Francis took the sword hilt out of its safe deposit box and studied it again, feeling the excitement, re-reading the script. Finally he sent Nicolá Massane a report on the disappointments of the last expedition out to the wreck site by email.

> Based partly on your story of the 'valley rimmed with walls of stone', I have a theory, two really. One is that at least some survivors of any wreck might have reached shore and left signs of their presence. The second is that local Indigenous people may be the best source of information on such an incursion. Shipwrecked groups have, in other places in this country been remembered both linguistically (ie by their language infiltrating local dialects), culturally, and in oral histories.

> I am planning to head back out to the
> field in the next little while, for a peri-
> od of some six weeks, to follow up on
> these theories.

Less than an hour after pressing send on the email, his phone pinged. It was Nicolá.

> I am available for five weeks from the
> end of August if you would consider
> me. Nxx

He replied with:

> Welcome news, perfect timing. Con-
> sider yourself considered.

> Thank you. When do you want to leave
> and what should I bring? Nxx

Camille, who had been quietly pleased at her brother's disentanglement from Lauren, was on guard as soon as he told her. 'You hardly know this person. Do you really want to spend more than one month in the bush with her?'

'She's nice,' Francis said, 'very natural. You'll really like her. Mum would have liked her too.'

Camille said nothing, just clamped her lips together and folded her arms.

DESANOVE

When I raised the matter of Duarte, the Prior agreed readily. 'Duarte is a restless and somewhat mischievous boy. He may be better suited to your journey than a life of peace here in the monastery.' The big Franciscan who had become more than a friend clasped my shoulder. 'Take him with my blessing.'

Back in my cell I arranged the personal possessions I was packing for the journey, and looked up to see Duarte at the door, excitement writ large on his face.

'Did you ask him?'

'Yes. You are fortunate, the Prior is more than willing to let you go. Now hurry and get ready.'

'I am ready now, Padre.' He gestured to the bundle tied up in rags that he carried, making me wonder what treasures he might feel compelled to take with him.

'Good, make yourself useful, and help me with my things.'

Thus burdened, we left the cell, and continued along the passageway. Before we emerged, however, I chanced to look ahead, and at that moment had an uninterrupted view outside, past the monastery itself and to the Setúbal road.

A group of horsemen neared the brush gate – nine in total, all big men on proportionate mounts. I did not need to see the weapons at their sides to identify them as warlike. It's strange how those who set forth to do God's work do so at the pace of an ass, or ageing palfrey, while those with violence and death in their hearts are borne by the best and fastest animals available.

The riders proceeded through the opening and into the monastery itself. I moved back into the darkness of the passage, only my eyes still staring outside as a small group of monks met the newcomers in the courtyard and two of the men dismounted. Both carried helmets with golden visors and I felt fear in my heart.

'Come with me,' I hissed at Duarte.

'Who are they?'

'The same kind of men as we met on the road. If you have been listening at the Prior's keyhole then you know that Dom Sebastian is in danger.'

'Yes, Padre.'

'Then stop asking questions.'

Together we ran back down that stone passage, passing by the cell I had occupied for several nights. Burdened as we were, our progress was slow. At any moment I expected armed men behind us.

Reaching the turn, I hurried to where Dom Sebastian still lay. Tonio looked up from his chair as we entered.

'They are here,' I said. 'Are you ready?'

Tonio scowled back at me darkly. 'Of course, but why did you not tell me of your plans to take the True King to the East?'

'Because you were not here, but out indulging your inability to keep still. Now hurry!'

In order to transport Dom Sebastian, the monastery carpenter had created a litter both light and strong, using green willow. This contrivance lay on the stone floor, ready for use. Brother Martinho arrived at the door with two monks, both strong men, with earnest but frightened faces. Under my watchful eye, they lifted Dom Sebastian onto the prepared litter. The wounded man uttered a mournful groan and I suffered an empathetic sharp pain in my chest.

The sounds of activity increased from outside. 'Hurry,' the Prior hissed, 'they are searching the balneary.' The monks lifted the litter easily, for Dom Sebastian was now a lightweight compared to his former self.

As we hurried down the corridor and to the back entrance we almost made the mistake of blundering out where three armed men loitered. Exit was now impossible at both ends, and I worried that our journey might end there, at the point of a sword.

Duarte touched my sleeve. 'I know a way out, where they will not see us.'

The Prior turned on him. 'Do not tell lies. There is no other way.'

'Yes, there is, sometimes at night when I cannot sleep I use it to get out and roam the hillside above the ocean.'

'You leave your cell at night, boy?'

'Sometimes, yes.'

'Your disobedience—'

'Stop,' I hissed, 'this is not the time. Duarte, if you know another way, kindly take us there, and hurry.'

Retreating down the corridor, accompanied by mutterings from the Prior about lies and wilful behaviour, we climbed the stone steps to the upper level. There we proceeded along a row of cells and on into the Prior's office.

'You dared enter this room while I slept?' the Prior demanded, somewhat loudly. Duarte, to his credit, ignored him and led the way inside.

'Close the door,' I told the still-affronted Prior, apparently more concerned with the breach of discipline than our dire predicament.

The room was equipped with a shuttered window, looming over the brush fence that surrounded the monastery. Within reach were the branches of a mature yew tree, each as thick as a man's waist, alive with green leaves in their full summer glory. This was the most sacred of trees, revered by man from the time of the ancient Druids, and in spite of the circumstances I admired the majesty of the massive trunk.

'We cannot climb down this tree, boy,' I said. 'Not with a sick man.'

'It's the only way.'

I looked at Dom Sebastian in his litter, and realised that however impossible the downward climb might be, it was indeed the only way. From behind us armour rattled as men hurried along the stone corridors. No time remained for thought or discussion.

'Go,' I whispered to Duarte, 'lead the way, and hurry.' Then to the monks. 'Tie Dom Sebastian down with your sashes.'

As soon as my new novice had leaned through the window and taken a grip on the nearest branch, I followed him through, smarting at the unaccustomed strain on my legs, arms and body. I made the mistake of looking down, swooning to see the earth far below. Only Tonio, just above me, settled my nerves.

'Easy Padre, hold on, and you will not fall,' he said.

Mailed fists pounded on the door, and a gruff voice commanded us to open it. Fear twined around my bowels like serpents, even as the monks emerged, manhandling the litter between them. All my senses concentrated on the difficult task of descending the tree, yet I saw the two monks close the window's wooden shutters behind them. The sound of muffled voices came immediately thereafter. I moved out of the way to help the litter past, while it heeled to a terrible angle. I was sure that Dom Sebastian must fall. I scarcely breathed until my feet touched the moist, leafy earth beneath that tree, the skin between my thighs burning – rubbed raw from scraping along the bark.

Together, we were about to make off when the shutter far above reopened with a squeal of hinges, and voices grew louder. We stood motionless, not moving a muscle, hoping that the foliage would blanket us from view.

The shutter closed again. I thanked God and turned to the others. 'Now quickly, let us get away from here.'

Gorse and heather grew in clumps and thickets sufficient to keep us hidden. The two monks, young and accustomed to heavy work managed the litter without fatigue, but my possessions were a burden to me. Sweat dripped down my body in hot sheets, and my tongue felt like a strip of dry leather.

As we entered a patch of more substantial vegetation I bade Duarte climb a tree and study the monastery for signs of pursuit. When he returned to the ground the boy did not speak, but his eyes were wide and fearful.

'What did you see?' I pressed him, 'what is it?'

Moments passed before I could coax a word from his lips.

'I saw the Prior,' he choked out, 'in the cloister—' He paused, 'I watched a swordsman ... cut off his head at the shoulders. Oh dearest God, Padre, they picked it up by the hair and held it aloft.'

As we hurried away towards the waiting boat, I felt the cold spectre of guilt settle on my shoulders.

Through the night I sat on deck and listened to wind in the rigging, staring at the stars in their heavens. I was upset about the Prior, and I prayed for his soul, but still it felt good to be amongst friends, with Dom Sebastian resting in the snug cabin. The voyage around Cabo Espichel and north to the Costa da Caparica was of no great duration and time passed quickly.

The manchua belonged to my Sebastianist friend Balthazar de Barbuda, who had benefited during Dom Sebastian's reign, amassing a fortune through the export of olive oil and importation of English textiles. The boat was fifteen varas long, with the exotic lines of a Moorish zabra. The prow had been carved and painted into the likeness of a soaring Angel of Heaven. Balthazar did not hurry his crew. Their quiet competence soothed my nerves.

When we crossed the Tagus River bar I stood in the bows, feeling our motion change from a steady glide across the swells to a sudden thump, thump, then slide as the boat took a wave. Occasionally the hull broached, and I held tight to the ornate rail.

To windward lay the heads, and the water was disturbed and racing. Still, that spirited vessel revelled in the conditions, sometimes dipping her nose into a wave, at which time cold spray would drift across the deck until I tasted salt on my lips.

Balthazar held the tiller, with his son close by. His shouted orders kept the crew busy with the rigging, climbing like spiders up the shrouds or along yards, making every breath of wind count. Soon enough, the hull skimmed across the flat water of the estuary. Far ahead, the Tower of Belém rose from the north bank.

A number of ships lay at anchor on the Tagus, thick anchor

hawsers limp in the still conditions. The largest was the *Nossa Senhora dos Anjos – Our Lady of Angels.*

Duarte stared, eyes wide. 'That must be the biggest ship in the world. Surely men could not build a vessel larger.'

'Who knows?' I answered, but she was certainly a sight to behold.

As we came alongside, Balthazar shouted his orders, dropping the foresail and mainsail in turn. The manchua came to rest with her stern sheets level to the cargo net. I admired the skill with which it had been done.

All cargo having been loaded, the customs officers were gone, yet a sentry shouted down a challenge. Balthazar must have answered correctly for two seamen clambered down to assist. Other boats lay alongside – open lighters, decks laden with the last-minute cargo of live animals. Men clambered up and down the net. Cages of shrieking pigs and fowls inched up on ropes.

I shook Balthazar's hand. 'I cannot thank you enough, for what you have done.'

'I need no thanks, but please, bring Dom Sebastian back. Let him return and lead us – deliver our land from tyranny.' He clasped Tonio on the shoulder also, for they were like-minded men.

'We will return,' I said, 'look for your rightful king when the morning fog is on the Tagus. One day you will see him sail in at the head of three score ships and ten thousand men.' I bent until my eyes were level with Balthazar's son. 'Be proud of your father, and grow up to be a man like him. You could do no better.'

The wrapped form of Dom Sebastian inched to the deck by way of a rope sling. I waited at the rail, while all around me men readied the ship for departure. I locked eyes with the Captain, Dom de Oliveira, who Dom Sebastian, when still king, had chosen to command this ship. De Oliveira was tall, with a full moustache and goatee. He carried with him an air of competence.

I bowed, 'Good morning, my name is Frei Pereira. This is my novice, Duarte.'

'You, your novice, and your injured friend are expected. I will escort you to your quarters myself, come this way.' With these words de Oliveira led us to a ladder and through the steerage room into a dark corridor, the smell of new timber and pitch strong in my nostrils. Behind us, Tonio and a burly marine carried Dom Sebastian on his stretcher, face well hooded from curious eyes.

The captain turned to speak. 'We have made available a large cabin. I trust that is acceptable?'

'Entirely suitable. Is the orphan Aletia de Calvez here?'

'Senhora de Calvez boarded this morning. Her cabin is down the corridor from yours.'

Now I allowed myself to hope, almost sighing aloud. 'I am pleased.'

Without warning, the Captain stopped, and leaned towards me. 'Padre, I must tell you that I know everything – I am for Dom Sebastian, as are all my officers. We sailed from India still believing that he was king, and wept to find Henrique on the throne. You can trust us.'

Our hands gripped in the darkness. My heart boiled over. 'Your words are more welcome than I can say.'

At dawn the next day the northeast wind rose, just a zephyr at first, then a steady breeze that was both welcome and auspicious. Passengers crowded the decks, while Lisbon's population filled the riverbank from the Palace Square to the Tower of Belém, turning out in their thousands to farewell the fleet, just as they had for a century. Pennants waved and ranks of soldiers wheeled to the orders of their officers.

Our ship carried somewhere between six and seven hundred officers, seamen, soldiers, slaves and priests. Nobody, not even the captain himself, knew for sure how many, for at least fifty stowaways, mostly boys down to the age of seven, had already been removed, though many more would remain on board.

The ship looked impressive that day – her teak decks scrubbed with holystones, three masts reaching skyward, thicker at the base than the width of a man's outstretched arms. The rigging was a maze – shrouds like giant spider's webs and halyards dropping down from the yards. The deck was so long that a loud shout would scarce be heard from quarterdeck to prow.

Riding close by, also underway, were the other ships of the fleet – the *São Pedro*, *São Jorge* and some smaller carracks. Smallest of all was the delightful caravel *Barbosa*, with her pleasing lines and raked masts.

Duarte stood beside me, cheeks flushed and lips parted in excitement. 'Look well on your homeland,' I said. 'Years will pass before you see it again.'

'Oh yes, Padre,' he said. 'Yet what wonders we will see in the meantime!'

'Wonders are all very well, provided we survive them.' I kept my mouth grim and voice level, yet even so, I could not deny the excitement that filled my heart at the prospect of the voyage.

The battalion of guards, dressed in ceremonial uniform, presented arms and stood at attention. Carried on a litter, a figure emerged from the Palace doors. I recognised Henrique the Chaste, the new King of Portugal and all her dominions.

Henrique climbed down from his litter and addressed the crowd. The breeze tore away most of the words, but we sensed the thrust of the speech – glory and riches – furthering the greatness of Portugal.

I remembered how Dom Sebastian had farewelled the fleets – from the age of three – the boy-king walking hand in hand with Catarina – the shower of petals and the roar of the crowd. Now, with Henrique on the throne the crowd stood dumb, unmoved, for they did not love him, nor Martin da Câmara who stood at his side. In fact if anything emanated from the people of Lisbon that day it was fear and hatred.

I was thus distracted as a barca full of late arrivals came alongside. A young man who worked for de Andrade the bookseller hurried up the nets and walked purposefully along the deck. His eyes widened as he recognised me. I clasped his arm.

'Estevão, I did not know you were with us on the voyage.'

He lowered his voice. 'I am not. A boat waits for me below. I came to tell you that Henrique is certain now that Dom Sebastian is alive. A monk of the Arrábida Monastery admitted it under torture. You must get under way before Henrique learns that the true king is aboard, as he surely will. Tell the Capitão.' He paused, 'And tell Dom Sebastian that we anticipate his return. All Portugal is waiting, with love in their hearts.'

I wanted to press him further, but he had already hurried away, down the nets to a waiting boat.

Clouds of black smoke billowed from the gundecks of all four ships, and the hull shuddered beneath my feet. The detonations were thunderous, bringing applause from the watching crowds.

Elfo, the ship's master of seamanship, a wizened little man with sharp, protruding ears, blew his orders with nuanced blasts on his whistle. Men appeared in the rigging, and sails dropped in rehearsed sequence – topgallants, topsails, the big mainsails and finally the spritsails. The river was thick with traffic, mostly waterborne spectators. The Carreira da India had made our country great, and commoners and nobles alike loved to see the ships sail.

Our Lady of Angels inched past the royal palace towards the Tower of Belém, passing the massive but not yet finished Jerónimos Monastery at Belém. The bells of the Church of The Wounds of Christ, patron of pilots and mariners, tolled for the fleet, and the soldiers, sailors and passengers who would never return.

> *Tlão ... Tlão ...*
> *Tlão ... Tlão ...*
> *Pelos que vão,*
> *Tlão ... Tlão ...*
> *Tlão ... Tlão ...*
> *E não voltarão.*
> *Tlão ... Tlão ...*

And the voyage was begun.

VINCE

Francis and Nicolá flew out on a Cessna 208 Caravan seaplane. Normally, a fourteen-seater, decked out for taking groups of tourists out over Darwin Harbour, Dundee Beach or the Coburg Peninsula, it was now packed full of camping equipment, four weeks' worth of stores, solar panels and a 4.28 metre Australian-made Porta-bote. A 20hp Honda outboard and cans of fuel had caused the plane to list a little after take-off, and Francis had to move them towards the centreline to even out the load.

Nicolá, never having been to Australia, let alone to the wild Top End, was as excited as any undergraduate volunteer on her first excursion. The panorama of remote coasts, islands and river mouths as they flew on past the Perron Islands to the Fitzmaurice and Victoria River estuaries, kept her face glued to the window.

After the third hour Francis tapped her shoulder. 'We've just crossed the Western Australian border, and that's the Ord River down there to the south,' he said. 'Not far to go.' A few minutes later they began a stabilized descent. The tilt of the craft enhanced the view over the blue sea, and the pilot executed a near-perfect landing, with the nose-up and the floats touching aft first in copybook fashion.

At taxiing speed the pilot carried them close to the nearest of several islands. This one had a welcoming beach of sand. 'Half your luck,' he said to Francis, with a private wink which was ignored.

It was necessary to assemble and launch the boat to carry their equipment ashore, and an hour passed before the pilot was ready to leave.

'October the second,' he said. 'I'll come for you then.'

'Great. If it's any earlier we'll call you on the sat phone.'

The engine started, and the plane moved to take off speed, swiftly leaving the water, then, receding over the ridges and away, echoes dragging behind, clattering off water, stone and sand.

'What an incredible camp site,' Nicolá said, standing with her hands on her hips and looking around the beach.

'Just for one night. Tomorrow we'll select a good spot on the coast. We can risk a quick swim here, too, if you like.'

Then, with the Porta-bote dragged up and tethered above the high-water mark, and a pair of tents standing tautly up on the sand, they dressed in swimming costumes and headed for the water. The sand was coarse but white, though dark multicoloured cliffs rose at the back of the beach to a sheer height of six or seven metres. Nicolá wore a lime-green bikini that showed deep cleavage and a smooth abdomen. The light breeze raised a rash of goose flesh across her upper arms, chest and body, enhancing the perfection of her skin.

Disappointed when the water swallowed her up, Francis followed her in, swimming on into the depths, pausing to tread water. 'Come out further,' he called.

Nicolá stood with her arms folded across her chest. 'Aren't there crocodiles here?'

'Some, and the odd shark, but you'd have to be unlucky.'

'I might be unlucky.'

'You've done a lot of diving, sharks come with the territory.'

'I don't mind when I can see under the water. I can't do that when I'm swimming.'

Despite further attempts by Francis to entice her into deeper water, Nicolá stayed resolutely in the shallows, and after stroking around for a while, he went in closer and joined her.

It seemed to be the most natural thing in the world when he took her hand and squeezed it. She did not refuse the grasp, but instead turned and looked at him seriously. 'Do you mind if we set some ground rules?' she asked. 'After all, we're going to be here alone for many weeks.'

Francis shook his head, releasing her hand and backing away a little. He realised that her use of the word 'we' in setting the ground rules was not strictly accurate. It was she who was in control.

'Please don't try anything, Francisco, even though I know we had a little goodbye kiss or two in Lisbon. Of course it's a romantic setting – here on a secluded beach, but we are working together, we have a wonderful and exciting mystery to follow, and any intimacy might ruin everything.'

The water felt suddenly cool, and Francis stared across at her, ashamed of himself. 'I'm sorry. I do like you, that's all.'

'I like you too, but I feel that we should leave things there until after the field trip. If we still have feelings then perhaps we could discuss it again.'

Francis smiled to himself. She appeared to be proposing some kind of formal meeting to decide if they might take things further. 'I agree,' he said. 'I won't try anything until after the field trip.'

'No,' she said. 'Until after the field trip *and* a discussion on the advisability of a deeper relationship.'

'I agree,' said Francis.

'Good, I'm glad.'

A little self-conscious now, Francis was the first to leave the water.

Later, Francis set up the satellite telephone to deliver a burst of internet data. Charged by the megabyte, this was expensive and used strictly for the despatch and receipt of communications. He checked and sent emails, along with a text message to Camille assuring her that he had arrived safe and well.

Nicolá went through her inbox, emitting a small groan of disappointment.

'What's wrong?' he asked.

'I was hoping for some information. 'Have you ever heard of something called the *Parcela de Lusitania*?'

Francis shook his head. 'No. What is it?'

'I don't know yet – it cropped up in my researches about Dom Sebastian a week or two ago. It's probably just a story, still, it's interesting. One of my colleagues has promised to follow it up for me and send me any information he comes across.'

'Interesting,' said Francis. 'I'll do another burst in a few days, hopefully he'll have sent you something by then.'

Nicolá closed the laptop with an audible snap. 'It may be nothing at all, and of course I'm more interested in what we'll be doing here. What's the first step?'

'As I suggested before, we take the anthropological approach. We ask the people whose ancestors have been here for fifty thousand years.'

'That sounds like a good plan.'

'Would you like a glass of wine?'

Nicolá smiled. 'You brought wine? You really are a clever man.'

The only real settlement in the area was a small Indigenous outstation located along the coast to the east, populated with Traditional Owners of the Yeidji people. Francis welcomed the opportunity to disclose he and Nicolá's presence, as well as to follow up his hunch that the original inhabitants of the country may have clues to past incursions by European seafarers.

As they neared the area, with the Honda outboard pushing the Porta-bote along on the plane, Francis pointed out a collection of corrugated iron buildings on the shore ahead, where smoke rose lazily past palm trees and a distant red ridge. The tide was high, making it possible for them to motor right up to the beach in the shallow-drafted vessel.

'There it is,' Francis said to Nicolá. 'Get ready for a big reception.'

Dark, smiling children splashed into the water to meet them – two dozen of them laughing, shouting and squealing – a welcome and a summons to members of the group not privy to the sight. Some of the older and braver children trod water in the depths beyond the beach, heedless of sharks.

The dongas were built from an assortment of corrugated iron, timber and hessian. Hearth fires burned, men and women at rest beside them. As the boat neared, however, they moved towards the beach area, watching and talking with an animation audible from the boat.

Cutting the engine in the shallows, the small boat wallowed in the wind chop while Francis grasped the painter in one hand. The muscles of his shoulder bunched as he beached the vessel. Children gathered, bursting with infectious laughter. This melee continued until a strong looking woman in her sixties walked down onto the beach. 'Hey, you mob. Leave 'em alone. Go swim and leave 'em alone.' The children backed off, staring now, chattering amongst themselves, dark bodies streaked with water droplets from the sea.

Francis took a firm hand in his own. The woman returned his grip, looking into his eyes. 'Welcome,' she said finally. She smelled of woodsmoke and earth.

'It's a privilege to be here,' he said.

She did not disagree with that observation. 'My people have lived here since time began.' She talked in rapid fire, and only Francis's talent for languages and nuances of dialect allowed him to follow.

Young men in jeans and Wild West shirts watched from a distance. A trio of teenage girls, giggling and beautiful, came shyly from behind trees.

'Come with me,' the older woman ordered. 'Have a cuppa.'

Francis smiled, liking her scarred dark skin and wise eyes. 'That would be nice, thank you.'

'Nancy's my whitefella name,' she explained. 'You can call me that if you like.'

'Of course, thank you. I'm Francis and this is Nicolá.'

'The Land Council called up,' said Nancy. 'They asked if anyone would mind if you people came and did some looking around on Country here so I was thinkin' you might drop in for a cuppa. I guess you were the same ones looking for wrecks off-shore not long ago?'

'Yes that was us.'

They sat on an eclectic range of chairs, talking about the finding of the barca while Nancy picked the billy off the fire with a short length of fencing wire shaped into a hook. Tendons tightened across the juncture of forearm and elbow as she sprinkled tea from a cardboard packet. She poured three enamel mugs full and topped her own with sugar from a jar and cold fresh water from a plastic cube to settle the leaves. Milk was powdered, from a tin.

'We don't see too many whitefellas here.' Nancy said. 'Sometimes big tourist boats, and now and then yachts go past. Not many stop by unless they want fresh water or to gawk and take photos.'

'We're looking for information about an old shipwreck,' Francis explained. 'It happened a long time ago. You might be able to help us, perhaps your people have found something on the beach, or maybe there are stories—'

'Old whaling boats?' Nancy asked.

Francis shook his head. Whalers had plied Kimberley waters for a hundred years or more up until the nineteen sixties. 'No. Long before that. Hundreds of years ago.'

'Not that I know of. Most of the songs are about us. The land, the animals. But you'd better ask old Henry. A doctor who came here from the city tried to work out how old he is. Henry can remember the old days, when the cattle first arrived. Now come on and meet him. He talks only Kriol and Gwini, but you'll work it out.'

The old man, Henry, bearded and clothed in jeans and a flannel shirt, was sitting in the shade, almost immobile. His feet were bare and dusty, and he held the stub of a roll-your-own cigarette between the thumb and forefinger of his right hand.

One of several tick-infested dogs had wriggled up beside him – a brindled, ugly brute, one eye clouded and blind, a tooth caught on his lip, making him look savage.

Francis squatted on the sand, with Nicolá standing behind him. 'My name is Francis da Costa. I'm interested in people who came here on a sailing ship a long time ago. I wonder if you might know anything about that.'

'Oldwan bot?' the old man asked.

'Yes, a boat. Long time ago. Do you know anything that might help us?'

Henry sucked in his lower lip reflectively, then kneeled on the sand, clearing a space with his forearm, like a teacher cleaning a blackboard. He picked up a casuarina twig, stripped away the needles, then passed it to Francis and looked at him expectantly. 'Oldwan bot?'

'You want me to draw what the boat looked like?' Francis added.

Henry inclined his head sharply once, lips set in a pugnacious line. Francis used the stick to draw the outline in the sand – towering castles fore and aft, the three masts and bowsprit. He took his time, adding detail. There was something about the importance of this discussion that warned him not to skimp on details.

Henry stared at the diagram for a long time, placing a broad hand either side and holding his face low over the sketch-in-the-sand as if taking a drink from the surface of a pool. Then he showed a mouthful of gums and stood up, walking resolutely towards the boat Francis and Nicolá had arrived in, now drawn up on the beach.

The tide had dropped since their arrival, and some of the youths came down to help them shove the boat down into the water, feet braced in half-mud, half sand, straining until the hull floated free and the prop had enough depth to spin freely. Francis took the tiller and started the engine.

One of the young men gestured at the space next to Henry at the bow and Francis gave him the thumbs-up, waiting until he had settled himself on board before motoring off under Henry's direction.

At top speed the four of them flew along the coast, the old man pointing the way through channels guarded by fangs of coral and sea-savaged rock, while Nicolá sat in the middle thwart seat, smiling back at Francis at the strangeness of the journey.

That hour with the Community had energised Francis. Filled him with hope. Maybe there was a chance, and in the meantime there was the spray and the sounds of seabirds and his love for the ramparts of stone that fortified this part of the coast. Those things were enough, right now, with Henry in the bows extending a long forefinger to thread them through the reefs, sometimes conferring with the youth beside him.

Henry didn't stop them there, but directed them through a series of shoals and bommies before pointing in at a beach between two high bluffs. It was mid-afternoon by then and the light was burning gold. Iron-rich stones surrounded the beach like clotted blood.

Francis was out first, grasping the handle at the bow while he waited for the others to swing their legs over the gunnel onto the sand. This done, he heaved it up onto the beach, the hull scraping softly on the substrate.

The beach between the bluffs was some three hundred metres long, rocky in places but grading at the northern end to a series of dunes, some ten or more metres high. At the opposite end a small creek emptied out in a shallow channel across the beach sand, staining the sea dark tannin shades where the waters met.

Henry led them towards the dunes, finally stopping at one of several outcrops of stone on the beach. He sat down. Francis and Nicolá did the same. The old man smiled broadly, half closing his eyes, looking up at the beach to the line of white and orange dunes. They were typical in shape, wider on the windward face, sculpted into rounded peaks by the weather.

Francis turned to Henry. 'What are you trying to show us?'

The old man waved an arm at the sand and sea. 'Oldwan bot. Speshalwan. Kaman salwada.' He followed up the Kriol with a stream of his own language.

The youth, standing barefoot on the sand with a smile on his face translated. 'Grandfather says that this is the place. A long time ago – before even his father was born – white people came here from the sea. He says that he saw parts of the ship here when he was a boy, but he can't see it now.'

Henry pointed down at the sand and nodded grimly. 'Yah. Here, this place.' He patted his pockets for a tobacco pouch, rolled a cigarette and installed it between his lips, then said nothing more.

They motored back to the community. It was slack water by then, and they were forced to drop the old man and his descendant fifty metres seaward of their previous approach. With a weather-eye out for crocs, Francis watched Henry's dark, tall form pick through the sandflats to the beach, assisted by the younger man, before they pushed off into the darkening sea.

Back at the island, after a cool run through the gathering dusk, they sat in silence around the fire.

'What do you think he was trying to show us?' Nicolá asked.

'I don't know, but I think we need to check the area out thoroughly. It's a good starting place, at any rate, and Henry knew exactly what he was showing us, even though it's not obvious.'

VINTE E UM

Six days out from Lisbon, the islands of Deserta and Madeira passed to windward. We had reason to believe that God would continue to guide and help us, even as the faster ships of the fleet disappeared over the horizon in a headlong rush by each captain to reach the Indies before disease felled too many of his crew. Others lagged behind and were likewise lost to view.

In the dark hours before dawn I bade Duarte hold his candle for me while I tended to Dom Sebastian. His forehead burned like a furnace. The smell of rotting flesh overpowered me. The cabin was dark but for that bare flame, and the deck tilted with the movement of the ship.

'I will bleed him again. There is nothing else left to try,' I said. As I readied myself I found the astrologer Rui Chanoca at my side, watching in that silent, quizzical manner of his. I was in no mood for his philosophising. 'Since you are awake you may as well help,' I said.

'Certainly, yet I cannot see the point of letting more blood.'

'Oh, and of course you are a physician of some note.'

'No, I am not, yet I have been in many prisons. I know the smell of a dying man.'

My hands stopped their work, and I turned to face him. 'You think Dom Sebastian will die?'

'I know he will, unless you do what needs to be done.'

His words sent a shiver of fear through my body. Amputation was a terrible business. I knew, for I had assisted in the removal of an arm once before. Even so, Rui's words worked powerfully on me, and I knew the truth behind them. I closed my eyes for a moment. The ship carried a physician of sorts – a médico, schooled in basic surgery – competent at leechcraft, yet still I would not entrust him with such an important operation as this. The amputation was my responsibility. Girding myself, I said, 'You are right. I will do it tomorrow.'

Rui's eyebrows rose. 'If you do not amputate, Dom Sebastian might be dead tomorrow.'

'Then I will do it now,' I snapped. 'Are you satisfied?'

Many of the priests were by now waking for Lauds, and I called for Duarte. He came quickly, rubbing sleep from his eyes and yawning.

'Yes Padre?'

'There is no longer any choice. I must take Dom Sebastian's leg. Bring candles, then fill a bucket with water. I need a knife and one of Leonel do Amoral's sharpest saws.'

When my novice had hurried away to find the ship's carpenter I kneeled at Dom Sebastian's side and gazed into his eyes. Already they had the glassy sheen of a man disembarking from the journey of life.

First I folded a cloth and laid it beneath Dom Sebastian's upper leg, then borrowed a scrap of leather. As Duarte returned and the time came to act I resolved to take the leg quickly – to be sure and strong with the knife. I forced a strip of leather between Dom Sebastian's teeth, then instructed my novice to hold both shoulders with all his strength. Next I wrapped a thong around the leg, a hand's breadth below the groin.

The thong I tied so tightly that Dom Sebastian cried out. Once that was done I lifted the dagger Duarte had procured. This was a fighting weapon, and the edge shaved hair from my wrists.

'Turn away if you have to,' I said to Duarte. 'I cannot risk you fainting.'

'I will not,' he said, though he looked ill and hesitant. Hurrying now, I bent to Dom Sebastian's thigh, first aiming a practice stroke at the air.

Just as I was about to slice into the withered muscle of that leg I heard a shout. 'No!'

Sighing, I lowered the knife, looking at the door, where Tonio Fonseca now stood, almost as broad as the doorway itself. Dark eyes chilled into me like frost on a winter morning. 'You cannot do this. I heard the lad attempting to borrow a dagger, and guessed that some devilment was planned.'

'The taking of a limb is not a pleasant thing,' I said, 'yet I have to cut to save his life.'

'You cannot take the leg. Dom Sebastian is twenty-five years old. He is a warrior. Can you sentence him to life as a cripple? How will he return in glory hobbling on one leg?'

Every word Tonio said was true, yet still I protested. 'If I don't take the leg he will die. Do you want that?'

'Of course not. Yet I cannot watch a great man's soul wither away either.'

My eyes closed as if to will this tragic dilemma away. 'Dom Sebastian incurred this wound many weeks ago. It has grown worse. Time alone will not heal him.'

Tonio came forward into the candlelight, and unwound the bandage, throwing it to the ground in disgust. Then he pointed at the wound. 'Look at it,' he cried. 'It festers from within. Something prevents it from healing.'

Though I had become hardened to the sight of that leg, the smell made me sick inside. 'You are suggesting that a fragment of the crossbow quarrel remains lodged inside. I can assure you that the good Franciscans of the Arrábida Monastery thought of the same thing and searched the wound. They found nothing. That cannot be the answer.'

'You have told me so before. And I will tell you again that they did not look hard and deep enough. What else can it be? Some remnant must lie inside. Cut for it Padre, cut for it now and see.'

'No. I will not.' My resolve to amputate the leg had hardened slowly. Once I backed away I might not find the courage again. Taking the limb was a hideous solution, yet Dom Sebastian would have a good chance of survival, provided the stump itself did not then become infected. 'I appreciate your concern, as I'm sure does the True King himself, but if I do not take the leg he will die. Please leave me now.'

'No,' he cried. 'Cut into the wound. Find the poison inside. Then he will live.'

I exhaled so hard my shoulder slumped. 'Very well, but if I find nothing, then I will proceed with the amputation.' My lips turned down at the thought of carrying out two very unpleasant operations instead of just one, yet now I had made the promise I would not go back on it. 'Now, help Duarte hold him down, this will not be pleasant.'

As my knife made the first stroke, Dom Sebastian bucked

and moaned. The faces of my helpers darkened with blood and the veins stood out on their necks as they struggled to keep our patient restrained. A foul-smelling mess of pus and watery blood eased out from my cut. This I wiped away with a rag.

The struggles subsided, then ceased altogether as Dom Sebastian fell into unconsciousness. Lowering the knife again, I sliced my way deep into the wound, using fore and index fingers to probe raw muscle, parting arteries and the thicker veins with my fingers. The blood flow made it impossible to see. My hands were sticky with fluids, and I looked at Tonio, who had turned pale.

'There is nothing there,' I told him. 'I'm sorry.'

'Cut deeper.'

Sobbing for breath, I did as he asked, and now my blade touched bone. Still my exploring fingers found nothing, and I was operating at the very limits of my emotional control.

'Nothing,' I blurted. 'There is nothing there. For the love of God—'

Men wept openly now, for the sight of my bloody hands deep in raw human flesh must have been horrible to behold.

'Please. Keep searching,' Tonio begged, his swordsman's arms were flexed, veins and tendons standing proud with effort.

My forefinger passed along the smooth surface of the femur, and along one side I felt an imperceptible nick in the bone. The find steadied me. The nick could not be natural, but had surely been caused by something striking it. The point of the quarrel had touched bone and continued on. Using the knife again to dig beyond the bone, I heard a click as the blade struck something hard.

'What's happening?' Tonio asked. 'I beg you. Tell me now.'

'Praise God, there's something in there.' I dropped the knife and probed the object with my forefinger, trying to dig it out.

It was, however, stuck fast. My cutting had quickened the flow of blood. This made my fingers slippery and useful vision of the wound impossible.

Again I used the knife to cut around the object, and now, to my relief, the thing came loose of its sucking bed of tissue. Even coated with blood I recognised the wicked iron point, still with a shoulder of wood attached. I dropped it in a bowl with a dull clink.

Passing the knife to Duarte, I said, 'Heat this blade in the cooking boxes on deck until it glows red hot. Hurry.'

Duarte returned a minute later, panting, holding the handle in rags.

Leaning forward, I lowered the flat knife blade onto the wound, the scent of hissing, burning flesh strong in my nostrils. The thing became a nightmare, with the blade needing to be re-heated two dozen times before the blood flow stopped, and I was satisfied with my efforts.

Finally, I washed the area and my hands from the bucket. Moving up along Dom Sebastian's body, I could scarcely believe that he had survived that operation. When I lowered my ear to his lips, however, I heard breath flutter through with quiet regularity.

'He lives,' I told Tonio. 'Thank the Lord God for His kindness.' Having uttered these words, I staggered from the bedside.

Duarte hurried beside me in concern. 'Where are you going, Padre?'

Unable to answer I hurried away from the reeking cabin. Reaching the stern gallery I bent over and emptied the contents of my stomach into the ocean far below.

Through two centuries as seafarers the people of our nation have forged a protocol for shipboard life. The ship is governed by three men. The captain, usually a political appointee, has overall responsibility, the master is in charge of the general running of the ship, and the pilot is concerned with navigation. Beneath these three are junior officers, each trained to carry out specific duties. Our ship, being large, also carried a médico, an officer in charge of the dispensary, and the commander of the hundred or so marines on board.

Subservient to all are hundreds of seamen and young apprentices, called grûmetes. Each wears a woollen cap, linen shirt and canvas breeches stout enough to last for a long voyage. Few have leather shoes. Most develop calluses so tough they can walk on broken glass. Down below, on the gun decks that doubled as sleeping areas, each man has his own locked liberty chest. Inside, amongst his private treasures, he keeps a change of socks, spare buttons of bone and wood, needles for sewing, and a woollen doublet for cold weather. Our seamen are the toughest in the world – some are Lisbon water rats, some born in the East, some Brazil, others mestiços of mixed heritage. Most are devout. Floggings and other punishments are rare.

The art of navigation, the responsibility of Nuno, the pilot, requires skill in geometry, directing the ship in a series of right angles, with the length of the hypotenuse being the distance travelled, and its angle the course. In this way the pilot can navigate to any point in the world, without knowing the exact time – knowledge that is necessary to calculate longitude with any degree of accuracy.

When Nuno deemed the sun to be at its highest point for the day, he opened the padded teak chest that held his instruments and brought out the balestilha. This instrument looked rather like a flat brass disc, and was used held low, adjusting the alidade so that a sun's rays passed through. The distance of the sun from the horizon, obtained in this way, gave the pilot an approximation of the ship's distance from the equator.

It was decorated with celestial bodies and the lines of latitude of the earth. This tool was as important to Nuno as an arm or leg, surpassed in value only by a rolled rectangle of artists' canvas, kept in a purpose-built, watertight receptacle. Nuno's chart was his most important possession, a document drawn from personal experience and the work of generations of navigators. It showed the land masses of the known world, shoals and currents, anecdotes and diagrams, even illustrations – a naked Khoikhoi of the African Cape and a mysterious Balinese beauty.

In addition, Nuno used a roteiro manuscript book, scribed in his own hand, which contained solar declination tables, directions for navigating by the pole star, a traverse table and a synoptic version of John of Holywood's *Tractatus de Sphaera*, sailing directions for the Carreira da India.

For my own part, I liked nothing better than spending time with Nuno, discussing the physics of our journey, angles and plots, as well as the geography of the world.

One day in November, when Nuno and I passed an afternoon in conversation, arguing on a matter of celestial arcs, one of the young priests came running from below.

'Frei Pereira,' he said. 'Come quickly. Dom Sebastian is asking for you.'

I hurried behind him, down the companion-way ladder through the steerage room and into the corridor. When I entered the cabin I saw that Dom Sebastian was sitting up in bed.

My eyes widened with wonder and I looked at Tonio, who stood at the True King's side, beaming as if his new vigour were his own achievement. In no small way, of course, it was.

'Praise God,' I said, and kneeled. Dom Sebastian extended an arm to me.

'Get up, and come closer.' His voice was weak, but as I arrived at his side he gripped my arm. 'I have many questions, but only one that matters. How fares Portugal under the yoke of a tyrant?'

My face darkened at the mention of Henrique, yet I spared him no detail – telling him of men hanging in the square, and the frightened, hungry faces of his beloved citizens. When it was done, Dom Sebastian was weeping, and I wondered if I should have cushioned the blow somewhat.

Even so, that night he ate a bowlful of stew and the bread that came with it. My heart filled with hope.

Mysteriously, the orphan Aletia de Calvez was welcome at Dom Sebastian's bedside. Whilst her skills as a nurse were considerable, as the young man healed I assumed that he would dismiss her permanently, for he was indeed a misogynist. He disliked and mistrusted the fairer sex to the point where he would not suffer a female horse, let alone spend time willingly in the company of a woman.

There were reasons for this aversion, of course. His father, as I have mentioned, died before his birth, and when he was three months old, Doña Juana, his mother, skipped back off to Spain at the request of her brother, leaving the tiny heir parentless in his adoring country.

The only female of note that remained present during Sebastian's upbringing was his grandmother Catarina, a stern woman who forced him to sleep in her own bedroom until he was eight years old.

Aletia, in fact, might have been the first personable, intelligent, and attractive young female he had met outside a very formal setting. Perhaps if I had realised this I might have understood why he responded well to her. If I had thought about his loveless childhood – his abandonment by both parents – I might have seen how ripe for affection he must have been.

I do know that even then, Aletia began to appreciate what kind of man Dom Sebastian was. His impressive looks had attracted her first, before she came to know his gentle side – his love of words, for example. When she read poetry he truly listened, and his face mirrored the emotion of whatever piece she happened to read.

A stirring ballad of war, for example, would compel his eyes to grow fierce beneath his brow and his lips compress into a hard line. If, however, she chose a gentle tale of love his face would soften, and a dreamy expression pass through his eyes. Once, when she read Euripides's masterful play, the Greek tragedy of Medea, acting out each character in their own distinct voice, a real tear fell from the corner of his eyes and she squeezed his hand, a pressure he returned.

Dom Sebastian rose like a leviathan from his death bed to take command of the ship, and the difference was apparent in a day. De Oliveira was made a special adviser, with all rights and privileges, and promised the next lucrative governorship that became available.

The previous captain was an administrator, the new one a warrior, at first using a stick to hobble from one deck to another or from bow to stern, driving his officers as hard as they, in turn, drove the men.

For two hours each day, Dom Sebastian, with Tonio his sergeant-major, red faced and stern, drilled the marines in the waist, shouting orders and communicating his general dissatisfaction with their performance. 'Raise your chins. Be proud. You are the core of what will one day be an army,' he promised. 'You will train ten thousand young men, and lead them in glory back to Portugal.'

The gun crew enjoyed Dom Sebastian's special attention, for battles at sea were won or lost on their performance. This force numbered over a hundred and fifty men – six to operate a single gun. The sergeant was responsible for priming and aiming the weapon, another man manipulated the barrel, one loaded the charge, one damped down sparks, and another passed ammunition. The youngest and smallest member of the team was the powder monkey, who brought the combustible powders up from the magazine. These were skinny lads, still shy of adolescence, built for wriggling through narrow hatches and confined spaces.

Dom Sebastian learned the first name of each man, just as he discerned their weaknesses and strengths. He knew that José, for example, had once lost a finger in a knife fight and Verissimo had a lazy eye that prevented him from seeing well to his left. He chose six of the best and fastest who, in the event of an attack, would leave the main guns to their comrades and race up to the deck to man the deadly verso. These swivel guns were packed with shot and scrap metal, designed to rake an enemy deck.

When the gun crew practised live firing I watched, spellbound. I am a man of God, and of peace. I had never killed a man in my life, and believed, at that point, that I never would. Even so, I thrilled to watch the guns recoil back against the ropes and the shot strike far out into the ocean, in a spout of white water. Dom Sebastian moulded that group of men into an effective fighting force. That was his talent. That was what he was born to do.

Ten men carried five hundred varas of the finest hempen rope up from the cable deck and set to splicing and plaiting a massive boarding net. These craftsmen sat with boundless patience, not questioning whether there would ever be employment for their handiwork, but intent on doing their best simply because they had been asked to do so. When I questioned Dom Sebastian on the need for this device he replied, 'Preparing for the worst is a trait that even you would approve of, Padre.'

I nodded my agreement. We both knew how much Henrique wanted not only the head of Dom Sebastian, but that special cargo we carried in the holds.

The stateroom that had been spotless under the command of de Oliveira became a mess of unrolled charts, with ever-changing gatherings of men at the table, for Dom Sebastian sought expertise where he could, and those with experience of the East were pressed for every scrap of information that might prove useful.

Leaving nothing to chance, Dom Sebastian kept two clerks at work on letters to Eastern leaders seeking alliances and treaties. Other missives were addressed to Portuguese viceroys and garrison commanders throughout the East, from Melaka to Tymor, signalling Dom Sebastian's intentions and asking for loyalty, which would be rewarded with promotion and wealth when power returned to its rightful owner. Of course, we were still months away from the Indian Ocean, and the correspondence built up, awaiting a reliable delivery method.

It wasn't long before Dom Sebastian, tired of borrowed cutlasses, wanted access to his own, beautiful weapon, and Duarte and I spent two full days in the holds, searching for the plain coffin. When we found it I wouldn't let even Duarte see what I was doing, levering up the lid and moving aside the body of the hapless monk whose eternal rest I had interrupted.

The sword was hidden in a false bottom in the coffin itself, and having retrieved it I was tempted to remove the *Parcela* also. There was, after all, a strong room attached to the captain's cabin.

Yet the *Parcela* had been packed not into a wooden cavity, but within the body itself, and the coffin had proved to be a safe hiding place. When we had finished packing goods back around it, no one would find it without attracting attention. I let the great treasure lie, and cleaned Dom Sebastian's sword carefully, polishing it with the grease it had been packed in until it shone.

The task of retrieval was worth it when my King's hand closed around the hilt. That was the moment in which he became a man again.

Strangely, even as he resumed battle training, Dom Sebastian did not turn his back on his former nurse, and Aletia was often a fixture in his chambers, reading nightly from the texts she borrowed from all over the ship.

Seeing them together thus gave me a strange twinge in my chest that even now I cannot put a name to. The two young people I loved most in the world, learning to see the magic in each other. Of course, back then I imagined that this was only a developing friendship, not the first tender shoots of genuine true love.

Now and then, sometimes for days at a time, the wind abandoned us, leaving our ship wallowing like a sow in her mud hole, seared by a tropical sun.

Dom Sebastian and the master, Elfo, tried everything from wetting the sails to filling the ship's boats full of oarsmen in an attempt to tow the não along – hunting the wind instead of passively trying to receive it.

During those burning days crew and passengers alike swam from the sides like children on the Tagus docks, trying to escape that merciless heat. Lethargy gripped us all. Even Duarte slowed to a walk. Fevers scoured the ship, and the first deaths occurred. The most common illness started with lumps around the groin, and soon after, the sufferer became delirious, often having to be tied to prevent a mad leap overboard.

At night we would form a procession that snaked around the decks, praying for God's forgiveness and a beneficent wind. First would come one of the younger priests, carrying the banner of Holy Relics. Then followed a line of priests, and finally Dom Sebastian and his officers, the merchants and those seamen and soldiers who chose to join in.

Walking at the rear I led the singing of the Psalm *Miserere Mei Deus*, all the while praying that our sins might reveal themselves. Most of all I prayed that God might accept the ordeal of the nightly processions as fair exchange for whatever had offended Him.

I spent much of my time tending to the sick. Scurvy claimed the greater percentage of lives. Even I had the gum disease, though Dom Coutinho, the ship's medico, assured me that I would return to normal once we reached land.

'The sea air causes it,' he had said, grinning to display his own swollen red mouth. 'There is no cure but firm ground under your feet.'

Others suffered from dysentery, characterised by liquid emissions that gushed from the bowels. Helpless to control the discharges, these unfortunates lay in pools of their own filth, so ashamed of their own malfunctions that they could not meet my eyes as I attempted to clean them.

The wind, when it came, blew out of the north, a howling torrent that filled our sails and purged the ship of the lethargy that had gripped it. This was no beneficent breeze, however, for it carried Henrique's desperate anger that Dom Sebastian had escaped his grasp — five ships of war, sails billowing, borne by that same devil's wind.

From the first shouts of the topmastmen, I felt my guts churn with the memory of battle. White sails resolved into hulls, bristling with dark gun ports.

'Henrique stretches his power across an ocean,' de Oliveira said, having already given the order to fetch Dom Sebastian from his cabin, there meeting with the ship's officers.

'Are you sure they are chasing us?' I asked.

'The India fleet has sailed. We are three hundred leagues past Brazil. They are Portuguese ships, and Henrique's pennant flies at the foretop. Besides, there is no difficulty in proving their intention.' He broke off to shout down at Elfo. 'Alter course ninety degrees starboard.'

The orders were relayed to the helmsman, and the ship responded to this preposterous change in course. Shadows cast by the masts, rails and rigging moved, and I found myself facing the sun.

'Now,' the former captain urged, 'watch those ships.'

At first the five shadowing vessels appeared to maintain their original course. Then, before I could make a confident and relieved prediction all five tacked back into the wind so their bowsprits looked like compass needles, so unerringly did they seek us.

'You are convinced?'

'Yes, unfortunately.' I lowered my voice and frowned. 'Our men are in no condition for a fight. Senhor Elfo can scarcely raise a full watch.'

Dom Sebastian, arriving from below, broke in, 'They will fight if they have to. Even the sickest man will a give good account of himself when his life depends on it. I fear, however, that five lighter ships will toy with us on the open ocean. Even with a full complement we could not match so many.'

'Then what can we do?'

Dom Sebastian's answer was typical of the man, 'Fia-te na Virgem a não corras – trust the Virgin and don't run.' The phrase, heavy with sarcasm, meant that we should do everything to help ourselves rather than merely praying. 'Henrique has defeated me once – I cannot let it happen again. We need islands – reefs – anything that we can use to advantage. Turning to Nuno he snapped, 'The nearest land – the isles of Tristão da Cunha?'

'That is correct, Dom Sebastian.'

'Give me your best estimate of our current location and plot a course for those islands. Senhor Elfo?'

The stocky master ascended the ladder from the waist. 'Yes, Dom Sebastian?'

'Set a new course according to the pilot, and give us all possible speed, even if you tear the masts from the deck. I want every man awake, fed, and ready for action. Gun crews should stand by to take their stations.'

'Yes Dom Sebastian.'

He turned to me, 'Do you know where Tonio is?'

'In his cabin, perhaps. I know he was on deck almost all night, for he said that the wind unsettled him, for all that it is fortuitous and welcome. He has had very little sleep.'

'Would you fetch him for me?'

'Of course.'

Coming upon the cabin I knocked gently, but noticing that the door was ajar I pushed it open. There I saw Tonio, kneeling, muttering under his breath, black eyebrows narrowed, overshadowing the eyes beneath. Praying but yet not praying: more like an incantation to some demon than to our father in heaven. I stopped, taken aback.

'Tonio, I am sorry, Dom Sebastian is looking for you—'

When he came back to himself, it was with the eye of a man who has journeyed far and did not wish yet to return. The scar on his upper lip glowed brightly. 'I am sorry, Padre, I was deep in prayer.'

I wanted to comment that it must be a bitter species of prayer, yet said nothing, instead touching one meaty shoulder. 'I know how you feel. Sometimes prayer can be a powerful thing – more real than speaking to someone in the same room. Even so, you must hurry now.'

Slowly, like a man recovering from the effects of strong drink, he rose and followed me to the companionway, to where Dom Sebastian waited. My brow creased in thought, for I could have sworn that I heard him utter the word 'vengeance' in the text of that prayer.

VINTE E TRES

The beach Henry had taken Nicolá and Francis to was a desirable base, partly because of the small freshwater stream that flowed in at the most easterly point. It also offered flat areas of sand up behind the foreshore where they would be safe from crocodiles and other dangers.

Transferring the camp to the new site took much of the next day, interspersed as it was with exploratory runs along the coast nearby that left the skin of their faces and arms a little sunburnt and gritty with salt.

In the late afternoon Francis, feeling the need for recreation, pulled on shorts and took out the soccer ball he had insisted on bringing. He carried it away from the camp then dropped and dribbled. Facing the waves, he bounced it from foot to foot.

Kicking the ball high and long, he chased it down, and was surprised to see Nicolá walking up from their new camp. Francis kicked it across and watched the young woman work the ball.

'You are good, really good,' he said.

She grinned, 'So are you.'

'Yes, didn't I tell you that I am Francis the magnificent, Francis the goal scorer?'

Nicolá tilted her head, hands on her hips, 'Listen to Francis the boastful. Kick it here and I'll show you how it's done.'

Francis kicked it to her on a low, flat trajectory and watched her trap it with her left foot, and kick with her right. He appraised her body, wondering how she kept herself fit, for she carried very little extra weight. 'I think perhaps I will let you on my team – you show some aptitude.'

'Oh thank you,' she said, and kicked the ball back to him off the flat side of her foot.

Francis controlled it then lofted it back, and for ten pleasurable minutes they kicked to each other across that expanse of sand, with the sunset turning the sky and their surrounds to bloody red.

'That's enough,' Nicolá said, hands on hips and chest rising and falling visibly, 'we haven't even lit the fire yet.'

Francis trapped the ball and bent to lift it, holding it under the crook of one elbow. 'You're right, there's work to do.'

That evening, moisture in the driftwood hissing and bubbling out the end grain of the larger logs, Francis spooned up the dregs of his dinner and laid the plate beside him, looking around with pleasure at the light dancing on the stone that surrounded them. Ripple-sized waves broke on the sand, a hundred paces away, and somewhere out in the water, a predator fish slashed at bait near the surface.

'I feel so insignificant here,' Nicolá said, 'as if the human species is not so important after all – that when we are gone the planet will shrug its shoulders and carry on regardless.

Francis picked up his plate and moved around to collect hers, along with the aluminium pan they had used to heat up the meal. 'While you ponder the universe, I'll wash up.'

'Wait, I'll help,' she said, tidying up while he carried a plastic bucket down to the water and filled it with seawater, first scanning the shallows with his torch for any sign of reptilian eyes. He washed up without suds, using handfuls of sandy gravel to scrub the pots, while Nicolá dried, arranging the plates and cutlery on a flat stone to dry.

When it was all done, Francis moved closer to the fire and extended his hands, splaying his fingers to dry them, while Nicolá cleaned her teeth on the edge of the firelight.

'The Sebastianists believe,' she said, coming back into the firelight, still holding her toothbrush, 'that we will reach a plateau, where the guns fall silent and we get on with life sustainably, without destroying each other and the planet in the process.'

'I hope to God they're right,' he said.

Rising at dawn, they ate the last of their bacon and eggs, washed down with orange juice — another perishable that they would soon have to live without.

After the meal they sat in silence for a few minutes, a changeable breeze whipping smoke from the dying fire this way and that.

'So how are we going to do this?' Nicolá asked.

'We'll start with the metal detectors, cover the beach, and after that I think we should penetrate inland.'

'I'll focus on the dunes, then the waterway and surrounds,' she said.

'And I'll stick to the sand and the tops of the headlands – keeping an eye out for any overhangs or other natural features.'

'Of course.'

'Let's get to work then.'

The metal detectors were second-hand, yet top of the range Garrett-brand units, able to discriminate between ferrous and non-ferrous metals, with the power to penetrate up to three hundred millimetres of sand.

The rugged instruments had taken a beating over the years. Unlike more modern machines, these were heavy, though a harness spread the weight over the shoulders. Francis pressed the power switch, and slipped the headphones over his ears. The unit emitted a steady low-frequency hum. When he moved the sensor plate over a tin mug near the fire the noise rose to a high-pitched squeal.

Nicolá smiled at him. 'You've found something already.'

'I wish it was that easy. Have fun. We'll meet back here mid-morning if you like.'

'Sure, you have fun too.'

Francis started at the far end of the beach, sweeping the instrument from side to side, soon finding a rhythm that was not too fast yet covered the ground at a steady rate. He looked up only occasionally to fix a point in his mind so that he did not wander too far from his search pattern. When he finally reached the rocks above the beach he turned and headed back towards the water.

The advantage of the deserted beach was that his footprints delineated the areas that he had already covered, making the survey rapid and efficient. The task became routine, and Francis found his mind wandering, looking across to where Nicolá was covering ground up near the freshwater stream.

An hour passed before the machine responded for the first time. He might have missed the sudden rise in pitch, so quickly did it return to normal. Retracing his steps, however, the change was unmistakable. The item, whatever it was, had to lie at near maximum depth for the return to be so weak.

Laying the detector on the sand, Francis fell to his knees and dug with his hands. He had decided against carrying a shovel around all day, the sand being so soft and the camp close by if he decided he needed one.

At a depth close to the rated maximum for the unit Francis uncovered a tin can so rusted that it fell apart in his hand. It might have been, he decided, fifty or more years old, left behind by some traveller pulling his boat ashore for a meal.

Throughout the morning he continued to work, interrupted near noon by the sight of Nicolá on all fours in the shade, staring intently at the ground. For the next few minutes he divided his attention between that sight and the metal detector, expecting Nicolá to cease whatever she was doing and stand up. When this did not happen, however, he gave in to curiosity and moved towards her.

Lifting the harness over his head he laid the detector down and walked across the stones and scattered vegetation. Even as he drew near to Nicolá she did not raise her head. He stopped to wipe the sweat from his face. The object of her attention was still unclear to him.

'What's happening?' he asked.

Finally she looked up. 'Can't you see? A thousand ants are killing this grasshopper. Come closer.'

Trying to hide a wry grin Francis too sunk to his knees and settled beside her, conscious of her fragrance now, yet also intent at the battle being fought in the sand. An uncountable army of tiny black ants had trapped a struggling grasshopper. It was obviously injured, for despite weak flicks of his powerful legs he moved only a handspan away, and the mass of ants soon caught up.

Nicolá reached out a finger and brushed dozens of the ants away. The grasshopper gained the upper hand for a moment, struggling upright.

'What are you doing?' Francis asked.

'I'm helping him fight the ants.'

'Why? He'll soon die anyway, they might as well get to eat him while he's fresh.'

'That's mean.'

'No it's not, just practical. All you're doing is prolonging his agony.'

Nicolá's eyes widened and for a moment Francis half expected a tear. Together they watched as the ants swarmed in. Slowly, over the course of minutes, the grasshopper's struggles ceased. Thousands of ants began to carry him bodily away to wherever they had planned to complete their feast.

'We'd better get back to it,' Francis said.

He stood up and offered Nicolá a hand. When she took it and rose, they stood for a moment, fingers entwined.

'Have you found anything?' she asked.

'One tin, an aluminium coke can and the remnants of an iron bolt. It's amazing, probably only a dozen white Australians have ever set foot on this beach, and three of them left rubbish behind.'

'You've done better than me. I've found nothing.' She disentangled her hand and pointed to the stream. 'That's a gorgeous little waterway, and it goes a long way inland. I've covered the banks for the first few hundred metres.'

'Freshwater draws humans just as it draws animals.'

'That's what I was thinking. We should walk up a little way later.'

By the middle afternoon the tide had dropped, leaving acres of sand exposed. Under two-hundred millimetres of wet sand Francis made a discovery he regarded as interesting, without being conclusive – a solid residue of rusted iron as long as a man's outstretched arms, and hollow. It lay deep against an underlying gravel layer, and was so soft that the slightest touch broke it into a thousand tiny particles.

Nicolá came across to study it, 'Could it be four hundred and fifty years old?'

'Judging by the state of that tin can, probably not, unless it was a very thick lump to begin with.'

'It's possible, though.' She paused. 'A cannon perhaps? The iron looks like it was thick enough.'

'Sure, it's possible, yet why would one lie under the beach here? There are a hundred other things it's more likely to have been. I think it's best to leave it there intact, but I'll take some samples and we'll send them for testing when we get back to Darwin.'

Before dark, mug of wine in hand, Francis walked with Nicolá along the stream. At first it was subject to tidal movement, but this influence dissipated. In those mangrove-lined lower reaches

Francis pointed out a couple of croc slides.

'Not big ones,' he said, 'but they are here.'

Ascending a few metres, they reached the first wide but shallow freshwater pool, and then another, shrouded by pandanus palms. The pair talked as they went on, stopping where a thin cascade fell from a height of five or six metres into a pool no deeper than their knees. Nicolá had her camera out, taking shots and offering exclamations of appreciation.

'How about a paddle?' Francis asked, still looking beyond the white feather of the falls. Here the water had stained the cliffs black, indicating that it must be a torrent in the wet season. Some signs of that copious moisture remained, however, in the small ferns and vines that clung to cracks and seams in the stone face.

The young woman hesitated, then shook her head. 'What about the crocodiles?'

'You can see the bottom here. It's safe enough.'

She was not yet convinced. 'By the time I get my trunks, it will nearly be dark.'

The bikini that Francis had seen her wear could hardly be called trunks, he decided. 'You don't need them, come on, I haven't had fresh water on my skin for days.'

'No, no, no, I am not going skinny dipping with you looking at me. Besides, we haven't even got a towel.'

'That's a shame, 'cause I'm going in.'

Stripping down to his shorts, he waded in, the sandy gravel soothing on his feet. The water was cold enough to make him gasp, but a welcome sensation. He continued on until he reached the cascade, letting the water pour onto his face. Perched on a smooth, rounded rock he stared across at Nicolá. She looked forlorn, insanely jealous.

'Come on,' he cried. 'Wear your T-shirt and undies.'

'My what?'

'Your underwear for God's sake.'

'Okay, I'm coming in. Don't look.'

Francis averted his eyes, but turned back in time to catch a glimpse of long legs and white briefs. The skin of her thighs was the same light brown shade as her shoulders, face and arms.

The water covered her body to the waist as she walked towards him. Crouching so that she plunged fully under the surface, she burst back through, smiling and shaking her hair. Sliding up onto a rock, she sat with her back turned, brushing her hair with both hands. Studying her, Francis enjoyed the inverted triangle made by her shoulders and trunk, along with the ropes of wet hair falling down past her neck.

She turned to look at him over her shoulder. 'We should have brought some soap.'

'Soap's a no-no in this kind of place. Not environmentally friendly.'

'You're right. Nothing should ever spoil this.'

Sunset was close now, and the sky turned blood red. The surface of the water, rippled from the falls, looked as vivid as the landscape itself. Francis swam across the head of the pool, pulling himself up on the rocks. The cliff above was not as sheer as it had appeared at a distance.

Still wet, he began to climb, gaining the top and staring inland in wonder. The afternoon air was filled with dust, or smoke, giving the vista an eerie distance.

The landscape that met his eyes was surreal, unforgettable. Pinnacles of red and yellow rose wraithlike from the surrounding earth, with hollows and shadows and secret places highlighted by the low-angle light. Francis's breath came faster. He felt that he was staring at destiny itself. As if all the works and trials of his life had led to that moment.

Francis did not turn when he heard bare feet behind him, nor even when Nicolá came up, her shirt clinging to her body., and eyes mirroring his excitement. 'What's out there?' she asked.

He pointed with his forefinger towards the wilderness. 'Everything. They were here. I know they were.'

That night Francis remained at the fire for more than an hour after Nicolá had gone to bed, before he walked to his tent and shimmied into his sleeping bag.

At first unable to sleep, he succumbed eventually, and thereafter managed a series of hour-long catnaps. Each time he woke it was to a strange kind of half-wakefulness, with the saudade pulling at his heart as if it were tied to the moon slipping down on its arc on the other side of the earth.

It was strange, but his mind returned to thinking about the beach itself and the sand dunes behind it. He thought back to long-ago high school geography lessons. The beach formations – littoral, fore-dunes and back dunes. The valley or slack between each dune.

It seemed strange that this particular beach had formed dunes, and most of the others in that area had not. Another snippet from those lessons came back. He could hear her plain as day: diminutive Miss Bolton with brown hair that seemed to hang to her knees.

'Dunes often form around an obstruction,' she had said. 'Windblown grains stop when they hit a rock, tree, or other hard object then start to build into the classic beach dune formation—'

Francis slept again at last, and this time his subconscious sifted through all the years of learning and reading. If this was truly, as Henry said, the site of a landing, there was one thing that those mariners would almost certainly have done …

When the subterranean glow of false dawn touched Francis's closed eyelids he came fully awake as if jolted by a cattle prod. He left his sleeping bag, dressed, then walked to Nicolá's tent. 'Wake up,' he called.

She appeared with her head in the entrance like a bear at its cave. 'What is it?'

'Come with me, hurry.'

Together they climbed the headland, looking out at where the sea met stone in puffs of white. There was a blue-white phosphorescence in the water that morning, visible even from that distance.

Being with the beautiful-to-him Portuguese woman in this magical half-light was recharging the cells of his soul, emptied by the quest, the relentless searching, and the bargaining, begging fund-raising that such an enterprise required.

Together they walked silently along the shining littoral to the top of the headland above the beach. There Francis started casting around, looking through and amongst the undergrowth.

'What are we looking for?' cried Nicolá.

'A pile of rocks maybe,' he replied. 'What's the first thing a Portuguese landing party would build?'

'A padrãos – a marker. Of course, you clever man.'

This was not a large area, and Francis found what he was looking for amongst the grass and turkey bush. It was a crumbling pile of stones at the very summit of the headland. He fell to his knees as if it were a shrine.

Nicolá, arriving at his side, squatted before the pile of rubble. 'You were right.'

'There's not much left of it,' he said, 'but I'm sure this must have been it. I'll come back later and do some measurements and take photos, but … it's just nice to know that it's here.'

Together they moved without speaking until they overlooked the beach again. Dawn came slowly, the brilliant orb finishing its journey across the ancient red continent, thousands of miles of weathered beauty. This was a different place now, with low light over the dunes, followed by sunbeams making yellow–white shafts of light into the sky.

At first, as Francis watched, he saw nothing new, but he was watching intently; hoping. Over those momentous minutes when night turned to day, the sand dunes captured Francis's eyes. Slowly they formed into a recognisable shape. Invisible yesterday, now it was plain, and so big that at first he could not believe it was true.

There was something under the dunes, something massive. The shape was unmistakable – a long keel, ribs and knees. Not complete by any means, but *there*. It was a ship, buried under the sands, and revealed by the angle of the dawn light.

'Oh God,' said Nicolá. 'It's here, after all – just like the Bom Jesus in Namibia.'

Tear spilled down his cheeks. 'We've found her. We really have.'

VINTE E QUATRO

The islands of Tristão da Cunha were located at the southernmost point of our long sweep across the Atlantic Ocean. Two of these isles were so insignificant as to not merit a name, while a third was named after its discoverer, Gonçalo Alvarez. More than that I did not know, save for reports I had heard of the islands' volcanic origin, and of the massive seas that pound the inhospitable and uninhabitable coasts.

Throughout the afternoon, in a headlong rush for our barren and unfamous destination, I scarcely left the deck for want of staring at our pursuers. Hurrying below in the mid-afternoon, I knocked on Aletia's door and spent a few minutes with her, not wanting to alarm her, yet anxious she be forewarned of trouble.

'I have a new test for your tongue,' I told her lightly.

Aletia's eyes narrowed suspiciously. 'Is it one you made up?' Over the course of the voyage, not having heard many new riddles or tongue-twisters, I had resorted to inventing them, and we both knew that the quality had degenerated.

'Not at all,' I said. 'This is a brand new one, told to me just today by one of the merchants. Listen carefully: "O tempo pergunta ao tempo quanto tempo o tempo tem. O tempo responde ao tempo que o tempo tem tanto tempo quanto tempo o tempo tem."'

Aletia clapped her hands. Then, with that sharp mind of hers she repeated the words back to me. 'Time asks time how much time the time has … What was the next bit? Oh yes. Time answers time that the time has as much time as time has.' She paused for breath. 'I like that one.'

'Say it quickly,' I said.

Smiling, I watched her face grow red with embarrassment as her tongue tripped on the repeated letters, then dissolved into laughter, touching my shoulder to steady herself.

'I'll practise,' she said at last. 'By noon tomorrow I'll be able to say it as fast as you like, Padre.'

'I'll look forward to that, but I came down here to give you a warning.'

Her eyes clouded over. 'A warning?'

'Yes. There are some ships behind us that may shoot at us with their cannons. Never fear, they will not catch us, and will soon fall behind, but if you hear gunfire, stay here in your cabin. You will be safe. If that situation changes I will come to get you. Understand?'

Aletia nodded her agreement, and I turned away into the corridor.

Night fell, and as Dom Sebastian had predicted, the closest of our pursuers eased within range of our stern falconets. Tonio led the gun crews in opening fire, and, having never seen cannon's discharge in darkness before, not up close at least, I was stunned at the tongue of flame that burst forth from the muzzle. Narrowing my eyes in concentration I discerned a spout of water fine on the starboard bow of that nearest enemy ship.

'The range is still marginal.' Dom Sebastian commented from beside me, 'yet the practice gives the men something to focus on.' A similar spurt of flame emanated from the enemy's lead ship, and a moment later a fountain of water erupted astern of our position.

'Their guns have greater range than ours,' I said.

'I do not believe so,' de Oliveira put in. 'I know that ship – the *Santiago*, a veteran of the Carreira da India. Her captain is a man called Simão. If her bow chaser is achieving greater range than our guns they are overcharging the bore – a dangerous practice.'

Our marksmanship, while accurate, proved ineffectual, and after half a dozen more volleys Dom Sebastian ordered a cease fire in order to save powder and shot. The crew stood watching the enemy's efforts, cheering when a shot went wide, and hissing and jeering when it passed close.

Spectacularly, I saw the bow of the pursuing ship suffer a bright explosion and across the water came the sound of screaming men.

'As I told you,' de Oliveira said, 'they were overcharging the bore. An explosion was only a matter of time.'

'They must be stupid to do such a thing.'

'No, not stupid. Simão is not a stupid man. Desperate, perhaps, or driven.'

Dom Sebastian added his own observation. 'Just before dusk I saw men on the forecastle. Their helmet visors shone gold in the sun. There are guarda-costras aboard.'

I crossed myself. 'I pray that you are wrong.'

'Would I ever forget those who killed my comrades, and left

me also, for dead?' asked Dom Sebastian. 'We will do our best to reach the islands. Otherwise, I'm afraid that tomorrow will see our destruction. We cannot fight five ships.'

The quarterdeck became a place of quiet tension, the ship flying desperately with little regard for safety. Nuno left his chart table to tug at our commander's sleeve. 'Dom Sebastian, the islands are close, we cannot afford to run at full speed in the night, there may be uncharted shoals and islets. You must slow down.'

'What is my choice?' Dom Sebastian snapped, 'to risk such hazards or let five caravels bring us to battle on the open sea.' Prudently, however, he sent three men aloft, and stacked the forecastle with men whose sole duty was to pick out a line of foam over breaking water, or the darker shadows of rocks in the night. The calm voice of de Oliveira could be heard in every corner of the deck.

Slaves brought food and watered wine, and no man left the quarterdeck for any reason. My mind was heavy with memories of Alcácer Quibir, and these I saw also in the face of Dom Sebastian.

Lost in my thoughts, listening to the leadsman's cry, there was an outbreak of consternation on the bridge. 'Satan's work,' someone cried. Others prayed aloud. Looking ahead over the bows I saw what had upset them – the entire south-eastern quadrant, sky and ocean alike, glowed with red fire, like the coming of some devil's dawn.

Making the sign of the cross I began a psalm, for the sea itself was ablaze. Dom Sebastian came up beside me.

'We should steer away from there,' I told him. 'This is something beyond us.'

'We cannot, if dawn finds us still on the open ocean we will be dead before noon. I must maintain our heading.'

As we drew closer, one half of the sky took on that crimson glow, and I saw things that both thrilled and frightened me – tendrils of fire reaching to the heavens, trailing smoke into the firmament. All around me men shouted and howled. Some threw themselves to the deck and prayed as if we were sailing into hell itself.

Other men begged our commanders to take them away from what, they reasoned, must be Armageddon. The smell of sulphur filled the air, reeked in my nostrils, so thick I wanted to dive into the water to purge it.

An explosion, still far away, louder than a thousand cannon, rocked the ship, preceded by a flash of distant fire and light so bright as to stun the eyes. The ship's company screamed as one. All eyes turned now from the pursuing ships, so close now, to this infinitely more frightful show of power.

The first of three massive waves struck us soon after the explosion. The lookouts shouted a warning just before the wave hit, and the deck heeled. Water washed along the deck. Striking unprepared, the wave knocked me to my knees, leaving me cold and frightened. Scarcely had I time to recover before the lookouts cried again, 'Another comes, save yourselves.'

This time I was able to prepare, gripping a rail with both hands, letting the water wash over me. Even so, the strength of that flow tugged at me as if insisting I return to the sea with it.

The mountain of Tristão da Cunha appeared, rearing a mile high over the surrounding ocean, and before smoke and brightness obscured my view I saw a tremendous crater at the peak spewing forth burning stone and fire. Between the place where

I stood and that mountain I saw burning rocks thrown high into the air, falling into the ocean with a hiss and splash.

Up until that moment my knowledge of the phenomena called variously vulcão or volcano had been theoretical. I knew that the Greeks believed that these were the fires of Vulcan's workshop spilling upwards from his underground forge, and it was indeed the single most frightening thing I had ever seen. My eyes sought out Dom Sebastian in the reddish glow that now lit the world like midday in hell. 'Turn back,' I shouted. 'To go on means death.'

Then I saw the direction of his eyes. The other ships were now visible, still with us, braving the terror to keep pace. If we turned, they would use the fiery light to shoot at us, yet to go on was unthinkable.

Dom Sebastian's orders made me reel in shock. 'Harden up – full sail,' he roared.

'Surely not!' I cried. 'Don't dare to defy the power of God.'

'I will not defy Him, but place ourselves at His mercy.'

Building up speed, we sailed not out of, but closer to that mount-of-hell, until the heat of it scorched my face as if I were leaning too close to a brazier. The red fire seared my eyes, and burning rocks fell so constantly that it seemed impossible we would not be sunk.

The deck became hushed. Men performed their duties, uttering vocal pleas for deliverance from the burning mountain.

Oh please, turn and let us battle men, not the devil. Lead us out of here.

I was not the only clergyman on deck, others had gathered in the waist with a yellow lantern in their midst. In deep, low tones they sang together, the beauty of their voices inspiring.

The Holy men sang the Twenty-eighth Psalm, and I closed

my eyes, letting tears flow at the deep sadness in the words: *Hear the voice of my supplications, when I cry unto thee, when I lift up my hands toward your holy oracle.*

We sang and prayed while men lowered leather buckets to the sea surface and dragged up water, before throwing it in all directions. Others carried buckets aloft and saturated the sails.

Still we sailed on as balls of lava pitched down ever more thickly, and the burning mountain loomed closer. In that extreme moment I fancied that I saw the pagan god Vulcan himself stoking the fires of his underground forge.

Molten rock flowed down from the crater lip, pouring down gullies to the sea itself, this last meeting obscured in clouds of steam. The air stank of that steam, as well as the increasing reek of sulphur. My cassock, wet from the near swamping, dried until it crackled like straw.

'They follow still,' Dom Sebastian shouted, and I turned to see at least three of the five ships, two of them coming within range now. Then, one of the caravels was struck by molten stone and transformed into a ball of flame. Unbelievably, it was consumed in an instant, the remnants pulled beneath the waves as if by a kraken.

Our company cheered, yet men of Portugal had died, and I could not feel pleased, no matter what their purpose, nor who commanded them. Dom Sebastian ordered our ship deeper into the inferno, where the very air appeared to be aflame. The quiet fear of our decks turned to noisy confusion.

The air became too hot to breathe, and fires broke out on the deck and in the sails. Sizzling fragments of rock rained down, until it became impossible to keep one's eyes open. Pumps clattered and buckets raised and lowered as two hundred men fought the fires. My skin felt as if it were ablaze.

Somewhere astern, another enemy ship caught fire, flaring like guncotton. As we loomed close to the steaming shore, waves inundated the molten rock, and my cassock flamed so that I had to roll on the deck to extinguish it.

Strangely, Rui Chanoca the astrologer looked at ease in that firestorm, facing the conflagration with a serenity that was hard to credit. Tonio Fonseca was also calm, busy helping to organise the bucket chains that were saving our ship.

At last, our bow faced away from the heart of that vulcão instead of towards it. Every heartbeat lasted an eternity as we inched towards safety – scorched, yet still sound. Soon the burning rocks fell only occasionally and the air in my lungs was good clean sea air in comparison to what we had breathed.

Dom Sebastian threw one sweaty arm around my shoulders, and the other clutched Tonio in a brotherly embrace. 'It was a test. If the Lord God wanted to destroy us he would have done so. We are fated to live on.'

'Are the enemy ships destroyed?'

'Not all. I do not believe that all five followed us into the inferno. Even so, it will be hours before the surviving ships can work their way around the islands and try to locate us. By then we will be far away.'

The manner in which Dom Sebastian navigated our ship through the fires of the vulcão only increased the awe with which the men held him. It was seen as a test akin to a labour of Hercules.

Tonio Fonseca summed up the general feeling in one sentence. 'Dom Sebastian's courage and faith in the Lord God is an example to us all.'

With precise navigation and winds that kept the sails taut, Table Bay soon welcomed us with her wild beauty. My eyes drank in the expanse of water, then the grey mountain rising up to a cloudy summit. The flat-topped giant did indeed resemble a table, but one immense beyond belief, dwarfing shore and ocean alike, its sides weathered and gouged as if it had been clawed by gorgons. That dramatic landscape shimmered in a bright reflective haze that pained my eyes.

Parties of extras crowded aboard the ship's boats as they set off to fill pipes and barrels with water and bargain for food. Everyone aboard was anxious to step on dry land, fill bellies with fresh water, and eat anything available. With them also went armed marines, for sixty years earlier my countryman Francisco de Almeida and scores of his men had been slaughtered by the treacherous Khoikhoi on these beaches.

Hours passed before Duarte and I found space aboard a barca heading in for the beach, and we were able to spend a pleasant afternoon strolling the shallows with Rui Chanoca.

This was a strange and thrilling experience, for when a man has sailed for months on end, his body cannot stop anticipating the pitch and yaw of the ship, so that even though his feet tread on firm ground, he still feels as if he is rising and falling with a restless sea.

Duarte, unconcerned with this phenomenon, rolled up the legs of his breeches and searched the beach for lion footprints. Once, when he was convinced that he had found the elusive marks a nearby sailor contradicted him. 'No lad, that is the print of a Cape dog. A lion's paw is wider than a grown man's spread fingers.'

That time on land restored so much of my inner strength that I wondered at how blue skies, copious water and fish straight from the sea can make a man feel good about himself in such a short time. While Dom Sebastian bargained for meat with the naked Khoikhoi, I stared at the mountains and wondered what might lie beyond.

'Tell me,' I asked Rui, as he walked beside me. 'Why did you choose to travel East? The heretics of Germany would have sheltered you.'

'And spend my days eating sauerkraut and drinking beer? Not my style. Besides, soon they would decide that my heresy is not as pure as theirs and burn me up. Men have blamed me for everything from plague to the infidelity of their wives. If it were not for priests of your order I might now lie in one of the Grand Inquisitor's mass graves.'

This was the first time Rui had used the word heretic to describe himself. Strangely, I felt a wave of companionship for him, and a measure of curiosity. 'What is your particular brand of heresy?'

'I am of the Illuminati.'

My ears burned. 'That is indeed grave heresy. I do not approve.'

'Yet you do not tie me to a stake and frizzle the fat from my bones. You accept that despite our different beliefs we can live together side by side. Perhaps be friends.' Rui pointed to his nose and wrinkled it like a ferret. 'I have a nose for the truth, and I seek it eagerly. I refuse to accept everything I am told. As you know, the word heresy comes from the Greek word hairetikos – to choose.'

'Ah yes, but as Saint Isidore wrote, "We are not permitted to believe whatever we choose, nor to choose whatever someone else has believed." Your views are confronting, to say the least.'

'Of course they are, and for that reason, I beg you not to repeat this conversation. There are some on board who would happily see a man of my beliefs thrown from the side.'

'Your secret is safe with me,' I said.

After a long pause he said, 'Are you familiar with the work of Bandarra?'

'Yes, the Shoemaker from Trancoso. I have heard of him.' Indeed I had. Bandarra was an unGodly man, charged by the Inquisition and his works outlawed before his death.

'To understand Bandarra you must go back to the same Saint Isidore you quoted a moment ago. He foretold the arrival of a hidden king – el Encuberto. Then you need to consider a twelfth century Abbott called Joachim of Fiore. He was the first man to postulate than he was living on the cusp of a final age – an Age of Justice. Bandarra also came to believe that mankind was heading towards a new period of glory. Do you remember Daniel's interpretation of Nebuchadnezzar's dream?'

'Of course.' This was an oft cited and mysterious passage from the Bible, yet not one I had made any particular study of.

'Please let me outline it in the context of this discussion; Nebuchadnezzar, the emperor, dreamed of a colossus, a giant statue, with feet of clay, head of gold, belly of bronze, legs of iron and a golden head. When Daniel interpreted that dream, he suggested that each body part represented an empire, the fifth of which was represented by the golden head. This empire will be the greatest of all – will succeed all the others – a merging of the intellectual and spiritual into a near perfect state. The lesser empires of Assyria, Persia, Greece and Rome have all come to be.'

'This is heretical talk,' I hissed.

'No, it is not, please listen. Bandarra was apparently capable of direct communion with God's angel Gabriel, and was told that a great king, the man who would lead the world to this wonderful new state, would campaign in Africa, then be forced to flee.'

'Yes, yes, I have heard some of this—'

'Then surely you can see who he must have been referring to. Who else but Dom Sebastian?'

'Inconclusive.'

'Not so inconclusive. I have spent years studying Bandarra and his forerunners.'

'We are warned to be wary of false prophets. The Inquisition has labelled Bandarra as such a one.'

'And who is the Grand Inquisitor but your good friend Henrique? Which side is right? The one that seeks the truth, or the one that kills and maims those who disagree.'

There was no doubting the sincerity of his words. 'I'll think about what you have said. Perhaps we will talk of this matter again.' With that I called Duarte, for we had wandered far from the protection of our marines, and turned back towards our landing place.

On the third day, the Khoikhoi returned to fulfil the deal they had struck with our king. These compact but proud people – men and women alike – were punctual, for the first warming rays had scarcely struck the beach before they arrived, along with a dozen more of their kind, driving mottled cattle and burdened with woven baskets of wild cabbage, sorrel, mustard leaves, and white flowers.

Duarte displayed his Ribatejo heritage, calming the cattle and bunching them near the boats, talking to the beasts in low tones and clicks of his tongue while other men carried the agreed quantity of trade goods over to the Khoikhoi – glass beads, axe heads, copper wire and cloth.

A swordsman approached a great humpbacked bull, whose dewlaps hung near to the ground. Strings of mucus fell from his nostrils. Despite its fearsome appearance, the animal was as tame as a dog, and did not react until the blade pierced vital organs. At that instant it dropped to its forelegs, bellowing. The butcher, spattered with blood, moved onto the next animal, waiting while it stamped nervously at the smell of death.

As soon as one animal dropped, the cooks swarmed in, cutting away hide and using axes to hack through the rib cage. Fires for smoking a portion of the meat had already been lit, and pickling vats waited. Portions of the meat were cooking, ready to be rowed out to the ship, where people would fill their bellies for the first time in months. The smell of fresh blood, cooking meat, woodsmoke and that peculiar bovine stench was intoxicating.

We were in the process of packing up on the beach when one of the ship's falconets discharged. Another followed seconds after. The emergency recall signal.

'To the oars,' someone shouted.

There are few more potent fears amongst seamen than to be marooned on a remote shore. Our seamen and marines came from all directions, cramming the bench seats, late-comers sprawling over the others. As we were about to cast off a lone grûmete ran from the bushes where he had been relieving himself, holding his breeches in both hands and screaming for us to wait.

The rowers heaved, shoulders straining, tendons proud in their necks and shoulders. The *Nossa Senhora dos Anjos* spun on an unseen axis as men worked the capstan to retrieve the anchor. Dom Sebastian was in a hurry indeed. We reached the hull just as the top sails dropped and filled. Rather than spending time retrieving the barca, our leader ordered a painter to be attached so it would trail from the stern.

'We have a problem,' Dom Sebastian informed me on the quarterdeck.

'What is that?'

'The lookouts have sighted two ships, both about three leagues distant and on a heading to round the Cape.'

'What manner of ships?'

'One is certainly the *Santiago*. The other is known to Dom de Oliveira as the *Santo Espirito*. Henrique's minions have found us again.'

'What do we do?'

'We run unless they force us to turn. I wonder how well they are provisioned, for they cannot stop for fresh water and food like we have done without losing us again.'

The wind did not serve for clearing the bay, and it was necessary to tack back and forth before the sea deepened into a healthy blue and the eastern horizon showed no land. I stood with Dom Sebastian while we ran at speed, with the two pursuers in clear view two leagues or more to the west.

'Perhaps we can scare them into abandoning the pursuit,' de Oliveira suggested.

'How might we manage that?'

'They cannot chase without men fit enough to climb rigging and man guns. Prudence dictates that we take the inner passage to India, hugging the African Coast. Instead we could boldly sail out past São Lourenço and into the heart of the Indian Ocean with the Southern trade winds. I doubt that Simão will wish to follow us for long, and later we can resume our northerly course.'

Dom Sebastian studied the charts for several minutes, scratched his chin and nodded, 'Then that is what we shall do.'

VINTE E CINCO

The stalemate between *Our Lady of Angels* and her two smaller pursuers became a matter of routine over the following days. Sometimes in the darkness, or when a storm thrust its grey fingers between the endless horizons of this great sea, we would think them gone, yet the following morning there they would be, sometimes hull down, showing just the stub of a mast. On other days they loomed close enough to skirmish with the guns.

In this way we journeyed into the northeast, past São Lourenço, crossing the Tropic of Capricorn on the Feast Day of Saint Cyril of Alexandria. On this leg of the journey Rui Chanoca lent me a slim volume of Bandarra's *Trovas*.

This was not a long book, yet each verse required thought and interpretation. I read it through, over and over again, reading in snatches when I was sure no one could see, even secreting the volume beneath my Bible, hiding it particularly from Aletia, who was always interested in what I was reading.

For a week I studied those cryptic lines, until I had some inkling of at least three or four of the more pertinent verses.

Waiting for an opportunity to catch Rui alone, we finally found ourselves in the cabin when the other priests were busy elsewhere. 'I have read it,' I whispered.

'And?'

'Bandarra prophesises that a great king will return to save Portugal, then lead the world to the glory of a Fifth Empire, with Portugal at its head.'

'And who is the great king?'

'It is not conclusive, one way or—'

'No? A man who fought a terrible but losing battle in the Reinos Africanos – the African Kingdoms, and was forced to flee? You call that inconclusive?'

'I do not believe that a man can predict the future.'

'Bandarra is but a mouthpiece for God. Have you not seen enough of war and death to believe that mankind's only hope is to move towards a new age, an age that God has promised us?'

'Please, lower your voice. Give me time to think.'

Rui's eyes became soft and sympathetic. 'Of course, Padre, yet do not think too long, for it is you and I, particularly you, to whom special duties will fall. I know about the meeting that took place before you spirited the True King away from Portugal. The coming together of the first Sebastianists. You must prepare the way for the millions who will follow.'

I backed away, needful of peace and quiet.

Snatching sleep between Compline and Matins, I dreamed of happy and inconsequential things – of springtime in Lisbon, when the air is filled with the scent of flowers, and girls walk in happy groups down by the square. Then, for the first time in many years I dreamed of she who I had loved so many years before. Images of her as she was when I first met her – eyes as large as trochus shells. I went deep into her arms and was smiling as I slept.

I am old now, but I recall her smell, her smile. No one can take that from me, or cheapen the memory. I welcome such dreams when they come, and that night I walked with her, hand in hand, in a fantasy that I would have happily dwelt inside of for the rest of my days.

When I did wake, however, it was not only to the usual sense of loss. As I came to my senses, I caught a scent of smoke – so faint it might have been a guttered candle, or mere imagination. I sat upright and swung my legs off the bed, dressing quickly.

As I did so I heard a faint and muffled shout, 'Fire! Smoke! Fire!'

Leaving the cabin, the smell of smoke intensified as I hurried towards the captain's stateroom. Others were waking now, and making for the deck. Once or twice I had to push my way through a press of bodies.

Approaching the stateroom the door opened and Tonio, followed by Dom Sebastian, appeared in the gloom.

'Can you smell it?' I asked.

Dom Sebastian flared at this pointless question. 'Why else would I be creeping through the ship at this time of the morning?'

Together, bent over like crones, we ran through to the steerage room. The helmsman, sweating and strong, overdeveloped arms bulging with muscles like newly-washed potatoes, looked up at Dom Sebastian. 'I heard men shout of fire, what shall I do?'

'Stay at your post until you are told otherwise. Do you smell smoke?'

His nostrils twitched like those of a dog seeking a scent. 'No. Not yet. I merely heard the cries.'

The steerage room, of course, was a well-ventilated area, open to the sky. Rather than returning to the cabin, we continued through into the lower gun deck. Most of the inhabitants were sleeping, yet some still played dice, or sat in small groups, talking. Some had gathered near the main hatch, talking urgently, relieved when they saw us approach.

'There is smoke, Dom Sebastian,' a young midshipman said. 'Growing stronger by the minute.'

'Was it you who raised the alarm?'

'Yes.'

'Well done. Now all of you. Do not panic,' Dom Sebastian soothed them, 'but wake those who are asleep and go up on deck – just as a precaution.' Then he picked out the midshipman again. 'Run to the quarterdeck and tell Senhor Elfo that there may be a fire. Tell him to turn into the wind and stop us cold, then get every idle soul on deck. Tell him to get twenty men shifting powder from the magazine.' As soon as these words were out, our leader strode for the companion ladder and descended into the dark void below. Tonio followed behind him, silent and dark, then myself, in the rear.

The smell of smoke intensified on the cable deck, but still we descended further, into the hold itself, where we faced a blinding, choking mist of smoke – and the first flames – leaping from the dunnage into wooden crates and barrels of pitch, blazing so hot it seared my skin. We all knew that the powder magazine was at the forward end of the hold, protected by a few inches of stout timber. If fire should penetrate through, the resulting explosion would gut our ship like a fish.

A cloaked figure came from nowhere, barging at Dom Sebastian with his shoulder. The young warrior recovered, stepping into the hold, drawing his sword in preparation for his assailant, who produced his own weapon and went on the attack, shoes clicking on the stone ballast that made up the floor of the hold.

Dom Sebastian met the first attack with a simple parry, stepping back until he was at the limit of usable space. The hold was packed with stores for the outposts, and trading goods held in crate and bale, along with hundreds of water pipes and food stocks. There was also that plain coffin, the contents of which had been on my mind since the first hint of fire.

Tonio also drew his blade, but Dom Sebastian shouted, 'No, leave him. He is mine.'

The treacherous fire-lighter, even to my untutored eyes, was an enthusiastic though unskilled swordsman. Dom Sebastian, sensing this, moved onto the front foot, forcing his opponent into the heat and clutter of the hold. The hooded man swung wildly as he retreated, however, and the True King sucked in his belly so that the razor edge barely flicked his shirt.

Dom Sebastian's response was to extend himself and offer a similar shot, but at neck level. The hooded adversary ducked, flexing his knees and thus passing under the blade. The movement, however, forced the cloak to fall away and for his face to be revealed. He was little more than a child – almost certainly one of the many stowaways that hid in the shadows of the ship.

Dom Sebastian struck, and the point caught the youth on the breastbone, driving inside like a skewer. Slowly, he fell, as if drugged with opium.

Kneeling beside the dying youth, I prayed that he would live long enough to answer my questions. 'Why did you try to kill Dom Sebastian? Who hired you?' I asked. 'Who paid you to light the fire?'

'The one … from … Leal,' he gasped, eyes as round and shining like newly minted silver coins.

Tonio took over, scowling, grasping the youth's shoulders and shaking them violently, 'What is the man's name?'

This violent movement, however, only hastened the blood flow, and I watched as the youth's eyes widened in fear of death, then all life left them, and his head slumped to one side.

I turned to Tonio, 'Well done. You killed him.'

'I am sorry, but I am angry. Look what he has done! Look at the fire!'

'Both of you stop,' Dom Sebastian said. 'There are more important matters now. Help me. We have to flood the hold – nothing else will extinguish this blaze.'

'How do we do that?' I knew that he had been involved in the design of this ship – if anyone knew how to save her, he would.

'We open the cocks at the stern. Follow me.'

We ran together, in a bent over fashion, mindful of massive squared-off beams and stopping to clamber over pipes or crates. Together we reached the place where the fire blazed thickest. Dom Sebastian threw his woollen coat over the narrowest stretch of flame, then tumbled over, grunting with pain as he did so. With the Lord's name on my lips I followed, my eyelashes and brows igniting in the terrible heat.

By firelight I saw Dom Sebastian's hand on the brass mechanism of the sea cocks. The wheel that controlled it was stuck fast.

'Help me,' he shouted. In response I fell to my knees and gripped the wheel with all my strength. Tonio beside me did the same. The wheel turned, and a jet of water blasted through. 'More,' Dom Sebastian shouted. One full circle later, and the water became a solid jet as thick as a man's thigh.

'Can we go?'

Dom Sebastian shook his head, and shouted to be heard. 'No, we need to turn it off again when the fire is out, or we will swamp the ship. Stay with me.'

From further up the hold we heard shouts, but since no one came, it seemed that they had not been able to cross the barrier of flame. The water, however, was soon knee deep, hissing against the burning crates.

'Help the water do its work,' Dom Sebastian shouted.

'How? What do you mean?'

Already he had moved across to the nearest flames, splashing water with his cupped hands so that they spluttered and extinguished. Empty pipes, spare timbers and small crates floated in the rising water, some still burning, extinguished only as the water seeped upwards through timber or cloth.

Other men burst through the barrier of fire. Some had buckets, and standing thigh deep in water worked with constant scooping and splashing action. I looked back in alarm at the rising waters.

'We have to stop the water,' I shouted.

Half swimming, staggering, weak from smoke and fatigue, we moved towards the sea cock. The water was at my neck, eyes and nose burning from the bitter smoke.

Taking a lungful of smoke-filled air, Dom Sebastian dived. I was paralysed by then. I could not have helped even if I wanted to. Finally, he surfaced, and I gasped with relief.

'Is it done?' I shouted.

'Yes, it is closed.'

I was almost at the limit of my strength when I felt a pull on my collar. Dom Sebastian dragged me through the water until I found myself on the floor of the cable deck surrounded by a dozen crouching men. His face was heavy with worry, and not just for me.

It dawned on me then that the fire had caused us to float uselessly, and that the enemy ships must surely be almost upon us. Lighting that blaze was a dastardly act indeed.

I turned to one side and vomited, wishing I was ten thousand leagues away from there.

Hours passed. The stink of smoke and burning trade goods filled the ship with an insidious, choking mist that brought tears to the eyes. Bucket chains of men arrested the flames spreading upwards from the hold, while the intentional flooding had doused the main blaze below. Rotating teams on the pumps laboured to empty the holds of water.

I stood on the quarterdeck with Dom Sebastian, while he whispered orders to junior officers. We knew that the enemy ships had closed on us while we fought the fire. An attack might come at any moment.

Apart from the usual sounds of ship and sea, I heard a faint rustle as fifty or more seamen climbed aloft in the dark, working silently, draping the massive boarding net from the masts to cover both sides of the deck. Others ran forward to lash it to every available anchor point.

Marines stood at their stations, Tonio at their head, grim faced and dark – solid and reassuring. The verso were manned. Down on the gun decks every weapon had been run out. Men stood ready for orders. Enemy lookouts would have seen the glow of our fire, and even now must be creeping upon us in the darkness.

Orders had been given that any man showing a light, or making excessive noise would be flogged. Even the grûmete who came to report on the progress of the pumps whispered, 'Still twelve span in the hold.'

Dom Sebastian's voice was low and harsh. 'Tell them to hurry. Tell Senhor Elfo to rotate the teams more often if necessary, but lift the rate. We need to make way as soon as possible.'

The wind had been rising through the evening. Now a sudden gust rocked the ship and sang through the rigging, causing our impatience to increase – with only a hint of canvas we could soon be sailing away from danger at great speed, instead we waited, helpless and vulnerable.

Dom Sebastian and Tonio clasped arms in the darkness. 'You are my brother, for my father was father to you also,' the former said softly, 'and together, as brothers we will fight and win.'

'We are indeed brothers,' Tonio agreed, 'and the kindness of your father has never left my thoughts.' There was a strange emphasis on the word kindness that confused me, but there was no time to remark or ponder, for de Oliveira pointed out into the night. Seconds passed before the enemy ship became visible – not so much a shape or a colour, but a greater darkness against the clouded sky. The sound of creaking ropes and timbers filtered out across the water.

I prayed that the other vessel might pass without seeing us, but I knew that was a vain hope. The tension in my heart rose to the intensity of a cable under strain, and when I saw Duarte approaching along the deck I snapped at him.

'Get below, boy. Soon there will be a fight. Wait in my cabin.'

I half expected him to argue, but he nodded his head and went below, just as Dom Sebastian ordered the match on the muskets to be lit. A burning torch was passed from hand to hand and matches spluttered to life, filling the air with sulphurous fumes and dangerous sparks.

The arming of these dangerous but efficacious weapons was

scarcely complete when someone shouted, 'Take cover.'

A heartbeat later the *Santiago*'s broadside swept across our deck – twelve spouts of flame – perfectly aimed and aligned, firing a mixture of ball and grapeshot designed to kill and maim as well as shred the rigging and wreak physical damage on the ship. I had heard what it is like to face a broadside from another ship, yet could never have known the feeling until that moment. It came at point blank range, smashing into our sides. Teak splinters flew in all directions. Men screamed. The concussive force kicked me to my knees. My ears rang as if the bells of the Sé enveloped my skull. Smoke washed against our deck like storm clouds around a mountain, and burned gunpowder stung my eyes and nose. I felt the thump of shot striking the hull low down, near or below the waterline. A plume of water erupted, drenching much of the deck.

Now came our reply – another burst of cannonfire that shook the ship. Already great damage had been done. The sight of those tongues of flame in the night filled my heart with fear, and for the first time I understood what Saint John's Beast from the Sea must have looked like. The *Santiago* was its very image, rising from the dark waters, spewing forth fire and death. Men screamed and wailed, and a yard fell from the foremast, dropping like a tree to the axe.

Light rain had begun to fall, I noted, as with a squeal of grating timbers the enemy ship came alongside. A hundred men waited ready to board us, grinning hideously in the night, screaming their war cries across the night as they hefted pikes and swords.

A verso fired from our aftercastle and tore a swathe of bloody carnage through the enemy ranks. Fresh boarders appeared from behind their fallen comrades. As those dozens of men crossed the darkness I wondered how even our staunch marines could stand against them.

Then, however, I realised the efficacy of our simple plaited boarding net, for the enemy fell headlong into the unseen strands, and were tangled, while our defenders cut them down. Our muskets extracted a deadly toll, and archers and crossbowmen fired down from the fore and aft castles.

My eyes focussed on one of the enemy fighters, and my mind went back to that terrible night at the Port of Faro when we were overwhelmed. Now, though we had the numbers and the preparation, still the foe struck fear deep in my heart. One man near me balanced on the rail and scythed his way through the net, screaming as he did so, baring his teeth like a carnivore. One of our marines engaged the man, piercing him through the throat so that he died with a gurgle of pain, falling back and disappearing in the narrow gap between the two hulls.

The carnage did not last, and the *Santiago* drifted away. Even those of their fighters who had managed to slash through the net jumped back to their shipmates in the darkness.

A murderous sound came on our starboard beam. This was the *Santo Espirito*, spewing fire and iron. Our guns, replying, shook the hull, yet I watched our retribution on that ship, holes appearing, planks flying, stays parting and yards falling, crashing to the deck, men mown down as if by an invisible hand. It seemed to me that our cannon fire had been more accurate than theirs, and the damage to the smaller ship much greater. The long days of practice had been justified, indeed.

Their next broadside was less effective than the first, and I could only imagine the damage our aimers had wrought on their gundeck. Even so, the gut thumping feel of shot thudding into our hull sickened my heart.

A trick of the wind exposed the *Santo Espirito* to our broadside, and with most of our guns still firing, the damage wreaked was almost impossible to see at first through the clouds of smoke, and the fires that had sprung up all over her deck. Men were diving overboard in numbers. The mainmast fell, crushing the remains of the aftercastle beneath her as she went. I felt sick at the destruction of so many of my countrymen.

I was no passive observer, but attended to wounded men, and helped souls on their journey to the loving arms of our Father. In the near darkness I bent over a screaming man. The lantern I carried made me a target yet I needed light to do my work. I pinned him by the shoulders, and felt blood splatter my arms. A charge of grapeshot had hit his face, ripping much of his cheek away.

The sound of his agony emitted from a gaping and bloody hole. I touched the man's forehead and murmured a benediction. There was no hope of saving him.

'They are not trying to sink us,' Dom Sebastian said. 'They want me, and something else that I will not name.'

Another volley swept across the quarterdeck, followed by the hideous cries of stricken men. The boards were slippery beneath my feet. I found Dom de Oliveira choking on the blood in his lungs. The only visible injuries were neat puncture wounds in his chest where individual shot had penetrated. One hand on his shoulder, one on his waist, I rolled that noble man on his side. Blood trickled from his mouth, clearing his lungs, but I knew that he was lost to us.

Musket fire sounded over the screams and shouts. The occasional blasts of falcon gun and verso overrode the melee, and gunfire flashed like lightning. Out in the darkness, however, the *Santo Espirito* was awash and sinking, fires flaring through her sails and rigging. The wind was stronger now, and rain fell on puddles of blood on the deck.

Dawn came so rapidly that the sea went from dark indigo to translucent blue in a matter of minutes. That eerie twilight illuminated the bows, carved as they were into the likeness of gorgons, dragons, cherubs and angels by the craftsmen of Baçaim. Slowly the rain parted and I looked beyond the bowsprit, that great spar of solid teak that aimed like a weapon at the horizon.

The lookout screamed his warning, and at that same moment I saw the tall masts and dull gunports of the *Santiago*, emerging from the mist of rain, drifting broadside and vulnerable, beam to the seas less than a cable's length ahead, plucking survivors from the *Santo Espirito* out of the water.

Elfo shouted orders that sent men scrambling to hoist what sail they could in an attempt to give him steerage. 'We will finish it now,' he told Dom Sebastian. 'We are in position to ram them.'

'No,' Dom Sebastian cried, 'the *Santiago* is picking up men from the water. They will drown otherwise. They are Portuguese men after all.' The code of chivalry was planted deep in his psyche, and this time I agreed with him.

'Listen to me, please,' Elfo urged. 'They have pursued you half way across the world – they will not stop.'

I added my voice to the discussion, agreeing with Dom Sebastian. 'They will not follow, not now, surely. These are our countrymen. We have a responsibility not to do as they would do to us.'

'With all respect, have you been down below to look?' Elfo persisted, 'the enemy guns have raked our lower decks from stem to stern – it is a place of blood and death. Have you seen the bloody bodies laid out in the waist? Let these murderers die also.'

'Steer away, I command you,' Dom Sebastian said. 'I will not ram.'

Bellowed orders carried over the maelstrom of battle. The hull swung, though for some moments we seemed not to turn fast enough to avoid a collision. Even in those seconds a part of me hoped that we might destroy them yet. At the last, however, a stronger gust of wind heeled us to the port side and made us miss by a cable-length.

As we passed by, achingly slowly, friend and foe stared at each other across that patch of churning ocean, shook their fists and shouted out their anger and fear – their remorse at those we had lost in a war cry that left a lasting impression on my soul.

Even as Elfo was calling for a damage report I turned to look at the wounded and injured on the deck. The médico and his assistants moved amongst them, bandaging and comforting.

I was about to return to assist with their care when my eyes fell on Dom Sebastian. He was easing down into a sitting position. His face changed, eyes staring, mouth opening as if he could no longer breathe through his nose.

'Dom Sebastian,' I called.

Turning to look at me, he crumpled completely. By the time his head hit the deck I was with him, cradling one arm in my hand. Tonio arrived beside me. I turned to him, 'For the love of God, help me.'

When I looked down at Dom Sebastian's eyes I knew that this time there was nothing I could do to stop it from happening.

Fortunately, however, it did not start until Dom Sebastian had been carried to his cabin and I had locked and secured the door. As he lay, spreadeagled on the bed, he began bleeding from both hands and both feet, moaning the pain of the Saviour.

'Oh dear Father,' I muttered. I crossed myself and fell to my knees, for this was a scene I had witnessed just three times since the day of Dom Sebastian's birth, and each time it had shaken me to the core.

The room appeared to fill with light as the young man began to mimic Christ's wounds from the cross, jerking and crying in pain. Blood seeped from a hidden wound in his side. Tears streamed down his face as he felt the agony of the son of God made mortal by His Father's hand.

Still it continued, bleeding from his hands, feet, brow and abdomen. I moved forward and embraced him, rocking, kissing his bloody brow. I touched the crown of his head with the tips of my fingers, trying to feel his power, ready for what I knew would come next.

Look down upon me, good and gentle Jesus, while before your face I humbly kneel, and with burning soul, pray and beseech thee ...

The weeping began with the gentle flow of a rivulet, gathering momentum until it became a river wider and faster than a snow-fed deluge of spring. At times he would cease breathing altogether until with a jerk of that great chest he would draw a rasping slab of air, his eyes staring into space like those of a deer struck by a hunter's arrow.

Even though I was prepared, the next stage was harrowing beyond the bearing of it, for the intervals without breath grew longer each time. At those times the skin of his face and neck turned blue before he again found breath and the great lungs rose and fell inside the massive rib cage.

By then, I too, was weeping, mumbling scraps of scripture and childishly comforting phrases beneath my breath. Deeper into the passion he fell, and I followed as a brother might guard his sibling in a terrible battle, wiping bloody perspiration away with my palm, kissing his cheeks and hands, seeking to supplement his strength with my own at every turn.

Finally, with his eyes still closed he began to speak. To my surprise I found that he was addressing that great friend of his childhood and early youth, Alvora de Castro; not a strong boy like Tonio, but one who was slightly built, his arms like those of a girl.

Yet, Alvora had a way with words. Already a fine poet, he was perhaps destined to be a great one, before a seemingly routine fever stole his life. It was only these strange rants that held any clue to how much Dom Sebastian missed him.

When the crisis was over, Dom Sebastian slept, at peace now. Blood no longer flowed from his skin. Praying in silence, I tackled the twenty mysteries of the Rosary. While the afternoon light lingered, I read the book of St John aloud, beginning with the Parable of the Shepherd.

By the time I had finished Aletia had forced her way into the room. She took a more practical approach, forcing liquid between his unresponsive lips, and requesting soup from the kitchens. To her credit she asked no questions, but took the True King into her care, as she would have any sickly orphan.

Later, he began muttering to himself – snatches of half real words – mingled Latin and Portuguese and some language of childhood that cannot be understood by any but the speaker. Abruptly, however, these unconscious sounds ceased, and the young king slept. It was after midnight when I chased Aletia off to bed and dozed in a chair myself.

The next morning Rui Chanoca offered me some insight

into the True King's mysterious affliction. He knocked on the cabin door as the sun rose, and I allowed him to enter watching him examine Dom Sebastian's sleeping face in that muted glow. When he was done he sat beside me. 'Tell me, please. What happened?'

I shared with Rui secrets that I had never discussed with any man, not even Dom Sebastian himself. I struggled for words to describe what I knew, yet welcomed the opportunity to discuss the young man and the stigmata that affected him so powerfully. Rambling somewhat, I did my best to inform Rui of what I had seen.

When I had finished he clasped his hands over his heart. 'There can no longer be any doubt,' he announced. 'Only a man so touched by the Lord could be entrusted with the honour of ushering in a new age. Dom Sebastian is indeed O Encuberto, the hidden king. Did you note the words of Bandarra? "Do leao, e seu bramido, demonstra que vai ferido, desse bom rei encuberto – the lion, and its roar, shows that it is wounded, this good hidden king." In other words, does he roar so loud, so purposefully pursue the manly arts because he is wounded inside? I think we agree that his life has not been an easy one, with expectations placed upon him even before birth. Who knows what else might have occurred behind those palace walls? Is there something deep inside his mind that he cannot speak of, not bear to think of?'

The idea of a wounded lion made me thoughtful. 'What do you mean?'

Rui stroked his chin so that I heard his beard rasp over the skin of his palm. 'I mean that from what you have told me of his uncle and his former tutor … well, men who are willing to send twenty thousand men to their death in order to seize power … what else might their perverted minds have done with a small boy in their care?'

My chest rose and fell in my effort to find breath. 'You are suggesting that—'

'Yes Padre, I am suggesting that he was mistreated, and also that this was prophesised in the *Trovas*. We cannot, however, be sure of the exact nature of that mistreatment.'

Looking down at the sleeping Dom Sebastian I felt a wave of tenderness for him. 'Most men can empathise with the pain of others, yet Dom Sebastian feels the agony of Christ himself. The deepest melancholy of all. How many men would have shoulders broad enough to do so?'

Rui clasped my shoulder, 'I will leave you now to ponder. I feel the need of sunshine on my face.'

'On your way,' I asked, 'would you tell Aletia that she may return again? Tell her to bring some books.'

'Love is the greatest healer of all,' he said on the way out, and I saw that his face was bright with mischief.

More than one hundred cadavers were sewn up in canvas for burial. These were merely the more significant among the dead, for countless bodies of seamen and slaves had already been pitched overboard without ceremony. This was a sombre time, and the deck resounded to terrible wailing. So many good mariners were already dead. Dom de Oliveira, particularly, was a huge loss, for his good sense and decency.

Under the tireless direction of Dom Sebastian, who rose, seemingly without ill effect from his bed, the carpenters conscripted another twenty helpers and much of the cosmetic battle damage was swiftly repaired. Sailmakers patched canvas, and men learned to carry out the duties of their missing comrades. The many dead could not be brought back, and nor could the serious leak below the waterline be fothered while at sea, despite numerous attempts. The pumps worked continuously to quell the rising tide of seawater.

'What will we do?' I asked.

'There is only one thing that might help,' Elfo growled, 'and it is a last resort. We must stop the ship and frap her.'

Frapping the ship required heavy cables to be drawn under the hull, and volunteers were first required to dive with lighter cords, called messengers. To this effect Elfo stood on the quarterdeck rail, and called for all those who were good swimmers by repute, or known to enjoy dangerous work. These men milled together, laughing, egging each other on.

'The hull is deep, and crusted with barnacles and sea moss,' Elfo explained, 'I need two men who can swim, who are not afraid of sea creatures, and can dive down and pass under the keel without scraping the skin off their arses on the barnacles. Can any man here do that and bring up a line on the other side?'

This was indeed a dangerous undertaking, and the field narrowed, blank looks exchanged. The more timid slipped back down the companionway. Elfo, eyeing the remainder, was experienced enough to sort the pretenders from the competent. He chose a lithe young Malay, and a long, lean fisherman's son from Nazare.

Lengths of cord were dragged up from the hold, and the two volunteers stripped to the waist.

'A new centi coin on the string-bean surfacing first,' one sailor shouted, and an eager exchange of wagers followed.

Elfo had chosen his men well, for it was a pleasure to watch them dive from the side, down fifty span and into the water, the messenger cord streaming from their waists.

The divers used arms and feet to drive themselves deeply into the water. This was no easy feat, for the ship's keel was far below the surface. As soon as they disappeared from view, with only the rope rattling down into the water, the spectators rushed from that side of the ship to the other to watch.

At least a minute passed with nothing but an occasional bubble suggesting that there was someone beneath. The Malay was the first to appear, to a chorus of cheers from his mates, and groans from the others. The fisherman, however, was not far behind, both soon scrambling up the gunports and over the rail, squatting on deck, chests heaving, accepting the congratulations of their comrades happily.

Next the cables were brought up – hempen ropes as thick as my arms and stiff as wire. Expert splicers attached the messengers to each of the larger cables and thus a dozen heaving men pulled the cables around the hull.

Finally, each rope in turn was attached to the capstan, that great mechanical wheel most often used for hauling in the anchors. Now, however, with a dozen men sweating and straining, it was used to draw ropes around the hull – much like the girdle of a woman, pulling the timbers tight and closing gaps.

When it was done Elfo expressed himself satisfied. 'That will slow the leak,' he said, 'God willing for long enough to find land and repair her properly.'

The *Santiago*, despite the mercy we had shown to her and all aboard, pursued us like a terrier. Now and then she would loom within range and open fire with her bow chasers. Most of the time the shot would fly wide and our men cheer. Our own guns would respond, most usually with a similar result.

Fresh food, taken on at Cape Town, was now exhausted, and the original provisions were all but spoiled. The net result, with four hundred hungry mouths to feed, was a tightening of rations to a point few of us, even those of us who had lived in monasteries, had ever experienced. Hunger became a new enemy, claws deep in one's back, breathing over the shoulder all night and day, sucking pleasure from the day like a parasite.

Dom Sebastian seemed preoccupied during this time, wandering the deck, deep in thought. Then, one morning he woke with a wide grin for which I could discern no reason, considering our dire situation. From childhood, nothing has delighted him more thoroughly than to have a plan with which to demonstrate his own cleverness.

After the day's Psalm was delivered from the forecastle he sequestered himself with the ship's carpenters, led by the masterful Leonel de Amoral.

The craftsmen and their assistants were soon busy hauling timber out of the holds, along with buckets of pitch, nails and various tools. Slowly, an object took shape that could only be described as a small boat, not much longer than a man, yet designed to be seaworthy, with a deep keel, hard chines and high gunnels.

Often, that day, in between caring for the sick and leading prayers for those who needed them I called back to see how the mysterious craft was progressing. By the middle afternoon the sail maker had rigged a single, square sail, lashed in place. The craft would thus be pushed downwind by whatever breeze might be available.

'Surely,' I joked with Dom Sebastian, 'you have not gone to all this trouble for a toy.' My tone was guarded for it was not inconceivable that he would do such a thing.

Shaking his head, still he would tell me nothing of what he intended, though my suspicions firmed as the blacksmiths affixed a solid iron hook to the diminutive mast, and hung from it a brass ship's lantern.

That night, sailing into the dark sky of a new moon the crew hung this new vessel from the davits under the direction of Dom Sebastian. It was a work of art, really, smelling of pitch and fresh-sawn teak. By then I had a reasonable idea of what the plan entailed.

At the last minute I saw Tonio climbing up onto the little vessel, carrying a small wooden bowl that he placed inside. This done, he jumped back on board ship, a huge and uncharacteristic smile on his face.

'What was it?' I asked. 'What cargo does our tiny ship carry?'

Tonio smiled broadly, and raised his voice so all around could hear. 'Our good ship carries a nicely formed turd, still steaming, from my chamber pot. This is a gift from me should the enemy have the opportunity to hoist her aboard.'

'The good ship *Excrementa*,' someone shouted, 'let us name her so.' Others clapped and clamoured at this good natured, if somewhat childish and repulsive humour. The mood was thus buoyant as the last preparations were made.

'Now,' shouted Dom Sebastian. Instantly, one man extinguished our ship's lantern, while another, on this toy boat, was lit.

The crew removed the ropes from the cleats, and our creation, lit up to resemble our own great ship, dropped towards the water. Dom Sebastian halted the procedure a mere span or two from the surface, waiting while his seamen performed a dozen final tasks. With the final order, 'Escorregar – slip,' the boat, lantern shining bright, entered the water with scarcely a splash.

At first it failed to move, but that was because our own massive hull blocked the wind from reaching the sail. As we moved away, however, it rocked once, then pulsed off towards the north-east in a businesslike fashion. There was no time to enjoy the view, however, for Dom Sebastian was already on the quarterdeck, where Elfo relayed a new course.

There was a new purpose in the crew, breathless and awed at the audacity and cleverness of their leader, knowing that they were witnessing something special, a trick they would one day recount to their grandchildren, should they live for such a happy moment as telling them of the night Dom Sebastian outwitted Henrique's guarda-costras and their ship's commander, sending them after a tiny decoy.

The wind now came on the stern quarter as Dom Sebastian ordered us to sail at the widest possible angle to the wind, thus distancing us from the trick boat as rapidly as possible. For an hour we could still see it, out in the darkness to the north, like some fallen star. When it had all but disappeared we saw another pinprick, and before long it was obvious that the *Santiago* had indeed followed our decoy.

Slowly, both lights faded into nothing. I was at Dom Sebastian's side as we searched the horizon for a final glimpse.

'It is gone,' he said at last.

'Do you think your ploy will work for long?'

It is amazing just how much light the stars alone can provide.

I saw enough – the flash of his teeth, and shining eyes, to know how pleased he was with himself. 'We will see,' he said, 'but from now we sail without lights.'

'Where to from here?' I asked.

'Land! Even now, the pumps can scarce keep pace with the leaks. Without safe anchorage to repair the hull we are doomed.'

As we sailed east I made surreptitious enquiries about the identity of the man from Leal, the one who had apparently hired the youthful pyromaniac who had almost ended the voyage for all of us with a fire.

Since Leal is an inland village, few men on board hailed from that place. After weeks of searching I had found only one man who was known to have lived there, and he was a lowly seaman of few wits. Under questioning, he wept like a child, and was so moronic that I could only pity him.

My enquiries proved fruitless, and were, after a while, buried by the more pressing matters of our position and likelihood of reaching land at any time soon. Our hull was in need of repair. We needed safe harbour, and urgently.

Nuno, the pilot, fortuitously among the living, and still in possession of his balestilha and charts, had tracked our eastward movement by taking his sights each noon, and measuring our drift with fragments of wood tossed over the side. Every few days, cloistered in a circle of friends, we studied the Indian Ocean and Nuno's estimates of our position. The chart showed our journey along the fifteenth parallel, sailing from the coast of Africa, across a thousand leagues of emptiness.

Given how relentlessly we had been pursued it was not possible for us to steer north to our colonies, even Timor. without intelligence of what fate might await us there. A place away from civilisation to regroup and repair seemed to be the best choice.

Nuno pointed on his chart to the incomplete outline of a land both large and mysterious.

This land was not unknown to me, for geography was our national passion. Parts of the large land mass to the south-east of Java had long appeared in our mariner's charts.

Speculation about this Austral land had begun back in the time of the Greek geographer Ptolemy. Two thousand years later Marco Polo fed public interest with his stories of a greater Java – Jave-la-Grande or Grão-Java, south of the Indies. Maps had often shown this Jave-la-Grande as an indistinct outline.

My own countrymen referred to this place as the India Meriodonal, or at times, by the fanciful title of the Isles of Gold. Our knowledge of it came from centuries of conjecture and experience gleaned from sources as diverse as the Chinese and Makassarese. Spaces in old charts had been filled with imaginative images of men ploughing fields, exotic princesses, and animals so bizarre they must have sprung from the artist's imagination.

Dom Sebastian's face showed the excitement of an adventurer. 'The Austral land – I never imagined that I might sail towards those shores. How far is it?'

'One week, more if God hoards the wind.'

'There is yet another name for that place,' I said, 'I have heard men call it Patalie Regio.'

Dom Sebastian raised his eyebrows. 'What does that mean?'

The trembling corners of my lips indicated my trepidation. 'The nether regions – hell itself.'

VINTE E SEIS

Francis had, while the dawn light still showed the ship's outline in stark relief, laid cairns of stones to mark the extremities and main features of the shape under the dunes. That precaution proved to be wise, for later in the day the site looked hardly prepossessing.

'I don't know, Francis,' said Nicolá. 'Now the beach looks the same to me as it did yesterday – no sign of any ship.'

'Right now it looks like that to me too,' Francis said. 'It seems to need the low-angle light of sunrise to fill the hollows.' He led the way up onto the dunes. 'If I'm right the hull is lying to one side, and we're standing on the waist area.'

'My God,' Nicolá smiled. 'That means the boat is huge. Perhaps fifty metres?'

'Maybe a little more. Remember that she carried six hundred crew and passengers.'

'I can hardly believe it.'

'Neither can I. Not just yet.' Francis said. 'Time to see what lies under the surface.'

Fetching the augur from the boat, Francis walked along the length of the marked-out hull, first in one direction, then in the other. The sea was a calm and glittering blanket past the beach.

Brows knitted together he made a decision and started walking back to the south, at which point he climbed to a flat little mount. 'This is as good as anywhere, let's see what's down here.'

The augur had been made to order from an Adelaide engineering firm, the business end of smaller diameter than the usual post-hole borers found in garden sheds, and the handle longer. This allowed it to bite quickly into the sand.

The problem was that those first layers were too soft to be lifted by the tool, and Francis had to fall to his hands and knees to scoop it out after a few twists.

'Here, let me do that,' Nicolá offered, and her help sped them through that first layer before the substrate became more stable, and the tool worked more effectively.

As the augur descended, the handle became lower relative to his body, and Francis was able to bring more of his upper body weight to bear, increasing the speed of the descent. The pile of spoil grew, and they waited, hoping for the hard impact of the augur on wood, but the steel teeth continued to bite through the sand.

'We've got a charcoal zone,' Francis called once. 'A thick one.' But there was no edge of excitement to his voice. The remnants of old fires were to be expected in almost any soil profile. 'Okay, through that. Plain sand again.'

By then Francis was on his knees, driving the augur deeper, twisting the blade with frustrated strokes, lifting it to dump the spoil, driving the blade around until his knuckles drew circles in the sand. He lifted the tool, releasing a final load.

'Looks like more charcoal now.'

'Maybe the hull was burned,' said Nicolá.

'That's a possibility.' Francis lifted the augur and strode back to the middle of the area he had marked out. Again he dropped the augur into place, spread his feet and began to work on the handle. He stopped for a moment.

'There's a sieve with our stores, would you go and get it?'

Returning a few minutes later she began to sift through the spoil as Francis continued to drill the augur deeply into the beach sands.

The sun was warm, and Francis stopped to strip off his shirt, already sheathed with sweat, clinging as he attempted to peel it away from his skin. Then, the muscles of his arms and shoulders flexing, he went back to work.

'More of that charred layer,' Nicolá announced, but the augur was getting close to full depth.

For the third attempt Francis moved just a few metres away. The sun continued to grow in ferocity, radiating up from the sand.

This time not even that dark, soft layer broke the monotony. Just dry sand dumped in a heap beside the hole. Francis felt cheated.

'We should get a plan going.' said Nicolá. 'Mark each of the holes.'

'Yes, good idea. And later we could launch the little camera drone and get an overhead shot.'

Francis looked down at the hole he had made then lifted the augur, walking back down towards the furthest extremity. He dropped the tool and leaned on the handles.

Nicolá looked up from the second hole. 'I'm getting a few wood fragments, I'll start bagging and marking them.'

A moment later, for the first time, Francis felt real resistance to the augur. They both heard it, but almost as soon as he backed off the pressure the teeth were through. He lifted the augur out of the hole and dumped the load. More of what they had been calling the charred layer.

'What is it?' Nicolá asked the question.

'It's the same thing,' Francis said. He lifted a semi-hard mass from the spoil and held it close to his eyes, pushing his sunglasses up onto his head. 'But I don't think this layer is all charred. Some appears to be wood that's rotted and dried out again.

'Can you see a grain, what kind is it?' They both knew what they were looking for. Two main timbers had been used for the construction of Portuguese ships in the Age of Discovery – oak from Portugal, or teak from India.

Francis tried to dismiss his most dramatic fantasies. 'It's most likely just a layer of dune driftwood that caught fire when a bush-fire pushed almost to the sea.'

'Of course it is,' agreed Nicolá.

That night, working through bags of samples on the camp table, Nicolá helped Francis prepare razor-thin slices for the dissecting microscope. Within an hour they reached consensus that the charred wood layer, as they were now calling it, was consistent across the site.

'I was right,' he said. 'The wood is charred in places, but basically it's just rotten.'

The samples, however, were too degraded to be definitive.

'I'm pretty sure it's teak,' Francis said softly. 'But we'll send it for final tests of course.'

Finally, however, one of the larger chunks of rotten timber yielded something that time and the elements could not degrade.

Nicolá's blade touched something hard within the chunk.

'Hey, there's something in here.'

Francis dragged his seat closer and watched while she started to shave away at the area, aware that he was breathing audibly.

Finally, the clinging tissue of rotten wood parted and something dark grey, almost black, clunked to the surface of the table. Francis lifted it between thumb and forefinger and examined it closely. Misshapen and heavy it told him more than any expert on medieval woods could have.

'What is it?' Nicolá breathed.

Francis couldn't answer, but a tear dripped down the side of his face and landed on the sand. He was conscious of Nicolá craning forward until she understood.

'Oh, wow. That's incredible.'

Before he knew it, she went into his arms, her lips close to the skin of his neck. 'I knew that we would find something concrete,' she said, 'but not so quickly.'

The lead musket ball, embedded in rotten hull timbers, courtesy of some long-ago sea battle or mutiny, was a strong artefact. After that, the presence of the ancient ship took just half a day to confirm. At first with shovels, and then with brushes and air blowers they shifted sand away from the tilted deck. Exposed like this, every aspect of the half-millennia-old planking was plain, from knotholes, to the grooves between them.

By evening, they had revealed at least four square metres of charred and rotted planking, and a kind of awed silence had descended over both Francis and Nicolá. After the tools were washed down and put away he lit a bright campfire and opened a bottle of champagne that he had not expected to open until later in the expedition.

'This is beyond us,' Francis said, pouring two mugs full of the bubbling liquid. 'We don't have the ability to even begin this dig. There's twelve months work here. Careful and exacting work for a large team – a museum team – and the wet season is only a few months away.'

'So what do we do?' she asked.

'We've got two choices,' he said. 'The first is to formally report this to the Western Australian Museum and the Land Council with the satellite phone, then prepare for an influx of archaeologists, enthusiasts, even news teams.'

'What's the second choice?' asked Nicolá.

He looked at her and smiled. 'We show Henry and Nancy what we found, then, with their blessing, cover over the work we did today, then fold the boat up and cache our supplies.'

'What then?'

'We go looking for a "valley rimmed with walls of stone." When we come back we report the find, making sure that Henry gets the credit for bringing us here in the first place. What do you think?'

Nicolá was holding the mug of champagne up close to her lips, and he could see the bubbles rise and bust in the air in the firelight. 'I don't like the idea of sharing this world of discovery with the press and other experts in the field – not just yet. I vote for the second choice. Let's go and find this valley.'

VINTE E SETE

The dawn sun burned through the firmament like flames, and I shivered in awe at the sight. At first I did not know what to make of the luminous white apparition that passed by in the near darkness.

Soon, however, I recognised it for what it was – sea mist – white and heavy. It brought with it the scent of sea life and brine, filling our senses. We were tired and hungry. Months at sea had exhausted the crew and passengers alike. Food and freshwater stocks were precariously low, and through the night a strong southerly breeze had carried us along before dropping in the early hours of the morning.

'Quarterdeck … masthead … the mist is thick … I can scarce see the bow,' shouted the lookout far above.

The days had passed uneventfully, and though once or twice a lookout had sworn they'd seen a sail by moonlight – far off near the horizon – by morning that phantom ship was nowhere to be seen, and we believed that the *Santiago* had lost us many days earlier.

Now I heard an unexpected sound – a low warble. Turning my attention back to the rail I found the source. The bird was an ungainly creature, streaked with grey and white, with a bright red beak – some type of gull, disoriented by the mist and happening upon the ship.

Others saw it too. 'A gull. Land is close.'

The bird took flight, circling as if to reassure us.

Elfo shouted, 'Leadsman, sound the bottom.'

This was now a dangerous situation – land nearby yet no way of seeing ahead in the mist. Dom Sebastian, standing beside me, issued further orders, 'The mist will be lighter down low. Launch a barca to pilot us through.'

'Stand by the davits,' Elfo roared. In response a dozen men removed the lashings that held the smaller vessel in its place.

I touched Dom Sebastian's shoulder. 'There is no need for you to go,' I said.

He smiled at me briefly. 'I lead by example, you know that.'

My heart swelled, for I had never seen him so happy and fulfilled. Much of this I had to attribute to Aletia and her nightly readings, with me as silent chaperone in the corner.

Tonio volunteered, 'I'll come with you.'

'Good, you can take the tiller for me. There is no other man I would rather have at my side.'

Together with Tonio, Dom Sebastian led a strong rowing crew down the cargo nets and into the barca. They took position ahead of us by a cable length, from where they would be able to see and respond to danger before even our masthead lookouts.

My heart leaping with hope, I stared ahead into the mist and tasted its cold freshness. As the dawn light strengthened, my vision was so enhanced that I saw every diamond-white droplet, swirling and spinning in the air over a sea so calm and thick it might have been honey.

Many minutes must have passed before the shout came back from the barca, at full voice.

'Rocks off the starboard bow.'

These were words to strike fear into the heart of any seaman. The sound of water on reef came as a soft, deadly roar, a hiss as white water slipped back into ocean. 'Hard a-port,' Elfo ordered.

Peering ahead, I tried to look low down, where the mist was not so thick. Land must be close, I told myself; an island perhaps – or that mysterious place called Grão-Java – the Austral land from the charts. Somewhere to repair and heal. I closed my eyes and prayed with my fists clenched so tight the nails dug into my palms.

As our ship continued to turn, something emerged through the mists, the reef itself, dark and menacing, exposed after a wave, a thousand rivulets of white foam running back down its face. It was not even a crossbow shot away, yet it seemed that the ship would never turn before being sucked onto that shelf of stone and coral.

The crew, even as they worked, had fallen silent, praying for their lives. Dom Sebastian stood at the bow of the barca, shouting encouragement. Slowly our ship swung away from the reef, sailing parallel into the white water, the swells lifting us before unleashing their pent-up energy on coral and stone.

As we continued on our way, our frightened, yearning eyes took in foaming reefs, pools and rivers of water on the kelp and coral faces. All eyes searched for a passage through.

'Our Father, who art in heaven—' I began.

The mists lifted sufficiently to reveal a red-gold coast, extending as wide as the horizon. The way in was now clear, albeit through channels winding between islands and coral.

'Thanks be to God,' I said aloud. We had stumbled on a major land mass. There we would find water and comfort. Somehow we had crossed two oceans, and lived to see a sight more welcome than anything we might have imagined.

'Will there be lions?' Duarte asked.

'I know not what we will find here,' I admitted.

Dom Sebastian's orders, shouted back from the barca and re-layed by Elfo, directed us into the passage. Here the boat's forward motion slowed and stuttered. Never have I seen such a tide, running like a mountain river. Only with the rising breeze, and every scrap of cloth sheeted home, could we make headway, tacking from side to side in the channel.

Dom Sebastian worked his oarsmen like dervishes, keeping us clear of the forbidding coral outcrops. This manner of coast was alien to us, red dust running with the tide, and islands in all directions.

The racing current slowed, and before long it stopped altogether, so that the wind pushed us along at a good rate. This slow drift towards the shore, however, as the tide turned, became a headlong rush, and now the risk from underwater obstructions was an unspoken terror. Elfo furled every scrap of canvas, yet still we sped on.

Without steerage, our ship drifted and spun out of control, at the mercy of the whorls and eddies of that capricious sea. I picked out the white sheen of sand between two high bluffs on the coast.

'It's like no land I've ever seen,' I commented.

This was a world of stone. Islets rose in strange-layered strata, fingers and humps worn smooth by millennia of wave action. Some looked like the hulls of half sunken ships, others like castles. The sea itself was a washed-out blue, calm and lovely, full of shoaling fish that attracted a multitude of birds, notably shags and terns, but also species I had not seen before.

Cliffs on islands and ashore rose like the defensive walls from under the sea, capped with rock strata so even that each layer might have been laid by masons. Stained black around the sea surface, they took on a multitude of red, white and yellow colours, sheer for the last hundred varas to the top, where I could have sworn stood buttresses and breastworks.

A terrible sound, a grinding roar, stole my attention from the view. A roar of distress went up as the barca that was leading us to safety hit a protrusion of coral. The collision opened up that small boat as easily as a fishwife's blade enters the gut of a cod. The barca began to sink. Two hundred mouths screamed in horror from our decks.

There was little we could do but watch as some of the oarsmen, unable to swim, sank without trace. Elfo shouted orders in an attempt to steer us away from the same razor-sharp protrusion, and yet when we passed we were so close to the sinking boat that we were in a position to help.

Men used boathooks and even boarding pikes to pull friends closer. Others floundered away. Dom Sebastian, having been pitched into the water, joined Tonio and the brave few who were helping to drag these unfortunates to the safety of our hull. He had shrugged off the clothes that must have made it difficult for him to swim. He sucked mouthfuls of air, then slipped beneath the water.

He surfaced at length, and gasped out the words. 'I cannot find them.' Taking a fresh series of breaths he descended again, and this time did not reappear for so long that when he did so, his skin was a rare shade of blue and his mouth gaped for air. Willing hands pulled him up to the safety of our deck.

When he was able to talk he shook his head in frustration. 'I could see no others down there.'

I saw distress in his face, and took his hand. 'We lost some good men there.'

I saw a tear in his eye, and my eyes fell to his waist where for most of his life he had carried his sword, the blade that had been passed down from his father. This he had sacrificed in the struggle to save lives.

Continuing that wild ride inshore, I resumed my study of the landscape. Up ahead, near an island formed of a single sheet of red stone, I picked out a watercraft – a slender raft, made of bundled timbers, sharpened at each end.

The vessel turned stern on as the occupants – so dark they appeared a purple shade of black – paddled away. The manoeuvre made it difficult to discern how many paddlers manned the vessel, but a quantity of spears protruded from the sides.

Dom Sebastian did not take his eyes off them. 'They look warlike. I wonder should we fire a warning shot?'

'They are not threatening us.'

'That's true.'

The crew grew rowdy, with some of the men wailing in fear. I too saw the scaly beast that had attracted their attention – as long as a manchua, gunmetal grey with hide that rose in ridges and patterns from its head along the back.

'A monster, surely,' someone said.

Shaking my head, I replied, 'I have heard them called tasha-cha – or crocodilus.' A marine aimed his musket over the rail and with a spout of smoke and loud discharge, fired at the creature. The thing, whether wounded or not, slipped beneath the water surface, and did not re-emerge.

'What kind of place is this?' someone asked, 'that such vile creatures exist.'

The shore was close now, the bottom a series of blotched shadows visible far below us. Hurrying, I descended the companionway to fetch Aletia, wanting her to see the moment when we first touched the beach ahead.

I had just arrived back on deck with her when the hull nudged sand bottom, swinging with the tide until we lay abeam to the shore. Some grûmetes threw down the cargo nets, and people clambered overboard even as the ship ran aground, crying with relief, using their last reserves of energy in that rush for solid earth. They launched themselves into the water without fear. The ship's company descended the sides, splashing towards shore, the fearsome tashacha forgotten.

The sand came as a shock under my feet. A wave of vertigo assaulted me. On the beach people fell to their knees, kissing the earth. Others staggered away into the rocks and mangroves looking for food or water.

Duarte and Aletia were at my side as I climbed the beach, the sands on the eastern extremity cut by a yellow-brown stained stream. Reaching the sandy bank I sank to my knees and cupped one hand to lift a small portion of water to my lips.

The taste was brackish, and my eyes were drawn upstream. We ascended a modestly steep slope, and atop the next rise I stopped in wonder, still with Aletia beside me. The pool here was a stone's throw across, daubed with green lilies and purple flowers. On the lower side water flowed to the next level in shallow runnels across smooth rock. The water entered with a cascade at the other end, shaded by rich green vegetation.

Like so many others I waded in to my waist, then sank to

drink the precious fluid, as fresh as the streams of the Serra Estrada. Others could not contain their delight, splashing and frolicking like children after a rainstorm. I felt my belly swelling, and for the first time in months I became satiated. Still I drank on, until my throat became reluctant, and swallowed only with persistent effort.

At sunset a miracle occurred on the sandy shore, where small waves lapped the coral sand. A multitude of shells sprouted legs and walked. Word spread, and every living soul came to exploit the easy meal, crawling through the shallow water on our hands and knees.

Even those prostrated from too much water in their bellies could catch and smash the shells between rocks. We ate the crabs inside raw, too impatient to cook, nor even pull the sweet flesh from the carapace, instead merely spitting out grit when we had extracted the goodness from inside.

The small creatures died by the hundreds, eaten hungrily by starving figures – gorging until the cracked, discarded shells lay scattered on the sand. Still, there was no limit to the largesse, the crabs attempting to scuttle off on spindly white legs, while others washed out of each receding wave.

Aletia crawled like the others, her dress sodden around her lower legs. Not even the seamen glanced away from the banquet to stare, so intent were they on the feast.

Eventually the tide changed, and the crabs retreated back into the waves where it was hard to find them, and our pitiful number fell upon bunches of kelp washed up on the sand. The taste was rank, yet taste did not matter in the burning and most satisfying quest to fill empty bellies.

Dom Sebastian forced Tonio and I to our feet in the dawn, and together, aching and fatigued, the three of us climbed the most westerly of the two bluffs that guarded the beach. At the summit, treated to a mast-head view of miles of flat ocean and countless islands, we gathered small rocks. The pile grew into a small pillar. This was the padrãos that my country had used to mark her landings for over a hundred years. When the structure was waist high we stood together. Three brothers of Portugal, proud and devout, devoted to each other as few men can be.

'As far as I know we are the first Christian men to set foot on this soil.' Dom Sebastian smiled, 'All my life I have dreamed of raising a padrãos in my own name. Now it is done.'

VINTE E OITO

Taking advantage of the calm seas after dawn Francis took the Porta-bote up to the Outstation and brought Henry and Nancy back to look at the site before they covered it with sand again.

Henry walked around the verge of the dig, studying it intently, brows moving like dark centipedes as he looked, nodding his head as if he had always known it was there. Afterwards Francis made mugs of tea back at the campsite.

'I intend to register Henry as joint discover of the site, and what I'd like to do, if you're agreeable, is to set up a trust fund involving my company and your community organisation, that would benefit jointly from any profits that flow from the venture.'

'That's very kind of you,' Nancy said. 'And I accept on behalf of the mob back there. Maybe there'll be enough to help get more housing, maybe a school, that'll bring more families out here.'

'That would be good,' Francis said. 'I'll do my best.'

Henry sat, cross-legged, on the sand. Nancy kneeled beside

him. 'Are you alright, Uncle?'

Something passed through the old man's trachoma-riddled eyes. 'Det olmen, on bot, him ded.' He raised a trembling hand to scratch at his white beard, then pointed out towards the west, and spoke in short staccato bursts of Kriol. 'Yolabat lukabat na Bunngawa?'

'What's he saying?' Francis asked Nancy, leaning closer.

'He wants to know if you're looking for a Lord, a Great One.'

'Do your people have a story about someone like that?'

Nodding, Henry smiled, as if satisfied. 'Bunngawa.'

'What do you mean?'

Henry grinned. 'Helbam burrum na Bunngawa kaman salwa-da. Longtaim dadiwan bot jingdan,' he pointed out at the sea. 'Dei Kaman dijkantri. Longwei kantrai. Brom den, mala bin trabul.'

Nancy said, 'Henry says that the Great One came from the saltwater, the sea.'

'That's interesting. What else?'

'Just then he said, "Ever since *they* came my people have been troubled."'

With that outburst Henry appeared to recover. He stood and poured the rest of his tea out on the sand as if it was not to his taste. Then he shambled back over to the boat and waited to be taken home.

As they followed, Nancy smiled at Francis. 'Henry's excited about this, you know. He's remembering things about them, just like he did then … it's like they get thrown up from his dreams, from somewhere deep in his mind.'

'That's a special thing,' Francis said. 'This is a very important find, and it never would have happened without him.'

'He told me before that you should follow that little stream that comes out on the side of the beach. Follow it right to the source. That's where you'll find things – just don't hang around up there too long. He says it's a bad place – even he doesn't like going there.'

Francis's agile mind was already moving ahead. He knew beyond doubt that there was more to this story than a hulk of a ship lying in the sand, stripped of everything human.

After the evening meal Francis called Camille, feeling warm in his heart at the sound of her voice. Next he turned internet data on for five or ten minutes, while he and Nicolá downloaded communications.

She was very quiet, reading on her screen, eyes widening. 'Whoa,' she said at last. 'I got some news on this *Parcela de Lusitania*.'

Francis lifted his head, deeply interested. 'What have you got?'

'Well, you know the history of Portuguese settlement in India as well as I do, so I will not insult you with a summary. Suffice to say that in their first decades in India, in the early 1500s, the Portuguese became interested in the famed diamond mines of Golkonda. These were the only diamond mines in the world until the South African fields were discovered hundreds of years later. For centuries the Bahmani Sultanate had profited from the mines, but not only that – they had handpicked the brightest, biggest and best stones. These went to the Sultan personally – the start of the greatest collection of diamonds ever assembled. When the Sultanate was defeated by the Qutb Shahi dynasty, they strengthened the Golkonda fort and sold off at least a thousand diamonds from the collection. Thousands more remained.

Francis's eyes focussed on her face in the firelight. 'Go on.'

'A Portuguese governor, stationed in Goa on the western coast, had been trading in Golkonda diamonds for years, and finally, tired of paying top dollar, he gathered a couple of thousand Portuguese men at arms, and their local allies, the Honovar. They marched east and besieged the Golkonda Fort. They captured it, but three days later a massive force arrived to reinforce the Qutb Shahi defenders. The fortifications were in ruins, and thus indefensible, so the Portuguese withdrew, but with them they took the contents of the treasury, including the diamonds.

'According to a written source, a scribe traveling with the army, there were, in the collection, some three thousand stones, ranging from flawless examples of around two or three carats, to those of up to thirty carats. He wrote that the diamonds shone "like the moon, like droplets of crystal ice falling from the heavens."

'The very biggest stones mined there were too valuable to keep in the collection, and had already been sold. The Daria-I-Noor, for example is 185 carats, and adorns the Crown Jewels of Iran to this day. Most of the famous diamonds of history came from mines within a few kilometres of that fort – the Hope Diamond, the Regent Diamond, the Noor-Ul-Ain. Yet imagine, the best of three hundred years of output from the most productive and famous diamond mines in history, all in one place.' Nicolá's lips were parted, her eyes glowing.

'What happened to them?'

'The Portuguese Governor, when he first set eyes on the diamonds, declared them to be so beautiful that they must be fragments of the Holy Grail. This, of course was probably either figurative, or a way of invoking a religious significance to the diamonds. Almost all Portuguese at the time, even common sailors, were intensely religious, as you know, and this would have made mutiny or attempts to seize the diamonds much less likely.

'Envoys from the Qutb Shahi demanded the return of the collection, or they swore to raise an army that would sweep the Portuguese from India forever. The Governor decided on a compromise. He split the collection into two portions – one for the rightful owners and one for the Portuguese. The Qutb Shahi accepted this deal.

The Portuguese portion – the *Parcela de Lusitania*, was carried back to Lisbon and added to the royal treasury of King Joao III. The *Parcela* was a secret entrusted to only a few.'

'What of the Indian Portion?'

'It was sold off, bit by bit, over the years. Some of it might well have included the famous diamonds I mentioned before.'

'How much would this *Parcela de Lusitania* be worth?'

'Remember that only twenty per cent of diamonds found are gem quality. These were all gem quality – rare stones – found when the world was younger, worth hundreds of millions. More taking into account the historical significance. The Portuguese portion disappeared in the mid 1500s, never to be mentioned again.'

Francis exhaled loudly. 'That's crazy stuff. But what makes you think that it was on the *Nossa Senhora dos Anjos*?'

'Only the possible presence of Dom Sebastian. A king fleeing his homeland, of course, would surely take this great but very portable fortune with him.'

Francis smiled into his cup of red wine, stirred but not convinced. He had been hearing stories of fabulous treasures since the day he entered the field of marine archaeology.

VINTE E NOVE

Francis and Nicolá left the beach the next morning, bound for the interior. He had a Garmin handheld chartplotter in his pack, but as they ventured beyond the dune zone and into the scrub, he preferred to navigate the old-fashioned way, with a compass and topographic map. Large areas of the coast here were marked as NOT YET SURVEYED, but the hinterland was accurately drawn.

Taking into account the standard deviation for the area it was a simple matter to stop occasionally, unbutton the big thigh pocket on his trousers, orientate the map with the compass, and make sure they were heading in the correct direction. Most of the time they followed the banks of the waterway that ended its journey beside the most northerly of the two bluffs. It wound somewhat but offered the easiest path.

It was obvious, from the start, that Nicolá was finding a new pair of hiking boots uncomfortable. 'I ran out of time, and bought them online,' she said. 'Hopefully they'll wear in okay.'

Francis grunted, 'The old leather boots took ages to shape.

Modern ones are usually pretty good right out of the box, but not as hard-wearing in the long run.'

Above the rocky bed, on the high banks, Francis found game trails, pads of bare red earth between spear grass, wattle, kapok and boab trees. Blunt termite mounds pointed to the sky in stark battalions between the roots of stone hills washed of colour by the burning sun.

At times the walls surrounding the creek rose, tall and sheer, with gaps in the rock, like human lips. The faces themselves, at this stage of the day, were pale pink and yellow, often shattered into jigsaw-like shards, blotches of black and grey running as if from the passage of tears to the earth. Shrubs and taller trees grew wherever they found purchase, forming a framework for the heavy cliffs as if to help support them.

Following the gully over the course of the morning they came to a substantial pool, with another waterfall at one end, cascading down from a smooth channel worn over aeons into the stone.

It was past noon, by then, and Francis was feeling the weight of his Karrimor Jaguar rucksack, the sixty-five litre capacity stuffed full, a billycan and folding shovel hanging off the back. Nicolá's load was a smaller unit, but likewise bulging with food and equipment.

It was clear, however, that Nicolá was struggling, trying to walk on her heels rather than her toes, and her face showing sharp little stabs of pain from her feet.

'Stop for lunch?' he asked.

'Definitely. This is beautiful.'

They shrugged their packs off onto a rock slab in the shade. Before they ate Francis investigated Nicolá's bare feet, holding one, then the other, feeling awkward at the intimacy. Some blisters were tight bags of fluid. Others had burst. The skin beneath would soon rub raw. Taking his time, Francis dabbed the blisters with Betadine from the first aid kit, and covered each with Elastoplast. Still not satisfied, he donated a thick pair of socks to use as an inner layer.

'You have to look after those feet,' he said.

'If I am a liability,' she said, 'then leave me here. I will work alone.'

'Don't be silly. You wouldn't last a day.'

'You think so? You are sexist, Francisco da Costa.'

They ate in silence: dry biscuits and cheese, the sound of a tiny ribbon of water falling over the edge into the pool coupled with bird calls and insects. Francis timed the break perfectly, enough to dry the ribbons of sweat on his shirt where the backpack straps touched, but not enough for their limbs to lock up.

When Francis stood, ready to go, Nicolá laced up her boots and made ready to follow. For more than an hour her feet caused no issue, as they followed grassy trails below the escarpment. At times the stone gorges again rose to shade them, the stream winding between rock shelves and plates.

Then, however, her limp became obvious, and Francis insisted that she stop so he could tend to her feet again.

'I have let you down once more – the great Francisco who can play soccer like Pelé, digs like a mole, swims like a fish, never gets sick and has feet made of leather.'

Francis lifted both hands innocently. 'I didn't say a word.'

'Oh, but you are thinking it.'

'Not at all. We'll camp here for the night – under the stars – attend to those feet, and go on in the morning.'

'Good, thank you.'

While Nicolá soaked her feet in the stream, Francis built a fire and laid out groundsheets and sleeping gear. Finally, he put the billy on to boil and prepared a simple meal of curry and rice.

Over dinner, Nicolá remained aloof, and later, as Francis unrolled his sleeping bag and spread it out at one edge of the ground sheet, she prepared hers at the furthest possible extremity, before sliding into bed fully clothed.

Within an hour, however, when a curlew screamed its dying woman scream into the night, Francis heard a rustle as she worked her sleeping bag closer to him. And when dingos howled in the distance, she gave up all pretence at giving him the cold shoulder and moved so close that her knees dug into the backs of his legs.

'They won't hurt us, will they?'

'No. They just want to be left alone, and we're no threat.'

'But Francisco … they won't know that we don't mean them any harm.'

'I think they can sense it. Animals know a threat when they see it. I remember reading about wolves just walking around among caribou in Canada when they've done hunting for the day, and the caribou just ignore them.'

Her face was so close to his neck that her hair tickled. 'That would be a beautiful thing to see.'

The next morning, with fresh Elastoplast on Nicolá's feet, the going was easier. The game trails were more distinct, and they could often walk on flattened areas of hard gravel, formed when the stream wandered from its bed in the wet season.

The waterway narrowed and the rock walls reared higher. They came to a deep cleft through the rocks. Here living and dead mingled – tree trunks entwined with stone, until it was impossible to see where one ended and the other began. The stream flowed through the narrow fissure. Francis did not hesitate, but walked on.

Boots sloshed against the current, and water penetrated, chilling his feet, as they wound along the dark grotto – so narrow he could extend his arms to brush weathered rock with both hands. The water was knee deep, and even in the dull light each rock and pebble stood out, along with strands of algae that hung on the edge. Horizontal cracks filled the walls, where mosses and ferns grew, and far above, the sky was a gash of deep blue.

Francis savoured the cool shade, and water dripped from the inward sloping walls. The passage widened, with sandy banks to walk on. The light strengthened gradually, until the darkness ended, and the crack opened out into a wide valley, surrounded on three sides by sheer, water-stained cliffs. Only the northern end was open. Nicolá touched his shoulder and they stared ahead, in awe at the scene.

Scattered trees covered much of the valley floor – boabs, cypress, ironwood and eucalypts. Broken rock and sand littered the lower slopes of the cliffs. Shadows at the bases indicated overhangs and ledges.

'A valley rimmed with walls of stone,' Nicolá breathed.

A pool filled the centre of that picturesque expanse. Reflected sunlight dazzled the eyes. The pool surrounds were of crimson stone, jumbled and piled together. An old and massive boab tree, as tall as a two-storey house, its bark as scarred and weathered as the landscape, grew on one grassy bank.

Francis set off towards the pool, with Nicolá keeping pace at his side. In the shade beneath the giant boab sat a sandstone boulder, embedded in the ground. It had a flat, rectangular top, at table height. The branch above was obviously a favoured perch, for white bird droppings stained the top and sides of the rock.

Francis slipped the pack from his shoulders, laying it on the cleaner end of the stone slab. Nicolá did the same, and together they walked over to look at the pool. The bank in that area was sandy, like a small beach, but the rest was lined with that same heavily-pigmented stone. The water was the fluorescent blue-green of Listerine mouthwash, yet so clear that every detail of the sandy bed was magnified and enhanced. An azure kingfisher swept across the surface, and dragonflies cruised erratically over the water.

No stream entered as far as Francis could see. This was the source, the fountainhead – the spring itself. Somewhere, in the depths, artesian water gushed upward, filled the pool, and created the stream they had followed. There was a faint smell of sulphur, and when Francis squatted and dipped his fingers into the water he found that the temperature was warm.

'Hot springs,' he said. 'What an amazing place.'

'Beautiful,' Nicolá said. 'But can we swim here? The water is quite deep. Are there crocodiles?'

'Only freshies – the smaller variety – and they won't hurt us. Waterfalls like the ones downstream keep saltwater crocs out.'

Francis pointed up at the cliffs that fringed the valley, which was perhaps one kilometre in circumference. Even from here he could see overhangs and ledges. 'Let's have some lunch and a swim, then I think we should split up and search the area. We'll cover more ground that way.'

'Okay, where do you want to start?'

Francis pointed back at the grotto through which the stream disappeared towards the coast. Let's start on either side, and keep going around. We could leave our packs here, and meet back down here at say three this afternoon. It'll be hard going and we'll need a break.'

'Fine, let's eat now then, and get started.'

As Francis had predicted, searching the valley walls was an intense effort. He knew from experience that every small overhang, even upturned boulders with gaps underneath could hide secrets. All were worthy of investigation. This, however, despite the sweat that stung his eyes, was a pleasurable activity. A sense of anticipation bubbled just below the surface as he looked. Sometimes he stood upright, sometimes crawled on hands and knees, head turned sideways to peer under a fallen stone slab and into the shadows.

Scratched from serrated grass and shins skinned from impact with sandstone ledges, Francis was back at the boab tree near the pool just after three. He stripped his shirt off and squatted at the edge of the pool, splashing his face and chest, drinking the earthy water.

He had his pack open on the sandstone table, dabbing at his face with a towel when Nicolá come back through the scrub. Her face was also bright red from exertion, streaming sweat, surrounded by a horde of flies.

'Any luck?' he asked.

'Lots of stone art – hundreds of examples. I also saw an opening up high, but I couldn't get up there without rope.'

'How high?'

'Maybe six or seven metres. It looked very interesting, but the stone art was worth it in itself.'

'One day maybe we should bring old Henry up and get him to help us to catalogue it all. How are your feet holding up?'

'A lot better, thank you.'

They were somewhat subdued as they sat in the shade, eating

dry biscuits and cheese. Francis allowed them forty-five minutes of rest before he got to his feet. 'I think we're going to need every bit of daylight if we're going to finish exploring around this valley.'

'I agree. Let's get into it.'

All through the afternoon, Francis searched thoroughly, leaving no shadow unexplored. Yet it was near dusk when he happened on a deep overhang, where the cliff face was sucked inwards by time and the elements, a place of shadow and red light heightened by sunset.

He entered that space like an acolyte into a cathedral. The overhang was substantial, at least as big as the one at the famous Nourlangie Rock a thousand kilometres to the north-east. Protected from the elements, the rock art on the walls had survived in perfect condition – representations of animals and mythical figures in brilliant red ochre and white clay. Fifty thousand years or more of habitation had left its marks on the wall – stories of life in a wilderness at once beautiful, bountiful and harsh.

The walls varied in colour from white, to pink and red, with the texture of the sandstone varying from smooth to coarse, sometimes brushed with lichen, or coated with random patterns of surface oxide. The scent of flowering trees wafted in, along with bird calls, magnified by the stone. Tiny marsupial footprints showed in the fine layer of silty dust on the floor and sloping sides.

The ceiling lowered, and Francis was forced to walk on, bent over as he penetrated deeper along the overhang. Now, at last, he laid eyes on a large human figure – very unusual, wearing what appeared to be a cloak and headgear that radiated importance.

It was then that Francis saw the script – letters a hand span high across the sandstone. Goosebumps rose on the skin of his arms, and he rocked back onto his haunches, hugging himself happily. The script was Portuguese, rendered in ochre and white clay, each letter at least eighty millimetres high.

A shiver passed through his body – a stirring of something long suppressed. Somewhere out there a curlew shrieked. This was the valley's centre, and Francis began to *feel*. The stone was infused with blood. Something had happened here, he knew with certainty. Lives had ended.

A roaring filled his ears and for a moment he thought he saw it all. The loneliness. The longing. Terror came in a rush so overwhelming that his senses reached saturation point and no longer responded. Time passed that he later had no conscious memory of.

The image in his mind was of a ship, pursued by hatred and avarice across a seemingly endless sea – of humiliation and pain. Something large and black circled, something more frightening than anything he might have imagined. In a flash of insight he saw the thing that hunts all members of his species from the moment of leaving the womb.

When he came back to himself Francis was running down the slope from the cavern – blundering through the dusk-dark evening, feet stumbling past stone pillars and termite mounds. His breath became loud and hoarse. Terrified shrieks issued from his throat. A thin branch cut across his face and wet blood dribbled down his neck. The effort made his legs feel like wet cardboard, and the burning in his lungs intensified.

There came the rustling of grass, and the yawning trees as they moved in a sudden wind. The shriek became a continuous sound, filling Francis's head until the faces and voices disintegrated into an angry mosaic of colour and light. When he fell, his jaw hit the earth with a thump, forcing sandy earth through his lips. Blood trickled from his nose, and only then did he come back to himself.

It took a minute or more for him to regather his equanimity, before standing and setting off for the pool by the boab tree. As he neared he saw that Nicolá had lit the fire.

'What happened to you?' she asked when he arrived.

'I fell over,' he said. 'I was running.' His breath was still coming hard, and he paused only to take a handkerchief from his pack and hold it over his nose. 'Get a torch and come with me, I want to show you what I've found.'

The overhang, by torchlight, seemed even more mystical and special than it had been earlier. The yellow of Nicolá's torch, and the white LED beam of Francis's head-light met and reflected from stone, air and the ferns and creepers that had colonised every crack.

Nicolá kneeled in front of the painting and traced the letters in the air. The script seemed to come alive, the letters dancing as if they were being painted before his eyes – her hand gliding through the curves and strokes as lovingly as an artist.

$$- os - a - e - ora\ d - A - os$$

'You see?' she cried, 'add an N and another S to the first word. It's the name of our ship. The *Nossa Senhora dos Anjos*. This is where their journey ended.'

Francis hugged his arms around his chest. 'You are a genius. Of course it is.'

Nicolá went on, 'And here's a date – 1579. God Francis, we

were right.'

'I have a lot of work to do in photographing and recording it all – particularly that human figure. It's similar to a Wandjina figure from the West Kimberley, but different.' He paused to blow his nose on a cloth handkerchief. It had stopped bleeding, but still left a smear on the cloth. 'I also think that we'd be justified in making a small excavation in the cavern here. There may be artefacts, both Indigenous and Portuguese.'

'I agree. It would be good to sink a small trench in here,' she said. 'I'd say that the soil is quite shallow, so it won't take long, but we're going to need our gear.'

'Tomorrow's job,' said Francis.

'Of course,' she agreed, smiling. 'Well done, this is almost as exciting as finding the ship itself.'

'Either of us could have found it. I just happened to pick the lucky side of the valley.'

Standing, he followed after her, casting a last look at the representation of the human figure and the mysterious script at its base. 'I'm looking forward to getting started on this – I really am.'

Careful study of the topographic map allowed Francis to prune several kilometres off the journey back to the beach and its stockpile of equipment. Even so, it was a rugged four-hour round trip to collect supplies and return, staggering under the weight of the gear he carried. In deference to Nicolá's blisters he left her in the valley, despite her protests, to begin work on the cavern.

Returning from a second trip in the late afternoon, Nicolá met him down past the grotto and helped take some of the burden. Back at the camp near the boab tree she helped stow the gear. Once this was done, Francis stripped off his shirt and ran towards the pool He jumped, raising his knees, and the feel of the warm water on his skin was more potent than any drug, more refreshing than any drink. He surfaced, dog paddling, staring back at the shore where Nicolá had changed into her swimming costume and moved to the bank, sitting, flapping her legs like a duck in the shallows before diving in carefully.

His face still hot from the work of the day, Francis submerged himself again, opening his eyes underwater, staring out at the misty-clean world below the surface. A school of bony bream flashed away as he kicked down to the pool floor and picked up a handful of coarse sand, rising only when the urge to breathe became a torment, bursting through like a broaching sea creature.

That evening, using just a handline rigged with a 2/0 hook, and a grasshopper for bait, Francis caught a fat sooty grunter from the pool. Cooked slowly over a smoky fire, he had to admit that it was one of his best efforts.

Long after the meal was over, he and Nicolá sat close together, staring at the flames and talking. The springs themselves steamed in the cooler night air, giving the place a ghostly feel.

'I had a close look at the stone around the springs,' she said, 'it is some kind of volcanic intrusion – not the native sandstone – very unusual – crystalline – a little bit like quartz but softer, and so very red. I bet that's what was used as a pigment up there in the overhang. I took some samples and I'll get them identified when we go home.'

'You seem to know a bit about it.'

'I did one geology subject in first year at University – but I can't remember much. I never had to.'

'I kept away from geology,' he said. 'Anything with chemistry involved gives me the horrors. I just don't have that kind of brain. I grew up loving books, stories and history.'

'I loved all those things too,' said Nicolá, 'but I wasn't too bad at chemistry and maths as well.' She narrowed her eyes. 'Those scratches on your neck look a bit red, I'll put something on them.'

And while he sat with his shirt off, she used a cotton bud to dab at the scratches, leaning her face so close in the firelight that he almost ached with the way it brought out the highlights in her face, and colour in her hair.

'You've never told me if you have a boyfriend,' he said.

'You've never asked,' she smiled, but when she had screwed the lid back on the Betadine, she replaced it in the first aid kit and sat opposite him. 'I've only ever had one serious boyfriend, and he turned out to be a pig.'

'In what way?'

'Miguel was from a good family. Very handsome. He knew how to make a girl laugh, how to have fun. The guitar? Oh, you have never heard such tunes, sung with the voice of an angel. He was easy to fall in love with.'

Francis dared not say a word, knowing that she was trying to tell him something important.

'I was stupid, and naïve, but I thought that I loved him, and that he loved me. Instead I was just part of a childish game that went on in his head.'

Francis wondered if the anger he felt towards Miguel was because of the pain he had caused Nicolá, or through jealousy at how strongly he had made her feel.

She stared at him. 'I think I'm starting to realise that you are different. You are more afraid of me than I am of you.'

Francis stared at the fire, wondering if it were true. His attention elsewhere, he scarcely noticed her stand up until she squatted in front of him, placing a hand on either side of his cheek.

'I like you a lot, Francisco, but you are a strange one.'

The touch took him by surprise, and his immediate response was a quickening in his breathing and an unconscious movement of his hands to her shoulders, wanting to pull her closer. With surprising suddenness, and in defiance of her own ground rules she moved her head forward and pressed her lips to his. He responded to her light pressure, losing himself in the strange and irresistible feel of her.

Then, as quickly as it had started she broke off, and returned to her seat. The pleasant heat faded, and he looked at the earth.

'I'm sorry,' she said, 'I should not have done that.'

Francis tried to smile, but the moment was gone. He wanted to kiss her again more than anything in the world.

Francis's sleep that night was broken and unsatisfying, and he woke in the stinging cool before dawn with a headache, limping from the tent to stand by the ashes of the fire. His skin prickled as he listened to the sound sifting into the valley. From far away came the cry of an animal, a dingo perhaps, howling out its misery to an uncaring world.

It was a cry of dispossession, of loss and physical pain, of madness and hunger. Francis smelled again the ancient blood steeped in the earth and the rocks, in the shadowy places below the cliffs.

The valley was no stranger to death. Men and women had died violently here before. He shivered, then kneeled at the fire and added sticks, blowing on the embers until they flared. The fire grew until he felt safe in the warmth and light. Only then did his fears recede – those fears that feed at night, drawing strength from the darkness.

When the eastern sky blushed red with dawn, Francis walked to the pool edge to watch the display reflected on the still surface, and the rainbow bee-eaters swooping low over the water.

Still quiet, he breakfasted on muesli and UHT milk. He was almost finished when Nicolá emerged from her tent, wearing a tracksuit and lacing up a pair of running shoes, warming herself with fingers splayed.

'Are you okay?' she asked.

'Yeah, fine.'

'I heard you moving around. Couldn't you sleep?'

'Not really, but who cares, let's get up to the overhang and start work.'

TRINTA

rew and passengers alike gained vitality and vigour over the weeks ashore, yet most remained thin – the work of survival was hard, despite our guns and the other accoutrements of European civilisation. We all felt the lack of belly-fillers like bread, and olive oil was sorely missed. Meanwhile the heat and biting insects inflicted red bleeding boils and carbuncles on our skin.

The ship's company could be likened to the contents of a sizeable village. Our tradesmen plied their arts in corners of the beach. Smoke rose from a blacksmith's makeshift forge, a cobbler was busy repairing shoes, and merchants tried to foist their fire-damaged goods on ignorant seamen. Groups of boys – stowaways on the voyage, or the miscreant sons of merchants – roamed in groups, pilfering what they could, fighting among themselves and causing trouble.

Aletia amused herself with reading, and sometimes sitting on a rock, threading tiny white kauri or cone shells onto lengths of twine. The necklaces she produced in this way were sought after by the small number of merchant's wives in our company.

Half a dozen men, under the supervision of Frei Botelho, himself once a fisherman of Nazare, used cord and hooks to pull big cod and mackerel from the water. A grûmete from the Azores specialised in finding bird and turtle eggs. Two Jesuits took upon themselves the task of eating wild fruits to test for ill effects. So far one had almost died and the other twice prostrated with diarrhoea, yet they had added many a berry and some tubers, including those of the elegant purple water hyacinth, to the company's diet. Rui Chanoca proved adept at fashioning ingenious snares from wire, thus adding to our supplies.

The abundant, dog-sized, hopping deer proved to be more than just a twist of God's art. Dom Sebastian's hunters had brought the first of these creatures to the beach camp, where a crowd gathered to stare. All four of the blood-streaked bodies were grey in colour, with soft fur and dark blunt claws.

Roasted on the fire however, the flesh proved delicious, with Dom Sebastian himself declaring it superior to any venison he had tasted. Of course, months had passed since we had eaten fresh red meat of any kind, so the comparison may have been generous. The thighs and forequarters were inclined to stringiness yet the fillets were tender and sweet.

Soon after the landing, we celebrated Mass on the cliffs, our people standing in rows – still weak, yet uncomplaining of discomfort. Together we thanked God for our deliverance, surrounded as we were by a shining ocean and stone hills. Dawn was only a short time past, and clouds flared orange and yellow in the east. The earth smelled damp and sweet. After the Confiteor our congregation burst into the Introit – the entrance hymn, voices rising and breaking against the cliffs.

'Dominus Vobiscum – the Lord be with you.'

'Et cum spiritu tuo – and with you too.'

When Mass came to an end Dom Sebastian addressed us all. He spoke of this new land, and how it would shelter us, and provision us for the journey onwards to Tymor and India. He spoke of bravery, and fortitude. I wiped a tear from my cheeks.

The watchers cheered, a sense of history descending on us all. For the first time we were not mere survivors but explorers and navigators. We Portuguese are an emotional people – dreamers, poets and adventurers combined. Dom Sebastian had caught the imagination of our bedraggled company.

With the industriousness common to our nation, crew and passengers alike worked from dawn to dusk for three days to empty the hull of everything moveable, including the cannon and ballast of heavy river stones. No one noticed Duarte and I remove a coffin, which we carried far up beyond the beach and behind a ridge, where we battled the hard ground for half a day to bury it deeply. Afterwards we replaced soil and plants in order to make the area look undisturbed. I warned Duarte to tell nobody of what we had done.

There was also the contents of the captain's lazaret to consider – a store of copper and silver ingots, coin and gifts for Eastern potentates. These were also buried beyond the beach, in a distinctive location known only to Dom Sebastian, myself and a dozen of his most loyal guards.

When the hull was empty, two hundred men hauled the hull of the great ship *Our Lady of Angels* high up on the beach, assisted by the highest of the spring tides and a channel we dug in the sand. The hull looked massive even against the cliffs as the work of returning her to seaworthiness began.

Curved futtocks made up the frame to which labourers attached new planks. Ribands held the futtocks in place, strengthening the overall structure. A furnace of burning coals, served by three sweating men, heated cauldrons of water. These provided steam which Leonel de Amoral used to bend new-cut timber to the required shape.

Logs were floated and man-handled downstream from the hinterland and laid out in rows. Men worked on sculpting the butts ready to be seated in the bilges or smoothing the sides. Beyond the beach were our living areas, with dozens of cooking fires and motley bedrolls taken from the ship. Liberty chests sat on the sand or stone, in clusters, beside piles of firewood and untidy hearth fires.

In the midst of all this activity one of the hunting parties returned from a foray along the coast. They were laughing as they pushed their captive, a black adolescent, from man to man. One of these tormentors had a leather whip, with which he delivered a vicious blow to the youth's buttocks.

Dom Sebastian had been interested, from the moment of seeing them offshore in their dugout craft, in the inhabitants of this land. Signs of their presence were everywhere: shell middens on the beach, the smoke of cooking fires, and several clusters of small villages along the shore to the east.

The True King had sent a party of six men, equipped with trade goods, along the coast on our second day ashore, and while there had seemed to be a willingness on the part of the locals to trade, a rash movement by one of the tall warriors, who became curious about the burning match of an arquebusier's weapon, resulted in a shot being fired into the scrub, and several spears were thrown.

Our party had left the trade goods and returned, but the desired cordial relations had not been established, and two hunters barely escaped with their lives after a silent party of spearmen crept up on them.

This adolescent captive didn't cease his high-pitched wailing as our men shoved him to his knees. Another took a handful of wild hair and lifted his head so his eyes enlarged, showing an expanse of white above his pupils. The crowd were laughing and shouting, egging the participants on.

Sickened, I seized Dom Sebastian's arm. 'Stop them,' I pleaded.

In response he stepped from the ring of onlookers and across to where the burly marine sergeant still held the boy by the hair. 'Let him go.'

The man stared back, yet maintained his grip.

Dom Sebastian drew his replacement sword from its scabbard. This weapon had been presented to him by one of our surviving merchants, carried for trade in the East. It was a fine blade, gilt with gold and silver, yet no real replacement for the one he had lost.

'Release your prisoner or hang from a tree. Make your choice.'

'I must protest, my Lord. We found this devil spying near the beach.'

'Release him.'

The sergeant shrugged and pushed the black youth away. Dom Sebastian went to the sprawled figure and helped him up gripping his wrist with one strong hand.

The youth stood, but held his hands before his face as if he were going to be hit.

'I apologise,' Dom Sebastian said, 'for the treatment you have received at the hands of these men.'

The boy must have understood the conciliatory tone if nothing else, and dropped his hands. Blood dripped from both nostrils, and snaked down over puffy, damaged lips onto his chest, finally reaching a sparse adolescent bush of pubic hair. His eyes rested on mine and something passed between us then, some unspoken pact that I could not fathom.

I pointed to my own chest, then at the others who stood at a distance around the beach. 'We are people of Portugal,' I said. 'Portuguese.'

The boy inclined his head, and gestured at himself, then down at the very soil. 'Yeidji,' he said.

'Yeidji,' I repeated. Then, 'Go with God. Please don't think too unkindly of us.'

The crowd, without instructions, parted, forming an avenue for freedom for the youth. He turned to look at the escape route then back at Dom Sebastian, who said, 'They won't hurt you now.'

When the boy was out of sight Dom Sebastian turned to the small, muttering group of marines. 'Are you dim-witted? Can't you see that we are a very small group surrounded by great numbers of skilled warriors. They have not yet chosen to attack us in force. You have just given them reason to do so.'

'We have guns, and they fear them.' The sergeant spoke belligerently, chin high, eyes impertinent.

'Perhaps they do, but that won't help us if they boil over into blind rage.'

Dom Sebastian turned on his heel and stalked away. When he had gone I also went to the sergeant and berated him.

'How dare you be so slow to obey Dom Sebastian. He is a king, remember.'

The man sneered, 'King of what? Of this wilderness? Surely not.'

I narrowed my eyes. 'Don't be fooled. This is temporary only. The day will come when he returns in glory to Portugal.'

There is a certain look a man sometimes displays when another is being a fool. I saw that look in the marine's eye. I turned away lest it provoke unpleasant thoughts.

The sea was ruffled silver as the crew plied the oars, taking us past the beaches and cliffs and out past islets formed of the same stone as the headlands. This was the first time I had accompanied one of these seaborne hunting expeditions, and I tapped my foot nervously, feeling the salt tang heavy in the air.

At the bow two lookouts searched the gloom for our quarry. Dom Sebastian perched between them, one foot on the prow, shirt off, with only breeches and his belt at his waist.

The harpoon Dom Sebastian held was a modified boarding pike, attached to a long coil of rope. The muscles of his back were tensed, and I sensed his excitement in the manner in which he edged forward. He had always loved the hunt, and the sea. On this afternoon he would combine both passions.

The oarsman drew us on towards one of the larger offshore islands, with expansive weedbeds on the lee shore, visible in the shallow, clear water. These were the feeding grounds of the dugongo, most favoured amongst all the foods we had discovered in this new land.

The dugongo, or sea cow, as some men called the species, was a startling animal, often longer than a man and bigger in girth, with dark leathery skin. They yielded oil from each carcass and large quantities of meat, similar to pork.

The two lookouts were amongst the sharpest eyed of our people, and the dugongo were common here. Most were of regular size, but our hunters had reported occasional giants – monstrous beasts almost as long as the barca. Dom Sebastian, of course, had focussed his thoughts on these greater individuals, as if only they were worthy of his efforts.

Because of this, when we first reached the area, Dom Sebastian ignored the first excited shouts of the lookouts. 'There,' one man cried, 'crossing the bow. See him?'

Gripping the harpoon tighter in one hand, Dom Sebastian shook his head. 'Too young and small, we will only have time to kill one beast today, we should make it the fattest specimen we can find.'

Dom Sebastian hissed at his rowers to slow down. 'Just dip your blades,' he ordered, 'walking pace. No more.'

This was a most pleasant thing, skimming over the sea surface, tension thick in the air. Even Dom Sebastian betrayed his excitement, curling and uncurling his fingers on the haft of his weapon.

The lookouts, focussed as they were on the sea floor ahead of the barca, were not the first to see the brown shape surface a stone's throw to starboard. One of the rowers, in fact, hissed out a warning.

'There, abeam of us. A giant, surely.'

Dom Sebastian responded with a gentle wave in that direction with his free hand, indicating urgency but silence. Even as we turned I saw him change grip on the harpoon, so his hand was at the point of balance. In the sunlight I saw minute scratches on the blade where it had been burnished and sharpened.

My attention moved back to the dugongo itself, yet it had dived. I saw apprehension on the faces around me – worry that it might have moved off. A moment later, however, a dark shoulder broached the surface.

The barca inched closer and the animal remained on the surface. I held my breath and the men around me must have done likewise. When a rowlock squealed the man at that oar winced and ceased all movement.

When we had crept to within a boat-length of the creature I watched the muscles of Dom Sebastian's shoulder and back contract as he coiled in preparation for the throw, head cocked forward, focussing on the target.

As we came into harpoon range the dugongo dived in a fluid motion so fast that it left a hole in the water larger than a vintner's barrel. Dom Sebastian launched his stroke, driving the harpoon down, his follow-through so extreme that a less agile man might have overbalanced and plunged into the water.

Rope spilled overboard in serpentine fashion, and the men cheered now, ready with their oars, watching their leader for orders. We had all seen the dugongo, and knew it was a large example of the species, yet what happened when the rope came tight on the cleat took us all by surprise.

The bow of the barca was pulled down as if by the hand of a giant, and at the same time the stern lurched into the air, tossing us from gunwale to gunwale like flapping fish. Our vessel made way as if rowed by a crew of devils.

'Cut the rope,' one man cried, yet when one of his comrades drew his knife and moved towards the rope to slash at it, Tonio brought his bare foot down on the man's wrist, pinning it. 'Do not touch it,' he screeched. 'No one will cut the tow. Move back into the stern, keep the weight aft.'

My right hand held the gunwale like a vice and I gripped the seat itself in the angle formed behind my knee. The hull lurched beneath me like an animal, and the sheer speed raised a bow wave of white water.

'Do not risk the barca,' I pleaded. 'We have already lost one.'

Dom Sebastian ignored me, not even turning to address this patent good sense. I have often noted that, when his maleness is aroused – a matter of pride, or something to be proven – wisdom flies away like a pigeon from her roost.

Even as the hull's balance changed for the better it appeared that the monster was dragging us towards a coral outcrop. Experience had already taught us just how dangerous this strange material could be – stunningly beautiful in life, yet in death forming a conglomerate of sharp, strong skeletons piled together. There were many different shapes of this coral rock – plates like knife blades piled side by side, others more like points, and still others jumbled geometrical shapes without rhyme or reason. The whole was glued together with abrasive cement, making it the most dangerous material for ships in all the world.

At the last moment we passed just a handspan away. Beyond that point we found ourselves into the clear yet there was no slackening of speed. Instead, however, the dugongo worked furiously from side to side, trying to throw the great dragging weight that must be tiring him. To punctuate this point, one of the lookouts, recovering his pride after being dumped on the deck of the boat, climbed to one knee on the gunwale.

'Blood,' he cried. 'Blood in the water.'

A cheer went up from the crew as it became apparent that the dugongo was leaving clouds of scarlet-tinged seawater behind him.

'Surely,' Dom Sebastian declared, 'it cannot bleed like that for long. Soon it will die.'

This pronouncement settled the nerves of the party, and with the weight of all but Dom Sebastian in the stern now she rode level. Tonio seemed to be the only other man enjoying the chase, laughing with Dom Sebastian as if they were teenagers again. My humour improved at seeing them like that.

Looking at the islands and shoals that surrounded us, however, I was surprised at how fast we sped through the water. The sun lay forty degrees from the horizon now, and still the dugongo showed no sign of dying.

The beast led us towards the open sea, the way often blocked by islands and reefs. Always the flow of blood was maintained, yet the pace slackened not at all.

Then, in the clear water, the barca stopped cold, and men fell over one another for the second time, overbalancing and tumbling to the deck so that they swore and called out in confusion.

'Has he died?' someone asked.

There was no time to answer, for the rope came taut and the boat spun back like a child's toy, again pulling the bow down and making the stern rise.

'He's swimming the other way,' Dom Sebastian shouted. Now the barca slowed, and ahead of us, the dugongo surfaced, head and shoulders rising from the water, gnarled skin brown and vibrantly alive in the afternoon sun.

Blood erupted from his mouth, and I saw the harpoon sticking like a pin from a cushion in the animal's back, where Dom Sebastian had driven it deep. I looked into the eyes themselves and saw such sorrow there that my heart went out to it. They were brown and huge, timeless as the sun.

It occurred to me that the dugongo must be a patriarch — would have fathered a hundred calves and lived on these shores for a century or more.

'I am sorry, old fellow,' I said softly, 'but your flesh will feed a hundred mouths, and your oil will make lamps and candles. Your hide will protect our feet.'

Resignedly now, as if knowing that his enemy was relentless, he dived deeper into the water and again the barca lurched into motion. We were ready this time, however, and there was a sense now that the end was near. Again it seemed that the beast was heading straight for the reefs, where white water surged against rock and coral. Beyond lay the open ocean, blue and serene.

A new nervousness permeated our small craft, yet still we hoped the dugongo would turn. Closer and closer to danger we loomed.

One of the younger sailors shouted, 'Save us, Dom Sebastian, I beg you, cut the tow. The beast is determined to see us destroyed.' Those thoughts were echoed in other faces as we continued on that path towards the coral. Miraculously, however, the shelves of rock opened out and I saw a gap. Into this narrow defile the dugongo dragged us.

Men screamed in fear, for the tide roared through this channel like a galloping horse, with jagged coral on each side so close I could have reached out and touched it with either hand. The strength of the creature that bore us was beyond belief, for he now had to battle against a racing tide. Remorselessly, however, he drew us into that channel.

The narrow passage twisted into a series of loops, and I relaxed my grip on the gunnels. Surely the animal's strength could not last. My respect for the ancient sea creature deepened.

Still the harpoon cord remained tight and the relentlessly strong dugongo drew us on through the twists and turns of this passage. The sound of prayer from those around me became a continuous moan of despair. I looked at Dom Sebastian and pleaded with my eyes, yet saw the out-thrust chin and steady eyes.

'The open sea,' someone cried, and it was true, ahead loomed the sea, with breakers piling on rock and spray drifting high into the air like gunsmoke. The barca scraped the sides with a tearing sound that set every jaw on edge. The channel ahead was choked with blood now, deeper red than the petals of a rose. It was obvious that the dugongo was close to finished, yet I wondered if we could survive this headlong ride for much longer.

Now the whisper of surf became a roar, and as we rounded a corner of stone we were almost though.

'Pray,' I cried over the movement of the sea. 'Let us all pray together.'

Our Lord widened the passage in response to our pleas. The first wave smashed and foamed into the bow. Riding low down as the barca was, we shipped a great deal of water. Men stopped praying and began to bail.

The dugongo dragged us out of the channel and seaward, while we bailed for our lives. 'The thing will take us a league off-shore then drown us,' they complained.

The blood flow increased, and finally, as the coast receded, the beast appeared to reach the limit of his strength. The barca slowed, then stopped. The dugongo rose from the surface, roaring like a bull. Rolling onto one side, he thrashed the water to bloody foam, and we could but watch the death throes, in awe at his strength – like watching the slow inevitability of a sunset, or an avalanche.

Finally, when it lay still in the water, Dom Sebastian ordered the rowers to bring him closer, and he administered the coup de grace with his sword. I watched his face then, as he took possession of the animal. There was compassion in his eyes, and respect for the dugongo's power and will to live.

'Tail rope him,' he ordered.

Tonio prepared a slip knot and manoeuvred his way through

the boat to the stern, where he drew the knot over the once-proud tail and pulled it fast, tying off to a brass cleat, muscles rippling in his arms and shoulders as he worked.

'It is too heavy to tow,' Dom Sebastian called, 'and we have company.' He pointed out the dorsal fin of a shark as it cut through the water, turning, hunting, seeking the smell of fresh meat. 'We will take what we can now.'

Every man had his azcumas dagger, and some of them swords. Even I wore a small knife on the rope belt that secured my cassock. Now, with the dugongo alongside we proceeded to cut and hack into the carcass, taking great bloody chunks that we piled on deck. Men clambered over the gunwale and onto the floating body so as to make their work easier. Someone pierced the gut cavity and the stink of half-digested seagrass mingled with that of raw meat.

The sharks, gathering and circling, were wary at first, yet I watched one brute come in, opening his jaws so wide that his gums were bared, lock onto the side of our kill, and shake his head to dislodge a massive chunk of flesh while men screamed and clambered out of the way.

'Hurry,' shouted Dom Sebastian, taking up a spare harpoon to fend them away, 'or we will have nothing.'

The work continued at a feverish pace. A man cried out when a knife slipped, cutting his thumb to the bone. I bandaged the wound as best I could, and he went back to work.

Ensconced on my thwart seat, I watched Dom Sebastian's face change suddenly from melancholy excitement to wariness. I was concerned enough to make my way over piles of red flesh and brown hide to the bow.

'What is it? What can you see?' I asked, yet still he stared down along the coast.

I followed his gaze landward, far to the west and south. A narrow band of woodsmoke rose in a wind-troubled line. This was what drew the eye, but what sent a chill into my chest was the unmistakeable sight of three bare masts, pointing skyward from the sea.

'A ship,' I breathed. 'The *Santiago*?'

'It seems so, and I just saw a flash of sun on metal on land nearby.'

I shivered, there could be no good in that. Not now. Not here.

'Tomorrow dawn we will take a patrol and find out.'

'I will come with you.'

'No Padre. We may need to fight.'

'Ah, but we may also need to succour desperate people.' I turned away, hoping that the flash he had seen was sunlight on water, not the weapon of an enemy sworn to destroy us.

TRINTA E UM

Nicolá and Francis planned a sample cavern dig, working on the assumption that if indeed the medieval visitors had taken long term shelter beneath those sloping stone walls they must have left evidence behind.

Cavern usage, irrespective of the ethnological makeup of the inhabitants, tends to form common patterns, with sleeping areas near the rear walls, hearth fires located centrally, and a broad trash zone in the outer regions. Nicolá sited the trench to include segments of all these areas, while taking in the cavern-floor closest to the mysterious script.

Two full days passed in the preparations – pegging a six by two metre area perpendicular to the cavern wall, taking levels with a theodolite and dividing the space into grids. Standard locus sheets were altered to suit the dig. Francis and Nicolá would make anecdotal notes in their notepads, but the locus sheets would formally record every detail as it became exposed, from the soil type and colour to the details of photographs taken during the dig.

The following day Francis watched Nicolá lift her trowel delicately with one hand and take a slice of sandy earth just a few millimetres thick. 'There,' she said, 'that's a start.'

Few people outside the profession of archaeology understand just how painstaking this process must be. The soil in the trench had to be removed and every grain sifted through a screen onto paper. Famous shipwrecks and tombs had given the field a glamour image when the reality was hard work and a mind-numbing focus on minutiae.

While Nicolá shovelled and sifted, Francis set up his Nikon D7500 on the tripod. Not only the script, but the indigenous art works had to be recorded and the photographs attached to forms for registration of the site. The first of these was UNESCO's World Inventory of Rock Art, then the Standard Rock Art Record File. All photographs had to be taken using natural light, since that was how the artist had originally viewed his work. On the dull ledge this meant using long exposure times.

With the dig in progress Francis would have to contend with dust generated by the excavation, but that minor irritation, he knew, was nothing compared to the possibility of raising something interesting from the sandy floor.

With only a brief respite for lunch, so absorbed did Francis become, that if it had not been for the camera he might not have noticed the declining light levels as day slipped into dusk.

At that stage Francis had moved on from the main image and the script to a smaller series of figures beside them. Fitting the flash in defiance of protocol he continued on, studying them carefully. Each one was shaded in white clay, and, as was common in this style of art, each possessed noticeable and exaggerated genitalia.

Only one lacked this attribute, and using his torch for light, Francis leaned forward and studied it breathlessly.

Nicolá squatted beside him. 'Come on, it's almost dark, we'd better get back down to camp.'

He looked up, then pointed. 'In a minute. See this figure?'

'Yes.'

'What is different about him?'

Nicolá coughed, 'He doesn't have the … ah, private parts, of the others. He is thinner, but drawn larger, as if he is important. Could it be that—'

Francis knew that she too was thinking of the snippet from a medieval journal she had read to him in the library. 'The eunuch? Let's not jump to conclusions. Besides, it's almost dark, and I'm hungry.'

'You're right.'

Nicolá leaned against the wall while he packed the camera equipment into the case. 'We don't have to finish everything in one day, there's always tomorrow.'

'I know.'

They walked together out onto the ledge, where the dying sun reflected crimson off the springs. Leaning so close to each other they almost touched, Francis felt himself relaxing slowly.

After five more days in the bush Francis became attuned to the sounds – the pure note of the butcher bird, the cacophony of the blue winged kookaburra, and the cadenza of a thousand varieties of insects. Any change in the pattern, day or night, registered like an alteration to his own heartbeat.

Photographing and cataloguing the script involved one hundred and seventy-two shots with the Nikon. This done, Francis used a fine brush and weak acid to tease away the salts that obscured letters. It was a painstaking task, and would seem tedious to an observer not conscious of the immense satisfaction inherent in this kind of work.

Lunch breaks provided an opportunity to swim in the warm waters of the pool and sit in the shade discussing the increasing number of items Nicolá turned up in the cavern – bone fragments, stone chips and charcoal. Then, in the evenings there were fish for the taking and long hours by the fireside. At night, both retired to their respective tents.

Nicolá took her work seriously, and any distraction during the day met with a sharp rebuff. 'Please, stop talking for five minutes and let me concentrate,' she would say, 'or better still, go for a walk. Give me some peace.'

Thus ostracized, Francis left the intriguing script and turned to the rest of the valley, searching for other ledges and caverns that might hold clues to the long-ago visitors.

On the eastern side, the rock walls extended to the ground, and the ochre-painted goannas, fish, kangaroos and figures that adorned those walls had weathered badly. Francis climbed a sloping ledge where a small soak stained the rocks and gathered in a pool at the root of the cliff. He walked along a stone step just above the ground and found his way barred by creepers, a profusion of berries in clusters along the stems. Wild grape. He plucked one of the plump, purple fruits and took a bite. Its flesh was sweet but left a dry aftertaste in the mouth.

Continuing along the shady lee of the cliff he noted that the wild grape climbers became common. He paused often to eat. Trees also grew along that cliff edge – woollybutt, boab, stinkwood, kapok, salmon gum and black wattles. At the valley's end he stopped, staring at the ridges five hundred metres to the west. He wiped sweat from his eyes and looked again. Steep rock walls rose at least thirty metres from the valley floor. Small trees and shrubs sat atop the massive sandstone edifice like a green woolly cap. It was not the vegetation that caught Francis's attention, but a rock formation that looked too regular – too perfect to be natural.

Crossing the valley floor, he stopped once to study the cliff for a possible place to climb. He had to move south for some minutes before finding a relatively easy route to the summit.

Minutes later, Francis picked his way along the cliff top, walking on great slabs of stone, and patches of sand. Reaching the structure, he circled it, scarcely able to believe what he had found. In essence it was a space some two metres by three, enclosed by an undressed stone wall at chest height. Grass had grown high in the interior, but the walls could not be a geological accident.

A low section at the structure's rear allowed entry and Francis walked in. He leaned on the stones with both elbows. A watcher from that point could observe anyone or anything approaching for some distance. An armed man, or woman, would be able to bear fire in any direction.

Francis walked back to the cliff edge, and, cupping his hands around his mouth, gave a loud series of cooees. The cliffs sent the echoes back and forward, dying at last into nothingness.

Nicolá arrived eventually, hurrying up the difficult slope with sweat beading on her forehead and cheeks. 'What is it?'

'Some kind of breastworks,' Francis said, leaning on the stone parapet, goose bumps rising on his arms. He pictured them here, alone in a hostile land. He pointed out to the north. 'They must have expected a threat from the coast.'

Nicolá saw the others before he did, pointing with one arm along the cliff faces. 'Look at that,' she squealed, 'this isn't the only one.'

'What?'

At first Francis could not see – one of the other structures had fallen to half its original height. Then, it came clear to him. This was just one section of a series of ancient defences.

The stone breastworks were spaced around the valley walls at intervals of between three and five hundred metres. Each stood a minimum of one thousand three hundred millimetres high and was made of natural stone blocks, some of which showed evidence of being split with iron tools. Post holes at each corner showed that they had been topped by a platform of wooden poles.

Four of the structures had survived the intervening centuries intact, while one had degraded into rubble. Lichen had grown on the stones, and generations of birds had left white heaps of dung in and amongst the blocks.

In the dusk when Francis walked with Nicolá between the breastworks, a chill wind blew in from the country's interior. The last remnants of the sun turned the stone a thousand hues of yellow and orange.

Staring out into the coming night, he felt danger in every breath. Wind-stunted trees cast surreal shadows on the stone matrix – malevolent shapes, like daggers on the edges of his vision.

Nicolá wrapped her arms around her middle, goosebumps rising on her skin. 'I can't believe I'm part of this,' she said. 'We're talking about mariners from an age when men wore armour and went into battle on horseback.'

Moving closer to her, as if for comfort, Francis stared out

again at the landscape. 'These people were afraid.'

Nicolá's face looked empty of all subterfuge. 'Why would they be afraid?'

'This is a bolthole, a refuge. Fear drove them here. Fear built these stone walls.' He squatted, using a finger to probe into the soft sand. Nicolá moved up behind him. He felt her hand on his shoulder and froze.

'Fear of what?' she asked.

'I don't know … not the Yeidji I don't think. Something or someone that was very bad.'

Nicolá's fingers kneaded his muscles gently. 'I didn't comment that first night you came back with a nose-bleed and those scratches, but something happened, didn't it?'

Francis wanted to tell her that this place made him feel things that he did not want to feel. That the valley had a memory of its own. Most of all he did not want to tell her of the terror of that evening, and how it lay beneath the surface, like magma seeking out a weakness in the earth's crust.

Closing his eyes he reached back to the people who had built these stone walls. He felt their presence nearby. His heart beat with excitement, knowing that they were on their way.

'Nothing happened,' he said. 'I am not afraid.'

TRINTA E DOIS

The forward members of our patrol moved through waist-high yellow grass and scattered bottle trees. Already we had walked a league to the south, with no sign of interlopers, and our fastest scouts roamed far ahead of our main column.

At length we came to a ridge. From there we looked across a broad expanse of marsh – a place of tall grasses and scattered trees – between the sea and higher ground further on. Surface water was visible in places.

As we descended onto that sodden plain I smelled the burning match of the musketeers. The men moved in formation, cautiously as if in hostile territory. Three armed men brought up the rear.

For a time we walked the hopping deer trails through the grasses, skirting the pools and bogs. In places moisture oozed through cracks and the grass changed to a short green mat that softened with each footfall. Birdcalls sounded in all directions, and if it were not for the attentions of mosquitoes and obstreperous black stinging flies, crossing one quarter of the width of that plain brought no real hardship.

'Ahead lies more bad ground,' a young marine pointed out.

Glutinous black mud, broken with mangrove trees, stretched into the distance. Seawater obviously penetrated to this point at high tide. The mud looked slimy and brown. Bubbles rose through the ooze in places, and pointed roots extended at least a span out of that malodorous surface.

Dom Sebastian conferred with Tonio for a minute before declaring, 'We'll walk to the east, and see if the ground improves.'

At first this ploy helped. Following the edge of the marsh we made substantial progress. Then, however, we reached a point where the channel widened again, and the mud was deep, but not impossibly so. With each step I sank to my ankles before transferring weight for the next. The mangrove trees grew more densely until they formed a dark canopy, and the tramp through mud became an endless chore, legs aching with fatigue and men sweating so they had to drink from foetid pools.

'Holy Mother of God,' someone breathed. 'Look!'

A giant crab, with elongated pincers like a man's thumb and forefinger, stood its ground on the mud nearby. The appendages looked strong enough to crush bone. The thing walked sideways, deadly weaponry held high, until the men had passed. No one suggested catching and eating the creature – it was too hot and oppressive to think of anything but getting through that terrible swamp.

I had come to accept that we would tread through that hell forever when we heard shouts ahead. At first our marines drew their weapons, but instead it was a party of our scouts, running hard. With them they dragged a prisoner.

He was a Portuguese man, bloodied with wounds and striped

with mud, naked as a newborn child. They threw him to the earth at Dom Sebastian's feet. My sense of dread increased. This could only mean that our worst fears had been realised – the enemy had indeed landed on the coast – still in heated pursuit.

One of our fastest runners, a man called Lourenço, spoke for the party of scouts. 'Far away, on the other side of the swamp, we observed the enemy camp, packing up for the day's march and their scouts already moving this way. With fortune on our side we captured one of their forward men just as he entered the marsh.'

'Good work. How far behind us are they?'

'No more than an hour.'

Dom Sebastian approached the naked man, now on his haunches, spitting blood from his lips, eyes wild with fear. Every few moments he would attempt to rise, at which time one of his captors would knock him back to the ground.

Dom Sebastian squatted in front of him. 'What is your name?'

'Filho da puta.'

I looked away. This was not his name, but a virulent insult.

Dom Sebastian looked at the nearest soldier. 'Put out one of his eyes.'

I felt a sudden sickness and fell to my knees. 'Is that necessary?'

Tonio turned on me, eyes hard as stone. 'Turn away, Padre, if you don't have the stomach. Otherwise, say nothing. Our survival may depend on what this man has to say.'

The prisoner's screams tore at my soul. When it was done he was on his knees, holding both hands to his face. Blood seeped from between his fingers. I could not believe that he would now be in any condition to answer questions, yet I underestimated fear, and its power.

'What is your name?' Dom Sebastian asked. 'Hurry, or you will soon be blind in both eyes, and thus as good as dead. Why is your force moving towards us?'

'Our captains plan to sweep along the coast, and if they find you they will kill you all.'

'How many of you are there?'

'Ten score at least.'

'How did you know to come to these shores?'

'When we followed the decoy ship our captain found a message hidden inside. It told of the trick and your sailing plans from there.'

I exchanged glances with Dom Sebastian. A message had been sent in the decoy ship. We both knew that a traitor, therefore, must remain in our midst. Someone who had access to the toy vessel that had so delighted the True King.

Tonio leaned forward, smiling grimly. 'Did you find also a human turd? That was my message for you.'

The men laughed, Tonio loudest of all. The prisoner, eye socket weeping a liquid so loathsome it turned my stomach, hissed back at him.

Dom Sebastian stood up, 'He has nothing more to tell us. Kill him.'

With both arms extended, Tonio placed the point of his sword on our enemy's bare neck.

I turned away before the thing was done.

My mind was busy on that forced march back through the swamp, following our own footsteps. The message in the decoy boat meant that our traitor was still with us, the one who had hired the arsonist on board, and now, with a written message, imperilled us all.

The man from Leal. It was senseless. A small village of no consequence. Who could it be? Someone high ranking enough to have got near the decoy at the last moment.

I put these thoughts aside as, finally, we reached the ridge that marked the beginning of the swamp where we had set off earlier that day. We rested on the high ground looking down onto that expanse of mud and mangrove trees, the men standing and sitting, or drinking on all fours from a small man-made well between the boulders and scrub of that landscape. Most were streaked with sweat, dried mud coating their legs to the knees. Few had the energy to speak in anything but low, tired tones.

Dom Sebastian stared grimly out into the landscape from which the guarda-costras soon must emerge. Despite the tough march he stood as tall as a spire, brow dusted with sweat, heavy jaw marked with dust and unshaven growth.

'Here,' he said, 'we will make an ambush, yet we need all our strength to do so. I need a runner to speed a message to the beach for me. Who is the fleetest?'

The runner Lourenço rose, clear of eye and still light on his feet after all our exertions. 'I volunteer, Dom Sebastian.'

'Leave your weapons. Go swiftly back to the beach and tell them of the danger. Bring every man with a bow or sword and a good arm to wield it. Tell the priests to take all those remaining far upstream and to find sanctuary where they can. Run now, with all speed.'

That worthy young man did not hesitate, laying aside his heavy leather jerkin, bow and sword, keeping only a short dagger on his belt.

'Go with God,' I said. 'You are a brave man.'

Even as Lourenço's footfalls died away, Dom Sebastian turned to face the men. 'They will soon be here, let us prepare. There is no time for earthworks, but a brush fence will keep arrows out — force them to fight hand to hand, and we have the high ground.'

Tonio bowed, 'With a skirmishing party in reserve on the right? That is a good plan, just as we once used against the Brigands of Paes da Veiga. Did we not win victory on that day?'

I coughed, 'These are not mere thieves, but trained soldiers. Is there not a danger that they will skirt your defences and encircle us? Would it not be better to hide your men amongst the slope so that they are out of sight — so that the enemy might walk up close and fall prey to our lead ball and arrows. I agree that they must exit from this general area, but you cannot fortify the entire slope.'

Tonio laughed, his voice ringing in the evening air. 'That might well be the behaviour of a hill bandit, or highwaymen, but we are men of honour. We stand and fight as such.'

'This is too important. You cannot throw lives away here for the sake of good manners. You face a superior enemy. I do not presume to teach you tactics, but beg you to remember last time. Chivalry or victory. Which is more important?' The shadow of Alcácer Quibir passed over the True King's face, and then our eyes locked. I pressed my advantage. 'Think of innocent Aletia, waiting with hope on the beach. What if she does not get away in time?'

Dom Sebastian inclined his head. 'You are right. We will never have another chance to engage the guarda-costras on such fortuitous ground. Tonio, issue the orders, for the men to hide in every hollow, crevice and trunk. As for you, Padre, seek shelter when the time comes — you will be safe behind the crest of the hill.'

Our reinforcements arrived, a hundred and fifty strong. Lourenço himself marched among the first ranks, still looking fresh despite at least two miles of travel. They carried arquebus – muskets from the ship's armoury, casks of powder and even a pair of verso guns. These weapons – each longer than a man and borne by four men, were set up on their swivels in dense cover, yet with a carefully devised field of fire down the slope.

A storm front formed out to sea, and, once night had fallen the lightning bestowed on me fleeting moments of vision. Men chewed dried meat and fish brought up by the reinforcements, and waited, scratching themselves deeper into the earth to pass the time, burning match-cord shielded from view.

I must have dozed at some point, for a hand fell on my shoulder, startling me. It was Tonio. 'Our forward scouts have reported that the enemy are almost through the swamp. They are coming. You must hide now.'

When I looked down into the marsh I saw nothing, yet heard what might have been distant voices. Curiously, I felt no danger, and would have stayed where I was, had I not been guided away by Tonio. When he turned back towards the hidden lines I clambered amongst the rocks until I found somewhere comfortable to sit, yet in full view of the slope.

Now the storm hit in full force, a juggernaut of heavenly power that raked the ground with flying debris. Lightning sheets filled the sky. Jagged forks sought targets on the ground. Thunder cracked like cannon shot – loud enough to frighten even the stoutest heart. Fireflies blinked and swirled in the darkness, and I shivered in premonition. I prayed to our God of hosts for victory, at little human cost to our side.

A thunderclap sounded, somewhat louder than the others. Then, as a dozen muskets fired, I saw their spouts of deadly flame shoot out into the night, illuminating the enemy on the slope.

The verso also discharged their terrible load, with a scorching long flame that scythed dark figures down like broken tiles.

Men shouted and cried, and screamed, then came the shrill sound of steel on steel as they engaged. Now and then lightning would dance off a sword blade like a sunbeam, or leave the impression of the confused scene on my eye, so that even once darkness returned I could still see men fighting and dying on that slope.

Often, Dom Sebastian's voice rose above those of the others. 'With me, loyal marines of Portugal,' he cried more than once, or; 'You are fighting for your country, and for righteousness. Do not yield.'

Oh, how battle nudges the human heart like no other enterprise. Such guilt I feel when I admit my exultation that it was I who had prompted these effective tactics of lying in wait and striking without warning, in denial of all the rules of fair-play.

Somewhat indecorously, I left my hiding place and moved closer to the battle, watching and listening, praying under my breath for our men to prevail.

Yet we had not reckoned on the efficacy of the trained swordsmen of the guarda-costras against a force of whom the majority were middle-aged seamen and raw lads.

Hearing the sound of men in armour running towards me, I cried out, 'Who is it?'

Dark figures in the night. Fear filled my heart. At least some of the enemy force, I realised, had come through or around the fight unscathed.

Turning on my heels I ran for my life, blundering, fleeing from them. I ran until my wind was gone, then turned, in vain hope that they might pass me by. Death loomed, and with a strange, pious thrill, I reached under my cloak, drawing the cross that hung from a chain there and moved to block their progress. This I lifted as if to ward off Satan himself.

'Stop. Creatures of Satan,' I gasped out.

Still they came on, whooping with killing excitement. They held their blades high, faces contorted with effort. The arms that held those weapons were sinuous and strong. Even at the last moment I did not waver, but watched the blade come down.

My crucifix and cassock did not give them pause, nor even provoke comment. The blow landed high in my shoulder, slicing through flesh and jarring against bone. The impact drove me to my knees. Even then, however, they were not finished with me. One of the men lifted his sword, and brought the heavy pommel down onto my forehead like a club.

This gang of guarda-costras were in a hurry to escape, however, and the blow was but a light one. The pommel is a heavy weight, designed to balance a long iron blade, and a hard blow would have crushed my skull.

The escaping enemy left me to die, for as I lifted the hand of my untouched arm to my shoulder injury, I felt my blood, thick, sticky and warm, seep between my fingers like the waters of the Styx.

I whispered the Lord's Prayer, and soon after, abandoning myself to His care, I slipped away into blessed unconsciousness.

TRINTA E TRES

Francis left the valley, picking his way along the trail as it wound through the trees. Standing beside one of the watchtowers on the cliffs he had seen smoke, and decided to investigate. Dry speargrass brushed his knees, and scrubby woodland continued uninterrupted on all sides.

Impatient, he broke into a fast walk, passing along an animal trail and through a patch of denser bush, on into a smaller clearing. A small fire burned in the centre, and the breeze chased the smoke towards him, stinging his eyes and nose.

Beside the fire sat the old Yeidji man, black as coal apart from a grey beard and hair. A dog, its coat riddled with fat grey ticks, lay in the shade nearby.

'Henry?'

The old man looked up, but said nothing. Francis settled down beside him. 'You've walked a long way.'

Henry shrugged as if distance meant nothing to him.

Francis persisted, 'Did you come to find us?'

The old man continued to stare. 'Mi bin weidingabat.'

'Waiting? Who for?'

'Da einjul talim det datbala bina kaman.'

The flesh on Francis's arms rose. 'Who is the angel?'

'Gel.'

'A woman?'

'Ya,' he said, then pointed back towards the valley. Exposing one lone tooth and a line of gums, Henry swiped his throat in the universal symbol of violent death. 'Dedliwan. Lukat.'

'What do you mean?'

'Don dringgim woda o don dagat bij.'

Francis frowned. 'The water is sweet, and the fish are good to eat. Why wouldn't I eat and drink there?'

Henry folded his arms in a superior fashion. 'Bad kantri. Lukat.'

Francis changed the subject. 'Tell me about the white men who once came here.'

'Kaman bot. Longtaim.' Using his arms as an extension of his voice, the old man indicated his land and people with a broad sweep of his arms. 'Longtaim. Siknis. Ded.' He stood up, and there in the dust beside the fire he started to dance, his bare feet thumping against the earth in rhythm, accompanied by a wailing voice as old and chilling as the landscape. Francis felt the hair of his arms rise against his shirt as he watched the skinny, dusty legs.

Even though he could not decipher a syllable of that song, Francis felt meaning through the images that crowded into his mind. Images of illness and death, murder and treachery. Henry's eyes rolled high so the red-flecked whites were wholly visible.

Finally, the old man stopped and settled back on the earth, his bony legs folded under him. The exertion appeared not to have affected him.

He touched Francis's arm, changing the subject. 'Yolabat gadem tubeka?'

Francis smiled. He had been asked the same question before. 'No, sorry. I don't smoke.'

Apparently unimpressed, Henry stood up and collected a long, thin spear that had been leaning on a tree. The head was made of iron, ground to an edge on stone. He kicked sand on his fire and picked up a plastic shopping bag that held an old cordial bottle of water, a knife, and a piece of meat.

Henry started to walk away.

'Don't go,' Francis called. 'Come back. I want to talk to you.'

The old man did not turn.

TRINTA E QUATRO

Once or twice, during the nightmare that followed, voices penetrated through the mists of sleep and unconsciousness. I tried to raise my head and call out, but found it impossible to do so. Pain assaulted me from all directions – I moved my left arm and winced. Hours passed before I was aware enough to be surprised that I was not yet making my journey across the black waters, Charon my pilot, dark and cruel, poling his way in ceaseless toil.

Finding my eyes gummed closed I worked them open, then raised myself on one knee. Looking around, I shook my head to clear my vision, before easing to my feet and staggering in an attempt to hold my own weight. I saw that I was in the midst of a patch of brush both thick and near impenetrable. The sun, however, was directly overhead, so it was therefore close to noon.

A wave of vertigo assaulted me, driving me down to my knees. Memories of the battle came back to me like the sketches of a deranged artist – the lightning flash of firearms, the shouts of men fighting and dying and the shapes of warriors in the darkness as they thundered towards me.

In that position I set out to explore my wounds. The gash in my shoulder remained open and deep, while the crown of my head was covered with a mound of dried blood. This injury had triggered an internal ache as dull as a blunt knife. Even so, I knew enough about the physiology of the human body to be confident that I was not in mortal danger, and this knowledge allowed me to force my body up and eastwards towards our haven on the beach.

In all my days there have been few terrors as intense as finding myself alone in a strange and vast land, with my comrades and friends nowhere to be seen. The sounds of bird and animal life, and the wind whistling through the needle-like leaves of the she-oaks, only added to my anxiety.

I staggered along for some time before I saw a pall of black smoke in the distance, on the exact bearing of my destination. Closing in on those twin bluffs above the beach I smelled the chemical stench of tar, and a most dreadful certainty came on me.

Lord protect them. Lord save them. Lord protect them …

Even in my pain and exhaustion I knew enough to be cautious, creeping close to the cliff edge until finally I looked down onto the beach where we had spent so many pleasant days. There I saw a sight that chilled my blood.

Our ship still lay careened just beyond the reach of high tide, but it was afire − burning and smouldering still. Our mode of escape from this place had been destroyed.

The men who controlled that beach carried or wore helmets with golden visors, parading and strutting like cock roosters. A pen had been constructed of beach driftwoods and spare timbers and inside that area were a score of prisoners. I recognised many of them, but try as I might I could not discern Dom Sebastian,

Duarte, Tonio or my beautiful Aletia amongst them.

On my knees, I did then weep, wondering what might have happened to those I loved so well. They were not here, that was all I knew for sure right then.

Through tear-filled eyes, I skirted the beach, mindful of the many sentries, wandering down to the stream some distance upstream from the beach. Rain had swollen this waterway so that it gushed between its stone confines, brown and churning, carrying sticks and other debris along with it.

The wound on my shoulder was already swollen, and my head pounded with the first stages of fever. I drank water, brown and discoloured as it was, like a drunk drinks wine. The air in my nostrils felt like fire.

Yet my mind was clear enough to know that I would find my people upstream, the only practicable direction in which to flee.

These first stretches of the waterway were familiar to me, and it was easy enough for me to follow the spoor of several hundred feet. When a waterfall or pool blocked my forward progress I selected the easiest route and struggled upwards. Soon, however, the stream spread out over a broad and sandy bed. On either side, rocky ridges rose in eroded clumps and outcrops – no longer red as they had been, but stained black by the elements. Dark holes and caverns beckoned, and sculptured blocks of stone reared. Always, on either side, pale yellow grass grew high as a man's thigh, sharp and crackling dry.

As I walked, the pain in my body fell away, replaced by a lightness-of-foot and a high-pitched whistle in my ears. I was alternately hot and cold. I found myself giggling.

When my hand probed the wound below my shoulder I was surprised to find it burning hot and slippery with clear fluids, a trail that continued down my belly and legs.

I don't remember leaving the clear trail left by my fellow shipmates, but at some stage in that day I pointed my nose for the wilderness and my feet followed.

The following part of my account will seem disjointed, for my memories of this period are dim. I cannot tell what is fact or fiction, as from the time I first wandered away from the stream I began to have visions. I had not eaten for a day and a night, nor slept, and had been walking or running for much of that time. My physical condition was thus extreme – my mind weakened and susceptible to the wiles of Satan.

Later that day, as I wandered I know not where, it was first with food that he mocked me, promising me sides of smoked ham and honey-glazed venison, or fresh bread from the bakers of the Alfama. As soon as the image appeared in my mind I would run towards it, then, realising the trick, change direction in the vain hope that he might not find me again.

Night fell, and Satan tried other tricks on me. Of these he knew my susceptibility. As I stumbled on into the darkness, he filled my loins with liquid fire until I hungered for the visions that filled my heart – shameful and beautiful – visions of one I had loved and others I had despised yet been fascinated by nonetheless.

This struggle was so acute that I continued walking through another night and into daylight, crossing a vast plain, thinly wooded and studded with the earthen homes of termites, many of which reared above my head. The madness that had visited now engulfed me. Through days and nights, whether one, two, or more I have no way of knowing, Satan tormented me.

Once I found myself at the top of a cliff, with all the glories of mankind spread out before me. One civilization rising. Another falling. I saw the great empires, and then the glory of the Fifth. The angel Gabriel came, with a promise dear to my heart. I knew for a fact then that Rui Chanoca was right; that a new world order was within reach.

Two or three times, in that maze of stone, I blundered into galleries of ancient art rendered in ochre and clay on the walls – the artistic expression of the Yeidji that I had earlier noted in the ledges beside the stream above our camp on the beach. Now, however, I sensed the depth of feeling behind those dancing brown figures and animal representations. I felt the bones of past generations, their struggles, births and deaths – drought and famine.

Strangely, I remember the moment when I fell for the last time. It was dark, and I had traversed a long stretch of boulders. I went down, realising that no matter how far I walked, I could not outpace death. It was time to lie down.

The Yeidji youth appeared, and at first seemed to be just another vision. Yet, I recognised him from the beach. He was thin but wiry-strong, with arms that thickened at the juncture of the shoulders. His bush of hair was plastered with clay, and ritual scars crossed his chest.

The bony hands held a matt of grasses, moistened with water, to my lips, over and over again, while I felt the life-sustaining liquid trickle down my throat in agonisingly slow increments.

Over the course of several days he came and went, while I slept fevered dreams. I know for a fact that he saved my life.

At the sight of Duarte's face I drew back and screamed in fright, imagining this as yet another manifestation of the Fallen One.

Yet, when his palm touched my forehead, his skin was warm and human. Empathy filled his eyes as he carried me to a comfortable nook on the stream bed and used flint and steel to strike a camp fire.

I had never thought of Duarte as a healer, yet if I woke with a thirst he was there with a whittled cup brimming with cool water, and when I hungered he snared young hopping deer and roasted the tender chunks. Days passed before I considered what he must have done for me in those first hours.

'How did you find me?' I croaked.

'You left a trail like a boar. I stumbled on it.'

'The Yeidji lad – I think he came to me – helped me.'

'Ah, I saw footprints behind cover. They were watching. They watch still. I don't think that they mean us any harm.'

In the dark night hours Satan returned to me in nightmares so intense I screamed out until Duarte comforted me with his arms and soft words. My thoughts turned often to Aletia and Dom Sebastian.

'Do not fret, Padre,' Duarte reassured me many times. 'They are together, and safe. Dom Sebastian found refuge inland, and is arraying his forces to protect us all.' He paused. 'He is heartbroken that he had to leave you – yet apparently he and the men searched for many hours.'

Each day I walked a little further, and gained more weight. I bathed in bracing cool water, and in the evenings I helped with the cooking. After several longer, brisk, exploratory walks I began to feel that I would cope with the journey back to those whom I loved and missed with every heartbeat.

'We will leave tomorrow,' I declared.

'Are you sure, Padre?' Duarte asked. 'You wandered a long way. We have a good distance to travel.'

'Please don't fret on my behalf – you have done so much. Further delay will cause me more heartache than the exertion will, surely.'

And so we left after a breakfast of roasted catfish. I carried a fresh-cut stick and a light burden. Duarte slipped a skin bag over his shoulder that contained some crudely-dried fish and those few of his belongings he had brought along.

In the middle afternoon I touched Duarte's arm and signalled him to silence with a finger on my lips. We had been crossing a woodland plain, with stone castles rearing high on all points of the horizon. A flock of the flightless birds, so similar to ostriches ran off in a group – the first time I had seen such a number of them. It was not those, however, that had caught my attention.

A broad, lily-filled lagoon, shady with those unusual paper-barked trees, lay just ahead. Three dark children, one no more than three or four years, and the eldest on the verge of adolescence, played along those banks – splashing, laughing, running, and diving far out into the water before repeating the experience.

After a minute of watching, I nodded to Duarte and we kept walking, changing direction in order to give the lagoon a wide berth. Their play was too carefree, too natural, to disturb.

On the second day we came to a waterway, with red and yellow streaked cliffs on either side. The current flowed in a westerly direction, and Duarte was quite certain that we needed to cross it in order to continue. Here there were substantial pools, however, with grey drowned tree branches emerging from the depths like dead men's fingers. After a difficult descent Duarte pointed towards a scaly head protruding from the water near the far bank.

'Tashacha,' he said. 'A big one.'

The creature's presence necessitated a decision on whether we should make a raft, or walk upstream until we found a crossing place. With little hesitation we settled on the latter option.

The riverside trail we followed had been used before and this made for easy going. The trees here crowded close, and the canopy grew thick enough to make the light dull.

'It's nice to travel in the shade, for a change,' Duarte commented.

I was enjoying the cool also, and my mind was far from my surroundings when the track narrowed and we found ourselves in the lee of a sharp-sided gorge, thick with overhanging trees and drooping vines.

The sight that confronted us turned my heart to ice. Moving without caution we ran into a large party of Yeidji hunters. All carried spears, and one had the carcass of a large hopping deer over his shoulders. The leader changed grip on his spear, bringing it into balance.

No words could stop the man from impaling me. The only option was to show that I was defenceless. I opened my extended palms. My eyes pleaded, *We are not a threat to you.*

Taking a step backwards off the path I motioned to Duarte to follow. In response, the leader relaxed his grip on his weapon, lifted one hand, and touched my cheek. He smelled of wood smoke and of the land itself. Encouraged, the other men crowded close, touching and looking. No one spoke.

One pawed Duarte's hair, entranced by the light colour and fine texture.

'Follow me,' I said to Duarte, 'and don't make any sudden movements.' I sidled up to the track, my eyes on the strangely gentle Yeidji men.

Walking on, we were half way into a small settlement before I registered what I was seeing. Smoke rose from a dozen or more cooking fires. The dwellings themselves were stout structures of cut green timber with bark cladding. The yellow dogs of that land lay in patches of shade, staring warily at us as we passed.

Children ran from between the huts, laughing. I stopped, my heart touched, wistful for the orphanage I had left behind. Ten months had passed since I heard the sound of very small children playing, and it seemed to me that the games and excited squealing varied little between cultures. They stopped and stared as if we had risen from the river itself.

Seeing the pelt of a tashacha hanging on a pole framework, I wondered at the prowess of those who killed such a thing with a spear. Moving as slow as a heartbeat we rounded the corner until the village was out of sight. I wiped away the sweat that had broken out along my forehead, but could not hide my excitement at this glimpse into their lives.

The sun had dipped low when we located a stretch of the river shallow enough to cross. The water ran deeper than it looked from the shore, and the hard pebble bed was coated with a green slime that made walking difficult. We had negotiated most of the distance successfully before Duarte fell backwards, landing fully in the water and floating down with the current for a dozen paces.

Laughing, he recovered his feet, though his sodden gear would have to be dried. The youth shook his head as if to acknowledge his carelessness, and made his way to the bank.

Stumbling from the water we both saw the big russet-brown serpent, coiled amongst the rocks. I pointed it out to Duarte. There were many varieties of snake in this land, from harmless patterned giants to thick and ugly killers. This species was unknown to me, and I had never seen one react like it.

Instead of retreating, the serpent went from a coiled hazard to an angry, striking monster in a fraction of time so short it defied explanation. I was not even certain that Duarte had been bitten until he cried out, dropped his belongings and hopped away, holding his leg. The snake still did not retreat, arching its body so its head was high off the ground.

'Oh sweet God,' Duarte cried, 'the snake bit me.'

The bite must have been severe, because blood trickled from between my novice's fingers. At my approach the snake turned and slithered towards me, before rearing up once more. I shrieked and danced back, frustrated in my attempt to assist Duarte.

Picking up some driftwood I tossed it ten paces behind the snake. The creature moved with the speed of lightning again, making for the decoy, yet stopping short of striking at it.

This movement gave me time to lift a rock with both hands – as much weight as I could bear. I did not risk moving close enough to give it any chance at attacking. Instead I launched the rock with all the force of my arms and shoulders. True to my aim it landed around the snake's middle and pinned it while I found a stick to crush the evil head. Finally, I left the dying reptile and ran to Duarte.

The pain came quickly, and I could do nothing but light a fire and fetch water while my friend gripped the wound in both hands and rocked, 'Help me, for the love of God. Help me.'

Taking a steaming tin pot from the fire, I bathed the wound. Two jagged puncture marks wept blood and copious venom. To hide it from view I ripped cloth and bound the area.

'I will die, Padre, won't I?' Duarte asked. His teeth chattered with shock.

'Of course not.'

'It's not far now,' he said. 'You will have to walk without me. Walk due east according to the sun and you will find the stream that meanders to our beach, follow it upstream and you will reach the stone valley where Dom Sebastian waits.'

'You will recover, and walk with me,' I said.

'No Padre—' His teeth started to chatter with shock, and he clutched at the wound and groaned.

We had both been there on the beach when hunters carried in a marine who had been bitten. He had lived for just an hour or two, his screams echoing from the cliffs.

Duarte moved both hands to cover his abdomen, groaning at the spreading pain. In an attempt to foil the surging agony he rolled forward onto his knees and stood. He stumbled forward and would have fallen but for my steadying hand. He vomited onto the riverside sand. I eased him back down to a sitting position. His eyes dilated and he moaned, 'Cut it off.'

I stared, not comprehending.

'Cut my leg off before the poison reaches my heart. It's the only way.'

It was too late. We both knew that.

Duarte leaned to one side and spat. Bright red blood showed in the sputum. He started to shake, his spine arching like that of a lunatic. I prayed for the end, but my novice hung on for a long time, sweating so profusely that it ran in droplets onto the sand below his neck and shoulders.

I held Duarte's hand as he died, choking, crying for his faraway mother, deep in the cattle country of the Ribatejo. While the fire burned down unattended I wept for the lost life and departing soul of a friend, lying awake in the darkness, hugging my knees, curled like an infant, wanting comfort – a womb to shelter me and take away the pain.

TRINTA E CINCO

The lack of Portuguese artefacts from the cavern surprised both Francis and Nicolá. When finally one appeared in the litter at the bottom of the sieve, however, it was more precious and informative than anything they had dreamed of.

Nicolá gave a shriek of excitement and called for him with a tremor in her voice, holding a small silver object between her thumb and forefinger.

Later, back at the camp table, Francis watched her enter the reference in the locus sheet, one hand on her forehead as she wrote.

> *Item number: 167*
>
> *Trench 1, Cavern,*
>
> *Item: Medallion, solid silver. 35mm x 27mm
> x 6mm,*
>
> *Provenience: Grid 2,5 Depth 98mm.*
>
> *Distinguishing marks: Likeness of Portuguese
> Saint Isobel.*

The medallion, newly cleaned, sat on a square of soft cloth. Nicolá examined the rear face with a magnifying glass.

'Here,' Francis said, 'let me see it.'

Nicolá smiled, and passed the medallion across. Francis concentrated for some seconds before he spoke.

'It has a representation of Saint Isobel and the Portuguese words, "Keep me safe."' He lifted the medallion close to his eyes as if to pry secrets out of the bright metal. Two, perhaps three minutes passed before he lowered the item, and handed it back to Nicolá.

Nicolá moved close and placed one hand on his shoulder, fingers curling close to his neck. Responding, he stood and allowed his arms to creep around her side until his hands linked at the back. He felt the faint damp line of perspiration along her spine. She smelled of earth and water. His eyes closed involuntarily as he breathed her fragrance.

The embrace lasted only seconds before she broke away.

In the evening, after a meal of rice and a rehydrated chicken curry, Francis opened a cask and poured two enamel mugs half full of grainy, harsh red wine. 'To the *Nossa Senhora dos Anjos*.'

'And to success.'

Francis swallowed a mouthful of the wine and raised his glass again. 'To the eminent archaeologist Nicolá Massane.'

Nicolá waved one hand. 'No more toasts, please. I get drunk so easy, and you don't want to see me like that.'

'Why not? Might be fun.'

They drank in companionable silence, but when Francis filled his glass for the third time, Nicolá begged off. 'No, it's water for me. I'm getting a headache. I think I'll get ready for bed if you don't mind.'

He sat alone, nursing his wine as if it were an aged classic, half watching as she cleaned her teeth then disappeared to the latrine area with a torch. When she came back she warmed herself at the fire then kissed him on the cheek and touched his shoulder.

'Good night.'

'A successful day. Let's hope for another tomorrow.'

'Yes.'

When she had gone Francis stared at the flames. Then, on impulse, he returned to his tent and collected the medallion from its place. There in the firelight, he held it so the flames reflected on the silver, then lowered it back to the bed of wool. Laying the box on the sandstone table beside him, Francis stood and returned to his tent, emerging with a sketch pad and 2B pencil.

Sitting again, he flicked through the few pages he had already used – a plan of the cavern and the location of the major rock art. Another page showed the basic orientation of the valley itself.

Taking up a fresh sheet Francis began to draw, scarcely aware of what he was doing. Working beyond his ability, the plane of a cheek formed out of nothing on the page. Then, curling tresses of dark hair fell around a shapely neck.

With his brows furrowed in concentration, Francis shaded in the eyes – the most difficult and personal part of any image. Time passed, wine sitting on the table forgotten as he poured everything into the pencil gripped between thumb and forefinger.

The eyes took shape, then the nose; full lips. Smiling now, Francis worked in the slender neck, then, nestling at the base he etched in the medallion itself.

The woman looked like no real person he had known. She was no more than eighteen years of age, and beautiful, her cheeks perfectly sculpted and her lips sensuous. Francis put down the pencil and stared, still unsure of what he had done. The quizzical smile on the face of his creation bewitched him. Time passed, and for that short interval the woman on the page might have been alive.

The realisation that she was not there – that he could not see her – made a sense of frustration grow within Francis. He screwed the page into a tight ball and threw it onto the fire. The flames consumed it until nothing was left but black ash.

When it was gone he felt very alone indeed.

TRINTA E SEIS

The day after the death of Duarte, I was welcomed back into the company of my friends and comrades, stumbling into the arms of Amador de Brito and a hunting party.

The valley they inhabited, I had seen from the outset, was a remarkable and special place, at least fifty acres in extent, surrounded on three sides by cliffs of stone, open to the north. Near the centre, a deep pool, warm with heat from the centre of the earth, bled away to the south in a narrow stream, ebbing through a narrow grotto, then flowing towards the distant beach, now in the hands of our enemies.

This valley was no wilderness, but an organised enclave. To Dom Sebastian, military encampments came as naturally as breathing. He designated this or that piece of ground for this or that purpose, and directing the construction of works that would enhance the defensibility of the valley.

The full complement of around three hundred souls – cooks, soldiers, slaves, stowaways, adventurers and seamen had become two separate companies. The Alto, or high company, had responsibility for defending the cliffs, while the much larger Baixo, or low company, remained on the valley floor to protect the grotto, the collection of rude shelters around the pool itself and the open northern end. There were also workers filling support roles such as cooking and logistics.

Most impressive of the defences were a series of rough breastworks on the cliffs, spaced some three hundred paces apart. Each was circular in shape, fashioned from piled-up stonework supporting a platform of poles and a watchtower above. We had no masons amongst us, and no access to the limestone necessary for mortar. Instead the cracks were filled with mud and ash, providing a smooth surface and an impression of solidity.

Soon after dawn on my second day in that place, I joined Dom Sebastian on his rounds, climbing the cliffs and moving amongst our defenders, admiring the way he could banter with his men – recalling the most insignificant problems and concerns.

'José, has your liver settled down? Does it worry you this morning?' or 'Now, Domingos, remember you promised me to leave the dice alone? Have you adhered to our bargain? Braz Coutinho tells me that you owe him fifteen centi and you cannot pay—'

In return the men greeted him with genuine pleasure, sharing minor news of the watch in the manner of men who have spoken little for many hours and have saved inconsequential scraps merely for the pleasure of telling their leader.

'Dom Sebastian, after midnight the strangest owl landed on that dead tree, just there … his wings were as wide as a man's spread arms and—'

Up here, on the cliffs, a man towered over the surrounding country, with a view that made him feel like a bird of prey – one of the multitudinous kite-hawks and eagles that hovered in the daytime thermals – looking down on that glistening pool in the valley's centre, surrounded by slabs of red stone.

Dom Sebastian thrust an arm towards the coast. 'They are out there,' he hissed, 'yet they are clever. Each time my scouts locate them they move. They want me to engage them – they want us to seek them out.'

'And will you?'

'No. There is nothing out there to sustain them. Soon they will have no choice but to attack. If they want me badly enough then that is what they must do, even though they know I hold the tactical advantage.'

Rui Chanoca occupied an overhang beneath the cliffs. I found him squatting on the hard stone, surrounded by the bright painted marks of the Yeidji. He had passed his time with recording the name of our ship and the date with the same tools and pigments as they.

'This is a place of power,' he told me.

'Indeed?'

'Men and women have lived here for a long time, perhaps since before the days of Moses. Each living being leaves his mark behind on the landscape. The land remembers. Blood stains the soil as surely as indigo stains cloth.'

Those words were difficult to reconcile with my own beliefs. 'You have an unusual perspective, for the land itself has no soul.'

'Oh but it has, close your eyes and you can feel the ghosts in your heart.' He pointed down to the centre of the valley, to the hot springs surrounded by the red stone that our people were so fond of swimming in. 'We should not stay here too long. That pool is not good for us.'

'Indeed? And why is that?'

'If you, like me, had been to the ancient mines of Almadén in my native Spain, you would know what I am talking about. The deep red stone, that you will see in veins and fissures of that rock, is cinnabar, the ore of mercury.' He paused to scratch his chin, as if irritated by the thought. 'It almost always comes with volcanic waters, like those down below, and must always be treated with caution.'

I looked unconvinced. 'Yet the Yeidji still come here.'

He pointed to the paintings on the wall. 'Yes, they have used the cinnabar as a pigment, which is why the colour is so bright, but I doubt that they would breathe its vapor, drink the water or eat fish from the pool.'

Even now, at the remove of several years, I still surprise myself at how little regard or thought I paid to that observation.

Soon after my arrival in the valley I awoke after moonset to see Aletia rising in the darkness, slipping out of the hut and away into the night. I almost rose to ask her what she was doing, but tiredness took me, and I was asleep long before her return. In the morning, when I intended to ask her about the incident she distracted me by smiling and lowering her voice as if to share a secret.

'I have found something I would like to share with you, Padre.'

Secrets had always intrigued me, yet I could not think of what might be worth dragging me across the harsh landscape to see. 'How far away?'

'Not so far, just a little way.'

'Is it an animal?'

'No.'

'A plant.'

'No, nor a bird, nor insect either, but a place.' Her eyes sparkled. 'Come and let me show you.'

Aletia led me towards the eastern cliffs, skipping ahead as if unable to contain her excitement. Finally we reached a place where a tree had fallen against the cliff side, enabling her to climb the trunk at a comfortable angle.

'I am not going up there,' I said.

'Please Padre, you will never see anything like it again.'

Muttering curses, I did as she asked, bending over in an undignified fashion to ascend that tree. At the top I found myself on a ledge, standing before the dark entrance to a cave.

Exclaiming aloud, I looked at her face, bright with excitement at sharing the find. 'Come in and see,' she said.

Hesitant, I turned to look towards the pool at our valley's centre. 'No, we'd best go back.'

Aletia pouted at me. 'Please, come and look with me.' She brushed past me, and moved through the entrance and out of view. A moment later her face reappeared. 'Come and see, Padre. God has made this way beautiful, I promise you.'

My eyes adjusted to the darkness as I moved on inside. Aletia scurried onwards like an animal, into the darkness.

The surface of that passage was of crusty sand, and my progress rapid. The air, however, was earthy, smelling of past aeons, of time and life itself.

Just as the darkness became complete, faint light glowed ahead, beyond the crawling figure of Aletia. The passage became wider and higher. I paused to catch both my breath and senses with just the top of my hair in contact with the stone ceiling. My guide stopped, restless with excitement, 'Come, Padre. I want to show you.'

Unafraid now, I walked on as the light strengthened. Then, seeing Aletia rise to her feet, I did the same, having to walk on in a stooped fashion until the ceiling rose further and I was able to stand erect.

I followed her into a widening chamber, fifteen or more paces across and so long as for the other end to be lost in the darker areas ahead. Light filled the main cavern from a ledge that opened up on the cliffs high above the valley floor, with tree roots slipping through, attached to the hard stone as if by cement.

Streaks of discolouration ran down along the cavern walls, where millennia of rain had seeped through, creeping along the stone to the earth, leaving white salts and green algae smears as it did so. As my eyes continued to assess that cavern I saw a sight that caused me to fall to my knees and make the sign of the cross. I cried out with shock and my eyes turned on Aletia who seemed to delight in my reaction.

I gathered myself. I had been to the Capela dos Ossos in Evora, where the very walls are made from the skulls and bones of the thousands of monks who have lived and died in the adjoining monastery. Only that sight could have prepared me for this — in every natural crack and fault that covered those walls were jammed dozens of human skulls, eye sockets staring vacantly into space. Some were fresh enough that dried skin still clung to the bone itself, and wrappings of papery tree bark half covered them.

'See,' Aletia cried, 'I told you that this was a place of death.'

'My dear God,' I breathed. 'It is a mausoleum.'

'The Yeidji,' she went on, taking my hand. 'They must come here with their dead.'

As the macabre remains loosened their hold on my vision I saw the ochred marks on the walls themselves. One was an enormous, many-hued serpent that wound for twenty paces along those walls, and others were of lizards, hopping deer and fish. These, however, were obviously of significance, for, unlike the rock ledges on the cliffs there were few of the images that crowded every space outside – the work, perhaps, of children and adults at play, or some lesser magic that had not the gravitas necessary for this place of death.

Most of the stone walls were bare of marks, though I searched assiduously. For a further ten or more minutes I walked around that cathedral-like space with Aletia, investigating several side passages and caverns, all dead ends.

'We'd better go now, but thank you for bringing me here.'

'You like it?' she asked.

Like was not the correct word. I felt privileged, as if I had peered into the soul of a people. Death is common to all cultures, it is only the reaction that differs.

That night I was determined to remain alert. When Aletia rose, again in the dark of the morning, I slipped off my bed of grass and followed.

At first I thought that she might be heading to the pool to drink, but once there, she made no move towards the water, instead skirting the edge, finally reaching a glade hidden from view by the trees, the tiny stream winding through it. Now I heard a soft whistle. A tall figure emerged from the trees and embraced the young woman. Voices drifted across, though I could not hear the words.

During my absence, I was aware, the relationship between Aletia and Dom Sebastian had altered. They met several times each day in this pretty bend in the stream. Aletia's eyes would drift often towards it, no matter what else she happened to be doing.

Here they recited their poems and prose, and at times, thinking themselves unobserved, they would hold hands. I suspected that they had already exchanged tentative kisses.

Daytime, however, was one thing. Secret night meetings were another. I hid in the darkness of the trees while they settled down, arms around each other, still talking softly. Their heads came together and they kissed.

My eyes moved from my beautiful Aletia to this giant of a man – a modern day Viriathus, and my beating heart calmed as I remembered what kind of man he was. I backed away from my hiding place, and returned through the night to my bed of dry grass in one of the huts.

The next day I tried to engineer a private audience with the True King. It seemed that every time I opened my mouth someone else wandered up to talk to him. Finally I sent away a needy marine corporal and gripped his sleeve firmly. 'Dom Sebastian,' I said. 'I want to know what you feel for Aletia. Is it something strong that will stand even when we return to Portugal?'

Dom Sebastian's mouth opened. All the sophistication fell away. 'What do you mean?'

'You foolish man. Do you love her? Do you really love her?'

'Love?' He rolled the word around on his tongue as if testing it for sharp edges. His eyes met my own, level and serious. 'All my life I have worn a mask. I have been a man to men, and a king to my followers. I have been pious in my cathedrals and dutiful in the presence of my family.' He hesitated. 'With this woman I am none of those things. I am just a man. When I am not with her, I count the seconds until I am. Is that love?'

The words dragged me back through the years to another place and time. My breath caught in my throat. 'Yes, Dom Sebastian, that is love.'

He embraced me so hard I felt that my ribs might snap. 'Thank you Padre. You are wise.'

'We will not waste time then, the ceremony must take place tomorrow.'

'Ceremony?'

'A wedding ceremony, Dom Sebastian.' The look on the great man's face was that of one who has just spilled a pail of boiling water on his foot.

Walking away, I pondered that many great men might have taken a girl as delightful as Aletia for a mistress in their later years, or as a diversion in their prime. Dom Sebastian, I suspected, would only ever have one love.

Rui Chanoca came down from his place of meditation and, using a sliver of bone for a needle, and thread picked from discarded clothing, he sewed up the tears in Aletia's best remaining gown. He also directed teams of flower gatherers, and when the time came our hearth area was decorated with garlands of all colours: the tiny but vibrant mauve flowers of a native heather that grew around cracks and boulders in the cliff sides, the round pink blooms of a small herb, bunches of flowering wattle and a spectacular type of sun dew flower that invites insects onto its treacherous petals then traps and consumes them.

The only impediment to the day was Tonio Fonseca, who scowled darkly when told of the upcoming nuptials and expressed his feelings when Aletia was at my side.

'You must call a halt to this foolishness,' he cried. I saw the hurt in Aletia's eyes as he said it.

'Why would I do that, Tonio?'

'Dom Sebastian does not love her. He is infatuated. Do you really think an orphan girl is suitable as the wife of a king?'

'You are wrong Tonio,' I said.

He looked as if he were about to interject and I raised one hand to forestall him. 'It is sometimes hard for a man to see his best friend married – worried that they will never share the closeness of bachelorhood again, yet I want you to think foremost of Dom Sebastian's happiness. Not yours.'

Strangely, his eyes had the moist look of a man who was about to cry, and abruptly he turned away. I squeezed Aletia's hand. 'He is jealous. It will pass.'

'Do you think so?' Her eyes were as innocent as stars.

'I am certain. He too will come to love you – how can he resist?'

At length she smiled back, and twirled so her skirt flared around her knees. 'Oh, I cannot wait, not for another minute.'

The wedding was conducted according to custom, in the open air near the huts we had built beside the hot springs, beginning with the rites that must take place before the ceremony itself. The best-loved of these saw Aletia on her hands and knees, lowing like a cow, while Dom Sebastian pretended to be the farmer who must find and recognise her as one of his own.

Dom Sebastian stood, sweating no less fiercely than if he were chopping down a tree or running five leagues. Occasionally he looked down and his eyes would meet Aletia's. In spite of Rui's efforts, the young woman wore rags for her wedding gown, yet they were clean, patched rags. The broad yellow blossoms of the plentiful local cotton trees decorated her hair. She smelled as fresh as morning, her skin as clear as that of any sought-after maid of Lisbon on the promenade.

For a gift Dom Sebastian gave her a silver chain with a medallion of Saint Isobel that had belonged to his mother, and a rough diamond that he promised would one day be cut to adorn a ring. This last had required a long and secret night walk, and the labour of both myself and Tonio with a shovel.

When I finished the ceremony Aletia's brown eyes were moist and lovely. The audience clapped while the dark-haired young woman, and the tall, strongly-featured man embraced.

Dom Sebastian took Aletia in his arms and kissed her. When they danced, he moved with easy grace, and the young woman complemented his movements. Even we priests, while too dignified to join in the dancing, clapped our hands to provide a rhythm. Dom Sebastian had halved the term of guard duty so all the men would enjoy their turn at the celebration.

For most of us the wedding was a reminder of home, and a slice of normality, in a new life that was both alien and strange. The party reached its peak when Aletia removed one shoe and passed it to Dom Sebastian. By tradition the male guests would place money inside, compensating the groom for a dance with his bride. The money would, under ordinary circumstances, start off her housekeeping fund.

I have to admit that when I lay down to sleep my mind touched on Aletia going to her husband's bed for the first time. Despite their nocturnal meetings I was as certain of Dom Sebastian's virginity as I was of hers and had considered speaking to him before the wedding night. The incongruity of a priest instructing a king on how to deflower a maiden had given me pause, however.

Still, I imagined that this night was made more special by their own inexperience, both of them learning and delighting in new pleasures at the same time, moving towards that moment of oneness that is, apart from life itself, the most special of all God's gifts.

The newlyweds filled the valley with hope and light. I came to understand just how well they suited each other. In the night they would gaze at the stars, and while Dom Sebastian named the visible constellations, in their unfamiliar southern positions, Aletia would tell the story behind them – perhaps of Scorpio or the Archer, reducing the gathering around the fire to tears with the emotion of her telling.

Those were the last happy days I would know on this earth.

TRINTA E SETE

Just before dawn Francis woke without the ability to breathe – as if he had forgotten how to draw air into his lungs. Sweat streamed out of him – flooded from his pores. Many things passed through his mind in those seconds – most significantly the notion that if he didn't breathe he would die. Finally the big wet bags in his chest inflated with the sound of a file drawn across metal. He breathed at last, still panicked, pain filling his head.

Sitting upright, he listened, cold night air on his bare chest. The familiar night noises were not so friendly, and the tent walls provided no refuge – only a trap.

Now came a growl; a hiss; a scream; a train of noise. Every hair on Francis's body stood erect. That sound was the single most terrifying thing he had ever heard, and when it stopped something moved stealthily outside. Then came the shriek again, louder now.

Stumbling out of bed, he groped for his torch, and gripped it in both hands. The noise came again, and Francis fancied that the tent shook as if from an earthquake. From the rustling grass he knew the thing was circling, and he shivered again. Standing behind the tent flap with the torch aimed out from his hip, he glanced nervously around, hearing a heavy clunk as the shape struck something solid.

Francis backed away. He reached the rear wall of the tent, and slid down until he was in a sitting position. His legs flopped down like bags of jelly, but the wavering torch still pointed to the opening.

Then came the sound again – this time so loud that Francis thought he would be deafened. The flap blew in, and he saw only darkness. He bent down, hands over his ears. It seemed that he could smell the decay.

Every hair on his body stood on end as he paused at the open tent flap. He saw her then, light overwhelming that of the stars and moon, standing spread-eagled, her face, limbs and clothes a ghostly white. Blood ran from her outstretched hands, wounds in her side and on her forehead. Plaintive cries filled the night.

For perhaps a minute he was rooted to the spot, watching the fragile beauty of her face and the delicacy of her limbs. He found himself crying for her, yet unable to move forward and release her from the pain.

The vision faded, and Francis felt himself return. Still he was not alone. He sensed this, and it seemed that he walked on past the place where the young woman had been.

Ahead stood a tree where none had been before. From one of the high branches a rope had been tied, and from that rope hung a man from his neck. The man was heavily built, and wore a leather jerkin such as a man-at-arms would wear under his armour. Blood ran from where the rope bit deep. Choking sounds emanated from his throat. Francis took a step towards the man then stopped, terror filling his heart. The man screamed, then went into a series of spasms, jerking from abdomen to chest, as if in a final attempt to keep death at bay. Francis knew that with a concerted effort he could have willed the thing away, but instead he allowed it to persist; still moving; still fighting.

'You are not real,' Francis said, clenching his fists.

The dying man did not respond, but his eyes mocked back, as if to question the notion of reality entirely.

'I'm real.' Francis dug his nails into his palm as if pain might affirm his words. 'I am flesh and blood and I feel each step I take on this earth.' He closed his eyes, and when he opened them again the man and his hanging tree were gone. The tent was silent and he was still in the sleeping bag. Nicolá's face was at the flap, her head torch on a low setting, shining weakly into the tent. 'Are you okay?' she asked.

'I think so,' he said, and the saudade, lurking below the surface, took him in its grasp and rocked him gently, lulled him away. 'I need to know what happened to him. I need to know.'

Nicolá came into the tent and drew both arms around his chest, the pressure so tight it might have squeezed the life out of him.

TRINTA E OITO

A handful of our people, men and women alike, took to this land in a complete and surprising way, becoming attuned to the environment, enjoying the harshness, learning to distinguish the pad marks of the various species of hopping deer and various pouched rats, becoming adept at stalking game, sourcing natural tree fruits and even making contact with the Yeidji and learning from them. Others wandered the plains, rivers and stony ridges – born explorers drawn by distant horizons. Some even found a major river some leagues to the east, which they named the Rio Grande.

These attributes were seized upon by Dom Sebastian who made these people his front-line scouts, bringing constant reports of the enemy and their movements. They were happy to accept these duties in return for freedom to roam as they wished.

The guarda-costras were now bivouacked on a bend of the stream that linked us to the coast. Our scouts reported that they made themselves busy brewing liquor from local fruits, and spent their days sparring and drinking, building up their strength and courage for an assault on our naturally fortified valley.

Dom Sebastian, never one to sit on his hands, called together a score of his best fighters, dressed in light armour, and led them out in the late afternoon, loping like cats through the grassy slopes, led by two of our willing scouts.

The patrol returned not long before dawn, bloodied, reduced in number, but in possession of two prisoners, ragged, howling specimens, who screamed promises of revenge that echoed off the hidden shadows in the cliffs with malevolent clarity.

At noon, Dom Sebastian had these two men carried to the highest point of the cliffs, in plain view of a hundred leagues of wilderness. There, he had a rope noose placed around each neck and with these devices he hung them from two trees. Both men choked and kicked for interminable minutes until death took them.

Aghast, I could not look in that direction. Our young leader, however, was pleased with himself. 'I have goaded the dog,' he said. 'Surely now the pack will come hunting.'

In the shadow of corpses hanging from the cliffs, this valley that had once seemed so sweet and peaceful became our hell. People became listless and argumentative. There was a surge in numbers of sick, complaining of difficulty breathing and bleeding gums, but also of strange hallucinations. Many told of visions such as seeing Satan or the Virgin Mary amongst those cliffs and hollows.

'I told you,' said Rui. 'The red stones around the springs leach mercury into the water. It is poison.'

I prevailed on Dom Sebastian to outlaw the eating of fish or drinking of water from the pool, but the small soaks on the eastern cliffs provided scarce enough water for us all and many disobeyed. After all the fish were plentiful and tasty, and ill-educated seamen could not understand the dangers of a rare metal they could not see or smell.

Food became scarce. The stone walls hemmed us in rather than protected us, and I smelled Satan's breath in the dry afternoon breezes. I thought often of the gentler landscapes of home. I read and reread the *Trovas* and the book of *Revelation*, pacing and weeping with frustration. When I asked Rui Chanoca for interpretation he said, 'My part in this is done, Padre. I can help no further.'

No happiness remained here for us. The Beast loomed close. Soon he would strike. This place had been innocent. Now it was sullied. Sin stained the very earth. Still I searched for meaning. I had not slept for some three nights, and scarcely eaten when a heron cried, and seven tiny stars fell from the heavens to earth. My breath was driven from my lungs, and understanding came as an insight so clear and real it seemed that I could touch it.

Leaning over, I scraped my fingernails through the dirt, feeling them break, this physical pain only serving to fuel my distress. The Beast was stirring, pawing the earth as he prepared to overcome us.

The confluence of evil gathered pace, just as storm winds collected dust and leaves as they swept across our valley. Men sought a scapegoat for our predicament, and their eyes fell on Rui Chanoca.

When I told the Spaniard of their accusations and begged him to leave he said, 'My dear friend. I have learned that you cannot run from the ignorance of men. They fear the unknown, that which they cannot rationalise, so they seek to destroy it. My time here is over. You must follow the will of the *Trovas*. Remember, you are the first Sebastianist. The first of many thousands – millions perhaps.'

Down in the valley some thirty men set off in a group towards us. Some carried unsheathed swords, others solid staves. Together Rui and I watched them come. When they neared he moved to the lip of the platform.

A topmastman called Queimado led the mob, his face coarse with whiskers, eyes burning with uninformed indignation. He halted below the ledge and signalled his followers to do the same. He cleared his throat and spoke. 'Rui Chanoca, you are a heretic and an enemy of God. We demand that you leave this valley or prepare to burn in a fire we will stoke for you. What say you to these charges?'

'No,' he said. 'I will not leave.'

Queimado grimaced. 'Then you will burn.'

'Yes, I will succumb to the flames to which I am fated. But first, look into your hearts and see if you have the courage to watch me fry.' When Rui's hands flew to the clasp of his robe I didn't know what he intended. Removing those rags he stood naked before us. The place where his genitals had been was a mass of scar tissue. His voice became strident. 'They took it all so that now I piss through a hole. They unmanned me, because I refused to believe precisely the same way as they. Do you have the stomach for that kind of work?'

The assembled faces betrayed shades of horror or revulsion. The sight of that mutilation was so obscene that I felt certain the mob would disperse, and leave Rui Chanoca to the private hell that I had heretofore only guessed at. Queimado, however, in his self-righteous pride, had no intention of letting the scapegoat through his grasp.

'Half man or whole, you will leave this place or burn.'

I saw Rui's utter loss of heart as he covered himself. I turned the glare of my eyes onto the speaker.

'Who, Senhor Queimado, made you judge, jury and executioner?'

The ringleader turned to me and snarled. 'Those who wear the cloth have failed in their duty to root out Satan where he appears. This man is an insult to our church.'

'Church?' Rui spat. 'A church which burns a man for what he feels inside his heart is despicable. I shit on your self-righteousness and I shit on your church. There is madness here. What do these things matter?'

No man made a sound until Queimado gathered his wits sufficiently to make ground from that pronouncement. 'He has surely condemned himself.'

Rui, however, had not finished. 'Then burn me, you insane dog. Here, I will say it again.' He lifted his robes and bent his legs so that his skinny behind faced the earth, 'I shit on you and all you stand for.' He turned to me, standing now. 'Good Padre, are you going to let them do this thing with God's name on their lips?'

I hurried forward and took his arm, then turned to the mob in an attempt to placate them. 'Rui will leave this minute. Here, I will help gather his things.'

Together we moved towards the valley floor. We were less than halfway down when the first stone struck Rui between the shoulder blades with a heavy thump. He staggered and cried out in pain.

Half a dozen men ran up, Queimado leading the way. Another stone found its mark, this time hitting Rui just below the ear, provoking a bright flow of blood.

At this he turned to face his tormentors, voice rising into that strident tone I knew so well. 'Farewell,' he cried. 'You are afraid of the night and you are afraid of death, but you are impotent against them. Instead you destroy that which is defenceless against you.'

His pursuers had paused to gather more rocks, and now the missiles flew again. One struck Rui in the nose and flattened it. The flow of blood was instant and copious.

'I hope God is proud of you this day,' Rui cried, 'I know you think He thrills to the sight of blood in His name.' A larger stone landed on the side of his head.

The Spaniard fell to his knees, but before the offenders could come up and finish him off I stood in front of their victim and glared. 'That is enough. He is leaving, and is injured. By the Grace of God, put down your stones and get back to work.'

Some obeyed, wandering off in silent groups. Others, anxious to expurgate their guilt through violence, grumbled and turned stones over and over in their hands. When I followed up with a threat to report individuals to Dom Sebastian they filtered back through the woodland towards our little settlement.

I took Rui's arm. 'Are you hurt badly?'

'Nothing that will not heal.'

'Hurry then, before they change their minds and come back.'

Together we waded through the grotto and beyond, past hard-eyed guards fingering their weapons. There, feeling safe from any pursuit, we paused.

'You never know,' I said. 'Perhaps you are the fortunate one – just be sure to give our enemies a wide berth on your way to the sea.'

Rui knelt at the edge of the stream and I used my dampened robe to wipe away the blood from his nostrils and various other cuts, including one deep incision below the eye.

When it was done he gripped my hand. 'Farewell.'

'Farewell,' I said. 'You have been a good friend to me.'

Rui started to walk away, but then, at a distance of some ten paces, he turned back and looked at me. 'Tell her the truth, Padre. You owe her that much.'

Before my startled mind could conjure a reply Rui had stepped out into the trees and stone and was gone.

Late at night, with the moon full and creamy yellow, mist rose from the deep pool and cracks between the rocks, filling the low ground like a white sea. Out there, I knew, the enemy was close, for Dom Sebastian's scouts had reported them moving up during the day. Our hidden refuge was hidden no longer, and an attack was imminent. I knelt in prayer while Aletia faced the world defiantly, her stance resembling that of a warrior.

How I loved her then! Eyes tragic and dark, hair falling past her shoulders. I longed to invade her thoughts. I would have given anything, at that moment, to transport us back in time and space, to the orphanage far across the sea, where even now I might be meeting and assessing suitors.

As I acknowledged that wish, I knew just as strongly that Aletia would not go back, would not trade the love she shared in this place, nor the experience of crossing the world, for the safety of home.

Aletia began to sing, her voice ethereal, resonating in the very stone itself. I felt the goose flesh rise under my robes, as she turned away – facing the outside as if the song were a declaration of defiance. Of the many hymns I had taught her over the years, this was her favourite, the Latin words attempting to express the unutterable beauty and sadness of this life as we are given to lead it. As always, words must fall short, and only the astonishing timbre of Aletia's pure soprano filled the void.

Men girt for war, standing at their breastworks, listened silently, their faces turning to stare as the young woman sang their fears, longings, hopes and dreams into the night. Even on the valley floor, warriors stood limp beside their fires, yearning for the beauty expressed in that voice. My eyes were not the only ones that ran with tears.

Mist-deadened echoes fell and died with each note, and at times, when I closed my eyes, a choir might have stood on those cliffs, not one woman. The song gathered towards the crescendo, and Aletia's voice leapt higher, into a soaring finale that had me choking for breath in the night.

The last note fell away, and I stood in the moonlight while the mist absorbed those final precious echoes that danced in the air like stars. Walking forward I became conscious of my unworthiness, for Aletia was free of sin, as pure as I was sullied. I gripped her hand. Her skin was cold and trembling.

'There is something I need to tell you,' I whispered. 'I have hidden the truth for too long. I can hide it no longer.'

Aletia said nothing, yet her eyes were huge in the moonlight.

'A long time ago,' I said, 'I loved a woman—' I choked up with tears, covering my face with both hands while sobs wracked my body, as if the effort of wrenching truth from the past was costing my soul. 'I have had the privilege of watching you grow, but—' The past filled my mind, images both sad and sweet. I had arranged the midwife, and a house in the village of Douro. The last time I saw Aletia's mother she was so weak that she could not lift her arm. I held my darling's hand as she slipped away, while the baby screamed in the midwife's arms.

My great joy, and eternal sadness.

'I don't understand. You loved my mother?'

I touched her hand to my lips, spilling tears on her precious skin. 'I loved her. I joined with her, and you are the product of that union.'

Aletia was my daughter, the child of a love so pure and precious that no poor fool such as me should ever hope to experience it. I have never, since she was old enough to say her first syllables, held her close and felt her warmth against mine, yet I have treasured each breath and every beat of her heart, valued it more than even the sweetest moments of my own life. Words fell from my lips, 'Let me hold you like a father holds his daughter. Just once.'

Aletia went into my arms, holding me tight. When I drew back, it was to place my palms on either side of her face to feel the downy softness of her skin – the warm, living body, conceived in love, and reared at arm's length.

The moist beauty of her eyes was the brightest jewel on this earth.

'To me,' she said, 'you have always been my father. Something inside me knew.'

My chest constricted so tight I could scarcely breathe.

TRINTA E NOVE

Nicolá had drawn the map in her own hand. The resulting A3-size diagram showed the valley in pencilled colour. Apart from the main geographic features she had marked the overhang and the defences on the cliff and labelled them in tiny, perfect script.

Francis leaned back in his chair. 'We're down to bedrock in the cavern. Today we'll spread the excavated soil back into place. There's nothing more to find there. We need to think laterally.' The original trench had expanded to include most of the floor area.

Apart from the medallion the dig had located dozens of flaked single or bi-faced stone tools and three glass trade beads, the latter almost certainly Portuguese in origin. They were both anxious to gather enough evidence so that even the most sceptical members of their profession would accept the find as significant. Public interest and acclaim was already certain, but it was the regard of peers they craved most.

'We are dealing with a party of Portuguese seafarers. If we

assume they did stay here then there must be further evidence.' Francis took the map from Nicolá's waiting hand. 'We need to establish a settlement pattern. As you know, people have common needs regardless of their situation: shelter, food, water and fuel. Their utilisation of this valley will reflect that.'

'The season would have a bearing on how people might use the valley. In the Wet you would expect people to take shelter in the overhang. In the Dry the pool would become the focal point.'

'Good point, though remember that our hypothetical group could quite easily have constructed shelter.'

'The Wet season is the most likely time for a shipwreck.'

Francis nodded, 'Cyclones. That's right. But let's exclude the caverns for a moment. Do we agree that any form of habitation would centre on the hot springs?'

'Yes.'

'Then I propose that we undertake a site survey on the western bank of the pool, up to forty metres from the waterline.' This area was clear of thick trees and rock platforms. It was the obvious choice.

'Are you suggesting shovel test pits?' Shovel test pits required a number of hand-excavated holes.

'No.' Francis lifted a hand to chase off a persistent fly. 'We simply don't have the manpower to undertake that kind of labour. I suggest we use the hand augur at three-metre intervals.' After carrying the heavy implement up from the coast Francis was determined it should be used. If the sampling activity did locate an area of interest it would be marked and later excavated with the shovel.

'Shovel test pits give better results,' Nicolá said, 'but the augur will be fast, particularly in this kind of soil. I do think, however, that we should narrow the grid down to two metres. I would hate to miss anything.'

'Agreed, I'll start marking the grid this afternoon.'

Even with the augur the site survey process was hard physical work. Francis, swearing and cursing, twisted the handles until blisters swelled in the pads beneath his fingers, while Nicolá recorded results in a clipboard and marked areas of interest with surveyor's tape.

The soil was sandy, and this made the work easier. Material dumped from the augur had to be screened, and the two archaeologists did this together, recording the grid reference and approximate depth.

By the third day Nicolá was able to annotate her hand drawn map with the patterns that had emerged across the site. Almost all of the profiles showed miniscule layers of charcoal – the remnants of blistering hot grass fires that had, for millennia, seared their way across the Kimberley.

Also, however, eighteen of the test holes showed a heavy charcoal layer at depths that varied only a little from four hundred millimetres. The conundrum was that the particular test holes that showed this consistent feature were not necessarily adjacent to each other.

That evening, by the light of a fluorescent lamp, Francis sat beside Nicolá while she shaded the charred layer zones, as they had started to call them. When she had finished it was possible to recognise three distinct patches, varying in shape from oblong to almost circular. 'Have you got a hypothesis?' Francis asked. 'Bearing in mind that the charcoal remnants are consistent with burned timber of a reasonable size.'

'It's possible that those areas represent large wood fires lit by the Indigenous inhabitants of this valley.'

'Traditional burn-offs?' Francis kept his eyes fixed on the map while he spoke.

'Yes, yet grass, and fallen timber consumed in a fire do not spread their coals in such a thick and structured manner. Therefore, if we are going to assume human intervention, we have to consider all the possibilities.'

'You might be right.'

'But … the largest of the charred layer zones is almost five metres across – that's a huge bonfire. There's another possibility and we're just too scared to say it.'

Francis broke the ensuing silence. 'Wooden structures, burned to the ground.' He coughed and looked up at the stars, wanting badly to be right. 'I think we can justify a couple of pits. We don't have to go deep. But where do we start?'

'Here,' she said, pointing to the most northerly site, but closest to the springs. It was the largest of all the charred zones.

Francis pictured the area – thick with small wattle trees and one young boab that they would have to contend with. 'A difficult spot; do you think it's worth the extra effort?'

'I've just got a feeling.'

'That's the most spurious justification for choosing the location of an archaeological dig I have ever heard.'

Nicolá smiled at him. 'Why Francisco, it seems perfectly logical to me.'

That night they played two-handed euchre, until long after physical exhaustion told Francis to stop. Each time Nicolá pleaded for sleep he pressed her to play a little longer, just to keep her with him, watch her brown hair falling over her eyes in the firelight. Walking off to the silent, lonely tent seemed too punishing to contemplate.

When she insisted on stopping for the night he grew sulky, and as if sensing this, she sat back down and shuffled the cards. 'It's not that I don't want to spend time with you, Francisco, but I need my sleep.'

'I know.'

'You do too.'

'Yes.'

Standing, she walked behind him, and for a luxurious minute she massaged his shoulders. 'Tomorrow the real work begins, we need to save our energy for that.'

When she had gone Francis walked to the edge of the springs. When he cleaned his teeth, he spat blood into the soil, clearly visible even in the torchlight. Surprised, he kneeled and examined the red-streaked sputum with the torch. With one finger he felt his gums and the tenderness there. Slowly he stood and walked back towards his tent.

The following morning Francis pegged a six by two metre trench running parallel to the pool. 'It's going to be hell to dig in this sand,' he said. 'The walls will keep collapsing.'

'It doesn't matter,' Nicolá said, 'we'll get there.'

Francis helped scrape off the top layers, and then, in the middle afternoon, deeply involved in the work, he paused with one hand on the shovel. A sound had come from across the valley with an intensity that filled the pit of his heart. He stood for a moment, and listened again, but the sound did not recur.

'What's wrong?' Nicolá asked.

'Nothing.'

'Are you sure?'

'Of course.'

An hour of sandy, gritty work passed before he heard it again. This time he felt the hairs of his neck and forearm rise and prickle against his shirt. He looked into the northwest, staring as if trying to make the sound come again.

Francis's head sagged low over the ground where they were working and his senses filled with the graveyard smell of disturbed earth. He fought to ignore the sound, but it invaded all his defences. Finally he sagged back onto his buttocks.

'Here, catch.' He turned to Nicolá in time to field the plastic bottle of tepid water. 'Have a drink. You look like you've seen a ghost.'

'Thanks,' he tried to smile, but when he returned to work the soil seemed lifeless – the act of disturbing it futile, perhaps dangerous. As if acting against his will he put down the shovel and stood. 'I just want to go and look at something. Do you mind?'

'No, of course not.'

Francis turned and walked away, moving in the direction he had last heard the sound that had so disturbed him. Almost immediately it came again, along with an accompaniment he could not quite place.

Crossing the valley, he remained conscious of the music, a strange and unlikely rhythm. His shoulders bowed with the weight of responsibility, knowing how it felt to be a leader of men. Knowing what it was like to love those who followed and fear their deaths above your own. When the great rocky face blocked his way he began to climb. His actions were mechanical, and he stopped trying to resist.

The cliff tops were sheathed with solid rock in platforms and sometimes strangely eroded shapes. Francis headed for and stood beside one of the stone breastworks. There he heard the voice again, calling for help, shrieking in the still air, rising and falling in some strange Doppler effect.

Francis walked to the edge of the cliffs, looking out into the surrounding hinterland, outside the valley, searching for the source of the sound. The bush extended to the horizon, green and grey in equal measure. In the evening cool the colours became more vivid and real. The precipice at his feet fell sheer and rocky, all the way to oblivion. *They* were close now, he sensed them looming.

The shrieks became constant – the piercing note of mortal agony. In his mind's eye Francis saw a young woman; the ethereal beauty of her face and her pleading hands. The cry for help affected him to the pit of his soul. If he had known in which direction to run for her he would not have hesitated.

Tears ran down Francis's face as he tried to tell the young woman that he could not help her, that he was far away, that she was lost to him. Her voice filled his mind. At first he did not want to go, but she was so pretty and so insistent. Her voice rocked his soul, and he vacillated.

Francis began to sway. With each motion his body came closer to penduluming over the edge, where certain death lay far below. The fear that he felt at first became a sudden elation. Ecstasy. The girl was close now, and her cries had become comforting. Finally he reached the point of balance and tottered on the edge.

A sudden force pulled his arm and shirt in the opposite direction. He fell backwards, and impacted hard, the breath forced from his lungs. He looked up, surprised, into Nicolá 's eyes – angry, frightened, running with tears.

She fell to her knees and leaned over him, almost lying on him, and her face was so very close now. 'What are you doing?' she cried, 'for the love of God.'

The young woman's voice receded, and slowly the earth ceased to revolve on an unfamiliar axis. 'I'm sorry,' Francis said. He sucked air into his lungs as if he had almost drowned. 'Please. I'll be okay now.'

'We have to be careful,' she said. 'I'm not sure yet, which is why I haven't said anything, but that red stone around the pool – I think it's cinnabar. Elemental mercury. That's why Henry told you not to eat the fish. It's affecting both of us – and I don't want to leave here – not yet.'

Francis stared up at her. He knew something about the symptoms of mercury toxicity – he had once studied the effects of the substance on slaves in the Roman-era mercury mines of Spain. Breathing troubles, gingivitis, hallucinations. She must be right. He knew also that the substance had been mined in southeast Queensland – and that cinnabar occurred naturally near geothermal activity.

Nicolá placed one hand on each side of his chin. 'We have to stop. We have to be careful. We can swim in the hot springs – elemental mercury isn't readily absorbed through the skin, but no more fish. No more drinking the water. We'll need to get it from that soak over near the cliffs. We can't let anything stop us now.'

QUARENTA

They came in the half light of dawn, creeping forward with the mist, daubed with mud and dust so they blended with the wild creatures, the trees and the earth itself. If not for the conscientiousness of our lookouts, we would not have known they were coming, for they were guarda-costras, and thus fighting men without peer.

Dom Sebastian woke me with a hand on my cheek, and when I opened my eyes the firelight caught the strong features of his face. 'My scouts have reported the enemy moving up. They will attack as soon as there is light to see.' I washed my face and ate before hurrying across the valley.

My eyes moved restlessly to our defences. The grotto, like the gates of a castle, was manned by dozens of archers and several musketeers, ready to rain projectiles into the ranks of any approaching force. Piles of cannonball-sized rocks lay to hand. Down on the valley floor, twenty or more of our best men made up a skirmishing party ready to deal with any guarda-costras who made it through.

This open end of the valley was sealed with tree trunks piled atop one another, and defended by a hundred stout men with most of our firearms, and many archers. This was the most likely point at which the guarda-costras might win through. There I intended to watch the battle, beside the best and fiercest of our men, and Dom Sebastian himself. Reaching the lines I stood back from the wall itself, yet close enough to hear and see everything that transpired. My knees shook with fear at what would soon happen.

'Steady, men,' a marine corporal called from nearby, his hands resting on the shaft of his bow – made of a fibrous tree branch – as strong and flexible as the yew of our homeland. The two-handed sword on his belt glistened with animal fat. 'Remember that they are men, not ghosts. They will die as easily as rabbits when your arrow finds the heart.'

An archer standing not five paces away from me turned and smiled. 'Day and night, for a full cycle of the moon, we have done nothing but practise our aim and make arrows. We have enough to kill them all ten times over.'

Standing there beside a small twisted tree, I felt the gritty texture of sand beneath my feet. The air was as still as a crypt, and the only scent that of stale wood smoke from my sleeves and skin. My belly was a hollow drum, tight with anxiety. My eyes moved restlessly from the mist-blanketed ground to our defences.

While we waited, Dom Sebastian called to his men by name, pausing to pray with one group or other. The men smiled to see him there, for he was idol and friend, leader and companion. As he came level with the place where I waited he hurried over and clasped my hand.

'I wish you would agree to hide, old friend, yet it does my heart good to see you here with us. Perhaps today we will be free of them.'

'Pray with me, please.'

Together we kneeled. Other men joined us until the rumble of voices resonated in the stone itself.

With the Grace of God in his heart, Dom Sebastian addressed the men, walking backwards and forwards before the defences, his voice so deep and clear that even our archers in our castros on the cliff tops crowded closer so they could hear. 'Today we fight for much more than fifty acres of earth on the far side of the world. We fight for what is right, and to avenge the wrongs that have been done. The guarda-costras are good fighters, yes, but we, as defenders, hold a substantial advantage over them. It has long been known that a well organised defence can rout a force at least five times its own size if their heart holds. We have greater numbers than our foe.'

This information had an immediate effect on the spirits of our warriors, looking at each other with new hope. Yes, they realised, they could win this battle.

'When you fire your arrow, hold steady and be sure of your target, aim high in the upper body to allow for the projectile to drop in flight. If you engage a man with hand weapons get close to him – that will make it hard for him to use his skills. Get in his way, kick and punch, use every limb as a weapon.' A wag on the flank made a comment that had his comrades tittering with nervous laughter. As far as I remember it involved using a private portion of the anatomy as a war club. Dom Sebastian laughed too, and the tension eased a notch. 'There is nothing more I can say to you except to fight for your country, fight for yourselves, and fight for each other. Tonight we will toast our victory.'

The guarda-costras came like ghouls from hell, with the wild anger of men who have pursued their quarry across the known world and beyond – of men impatient for blood and victory. Seeing them come was like watching the legions of Satan – the Devil's foot soldiers. This was indeed the Beast, black and terrible. They came with blades of the finest Toledo steel, and matchlock guns smoking brimstone in the dawn air.

O God of hosts …

They came at a run, contemptuous of the arrows that flew like hailstones into their ranks. Firearms exploded their concussive power into the melee. Blinding clouds of powder-smoke drifted through, noxious and thick.

'Hold your lines,' shouted Tonio, his voice carrying through the clamour.

A musket ball took the archer I had been previously talking to in the chest. The projectile tore its way out, due to the obtuse angle, between his shoulders, at the base of his neck. In so doing it carried a chunk of flesh and tissue the size of a melon and smeared it on the rocks behind him. I leapt forward to help, but by the time he had fallen he was as dead as any man can be.

Apart from the skirmish back at the marsh, my only other experience of battle on land was at Alcácer Quibir, which differed not only in scale from this encounter. That clash had been a meeting of massed foot-soldiers and cavalry on a vast plain, with room to manoeuvre for both parties. This, however, was less measured, and infinitely more savage, as if the aggressors knew they had limited time to surprise and overcome the defenders, and the latter were aware that they faced only victory or death.

QUARENTA E UM

Francis's spade contacted something solid at the edge of the trench, some distance beneath the surface. Lowering the implement he bent down, choosing a small trowel to investigate. Again metal touched an unyielding surface. 'Nicolá, there's something here.'

'What is it?' she asked, already on her knees beside him.

Francis looked at her. 'I'm not sure yet. If you can brush the sand away as I go we'll get down there faster.'

An hour passed in uncovering the object, and even then Francis was unsure as to what they were looking at – something cylindrical in shape, with an average diameter of 220 millimetres. It was solid charcoal – burned timber, and had been set into the ground to a depth of 360 millimetres. Francis might have dismissed the find as natural but for another row of charcoal leading off at ninety degrees.

'Any ideas yet?' Nicolá asked.

Francis stood up to relieve the pins and needles in his leg. He had hardly been conscious of the sensation. 'I'm not sure yet, but it looks like a post – some kind of construction.

'A building?' Nicolá almost shouted.

Francis broke into a grin. 'That's the word I was looking for.'

Over the following days, strip excavating the site, the charred foundations of a single hut took shape. Six poles enclosed a space six point three by two point one metres. At a depth of one hundred and eighty millimetres the sand was infused with a thick layer of charcoal that Francis hypothesised as belonging to the burned roof and walls of the structure. Soil samples showed elevated levels of nitrogen and phosphorus, both indicators of human activity.

In the centre of that space Nicolá struck the archaeological equivalent of gold. Francis, standing five paces away, heard the click of contact as the steel of her trowel struck something harder than fragmented charcoal. He was beside her on the sand in just moments, watching her use a bicycle pump to blow the last grains of sand and dirt away.

The skull was grey with age, but untouched by the flames that had consumed everything around it. Francis's mind leapt ahead – did that mean the corpse still had a protecting layer of flesh when the fire came?

'Have a look at this.' Francis had never seen her so happy, but moved his eyes from her face to the grotesque remains before him. The skull had been cleaved through in a line.

'He was hit with a sharp object,' Nicolá breathed, 'murdered.' She pointed at a trace of rust that lay in a circle around the base of that skull.

Francis hugged her then, over the hapless remains. This was the big one. They both knew it. 'You'd better slow down now. I need to get this on film.'

Nicolá smiled, 'I just want to go at it with my hands.'

'So do I, but we'll have to be patient.'

The man had been kneeling when he died, his head almost touching the earth. The bony fingers of his hand held the remnants of a weapon, so badly rusted that it was not salvageable.

No trace remained of any clothes he might have worn. His twisted spine looked as if he had turned to face his killer at the moment of death.

'How old?' Francis asked.

Nicolá squatted close to the skeleton, her sunglasses pushed high on her nose and silk scarf knotted loosely around her neck. 'He's a young man, probably in his twenties. From my measurements I estimate that he would have been about average height for a medieval Portuguese. You can tell the sex from the pelvis. In females the sacrum is wider, and the body of the pubis is narrower. Also, you can see that the skull is quite robust – distinct brow ridges. He still has all his teeth, which indicates youth, though there are signs of hypoplasia – a symptom of childhood malnutrition. From that we can deduce that he came from a poor background.' Nicolá leaned down to touch the jaw. 'I'm pretty certain about the age; in those days, by the time a man reached forty he would have lost half his teeth, particularly a seafarer.'

'Okay. What do you think we should do now?'

Nicola sighed. 'He needs to be excavated slowly – every part coated in PVA and labelled so it can be assembled later.' She paused and sighed. 'I've dug a little way around him. There are more skeletons here, on either side and underneath.' She paused. 'This is some kind of mass grave. I wouldn't know where to start.'

Francis, lost for words, just nodded dumbly, and as they walked back towards the camp Nicolá placed one arm around his shoulders. 'We are a good team, you and I.'

'The best,' he smiled back. That casual contact enlivened him, making him bold enough to slip his arm around her waist, feeling the movement of her hips as they walked.

At the threshold of the camp Nicolá stopped and faced him, moving her hands to both shoulders, resting them there.

'You do not need to be lonely, Francisco. You have so much to offer.'

Embarrassed, he kept his eyes averted, yet wondered if she would let him kiss her again. 'Thank you,' he managed at last.

'We'll have fun,' she said, 'you cook and I'll pour the drinks.'

The wine that so often made her melancholy, tonight made her playful. Long after dinner she brought the precious medallion they had found in the overhang from its hiding place and unclasped a plain gold chain of her own. The item had a strong ring at the top and the chain slipped through. She lifted it around her neck and shook her hair as the medallion settled on her chest just above her breasts, bright in the firelight against her white cotton blouse.

Turning towards Francis she shook her hair. 'What do you think?'

'Suits you, leave it on.'

Nicolá smiled. 'No man I have ever known looks at me the way you do,' she said. And when he didn't reply, just moved his gaze shyly to the ground, she went on, 'It's hard to believe that another woman wore this medallion four hundred years ago.'

Nicolá wore the medallion for an hour or more, then put it away, but she retained the mood, even after she refused any more refills of her wine glass.

'Let's have a swim, a late-night swim,' suggested Francis. 'The moon's so bright. It might be fun.'

She looked at him levelly. 'If you want to,' she said.

He changed in his tent, then waited in the pool, treading water a few metres from the bank. The water was so warm it steamed fragrantly from the surface, filling his nostrils with the scent of earth, sulphur and fire.

Nicolá gasped when she pushed away from the bank, and dog-paddled towards him. 'It's delicious.'

Francis nodded in reply. He ducked his head under the water and moved parallel to the edge, where a rock outcrop extended from the shore, a hand's breadth beneath the surface. He sat, en-joying the sensation of the hungry little fish and their tickling.

'We'll be tired tomorrow,' Francis said.

'I don't mind, I feel good now, as if I could stay up all night.'

Francis felt the same. Alcohol roared through his veins, and the water enlivened him. Still he was not ready when Nicolá moved up behind him. She put her arms around his neck with her legs extended on either side of his trunk. Her half-covered breasts pressed against his back. Francis shuddered, and knew she had felt him do so.

Her hands started on his shoulder, caressing his skin so that he sighed. She nuzzled the side of his neck and tilted his head so she could kiss the skin below his ear. Francis felt something he had never felt with such intensity – a dreamy mix of pleasure and anticipation. He was aware of every cell in his body strumming with pleasure. He reached down and stroked the side of her thigh.

She stopped kissing his neck and, still partially entangled, moved to his front, one hand on each of his shoulder blades. In that position their lips met. Nicolá moved back for a moment, hovering.

'What about the ground rules?' he asked.

'Sometimes,' she said, 'it's necessary to change the rules as time goes on.'

In response he ran his hands to the back of her wet hair, holding and stroking, reaching for her, wanting more, but still she resisted.

'Francisco, if I let you into my tent tonight will you promise to be patient with me?'

'I promise.'

'I am not a virgin, but … well, my sexual experiences have not always been pleasurable.'

'I understand.' Francis felt a cloud-burst of tenderness for her.

'Maybe if you bring your sleeping bag we can zip them to-gether, then we'd have more room.'

'Okay.'

'I'll get out now. See you in a minute.'

The act of joining the two bags together necessitated two torches and almost ten minutes of work before Francis acknowledged that the two zips were incompatible. 'It won't work, sorry.'

'Okay, we'll lie on one, and have another over the top like a blanket.'

'Sounds good.'

This proved easier, and moments later Francis found himself beside her under the pleasant warmth of the spread-out bag. The only negative was that he had neglected to bring his mattress and there was room on Nicolá's for just one person.

'Oh sorry, do you want to swap places?' she asked.

'No, I'll survive.'

'I was hoping you'd say that.'

Francis lay breathless while she burrowed against him, the muscle of his bicep providing a cushion for her head, her hair tickling his neck and ear. The rest of her body lay close against him.

'This is nice,' she said.

Francis scarcely breathed in case the movement might disturb her. The moment was so exquisite that he closed his eyes and tried to implant it on his mind. For a while he was content to remain like that, but when he felt her breath against his cheek he turned his head and kissed her. Making no effort to touch her elsewhere, he concentrated everything on her lips, making love to them tenderly.

Only when he felt her body melt beneath his hands did he explore further, touching parts of her body that he had only dreamed of rouching. Still, he let it happen without haste, being sure of each step as it was reached. An hour or more passed before they were ready, and the moment at which they became lovers was good for both of them. When it was over, and they lay silent together, Francis's mother's words stole unbidden into his head.

> *One day you will find someone, and there you will see a beauty that is unique to your eyes; the wonderfulness of them will be your secret alone, and that is love, when you see someone in a way that the rest of the world can't see. You will know things about them that no one else can know. So it was with your father and I. Not even his death could make me stop loving him.*

Before he drifted off to sleep he felt tiny shudders in her, and felt the wetness of tears on her cheeks. Concerned, he pulled her closer. 'What's wrong,' he asked, 'why are you crying?'

'Nothing,' she said, her lips pressed close against his cheek. 'I have just never felt so alive in my life.'

Whenever he had a chance Francis turned again to Bandarra, reading the *Trovas* aloud to Nicolá, searching for meaning, finding nothing new. The words of the Shoemaker soothed the terrors that gripped him in this place, and it did not seem incongruous to have the words still resonating in his mind as they made love into the night, the glow of the moon on her body, and all reticence now thrown to the winds, their bodies sweating in passion, finding true pleasure in each other. They were children of mercury, slaves to the unusual synapses in the brain and the shaking of their hands in the mornings.

The Trovas linked the Bible story of Daniel's interpretation of Nebuchadnezzar's dream, with the legend of Dom Sebastian, promising that the fifth great empire of history would lead the world to a state of perfection, when wars and wrongdoing would be a thing of the past – when life would be lived in a state of ecstasy.

The work promised that O Encoberto, The Hidden King, would sail into Lisbon on a foggy morning and save Portugal, giving it leadership of the Fifth Empire. The old Sebastianists at the balcony over the Tagus had believed – had spent their lives waiting – the last of thousands who had done the same thing.

All his life Francis had watched the television news in horror – the tragedy and death that unfolded every day. Revolution and war. The Fifth Empire became a vision to him, of a new world of cooperation and friendship.

Nicola held his hand at the fireside, 'I've been thinking about the *Parcela de Lusitania*.'

'Don't expect to find a hidden treasure here,' Francis replied.

'We don't know that for sure yet. There might be, and if there is, it'd be worth hundreds of millions of dollars. I know that some of it would go to Australia, a little to you and I perhaps, but surely most would flow to Portugal and India – money that is sorely needed by both countries. I know it's silly, but that kind of fulfils Bandarra's prophecy doesn't it?'

Old Henry came one last time. Francis found him seated on a log near the open northern end of the valley.

Henry looked up as the archaeologist arrived at the fireside.

'Dei Kaman oredi.'

'Who?'

'Ghost. Ai lukum minminlait.'

Francis sat down and leaned forward. 'I saw the light too.'

'Da gel einjel kaman yesterdei. Samtaim ai hop datgel gowei. Den da kantri kin bluin egen.'

Digesting the meaning took some time. Francis walked forward, then squatted in front of the old man. 'Who is she?'

'Einjel.'

'Why will the country breathe again when she goes?'

Henry said nothing, but his expression clearly communicated the thought that it was obvious why she should go. 'Yolabat wandim wolabi?' The old man gestured at the animal roasting in the fire.

'Yes thank you.'

Henry grinned then, and pointed down towards the springs, shaking his head vehemently. 'No bij.'

Francis broke into laughter. 'You brought me meat so I wouldn't eat the fish anymore?'

Eating in companionable silence, tearing at the bloody chunks, Francis soon became satiated. 'Tell me everything,' he said, 'tell me what happened in this place.'

Henry looked down at the earth, then at the stars, as if seeking permission from the natural world. When he began to speak, Francis closed his eyes and let the words build a vision of a long-gone world, when foreigners walked from the sea, and stepped ashore, white as ghosts, some dressed in shining steel that reflected the sun like the surface of a still pool at midday. The old man spoke with his eyes closed, expressionless, pouring forth in an unbroken stream from memory – the particular skill of those for whom deep memory is the most thorough transmission of history.

The old man told of how the valley became a last sanctuary, and Francis imagined men at the stone watchtowers, saw the fear in their faces as they stared outwards, waiting for their enemy to come. When Henry had finished, Francis was silent for a long time.

'There was a king, wasn't there?'

'Bunngawa.'

The Lord – the great one. Francis screwed up his eyes. 'There were others, weren't there? A wise man?'

Henry nodded sagely. A half smile formed on his lips, as if at a memory of his own.

QUARENTA E DOIS

oving from wounded man to wounded man I blundered through puddles of blood, holding hands and staunching wounds, promising to take messages to a mother, a sweetheart, or a wife.

Always, the tall figure of Dom Sebastian showed in the thick of the fight, sword arm rising and falling like a gardener's scythe. I lost sight of him as I tended to a fallen youth who had taken a quarrel through the belly. Curiously he felt no pain, and his eyes were placid as I examined the entry wound, blood seeping like tar from around the shaft.

'My place is on a ship,' he whispered. 'I wouldn't mind so much if I had the sea to swallow me up. I don't like this place Padre. Would that I didn't have to die here.'

When I asked him to move his legs he could not do so. 'I feel nothing, but, oh dear God it is cold, colder than winter in Galveias,' he said. Even when I worried at the quarrel with my hands he made no sound. I realised that the point was hard up against his backbone.

'So cold,' he repeated, and his teeth chattered.

Removing my cloak I laid it over him and whispered a benediction. 'I will be back soon,' I said, wishing I could believe my own words, 'then we will dig that shaft out and get you back on your feet.'

In spite of the death toll, our men held their own, and even the enemy captains were unable to rally their men sufficiently to beat through our defenders. The most conspicuous of these leaders screamed above the din of battle – a shrill sound that chilled the blood. Standing perhaps a hundred paces away, every blemish of the man's skin, and the stains on his breeches and shirt were visible to me. A suppurating sore marred one side of his face and his eyes were bloodshot.

Our stronghold weathered a series of determined charges from the enemy. Each time our topmastmen, cooks and marines pushed them back from the brink. The height of our barrier was sufficient to confer advantage on our forces, protecting our fighters from arrows and forcing the enemy swordsmen to engage a man on higher ground.

The effort could not last indefinitely, and in the middle morning a series of shouted orders saw the guarda-costras withdraw and disappear into the broken ground from whence they came, dragging dead and wounded men behind them. A cheer went up from our ranks at the sight.

'They will be back,' Dom Sebastian promised. 'Pass the word down the line. Drink, eat, and prepare to fight again.'

Each of the men carried food rations. Water had been brought up in shallow bowls fashioned of bark, such as we had seen the Yeidji use, and from these the men drank thirstily. In relays, they rested in the shade. Dom Sebastian's lieutenants came together, bloodied and exhausted, yet still eager to talk tactics with their leader.

Within one turn of the hourglass, however, our men were back at the lines, honing their blades and staring eagerly into the woodland from which the enemy must soon emerge. Strangely, despite how well the fight was going, something was bothering me a great deal – a nagging thought that I could not articulate, or pinpoint, yet it dragged my spirits down.

The word Leal, something told me, was not as simple as it sounded.

Finding a handy termite mound I sat, face in my hands, bringing all my intellect to bear, dragging my thoughts from deep in my soul to the open. I thought of the word games that Aletia and I had been so fond of. There was one she had shared with me a long time ago.

As leal from Leal does, as leal from Leal says, and loyal leal must save the king.

I had assumed that 'the one from Leal,' uttered by the dying pyromaniac, the grûmete who had tried to set afire our ship, was referring to the village. Yet the same word means 'loyal' in our tongue.

There was only one man I knew who was known by that nickname.

When I first reasoned through the connotations of what I was thinking I almost chuckled, so preposterous did it seem. The idea, however, took hold, and I could not get it out of my head.

QUARENTA E TRES

rancis had tied the rope off to an ironwood tree at the top of the cliff, then thrown it down to where Nicolá waited below, before descending at an easier slope. He was now using the rope to help access some of the smaller overhangs they had earlier spotted on the eastern cliffs.

In the previous days, as lovers, comrades and friends, Francis and Nicolá had worked on the pits until they struck a hard clay layer. Beyond this it seemed unlikely they would find anything. Now they were spreading the net wider, and these beckoning dark spaces were at the top of the list.

Using the rope, Francis began to climb, using cracks and narrow chimneys as foot and handholds. He avoided looking back at the valley floor. Once or twice his hands touched loose rock, dislodging a dozen or more clumps. They fell, clattering as they went, to the ground, fragmenting into smaller pieces.

'Are you alright?' Nicola called from down below.

'Yes, all good.'

Reaching the substantial ledge at last, he realised just how far above the ground he had climbed – eight or nine metres, all of it sheer. There, however, he stood in the entrance to a deep cavern. On the surface of the shady wall he found Portuguese script – not just a few letters, but many words, some obliterated by time and water.

O God our Father, save us all from this calamity. Enter only the righteous of spirit, come to celebrate the life of one who we loved.

The words chilled to the bone, like ice swallowed whole. Francis waited, reverently, before he took the first step into the cavern. The interior was gloomy, despite another smaller entrance far ahead. The heavy taint of bats mingled with that of earth in his nostrils. Through that gloominess he saw a litter of fallen stones. His torch beam probed the shadows.

No feature stood out, certainly nothing of human origin. Surprised, and somewhat disappointed, he walked on, circling the darkened space, his feet crunching in shallow sand. He examined the area up close to the walls, hoping for an opening that might lead deeper into the shadows.

For an hour or more he searched that cave, knowing that the answers must lie here, yet unsure where. Then, towards the deepest sections, he stopped to stare at a wrecker's yard of stones and boulders.

When he stepped forward and touched the stone it was soft and chalky. Surely this was the site of a rockfall, and beyond that litter of stone he would find more.

He went back to the edge to call for Nicolá to climb up and help. Then, falling to his knees, Francis hefted the first stone and carried it away.

QUARENTA E QUATRO

The next attack was hesitant, probing the weakest sections, each wave controlled by the captains. Their musketeers held back, hidden in the trees, keeping the heads of our swordsmen low with constant volleys.

Dom Sebastian stood tall and unstoppable on the barricades, swinging his blade like a dervish. I saw him slay one man with a single massive stroke, laying him low on the earth and following up with a stab to the chest. Again we beat the enemy back.

De Brito and several of his marines engaged a ferocious troop of the enemy who gained the wall itself. They may have begun to exploit this advantage had the rest of their forces fared as well. Instead, however, their comrades retreated, leaving them exposed on all sides, and were thus forced to retire. I came up to the barricades to watch the last of their forces withdraw.

Dom Sebastian leaned on his sword, and I saw the satisfaction in his eyes at our efforts to that point. 'They will rest longer before they try again. We have a chance to eat.'

Platters of meat and fish were brought up from the cooking

fires, and relays of men went back to bathe in the springs and drink. Most returned heartened, and bold, ready to face another onslaught.

The expected attack, however, did not materialise until late in the afternoon, and began with a controlled volley of sniper fire – men who had climbed trees to gain height for accurate musket fire. We lost three or four men in a matter of minutes before all heads were safely behind cover.

Only then did they come again, determined and grim, aware that victory would mean they would sleep that night in our shelters, warmed by our furs, bellies full with the contents of our larders. Our defenders, conversely, stood at the breastworks, fighting like devils. Often wounded many times, no man allowed another to shoulder any more of a burden than he.

A rainstorm came and went, and still the battle continued. Even when the enemy captains let loose their reserves and stood behind, haranguing and shouting, they could not break our lines. When they crept forward and attempted to set fire to our barricades the wood was too green, and damp from rain. These men died with their glowing sticks in their hands.

The attack continued, but was beaten back by our defenders, and our men cheered. Night had fallen, and for a full day we had kept the best soldiers in Portugal, if not the world, at bay.

Dom Sebastian walked the defences, praying in thanksgiving as he went, shaking the bloody hands of every man, offering soothing words for those who had lost friends and comrades.

'This is not yet victory,' he said at last, 'but tomorrow we will finish it.'

The meal was different, of course, to that which it might have been at home – halls bursting with men, shouting and cheering. No pretty girls danced nor musicians plucked their harps. Our fighters were fatigued and most were wounded to some degree. The food was whole roasted hopping deer, oily catfish flesh, and tubers from the numerous water hyacinths. Dom Sebastian rotated the watch hourly so that no man missed out.

A sheet of lightning filled the sky from glowing clouds in the west, and a thunderclap shook the ground. The scent of rain filled the air, and the smell was like a reawakening. Was it God's way of warning us, or a signal that we would soon be free? I did not know the answer.

Even as the festivities continued under a flickering sky I was troubled, unable to think of anything but the identity of our traitor. The man of Leal – the man of loyalty. For the last hour or more of the battle I had watched my suspect fight, and under scrutiny, for all his talk and shouting, he had been surprisingly ineffectual, and while there was blood splashed on his arms and chest, I had seen no wounds there. Most suspiciously, right then, he was nowhere to be seen.

Making up my mind, I walked over to Dom Sebastian. 'Excuse me, have you seen Tonio?'

'Not for a while. Surely he will be nearby.' The young man filled his lungs with air and shouted. 'Tonio, my friend, where are you?' After no obvious result, he turned back to Aletia, who had been giggling as he told her a story.

Filled with a strong sense of foreboding I turned and walked away, moving back towards our barricades, feeling the warm pulse of daytime air that was yet to rise and let the night cool return. On the way I met men returning in groups. 'Why are you leaving your posts?'

'Tonio Fonseca told us we were to be relieved, that we could join in the feast.'

Swallowing, worried that I might overreact and cause an unnecessary scene I calmed myself and said. 'Then I'm sure he was right to do so. Go and enjoy yourselves.'

Still I hurried towards our lines, and my mouth went dry with shock. All the sentries were gone. I called softly and got no reply. Walking closer I saw the body of a man dead on the ground. In a flash of lightning I saw that his throat had been cut, with a spreading stain over his shirt.

Tonio Fonseca's father had been called Leal, the loyal one, for his support for King João. For many years the child had been named for the father. Could our traitor be not the man *from* Leal, but the one men *called* Leal?

That nonsense verse came back into my head. *As leal from Leal does, as leal from Leal says, and loyal leal must save the king.*

The stink of treachery filled the air. In that moment I saw it all. I understood why Tonio had not wanted me to amputate Dom Sebastian's leg – hoping that exploratory surgery would end his life. Now I knew why he killed the arsonist on board the ship, with his rough shaking, before he could speak, why he had promoted those pointless tactics above the marsh – the foul message on the decoy boat – a decoy within a decoy. More signs occurred to me, including his proximity to Henrique on that day I had surprised the conspirators making their plans. I berated myself for not seeing it before.

My thoughts were cut short by the sound of armed men moving across our lines, and such was their discipline that no sound could be heard apart from the light jingle of arms and armour.

I froze, for this was the enemy, crossing our deserted barricades. There was nothing between here and our defenceless settlement to stop them, nor to give warning. Only my own self – and I was a man of peace, or so I thought myself to be. What could I do but open my mouth, fill my lungs with air and turn back to face the inner valley?

'They are upon us,' I screamed. 'Treachery. To arms, to arms.' Even as I did so, I saw the guarda-costras coming for me, desperate to cut off my warning. Even now, however, I am proud to say that I did not cease to give voice until the first man reached me, charging in with his shoulder, slamming me to the ground, where I lay winded, staring as he drew a sword and raised it above his head.

Then came a voice, and I looked up at the frightening visage of an enemy captain, dark and merciless. 'We have no time, leave him. The damage has been done. Now we must make haste.'

As soon as they had gone, loping darkly through the night, I came to my feet and followed. At that moment, the heavens opened and light rain began to fall.

Coming upon the conflagration from the rear, it was a confused, terrible sight. Warriors in silhouette fought beside the first of the shelters already in flames, casting a sunrise-orange glow on the fight itself. I saw that my warning had been enough, at least, for our men to fetch weapons.

Running from cover to cover I made my way towards the secluded hut that Aletia had shared with Dom Sebastian. As I approached I almost collided with her, and she came into my arms, face wet with tears.

'Go,' I said, 'to that hidden cave in the cliff that you found, and do not come back until I tell you to.'

'But—'

'Please, trust me.'

When she had gone I moved back towards the fight, shaking with fear, knowing that my life might soon be over.

This was a battle that no bards will sing of, nor poets compose a stirring verse in praise. No artist will pick up his oils and capture the final conflict there, fought by firelight, light rain falling, men screaming and dying, seeing their comrades bleed and weep.

My anguish increased a thousandfold as I saw one of my Jesuit brothers kneeling at the opening of our burning chapel, struck on the forehead, falling back into the burning structure, his clothes flaming bright, hearing his screams over the general commotion. Worst of all there was no time to say a prayer for him, nor to anoint his lips and eyes. Only to see him burn.

Dom Sebastian and his twenty best fighters formed an indomitable ring that the guarda-costras could not penetrate. Back to back they fought – men who loved one another beyond life – comrades of many years. Of course, Tonio was not with them, and I saw how Dom Sebastian's anxious eyes searched for his friend.

Our leader himself slew the captain of the guarda-costras, in desperate, hand to hand combat. As the man fell, however, he was replaced by two more. Slowly our group was whittled away, until only Dom Sebastian remained on his feet, bloodied and exhausted, wet from the rain and perspiration, fighting himself to a standstill. The enemy hung back, surrounding him, yet none risking his blade.

The stalemate continued until the enemy ranks opened, and

through them walked Tonio Fonseca, sword held loosely in his hand, and the scar of his hare-lip lit like pale fire. Oh, how I hated him then – he who I had loved as a comrade, yet had betrayed us all – causing the death of so many.

Dom Sebastian lowered his weapon and stood, panting, his eyes wide with surprise. 'Tonio, my friend, what has happened? You walk among my enemies as if you were with them. Have they charmed you somehow? Or have you taken leave of your senses?'

'No. Nor yet am I your friend, but your destroyer. All my life, I have grovelled at your feet like a dog. I have made myself indispensable to you. I have worn your cast-off armour to remind me of my hatred, so that when I inhaled your smell it reminded me of my hate. I have learned everything there is to know of you.'

Dom Sebastian's eyes widened as if wondering if he might soon awake from a nightmare. 'You have been my best friend, and all the time you hated me. Why?'

'Your father pushed mine from his sailing boat into the water, knowing he could not swim … your father took my father from me. That very night my mother whispered the truth to me, and I wept with rage.'

Dom Sebastian turned to me, 'That is a lie, is it not?'

There were things I had scarcely admitted to myself over the years. All the signs had been there. 'There had been rumours that Tonio's father was in the pay of the King of Spain. Your father found out, I knew that—'

Dom Sebastian stammered. 'Whatever happened, my father treated you like a son.'

Tonio hissed out the poisonous hate from inside. 'Guilt. Everything he did for me he did from guilt. That is all. The family of Aviz is a cancer. You are the last one capable of breeding, and I will remove your head. Henrique has offered me nobility. When I return I will be a Duke with vast dominions, and you will be dead.' He lifted his sword. 'All my life I have been Dom Sebastian's dog – I have borne the weapons he grew bored of. Now he is weak, and I am strong. All my life I have waited for this moment.'

Slowly, realisation dawned on Dom Sebastian's face and he lifted his blade.

QUARENTA E CINCO

The cave-in had obviously occurred some centuries earlier, Francis realised, for a thick layer of dust lay on every surface. Most of the stones were easily carried, though others had to be rolled and manhandled away, leaving his and Nicolá's fingernails cracked and bleeding, their arms aching with strain.

Francis knew in the pit of his stomach that this must be the way. They rested at long intervals, but almost as soon as the sweat cooled on their brows, and their hearts stopped pounding, they swung onto their feet and went back to work.

Stone by stone, the cavern expanded. The floor area had been exposed at an earlier time, because the litter of artefacts from two different cultures continued unabated.

They worked like slaves, scarcely speaking, deep under the spell of that place.

QUARENTA E SEIS

oets and raconteurs have made much of the business of sword play, glorifying it into a romantic art – a thing of beauty and grace. Sparring, and fencing, as the sports of gentlemen, may indeed be so. In a filthy rain shower, with mud on the feet, beneath an angry sky, it was a dirty business indeed.

With a flick of his arm and a shout, Dom Sebastian signalled the beginning of the engagement and the two men circled each other, sizing each other up like street tomcats. Both held their weapons extended, palms downwards, arms bent, crouching. I stepped back close against the shelter and felt the heat of the fire that now consumed it.

An exploratory lunge was deflected off the blade by Dom Sebastian, purely by rolling his wrist. At the same moment he advanced a pace, now lifting his weapon so that Tonio was forced to parry.

The ingenious footwork that was a hallmark of Dom Sebastian's style was made difficult by the rain and soft ground so that he fought almost entirely with his wrist and arm.

Tonio ducked, flexing his knees. He matched the True King, blow for blow. Such was Dom Sebastian's skill, however, that he caught Tonio's shoulder a glancing touch, slicing into the muscle there, provoking a rivulet of blood.

The pain was obvious on his face, yet Tonio did not cry out, nor otherwise make a sound. Nor did he grip or even look at the wound. Instead he launched a stroke that saw Dom Sebastian lunging backwards. These two had sparred so many times – knew each other so intimately that each feint and response was launched before the other's stroke was complete.

I was not fully confident of the outcome. Dom Sebastian was the better swordsman, though he was tired from fighting and still shocked to be mired in deathly combat with a man who he had believed to be his friend. The flow of blood from Tonio's wound, however, might yet weaken him.

Dom Sebastian forced his adversary backwards so that the watchers had to move back to give him room to retreat. Their calls of encouragement became more strident; less confident now.

'Take him,' they urged, yet Dom Sebastian's defence was so certain that their champion simply could not find a way through.

For my part I wished that the fight would never end, for it was a delay of everything – of what must be my fate at the end if the True King was defeated. Tonio was a crafty swordsman, yet again he was cut, now in the side of his chest – another shallow wound.

'Do you remember your childhood friend?' Tonio shouted, the scar on his upper lip now bright red. 'Alvaro de Castro?'

'A *true* friend,' grunted Dom Sebastian. 'Unlike you.'

'Castro did not die from fever in his sleep.'

'No?' asked Dom Sebastian, but I could see the shock in his face. I remembered how he had mourned when his best friend died. In fact it was one of the saddest episodes of his young life.

Tonio timed his next words as perfectly as a matador times the movement of his cape.

'I killed Alvaro de Castro myself. I wanted to be close to you like he was. I smothered him in the night.'

This terrible revelation distracted Dom Sebastian for an instant, long enough for a fighter of Tonio's calibre to shift his weight to his left leg, then fully extend his right arm and shoulder, the point of his weapon finding the gap in Dom Sebastian's rib cage and angling upwards. For long, terrible moments it remained there, until Tonio withdrew the blade with a heave of great strength. Exultation filled the traitor's face.

That deep stabbing stroke must have invoked a sudden and terrible agony, for Dom Sebastian dropped to his knees, staring at the ground. His face lost all colour and a line of blood darkened his lips.

'You are dead already, maggot,' Tonio said, 'though your heart still beats, it won't for long. Then, with a snarl as vicious as that of a circus leopard he kicked Dom Sebastian to the ground.

Standing at his full height, raising his bloody weapon in the air the traitor screamed out, 'Spare the priest, for I need information from him, but leave no one else alive. Kill them all.'

It was a night of massacre, when the wails of dying men, women and children echoed from the stone walls of that valley, and blood met blood, from living veins to ancient rock. I saw acts of depraved death–lust like shadows on a silken screen, as if they were happening in some other dimension of reality.

This was a crime to rank with the most terrible deeds of history. Blood mixed with rain to stain the soil.

There is no word to describe my anguish as I fell to my knees beside Dom Sebastian. Each sob was the sound of my heart tissue being torn from its bodily cave, and each tear a lake of sorrow. Desperately I smoothed back the sodden hair on my friend's head, while rain fell from the sky and onto my own face.

'No,' I cried, 'not now. Save your strength. You will need it all.'

Yet even as I spoke blood began to weep from tiny scratches that appeared on Dom Sebastian's forehead, mingling with moisture to run down his neck and into the greedy earth. Dark fluid pooled in the rawhide sandals on his feet.

'Please,' I cried. 'Share your pain, you cannot bear it all. No man can.'

The massive chest rose and fell irregularly. The moans that escaped his lips were not of his body. The flesh of his hands parted as if to the nails driven by Pilate's soldiers.

Dom Sebastian began to speak in that strange tongue that I had never been able to fathom. Now I understood. It was Aramaic, the language of Christ himself. Yes, he was dying, and reverting to that state that so awed and frightened me.

When I looked up I saw Tonio Fonseca, the king's murderer, talking to one of his captains, directing the last of the killings. I saw him in Satan's form, outlined by the flames of our destruction.

Watching myself as if with a stranger's eyes, I found myself picking up Dom Sebastian's blade, and standing.

'You,' I shouted. 'Traitor! You must answer for your crimes.'

Tonio was focussed on the reaction of his minions. He turned slowly, and did not appear to notice the heavy sword that felt like a feather in the strength of my rage.

'I do not answer to you Padre,' he said. 'Only to God.'

'You,' I spat, 'had a thousand opportunities to kill Dom Sebastian before today. Why did you not do so?'

His eyes slitted, and his nostrils enlarged. 'Because I wanted him to see his kingdom in tatters, his followers destroyed, his dynasty finished. Today is the right day. Here in this wasteland, with the cries of his dying comrades ringing in his ears. More importantly, I want the *Parcela*. Tell me where it is and I will be on my way.'

Tonio Fonseca, that consummate warrior, made a mistake. Answering a shout from one of the captains he turned away from me. I steeled myself, rose, and broke into a run, lifting the sword as I did so.

Tonio swivelled his head, so surprised he did not move at first, but I came so fast he must have realised that he could not avoid the stroke. The blade entered the side of his chest, just behind his breastplate. I will never forget the sickly hiss as the steel in my hands slid through his ribs and on into that black heart. It did not disgust me then, forgive me Lord, instead I revelled in that sound. I revelled in the light of life fading from those eyes. I killed a man, Lord, and I was glad.

The enemy soldiers watched as they might a vision of God himself. I let go the hilt of that bloody sword, and lifted the crucifix that hung beside my breviary. These men were tired. Their leaders were dead. They were seeing things beyond their experience and they had a ship, still moored on the coast, with which to sail away.

One of them stepped forward from the others. He was an ugly brute, with long sideburns, and a flat nose. Blood from the business of killing covered his armour. 'Henrique wants the *Parcela*. I dare not return without it. Where is it hidden?'

Before answering that question I gathered myself, aware that this was the most important untruth of my life. I had to not only tell it, but sell it, like a born liar, or an actor of the stage.

I threw back my head and laughed. 'Foolish man! You think such a fortune is here? Trusted to one ship? Both you and Henrique have made ill-advised errands.' I lowered my voice to the tone of that of a learned man confiding in his friends. 'It was split, and carried on the lead ships of our fleet. It will now be safe with the Governor in Goa, a sworn loyalist of Dom Sebastian. Your intrigue and murder means nothing except to incense God.'

They were half convinced, and I cast the dice one last time. 'Instead of Henrique's desire, instead I will give you wealth of your own. Go back to the beach, and behind it you will see three bottle trees that stand like brothers, with sand drifting around their trunks. Dig at the bottom of the most northerly of the three and you will find the contents of our ship's strong room. You will find ingots of copper and silver. Thousands of coins. Take them, and pray you can find somewhere to spend your riches quickly, for I pronounce you cursed, one and all, and foretell that you will gather again in hell before the year is out.'

The guarda-costras turned to look at each other. The thing was over. The promise of easy riches was enough. Some walked away, and others ran headlong, for those first on the scene would have their pick. If my suspicions were correct they would be at each other's throats with knives by dawn.

QUARENTA E SETE

The stars shrink away from the greater glory of the moon, like lesser nobles kneeling before their king. The valley responds to the changing light, shadows softening the hard edges, red stone glowing with energy borrowed from the heavens.

Francis feels his breath acutely in his chest, conscious of how close the past is now to his grasp. The removal of the last stone has created a void between the rocks – with dank, dark air beyond. He lifts and removes individual stones until he has sufficient space to crawl through. Sitting up, he fixes the head-torch to his forehead.

Sharp rocks bruise his side and graze his knees, and he inhales the long undisturbed air filtering through from the dark spaces ahead. A drop of water falls from the stone ceiling to his scalp. Still he wriggles on, the torch beam illuminating more of the broken sandstone slabs.

Now there is room enough to sit, then to stand. Nicolá comes up behind him and he reaches back to take her hand. Water seeps from both ceiling and walls. The stones here are scattered and small. Not for a moment does he doubt that he is entering a womb. It is so dark and moist that he feels as if he is crawling back into childhood, into the body of the mother who bore him.

Ten paces on, and still the passage continues, narrowing sharply. The sides close in, and after a single turn a wall made inexpertly of small stones mortared with mud blocks the way. The script on that wall looks fresh – as if it had been painted an hour earlier – still clear and easy to translate.

> *Beyond lies Dom Sebastião, of the House of*
> *Aviz, rightful King of Portugal.*

Francis shivers as if the earth itself were shaking, knowing that he is about to find the remains of a man who was prophesised to lead a new world order. A man who will rid the world of the evil of war, exploding cars and maimed children. To follow him is to find a better place. A better world.

Sitting, breathing hard, afraid of what he might find, he sees dishonest politicians and corporations squeezing the men and women of goodwill that they rely on for profit and gain. He sees oil wells on fire and giant submarines that lurk beneath the waves, carrying the destructive power of Armageddon; missiles that fly through the air and destroy cities, killing men, women and children alike, leaving the land poisoned and sick. Throughout the world he sees and hears a babble of voices raised in anger so loud he has to cover his ears.

Coming back to himself, he sees that the wall looks flimsy, as if small stones have been deliberately chosen for their lack of weight. The mortar has long since dried to chalky softness. He lifts one hand and runs it along the sensuous cool stones, apologising for what he is about to do.

'We shouldn't,' says Nicolá.

'We have to. I cannot stop now.'

Almost reverently, Francis pushes at a corner of the structure. The lack of resistance surprises him. A section crashes onto stone on the other side. The hole is still not large enough to climb through. Now, however, he can work individual stones away, without disturbing the script itself.

Francis forces a passage large enough for their bodies, and with the lamp cutting a swathe through swirling dust he slips on through, breathing hard, snapping his gaze around in awe and excitement. This, he decides, is not the tomb itself, but an ante-chamber – a massive natural gallery of stone. Most of the available wall space is covered with words – all in medieval Portuguese.

Staring, mouth open, with Nicolá beside him, he circles the panoramic beauty of that work. In places the words have been obliterated by runnels of moisture oozing down from above, but the greater part is wonderfully, perfectly preserved.

> *How can I rest until this story is told? Can I let such a tale slip unnoticed into history, or allow men to take liberties, inventing lies about that which is precious to me? I, Luis Pereira, Dom Sebastian's friend and confessor, can alone let the truth stand for posterity.*

Francis translates in snatches, realising that this is an entire text, tens of thousands of words. Sweeping through it all is a massive ochre rainbow snake, so real it might have been alive, rendered in bright red cinnabar pigment. Ancient skulls grin from cracks in the walls. Here two cultures have met and joined in that which makes all humankind equal.

At the far side of the cavern larger openings beckon. The torch beam alleviates the darkness. The musty smell thickens as Francis stumbles forward, afraid of what he must find yet drawn by the compulsive curiosity of the living for the dead.

Walking into the largest of these secondary entrances, he follows yet another narrow passage deep through the stone and into the crypt itself. The skeleton of a tall man lies stretched out on a well-preserved timber platform. Beside it rests a rusted broadsword of the medieval style. Moving closer Francis looks down on the remains of Dom Sebastian. The bones have yellowed over the centuries and still carry traces of clothes, hair and skin. The head lies askew. White teeth grin from fleshless lips. A spider reacts to the light, scuttling from the nostril hole along the side of a jawbone.

Next to the great king's bones lie those of two other humans. One is smaller. A woman perhaps? Then the skeleton of a man whose hands are still joined, holding a bronze crucifix on his chest.

> *Look down upon me, good and gentle Jesus,*
> *while before your face I humbly kneel, and*
> *with burning soul, pray and beseech thee …*

In the rear of the cavern Francis sees bundled weapons in a state of decay, from cudgels to muskets, and a small pile of books. His eyes rest on four wooden boxes, cracked with age. One has split right through and crystal stones litter the floor. Diamonds. Some the size of bantam's eggs. Thousands of them.

This is a fortune beyond imagining, one of the great treasures of all the ages of humankind. Enough to buy and sell kingdoms. And it has sat in a cave for almost five hundred years.

Francis kneels beside the body of the king. He takes Nicolá's hand, and with the other touches the uncut diamonds, feeling the hardness, and seeing the cold fire in their depths. Dom Sebastian's legacy, the means by which he might help both Portugal and India, and their economies ravaged by pandemic and debt.

There, with Nicolá, time and distance become immaterial. Francis's mind moves back to the dawn of time. Now there are shapes in the darkness, at first amorphous and vague, then as clear and focussed as a mountaintop on a spring day. He sees primates descend from the trees. Humankind taking its first hesitant steps towards agriculture. Scattered seeds fenced in and watered. Tamed animals herded and tended. In a moment of clarity that makes him gasp he sees the births and deaths, the trials and agonies of fifty thousand million souls.

He sees a man, bent over with the strength of his burden, bearing a cross to the hill of Golgotha. Grim-faced soldiers walk on all sides, many of them far from home and afraid of the unknown. Francis sees Jesus Christ on the cross. He feels the blood and sweat that infuses the soil. The essence of the Son of God. The unsupportable pain and sadness.

A vision comes to him of twenty generations of Sebastianists – all believers in the rise of a king and a new world. Each carries a burning torch. As one, they fall to their knees and begin to weep, until their wailing fills the valley, calling to their God and the long-dead king who they want back beyond reason and beyond nature.

These images swell in Francis's heart. He feels the strength of the yearning hearts of a billion souls. The saudade. The longing.

The colossus of stone rears before his eyes. He sees clearly the great empires of history. The Assyrians, Persians, the Greeks and Romans. More than four in reality, for there were others – some undreamed of by the old prophets: Chinese dynasties; the Mongols, and the British.

The last empire, the Fifth, shines with a fire far brighter than the others – for this is not one of selfishness and greed, but of hope and friendship.

Francis blunders towards the flame, reaching out for what he now believes to be not just possible, but imminent – a new age. The angel appears, drifting above the ground as if she needs no legs to support her, weeping tears so bitter they erode the flesh of her cheeks as they fall. Fragile beauty shines from her eyes and blood stains her hands and feet.

The mercury in Francis's veins has come to inhabit his mind. He sees himself as a child, running on a beach towards his mother, so close now that he can hear her voice. *The ancient blood of the mariner runs thick in your veins,* she whispers. *Five hundred years ago the people of Portugal discovered the world.*

The response came to his lips: *I learned of those men and what they did,* he tells her, *I feel their pain. I know what it was like to live and die in their shoes.*

Nicolá's hand is on his neck. The exquisite touch that is unique to her. Her tears spill on his face, calling him back. His soul swells with the beauty of her eyes.

'Francisco,' she cries, 'we found it. Is this not the most remarkable thing that could have happened? Now it's time to go home. Time for you and I to heal.'

Francis, however, is aware that the story in not quite finished. He sees the girl angel again. Her face is no longer benign, and suddenly he understands what inhabits the darkness – the fourth horse. Death.

QUARENTA E OITO

Weeping, I cradle Dom Sebastian's upper body, holding his wrist, seeking and finding a pulse in the vein beneath his skin. I look into his eyes, glazed over like cheap glass. His lips move without sound. 'My king; my friend,' I cry. 'Speak to me. Look at me.'

His eyes stare, trying to focus. Finally, he forms a sentence: 'Uncle … no more, please.' Drawing his knees up to his chest, he attempts to hold an invisible assailant back with his crossed arms. Instead of the dull, lifeless, choked expression he has heretofore worn, he begins to weep – not as a man weeps, but as a child – with abandon, and every part of his soul.

Crossing myself, I mutter, 'Oh dear God, what did they do to you?' His hand tightens in mine until it feels as dense as a cannonball, and I whisper, 'Do not let Henrique win. Live for me, live for her. Do not desert us now!' Yet Dom Sebastian is dying before my eyes.

Aletia runs through the clearing, already sobbing, and when she goes to him her hair falls over his chest like a cloak to shield him. Dom Sebastian's feet tear to the sharp iron spikes and he cries out, a sharper and more poignant sound now. I feel God's presence – the wind of his movement, angry that his children, the men to whom he had given free will could use that freedom to perpetrate an act such as this. To destroy the man that He has chosen to mark as His own.

While the poison suffuses Dom Sebastian's body, Aletia's heart shatters into a thousand glass shards. She presses the palm of her hand against the bleeding hole in an attempt to suppress the flow of blood and prays aloud; 'Hail Mary, full of Grace, the Lord is with thee ...'

The prayer is not enough, and grief claws at Aletia's heart. One hand creeps to her throat. Then the first sob catches her. The thing in her soul grows too large to contain. It escapes as a groan, then a whimper and finally a howl as terrible and bloodcurdling as the monsters of a madman's nightmare.

Tears continue to flood from Dom Sebastian's compelling eyes, and he speaks for the last time – the voice of a man who has looked in every corner of his mind.

'My love,' he cries, 'you chased the darkness away. You brought me light.'

I cannot not bring myself to look at his face, but I know that he is gone.

EPILOGO

Two years after the finding of Dom Sebastian's remains, Lisbon's Sociedade de Geografia invites Francis da Costa and Nicolá Massane to accept an award from the illustrious organization. The ceremony takes place at the Centro Cultural de Belém, a modern building sandwiched between the Jerónimos Monastery and the River Tagus. After a luncheon at tables overlooking both gardens and the water, the function moves to a spacious conference room in the exhibition centre.

The President of the Sociedade unveils a secure glass case in which sits the hilt from the sea, coins, weapons and other, lesser relics, speaking with shared pride of the work behind the discovery. The earlier members of the team are there also: Jeff, Lauren, and half a dozen volunteers who helped in the early days.

Camille, also, returns to the land of her birth for the ceremony, honoured with a seat in the front row, her active eyes roving from the man at the dais, to Francis beside her.

Later, back at the hotel, Francis and Nicolá fall into bed in each other's arms, breathing harmoniously through the night.

After four-hundred-and-fifty-years Dom Sebastian will receive a State funeral. The empty tomb long ago prepared at the Jerónimos monastery in Belém will hold his remains at last. The Portuguese newspapers have printed news of little else for days, and the populace is expected to turn out in force – perhaps five million souls, spilling out onto the square and surrounds in a celebration of national identity.

Before the time comes for that ceremony Francis has something else to do – something important.

Stepping from the taxi Francis and Nicolá cross to the miradouro below the Castelo São Jorge. It is dawn, and a deep white fog rolls across the river to the terra cotta tiles and whitewashed walls of the ancient Alfama district. The Sebastianists are there, just as Francis remembers them.

Leaning on the rail he too stares out at the river, feeling the weight of generations of men and women who have waited in that place. 'Why do you still wait?' he asks one old man. 'You know that Dom Sebastian is not coming back.'

The Sebastianist shakes his head. 'That does not matter. This is not about reality.'

'You have sacrificed so much – for nothing.'

'Sacrifice is the fuel on which dreams feed. One cannot be without the other.'

'Where is the empire that you yearned for?'

'Oh it is not on the outside, but in the hearts and minds of the people, can you not sense the change?'

Francis feels as if he is going to cry, taking several deep breaths before he goes on, 'I have learned something important. There are things most people cannot see or hear. We leave something behind when we go. All of us. Some are fated to sense the lives that have passed.'

The old man's eyes are as dark as the night sky. 'That is the basis of saudade,' he says quietly, 'the nature of yearning.'

Francis again shifts his gaze to the river and the mist. Still he cannot see Dom Sebastian's ship return. Concentrating harder, however, his mind fills with images.

He sees the tomb take shape in the stone cave, the old priest labouring on his hands and knees. The young woman, belly rounded with her pregnancy, living in the ledges.

He watches the old priest deliver Dom Sebastian's son with his own bloody hands, holding him up to the light to view his sturdy limbs, bathing him in the water of the pool, allowing the golden sun to dry the droplets from his skin, while his mother's life ebbs away with the blood that will not cease flowing.

Nothing can stop the child's screaming anger at how bitterly the world had treated him. Firelight dances across his eyes. Somewhere, out in the east, lightning flickers, illuminating the cliffs. Fat drops of rain fall from the sky.

Then, while the priest sits in despair, help comes from the people of that land. They come from the hidden places, gentle and calm. A nipple slips between the boy's lips. While the child grows the priest spends his days with brush and red cinnabar pigment, recording the story of the last days of Dom Sebastian on the walls of the tomb's antechamber.

Francis sees Henrique's soldiers on the beach, knives sticking from their bodies like quills. He sees just one man, the heretic and eunuch, almost mad with grief and privation, reach Timor alive.

Finally, he watches the old priest climb to the highest cliffs, facing the storm, and with tear-stained cheeks bring his God to account. His grey hair has grown long and wild, and his eyes become desperate.

'Why?' he shouts. 'Why? Where is your goodness, your munificence? How can you treat us this way? Are we not your creations, your children?' The rain continues to fall unabated, the lightning to flicker. His voice falls away to a whisper, 'There is no glory in heaven worth living without her.'

The priest and boy fade into time, and the last thing Francis sees is a tall Yeidji man, with a wild bush of hair and beard, bearing a spear both thin and graceful. The man enters the stone overhang and lifts a sedge brush. The image of the priest takes shape in ochre, clay and charcoal. Frei Pereira in his coarse robes becomes that representation on the walls of a stone overhang.

The images fade, and Francis da Costa slips one arm around the shoulders of the woman who is special and unique to him. Together they walk away from the miradouro, away from the mist, and the river. Nicolá's heels are loud on the stone tiles. The king is dead, but the dream can live on.

AUTHOR'S NOTE

Dom Sebastian did indeed exist, becoming King of Portugal at the age of three. Before his birth he was known as O Desejado, The Desired, and after his disappearance as The Regretted. The Sebastianists swelled in number and remained a major political force for some centuries. They surfaced in Brazil several times, most recently in 1897 where a peasant called António Conselheiro predicted a return by Dom Sebastian to bring food to the hungry and justice to the maligned. A small scale war broke out, followed by the massacre of the imaginative Conselheiro and his hapless followers.

I am particularly indebted to C.R. Boxer's translation of the medieval text, *História Trágico-Maritima*, which provided much of the detail and colour, including the lament to the departing fleet. The journals of early Australian maritime explorers, in particular those of John Lort Stokes and Augustus Gregory, helped me understand what initial contact between Europeans and the Indigenous Nations of this part of the Kimberley might have been like. The Admiralty handbooks of seamanship were invaluable in their detail about how sailing boats were handled. For those interested in the likelihood of one or more Portuguese landings on Australia's coast before the Dutch, the excellent "*Secret Discovery of Australia: Portuguese ventures 200 years before Captain Cook*," by Kenneth Gordon McIntyre makes compelling reading, as does the century-old, "*Discovery of Australia*," by George Collingridge.

Most of the action in *The Last Days of Dom Sebastian* takes place on a fictitious stretch of the Kimberley Coast. I have used elements of nearby areas to create a setting that is faithful in spirit to the Kimberley, but is not exact to any particular locality. I have retained the Yeidji people as the traditional owners of this general area.

Frei Pereira, Aletia, the guarda-costas and the occupants of the ships as they sailed off to the East are figments of my imagination as are all the events following the calamitous battle in Morocco.

I have received help from many people over the years in the preparation of this manuscript, mostly through reading and making suggestions. My wife Catriona was, as always, my most trusted proof reader, along with my father, Bob Barron. I must also thank Brian Cook (who helped nurture those early drafts), John Carroll, Steven Russell, Gerard Clohesy, Mark Shepherd, David Barron, David Hall and Fiona Barron. Chris and Vicky Fay gave me the Sesame Street line from the taxi driver after a visit to Portugal.

I'd like to thank Gabrielle Battistel of TMP Media, the mastermind behind the book trailer, and Andrew MacRae for the voiceover. I'd like to thank Len Zell and Greg Hill for allowing us to use some of their images and video footage in the trailer.

I always appreciate the support of my writer friends, even when we don't talk very often. Peter Watt, Lily Malone, Jenn J McLeod, Annie Andrews, Annie Seaton, Cameron Raynes, Don Douglas, Fiona Macarthur, Tamara McWilliam, Karly Lane, Chris Allen, Chris Morphew, Jules Faber, Desley Polmear, Rachael Johns and many others.

I must again mention my father Bob, who does such a great job at warehousing and despatch. It would not be possible to do what I do without you. As always my wife Catriona and sons Daly and James are my greatest inspirations and best friends.

My late mother, Faye Barron, always loved this story, and helped more than she knew with its development. As stated at the frontpages it is dedicated to her, with love. I'm only sorry that she didn't live to see the release, but even so, this is your book, Mum. I hope it's worthy.

Greg Barron
Eungai Creek
September 2021